A.J.

A SAGA OF SOVEREIGNS AND SECRETS

THE AEGIS SAGA

This is a work of fiction. Names, characters, places, and incidents either are the product of the author's imagination or are used fictitiously. Any resemblance to actual persons, living or dead, events, or locales is entirely coincidental.

Copyright © 2024 by A.J. Shirley

All rights reserved. No part of this book may be reproduced or used in any manner without written permission of the copyright owner except for the use of quotations in a book review. For more information, address: ajshirley@ajshirleyauthor.com.

Cover design by Miblart

Map by Natalia Junqueira

ISBN 979-8-9897874-3-2 (paperback)

ISBN 979-8-9897874-2-5 (ebook)

LCCN 2024917289

https://ajshirleyauthor.com

To the grandmothers who shaped me, nurtured me, and loved me. Thank you.

The Kingdom of Kōsaten

Content Warnings

This book includes explicit sexual content/open door spice, violence, death, child abuse, and child death. You can find more detailed content warnings for all of A.J.'s books at https://ajshirleyauthor.com/content-warnings/ or by scanning the QR code below. (Content warnings webpage may include spoilers.)

https://ajshirleyauthor.com/content-warnings/

A Saga of Sovereigns and Secrets Playlist

If you like how music sets the tone in your favorite movies and shows, scan the QR code above to follow along to a playlist cultivated by the author (available on Spotify). Parenthetical numbers in the text indicate when to play each song. If the music is distracting to you, simply ignore the numbers and enjoy the story.

1. "Lay Lady Lay" by Magnet feat. Gemma Hayes

2. "Say Yes" by Floetry

3. "Halo" by Beyoncé

4. "Mad Hatter" by Melanie Martinez

5. "Mind and Body" by Ayelle

6. "Can't Help Falling in Love" by Haley Reinhart

7. "Blood in the Water" by Joanna Jones as The Dame

8. "Beauty" by Dru Hill

9. "Call Out My Name" by The Weeknd

10. "River" by Leon Bridges

11. "The Beast" by Old Caltone

12. "Say Something" by A Great Big World

A SAGA OF SOVEREIGNS AND SECRETS

13. "Ready for Love" by India Arie

14. "Every Kind of Way" by H.E.R.

15. "First" by SoMo

16. "Game of Survival" by Ruelle

17. "Something in the Way" by Nirvana

18. "Sippy Cup" by Melanie Martinez

19. "Eat Your Young (Bekon's Choral Version)" by Hozier

20. "Monster (Under My Bed)" by Call Me Karizma

21. "Trampoline" by Shaed

22. "Forsaken" by David Draiman

23. "Wicked Games" by The Weeknd

24. "Fantasy" by Black Atlass

25. "Enemy" by Imagine Dragons and J.I.D

26. "The Scientist" by Corinne Bailey Rae

27. "Unholy" by Sam Smith feat. Kim Petras

28. "Sacrifice" by Black Atlass feat. Jessie Reyez

29. "Take Me to Church" by Hozier

30. "Turning Page" by Sleeping At Last

31. "Lay Me Down" by Sam Smith

32. "Golden Hour" by JVKE

33. "Not Afraid Anymore" by Halsey

34. "Carousel" by Melanie Martinez

35. "Small Cuts" by The Brobecks

36. "My Songs Know What You Did in the Dark (Light Em Up)" by Fall Out Boy

37. "Last Stand" by Kwabs

38. "Any Time, Any Place" by Janet Jackson

39. "Copycat" by Billie Eilish

40. "Only Road" by SUR

41. "Something I Can Never Have" by Nine Inch Nails

42. "God is a Woman" by Ariana Grande

43. "Gasoline" by Halsey

44. "Do It For Me" by Rosenfeld

45. "everything i wanted" by Billie Eilish

46. "Slept So Long" by Jay Gordon

47. "Unstoppable" by Sia

48. "High for This" by The Weeknd

49. "Movement" by Hozier

50. "you should see me in a crown" by Billie Eilish

51. "No Time to Die" by Billie Eilish

Prologue

It is easy to forget that Aegises have been vital to Kōsaten for as long as the kingdom has been inhabitable. From the moment Khalid brokered peace between the gods, the Aegises were a necessity—our first line of defense against the creatures that would prey on our inherent weaknesses. It is odd, then, that we have deceived ourselves for so many years believing that Aegises lack human emotion. How could that be so when their commitment and sacrifice are so clearly indicative of a deep love for humanity? How many of us would be willing to give up our own comfort, stability, relationships, even our lives, for thankless strangers? Dear reader, if you have learned nothing else from my writings, remember this: Aegises are the most human of us all. They are the very best of what humanity has to offer. And if you should ever have the privilege of knowing and loving an Aegis, never, ever let them go.

-From *The Epic of the Aegis and the Wanderer* by S.S. (The Shield's Scribe)

Macella awoke suddenly, feeling the bed shift under another's weight (1). For a moment she was transported to a different place and time. She was in a rented bed at the Hurstbourne Inn, where she and Aithan had concealed their relationship to spare her from the scorn of the townspeople.

Then, as now, Macella felt Aithan's comforting warmth as he slid into bed behind her. Macella remembered how he had slid his hands beneath her gown, his touch spreading heat across her skin. Soon, he'd slipped inside of her, and they'd make love in a quiet frenzy, trying not to wake any of the inn's other inhabitants.

But so much had changed since that first adventure. Back then, Macella had just been introduced to the ways of Aegiskind. Hurstbourne was where she saw her first rift between realms and the snake-like demon that came through it—a demon that she and Aithan had defeated together. That undertaking was the start of their beautiful, tumultuous journey. They'd discovered a prophecy that foretold their Fate, unearthed hidden powers, stood against foes both human and demonic, and, most importantly, fallen deeply, irrevocably in love.

Macella was no longer the solitary, directionless wanderer she'd been when she'd met Aithan of Auburndale at a second-rate brothel. Aithan had taught her how it felt to be loved. She'd found her home in his amber orange eyes and honey skin, had found peace and stability in his strong arms and steady countenance. Macella had been chasing Fate, not love, but she had found both.

"I did not wish to wake you," Aithan murmured, the familiar rumble of his voice bringing Macella back to the present.

They were, of course, in their chambers at court—a suite of luxurious rooms near the apartments belonging to the king and her spouses. This proximity was necessary so that Aithan, as Protector of the Crown, could reach his charges quickly if any threats arose in the night. Thus far, nighttime summons had only meant King Khari had some matter of business on her mind. Aithan often came to bed after the hour of Nyx, well past the darkest part of the night, having spent the intervening hours accompanying the king in her tireless plotting.

Macella wondered what the king had kept Aithan for tonight. The remainder of the Crown seemed rarely to participate in these late-night sessions, leaving King Khari to her own devices. Macella was only required to keep record of official proceedings as Royal Scribe and, thus, was excused from the king's nightly whims. Sometimes, Aithan had told her, King Khari held tedious counsel with the castle's mages, inquiring minutely into their latest discoveries and advancements. Other times, she spontaneously assembled her advisors to discuss strategy based on some epiphany she'd had while she pored over her letters, ledgers, and tomes all evening. And on the rare occasions when Aithan sensed an actual rift near the capital, King Khari would insist on accompanying him to seal the fissure and slay any hellspawn that had already emerged.

"You know that I sleep but lightly until you join me," Macella replied, scooting back against Aithan, instinctively fitting her body to his. "She kept you exceedingly long this evening."

Aithan draped an arm across Macella's waist and kissed the nape of her neck. "The king received intelligence of some unrest in the north. She convened the small council."

Macella shivered at the feel of his warm breath against her skin. She felt herself relaxing, the part of her that could never truly rest in this castle without Aithan beside her finally loosening its grip. Macella touched the star charm that she wore around her throat on a length of braided leather. It was cool to the touch. It was always cool now—had been so since the day Aithan was appointed Protector of the Crown.

"The small council?" Macella asked. "It is a wonder I wasn't summoned."

"The official conversation will occur in the morning, so you were spared. But I regret that my duties nonetheless deprived you of sleep," Aithan murmured against her neck, sending shivers down her spine. "I do wish you would take a sleeping draught or some other aid on occasion. You need and deserve rest."

Macella laughed softly at the seriousness in Aithan's tone. "You fool. I am no more tired than you are. Or hadn't you noticed our bodies adapting?"

Macella could hear Aithan processing her words quickly, memories of the past few weeks flashing rapidly through his mind. When they'd first stepped into their new roles—him as Protector of the Crown and Macella as Royal Scribe—their duties had exhausted them, filling their days with busyness, and decreasing their periods of rest and recovery. However, but a short time had passed before they found themselves less wearied by their daily tasks, less in need of sleep at day's end.

"Aegis bodies can endure much more than humans, and we require less rest in general." Aithan spoke slowly, sorting through his thoughts as he did so. "But I believe this exceeds what is typical."

Both Macella and Aithan's bodies seemed to be rising to increasingly challenging conditions by steadfastly growing stronger, faster, and more efficient. This was more than the result of rigorous training or of their passing through literal hell to become Aegises. Their gifts flowed naturally through their veins.

It is because we are crossbreeds, Aithan agreed mentally.

Macella added this to the list of discoveries about their natures as "forbidden children." Aithan of Auburndale and Macella of Shively had both been born of unions between humans and Aegises. Because their existence was supposedly impossible, they knew little about the full extent of their own capabilities.

"I will make note," Macella whispered.

She and Aithan had instinctively learned to slip in and out of mental and verbal communication, keeping their secrets safe from the eavesdroppers and whisperers who seemed to inhabit the very walls of Kōsaten Keep. Macella's private writings, in which she gathered dangerous information, such as facts about Aegisborn children, were carefully encrypted, hidden, and warded. One day, the histories would include the truths she and Aithan were gathering, but they must first survive their sojourn at court if that day was ever to come.

Aithan hummed a sigh against her neck. "I still believe that more relaxation would do you good. This season has been far from easy."

Macella heard the worry lacing Aithan's voice, sensed the guilt beneath his words. She knew that he faulted himself for their confinement to the capital. If he had not earned the title of Protector of the Crown, they would still be freely roaming the kingdom, living as they pleased. Out there, though rifts dictated their path, time not spent killing monsters was theirs to do with as they wished. Far from the capital, Macella and Aithan hadn't needed to be on their guard at all times, hadn't had to carefully consider every word and action lest they provoke the Crown's displeasure.

Of course, if he hadn't earned the position of protector, he would be dead. No matter what challenges they endured at the keep, she would be grateful that Aithan had survived the Crown's cruel test. Macella didn't blame him in the least for their altered lifestyle. It was enough that they were alive and together. It was more than enough.

"I relaxed during the cold season," Macella replied lightly, hoping to distract him from his guilt. "We had much time to rest and revel."

It was true that the cold season had been relaxing in comparison to their current routine. While the kingdom's nobles and the other Aegises had been present, the Crown had been preoccupied with entertaining and pampering their guests. Even that, of course, was as calculated as anything else the rulers did. Macella imagined that King Khari, Queen Annika, Monarch Meztli, and Queen Awa had all formed or solidified alliances while charming their distinguished visitors.

Meanwhile, Macella had mostly passed her days among the other Aegises, listening to their stories, imagining how her life might've been if she'd grown up among them. She wondered how the other Aegises would react were they to learn the truth of Aithan's and her parentage. Diya, Kai, and Finley had kept the secret, but Macella knew they'd been disgusted and terrified by the truth.

"The cold season was far too short," Aithan reminded her. "So that brief respite hardly counts."

It had been the shortest cold season in memory. Seasons tended to linger in Kōsaten, but this most recent cold season had come and gone with striking swiftness. Aithan believed that hell refused to slumber because of the coming conflict. Though Macella and Aithan had convinced Kai, Diya, and Finley not to proceed with their mad plan to raise a demon army and challenge the Crown, there were still consequences. The rebellious Aegises had awoken some exceedingly ancient evils while plotting their uprising—evils that would not be easily subdued.

"Perhaps I am not the one in need of relaxation," Macella countered, squirming against Aithan's warmth. "Stop fretting about me and let me enjoy my time with you before Khari summons you away again."

(2) Aithan hummed thoughtfully, the touch of his lips setting her skin abuzz. "If you keep squirming that way, I am unlikely to grow calmer."

"Not at first," Macella countered coquettishly, wriggling against him once more. "But eventually you will feel extremely relaxed."

Aithan's cock twitched in response, stiffening immediately. She rolled her hips, grinding against the rigid bulge she felt growing behind her. Aithan groaned, his lips against her ear. Macella shivered as he slid a hand beneath her gown and trailed it up her thigh.

"Stop fretting and let you enjoy this time?" he purred, slipping his hand between her legs. "Do you enjoy when I do this?"

He deftly worked his fingers through the thatch of her pubic hair until he found the nub of her clitoris. Macella gasped, her hips spasming involuntarily as Aithan rubbed feather soft circles over her clit. He held her tight against him, his erection rigid against her ass.

"Do. You. Enjoy. This." Aithan growled, punctuating each word with the press of his fingers against her clit.

"Y-Yes," Macella moaned, reaching up to clutch the back of his neck, her fingers tangling in his hair.

Aithan slipped his fingers lower, dipping into her wetness, and circling back to her clit. Again and again, he rhythmically caressed her, letting the sensation build slowly. Macella gasped for breath, arching her back, and grinding her ass against the hard bulge of his cock.

"What about this?" Aithan whispered, his warm breath on her ear making her shudder. "Do you enjoy this?"

He moved his fingers more quickly, massaging her clit more firmly.

Macella cried out, her hips bucking. "*Fuck*. Yes."

"How much do you enjoy it?" Aithan prompted, his fingers nimbly moving against her, faster and faster. "Enough to cum for me?"

An electric warmth was spreading from deep in Macella's belly. She rolled her hips in sync with the movement of Aithan's fingers. He bit her earlobe gently before running his lips along the curve of her neck. Macella felt the buzzing spreading through her torso, her pleasure nearing its peak.

"Cum for me, love," Aithan murmured, his fingers practically vibrating. "Show me how much you enjoy it."

Macella came moments later, her body quaking, her face turned aside, her cries muffled by her pillow. As she caught her breath, she felt Aithan move away. After a rustle of fabric, she felt him return, his bare skin hot against hers. His lips touched her ear again, sending another thrill of pleasure through her core.

"Is that enough enjoyment?" Aithan murmured, his hand resting lightly on her waist. "Or would you like more?"

The press of his erection against her ass made it clear how very much more he was offering. Macella moaned and arched her back, allowing Aithan to slide his cock between her thighs. She felt his fingers positioning the hard press of his manhood against her waiting wetness.

"Would you enjoy it if I fucked you?" Aithan murmured, teasing at her entrance with the tip of his deliciously rigid cock.

"Yes," Macella panted. "Please. Fuck me, Aegis."

She could feel Aithan's answering smile against the back of her neck. Then she felt the exquisite agony of him easing inside of her with excruciating slowness. Releasing a hum of pleasure, Aithan drew back and then entered her again with that same maddening slowness, probing just a bit deeper. Again and again, he slid his throbbing cock in and out of her quivering warmth, each stroke a bit deeper, but always the same slow, savory, tormenting tempo.

Macella shuddered, breathless with yearning. She wanted every inch of Aithan's gorgeous cock inside of her, wanted him as deep as he could reach, wanted him to fill her in the way only he could. She could feel fire building beneath her skin, her desire blotting out everything except the sparkling, quivering juncture where their bodies met.

"Do you enjoy this?" Aithan growled, his hand moving from her waist to cup her breast. He teased her nipple between his fingers, sending a spasm of sensation through her torso.

Macella moaned, the fire in her belly growing. She felt herself trembling with desire, nearly whimpering with desperation.

"Aithan," Macella managed, her voice jagged. "Aithan, please *please* fuck me."

Aithan hummed again, taking one more long, slow stroke. He squeezed her nipple, eliciting another moan. Macella was sure she would implode if he did not go faster and deeper immediately.

Suddenly, Aithan thrust into her, hard and deep. Macella cried out as he held her close, reveling in the depth of their union. His breath on the back of her neck was ragged. Macella could tell that he'd been torturing himself just as much as he had her with that slow burn. He wanted her as badly as she wanted him.

Always, Aithan promised, and then he was thrusting into her again and again, giving her the depth and speed she craved. She felt full and weightless as the buzz in her torso spread. It grew to a fever pitch, blotting out all her other senses. Then the orgasm took hold, and she exploded into a thousand shards of sensation.

As the world rematerialized around her, Macella found herself lying on her back, Aithan still on his side next to her. He'd propped himself up on an elbow and was gazing down at her, his amber eyes smoldering in the semidarkness. She could still feel the hard press of his cock, now resting against her leg. She felt her vagina clench in response, her need for him as intense as ever.

"You are exquisite," Aithan murmured, the low rumble of his voice mixing with her lingering sighs of pleasure. "I cannot look at you, cannot touch you enough."

Macella shivered as Aithan ran a calloused hand over her stomach and across her hip, his touch igniting little fires on her skin. She stared up at him, her eyes moving from his burning gaze to his full lips. Obligingly, Aithan leaned down and kissed her, slow and soft.

"More," Macella whispered against his lips.

She pulled him toward her, spreading her legs and lifting her hips in eager welcome. She felt him smiling as he positioned himself atop her. He slid his tongue over her bottom lip, then caught her lip between his teeth as he entered her again. Macella cried out, wrapping her arms around him tightly.

This time, the slow grind was delicious, their bodies moving in rhythmic unison. He plunged deeply, again and again, each stroke hitting that place that made her feel as if she were falling into some vast weightless expanse. Macella's body trembled, her pussy clenching and throbbing as she clutched at Aithan's muscled back.

I love you, Macella. I love you, I love you, I love you, Aithan thought at her as he finally came.

Macella's hips bucked, an intense glittering warmth spreading through her. She clutched him tightly to her, reveling in the sensation of his closeness, his pleasure.

I love you, Aithan, she thought back. *I love you always.*

Afterward, Macella lay in Aithan's arms, her head on his chest, listening to the steady beat of his heart. He kissed the top of her head, burying his face in her curls and inhaling deeply. Macella sighed contentedly. She never tired of this feeling.

"I know you do not blame me, but still—I am sorry," Aithan said softly. "I know how much you enjoyed our wanderings and how difficult it is to be confined to the keep."

Macella ran her fingers through the soft, silver hair on his chest. "You know that you need not apologize, Aithan. It isn't easy here for either of us, but it is our Fate. I believe we are where we are supposed to be right now and that is all that matters."

Aithan sighed. "Nevertheless. I wish we could follow Fate somewhere else. Preferably somewhere far from Pleasure Ridge Park."

"Me too," Macella replied. "We shall spend the next few decades wandering the farthest reaches of the kingdom once we finish our business here."

When we finish the business of stopping a war, overthrowing a king, and creating a peaceful society where Aegises and humans are equals and everyone thrives? Aithan thought wryly. *That simple business? I'm sure we will be back to our wanderings in no time.*

Macella laughed, thumping him lightly on the chest. "Well, when you say it like that, it sounds a bit daunting, doesn't it?"

Before Aithan could reply, they heard the tinkle of chimes. Macella groaned. That was the sound of a servant summoning Aithan on the king's behalf. Aithan sighed and climbed from bed, planting another kiss atop her head as he rose.

Macella caught his hand, pulling him back down until their foreheads touched. "Listen to Fate, my love," she told him firmly. "It has not led us astray thus far. Fate led us to one another, to the truths of who we are. Fate led us here. Listen, watch, and wait. We will know what to do when the time comes."

Aithan kissed her, filling her mouth with his smoky sweetness. "I am so proud to be your partner in this life and this quest. I will not fail you."

And thus continued the Epic of the Aegis and the Wanderer.

Part 1
Darkness Gathers, Trouble Brews

Each of Kōsaten's four regions are represented on the Crown. King Khari left the upper eastern region to rule and has reigned for nigh a century. Presently, she rules alongside three other monarchs. Queen Annika of Edgewood is the newest, hailing from the west. Monarch Meztli of Park Duvalle has defended southern Kōsaten's interests for several decades. Queen Awa of Highview has represented the northern territories for most of King Khari's reign. It is a heavy burden, giving one's life to the kingdom, but King Khari and her chosen partners do so willingly and selflessly.

The Crown serves the people, at the people's will. King Khari, Queen Awa, Monarch Meztli, and Queen Annika have but one duty: to secure Kōsaten with protection, peace, and prosperity. It is a duty they do not take lightly.

-Excerpt from Royal Bulletin, Warm Season, Year of the Serpent

Chapter One

Dear Finley,

Thank you for your last letter. I am glad to hear that all is going well in Smoketown and that the recruits are growing healthy and strong. Have you any update on how soon some might attempt to cross into Duànzào? I am sure all of Kōsaten will feel safer when the Aegis ranks are full once more. It was wise of King Khari to move Valen and Cressida from the recruiter roles and into the seven shields, but it's still strange not having the full Thirteen. Although, as you said, since mortality rates in Smoketown have been greatly reduced, we are not in need of many new Aegis recruits, and so the two vacant positions aren't missed. I'm certain Valen and Cressida are thrilled to be finished with their time on recruitment detail—they seemed to crave adventure and will find

> *plenty of that among the shields. Recruitment may soon cease to be a necessity at all, since the scribe's writings seem to have inspired many patriotic parents to volunteer their children for service...*

Macella swallowed hard against the bile rising in her throat. Her hand shook as she gripped the pen, clenching her teeth against a scream or tears, she did not know which. She wanted to finish responding to Finley before the morning's business began, but she was not sure she could.

The scribe's writings seem to have inspired many patriotic parents to volunteer their children for service.

No, she would not finish her letter this morning. She would need all of her remaining downtime to compose herself. It would not do to appear so distressed before the Crown. There were always eyes watching, probing for weakness. She could not afford to betray any vulnerability.

Macella leaned her elbows on her writing desk and buried her face in her hands. After all she and Aithan had done to improve the lives of the children in Smoketown, had she inadvertently created a larger problem? The scribe's writings had unintentionally made it a matter of pride to give up a child to Aegis training. No longer were only the poor and desperate sacrificing their children, but many in the higher classes as well. Those who would have hitherto been scorned for thus disposing of their unwanted progeny were now hailed as honorable and selfless.

Since improved conditions meant fewer fatalities in Smoketown, there was now a growing group of children who survived the grueling training but did not take well enough to the transformations to enter Duànzào. These survivors would eventually be enlisted in Kōsaten's traditional army. While not fit to endure hell's scrutiny and join Aegiskind, these new soldiers would still be fierce and well-trained. And their useless parents could sleep soundly at night knowing they had not sentenced their offspring to near-certain death as before.

Well, Macella thought sardonically, *I've certainly fulfilled my Fate.* She'd condemned more children to a painful life. No matter how much the training in Smoketown had improved, it was not for the faint of heart. Becoming an

Aegis involved unbelievable, unendurable suffering. Many would still die in the attempt. Those who survived would live dangerous and often lonely lives.

In addition to her many other mistakes, she could now add the sin of growing the Crown's army. If the day came when Aegises had to stand against the Crown, Macella would know she had strengthened the army pitted against her brethren. Raised to be Aegises, settling for being soldiers, the former Aegis recruits would undoubtedly be the army's best fighters. And Macella's words had created them. Were it not for her, such soldiers would not exist.

Because they would be dead. The voice in her mind was gentle and familiar.

(3) Macella had sensed Aithan approaching but had not expected that he would so clearly hear the turmoil in her mind. Her grief must have been blaring from her tortured thoughts. Her Aegis came to stand behind her, his big hands kneading her shoulders. He bent to place a kiss atop her head, lingering to inhale and then sigh contentedly against her curls before straightening. Macella's shoulders relaxed involuntarily at his touch. The tears that had been prickling her eyes spilled over and ran down her cheeks. She turned in her chair, wrapping her arms around his waist and burying her face against his firm stomach.

"There were *never* survivors before the scribe forced the Crown to take better care of the child recruits," Aithan said, stroking her curls. "You have done so much more good than harm. Your writing is changing everything."

Macella breathed him in, taking comfort in his familiar scent. She could feel the deep rumble of his voice against her tear-streaked face. It soothed her as nothing else could. She felt herself growing calmer already.

"Kōsaten's unwanted children have always been sacrificed to Smoketown, even if it was in a quieter fashion," Aithan continued. "You have done more toward changing their fates than anyone else has ever dared. No one could do more without dismantling the entire system."

And we're working on doing that, as well, thanks to you, he added mentally.

Macella sighed heavily, forcing herself to hear the truth in his words. Things had taken an unexpected turn, but that did not nullify the good they'd done. She must believe that. She believed that Fate had led them down this path—she'd have to trust it was the right track.

"Listen to Fate, my love. It has not led us astray thus far," Aithan agreed, parroting words Macella had said to him in the early weeks of their first warm season at court. "Fate led us to one another, to the truths of who we are. Fate led us here. Listen, watch, and wait. We will know what to do when the time comes."

"I will never grow accustomed to the exactness of your memory. Why must you be so rational?" Macella grumbled, lifting her face to look at him.

Aithan brushed tears from her cheeks with a calloused thumb. "Because you are your own harshest critic. Someone has to defend you against such baseless claims."

Macella sighed again, giving herself a little shake. "I've no time for this pity party. I assume you've come to fetch me for the small council meeting?"

Aithan helped Macella to her feet, pulling her into a warm embrace. She wrapped her arms around his waist, leaning into him, her head against his chest. Her Aegis's heartbeat was as reassuring as always, steady, strong, and true.

After a few long moments, Macella reluctantly pried herself away. She splashed her face with water, attempting to disguise the evidence of her teary breakdown. She would not, could not show weakness here.

The pressure of Aithan's arm and his quiet, solid presence at her side further grounded her as he escorted her to the meeting. By the time they reached the council chamber, she felt nearly like herself—or as nearly as she ever felt to her true self while amongst the Crown and their entourages. She gave Aithan's arm a squeeze at the chamber's double doors, then slipped away to take her place at a small writing desk near the head of the table.

Aithan spoke briefly to the members of the Royal Guard stationed on either side of the chamber's doors. As Protector of the Crown, Aithan was also the high commander of the Royal Guard. Since his duties kept him constantly occupied with the monarchs, his captain primarily handled the regiment's day-to-day management. Still, Aithan took every opportunity to speak to the knights, not only offering guidance or encouragement, but simply asking about their needs and their lives. Despite his mostly solitary existence prior to this appointment, Aithan was proving himself a natural leader.

Aithan glanced away from the knight he was speaking to and caught Macella's gaze, a smile quirking at the corner of his mouth. *You realize I can hear you, right? You are practically bursting with pride.*

Macella smothered her own smile as she arranged her parchments and pens. Their easy mental connection often meant that they caught intense thoughts the other hadn't meant to share. But Macella *was* proud of him, and she wanted him to know it.

I love you too, Aithan thought at her, before turning back to the guards.

Macella's heart fluttered. Her mood had taken a drastic turn in the brief interval she'd been in Aithan's presence. For the millionth time, Macella thanked the forces that had brought them together. Aithan of Auburndale was the greatest gift she'd ever received.

(4) "Dear Macella looks a bit tired today, does she not, Lord Anwir?"

Macella sobered immediately. That high, tinkling voice was one of her least favorite sounds. She forced a pleasant smile before looking up.

Short, plump, and pretty, Queen Annika stood looking sweetly down at Macella. The queen's bright blue eyes were cold, despite her lovely smile. With her pale skin, wide eyes, and rosy cheeks, all framed by long hair flowing in shiny golden waves, there was something innocent and childlike about the young monarch. Macella knew that perception could not be farther from the truth.

The beautiful young ruler had taken instant issue with Macella, out of some misplaced jealousy of the king's admiration. Likewise, Macella had immediately distrusted the young queen—a feeling proven justified when Queen Annika manipulated King Khari into a power display that ended with Shamira's execution. Thus, it was the young queen's folly that led to Aithan being appointed as Protector of the Crown, trapping him and Macella in Pleasure Ridge Park indefinitely. Her relationship with Queen Annika had only soured further since that disastrous day.

"Lady Macella and her grace, Queen Annika, look as lovely as ever," simpered Lord Anwir with a small bow.

Macella acknowledged the compliment with a small nod. "You flatter me, Lord Anwir."

In truth, Macella despised Lord Anwir nearly as much as she did the young queen. Tall, pale, and gaunt, with dark hair growing increasingly gray around his temples, and sunken, cornflower blue eyes, he had an unpleasant look about him. As Grand Vizier, he was King Khari's most trusted advisor. Though his closeness to the king was enough to ensure Macella's disdain, the man himself was insufferable. Calculating and cunning, Lord Anwir made a point of ingratiating himself to the most powerful person in any room, by whatever means necessary. It was never clear if he was giving his true opinion on any matter, or whether he even had his own opinions. Lord Anwir agreed with any course of action that benefited Lord Anwir.

Macella turned from the Grand Vizier to bow her head at the queen. "Her Grace, Queen Annika is most gracious to concern herself with my well-being. I assure you I am quite rested. With the lovely accommodations the Crown has so generously provided, how could I not be?"

Queen Annika's cobalt gaze hardened—doubtless due to her disappointment at not getting a rise out of Macella. Macella gave her a sugary smile. Queen Annika sniffed and turned away, imperiously taking Lord Anwir's arm so that he could escort her to her seat at the council table. As soon as the queen's back was turned, Macella let her smile shift into a smirk. She would not give Annika the pleasure of nettling her today.

While Macella was preoccupied with the queen, the chamber had slowly filled. Queen Annika took her seat to the left of King Khari's place at the head of the table. Lord Anwir sat across from her, at the king's right hand. King Khari's other spouses—Monarch Meztli and Queen Awa—soon took their places beside Annika.

As always, Monarch Meztli looked inscrutable. They sat between Annika and Awa as they did whenever the Crown gathered. The entire court knew that Awa and Annika disliked one another immensely. They never sat near each other, only speaking to one another to the extent the conventions of politeness required. Meztli never seemed to mind being the buffer between them—but then, Meztli never seemed to mind much of anything.

Of all the Crown, Monarch Meztli was the most mysterious. They seldom showed any emotion aside from boredom. They were as uniquely beautiful as Annika and Awa, with copper skin and long, straight black hair. Fathomless black eyes shone in their solemn face, complemented by high cheekbones and full lips.

Queen Awa was Macella's favorite, despite her cold beauty that was somehow simultaneously attractive and repellent. Awa was tall, with smooth blue-black skin. Her teardrop shaped face was haughty and forbidding. She favored gowns of white or silver. Today's pristine white dress was complemented by a white and silver headdress that wrapped intricately around the queen's bald head. Awa caught Macella's gaze and gave her a brief, tiny smile that was gone before anyone else could see it.

As all the king's spouses seated themselves, other members of the small council filed in. Aithan took his place behind King Khari's chair at the head of the table. He looked handsome and intimidating with his chiseled features, broad shoulders, and tall, muscular frame. The crimson tips of his silky silver hair blended with the deep crimson of his surcoat and tunic. His golden skin shone, complemented nicely by the colors of his guild. He stood at attention, only his orange eyes moving, scanning the room.

The Grand Mage and Grand Treasurer seated themselves beside Lord Anwir, calling for servants to fill their goblets. Additional staff entered with light refreshments of cheese, pastries, and fruit. The servants were swiftly followed by the captain of the Royal Guard.

"High Commander." Captain Drudo gave Aithan a respectful bow as he entered.

"Captain." Aithan nodded in acknowledgment.

Before positioning himself at his post against the wall behind the seated monarchs, Captain Drudo bowed to Macella. He took her hand fondly, glancing over at Aithan before giving Macella a saucy wink. She rolled her eyes and looked at Aithan, who observed the exchange with veiled amusement.

"Lady Macella." Captain Drudo greeted her in a low voice laced with his easy charm.

"You continue to make these meetings the brightest part of my day."

Macella blushed—more from her discomfort with her title than any effect of the captain's attentions. Her position as Royal Scribe had elevated her rank, but given her modest upbringing, she often felt like an imposter.

"Good morning, Captain." She smiled. "Stop your flattery and get to your post before your commander has you sent to the brig."

"A few extra moments with you would be well worth the punishment," Drudo replied.

He kissed her hand before moving away, his lips lingering an extra moment on her skin.

Drudo seemed a good man to Macella. Unlike some, he took no issue with being commanded by an Aegis. He and Aithan got along so well, in fact, that Drudo often joined them for a meal or an evening drink. He was young and quite handsome, with olive skin, a neat goatee, and thick, dark hair with golden highlights that glinted in the torchlight.

Captain Drudo found Macella equally attractive, and he made sure she knew it. He kept up a good-natured flirtation, playfully trying and failing to get a rise out of Aithan. Macella appreciated that they had at least one person in the castle with whom they could maintain a casual friendship, free of pretense and conniving.

He is thinking that you look especially fetching today with your curls unbound about your face, Aithan informed Macella mentally. *And now he's noticing how inviting your collarbone is and thinking how soft your beautiful brown skin must feel beneath your bodice. One day, I'm going to give him a good thrashing.*

Macella stifled a laugh with a cough. It was certainly a double-edged sword that Aithan could hear more than just Macella's mind. As an Aegis from the guild of Lucifer, one of his gifts was telepathy. Here in the castle, it proved extremely useful to be able to hear minds. His gift helped them to avoid many a misstep and often guided them in meeting the whims of mercurial nobles.

Unfortunately for their plans of deposing King Khari, the minds of the Crown were closed to Aithan. After passing through the trials administered by the gods of light, King Khari was blessed, and shared that blessing with her spouses. The Crown had all been enhanced in a variety of ways. Like Aegises and mages, they did not age. They were also graced with good health and other protections Macella and Aithan had yet to discover. What they did know was that the Crown's minds and bodies were shielded from Aithan's gifts.

Once Aithan was appointed to his position as Protector of the Crown and took his vows, he was beholden to certain magical bindings. He could not intentionally harm any member of the Crown, even if he wished to. The attempt would cause him excruciating pain and possibly worse. King Khari's spouses had taken similar vows upon their marriage. Macella was sure that, had it not been for the binding, one of them would've murdered another by now.

Don't look so serious. I am no stranger to the minds of men, and Drudo's fantasies are far more honorable than many I've heard. I will not hurt him too badly. He's still a fine captain, and I need him.

Aithan's mental teasing brought Macella back to the moment. Without looking in Aithan's direction, she straightened her neck and shoulders. Feigning nonchalance, she trailed her fingers lightly across her collarbone. She gazed down as though in concentration and brought her other hand up to press her pen against her bottom lip absently. Then, wetting her lips with her tongue, she resumed readying her papers.

Perhaps you're the one who is going to kill him, Aithan scolded. *I am not even going to repeat what he's thinking now—though I might actually be forced to throttle him if he doesn't rein this fantasy in soon.*

Stop listening to him, Macella replied, giving Aithan a stern look. *Surely there are more useful minds to study at present.*

Aithan flashed her a grin, then schooled his face back into its customarily stoic expression. Macella resumed her perusal of the assembled council. While she couldn't hear human minds, Macella was still an astute observer. She, too, had helped keep them in good standing with the rest of the castle's inhabitants through her careful scrutiny.

There were but a few remaining small council members. Next to Lord Anwir, Grand Mage Kiama had taken her place. Kiama was a large, lovely woman—tall and broad with generous curves. She wore her hair in hundreds of small braids that hung to her waist. Her light gray mage's eyes looked especially striking against the rich mahogany of her skin. Though Macella didn't trust the Grand Mage, she had no reason to dislike her. While it was wise to be wary of everyone at court, Kiama didn't present as exceptionally perfidious. The Grand Mage was a powerful woman who kept herself to herself.

Finally, there was Grand Treasurer Theomund. While Macella knew no ill of him, she was skeptical of anyone who'd remained in the king's good graces for so long. Like Kiama, Theomund had served for much of Khari's reign. Unlike Kiama, the Grand Treasurer aged as a regular human.

Thus, unlike Grand Mage Kiama, he probably wouldn't be in the king's service much longer. Theomund was incredibly old and in poor health. As a pair of servants helped him into his seat, a coughing fit racked the Grand Treasurer's body. He gulped his water, hacking and spluttering all the while.

Macella felt a stab of pity for the elderly man. He should have retired decades ago. She knew that he had long wished to relinquish his duties. However, since the Crown could not agree upon a successor to his position, Theomund was forced to continue in the role. Macella knew he would likely die as Grand Treasurer, because each member of the Crown had their own candidate for the position and their own self-serving reasons for so choosing.

There was a general stir as everyone rose from their seats. Macella quickly followed suit. King Khari had entered at last. She swaggered to her seat at the head of the table, her crown perched precariously at a rakish angle on her shorn blond head.

As beautiful as she was dangerous, King Khari effortlessly commanded the attention of everyone in the room. Though shorter than many present, the king still somehow seemed to tower over everyone else. She wore her power like armor and wielded it like a sword. One must be on constant guard in King Khari's presence.

"You may sit," the king announced imperiously, after she settled into her chair.

While the small council reseated themselves, a page appeared at King Khari's side. Carefully, the child used a silver spoon to scoop wine from the king's goblet. After tasting it, the page waited for several long, silent minutes. When the king was sure they suffered no ill effects from the drink, she waved the child away. The remaining servants exited behind the page, closing the door firmly behind them. Small council meetings were private, despite the fact that secrets tended to spread through the castle like wildfire regardless.

"Lord Anwir." King Khari motioned for the Grand Vizier to begin the day's proceedings.

Chapter Two

Macella had learned a great deal in her time as Royal Scribe. She now knew when to record someone's words exactly and when to revise or omit certain details. Some of her copious notes would eventually become news items for the official monthly bulletin, while others would join the historical records in the castle's library. Sometimes, King Khari would redact or destroy her reports, but mostly Macella had learned which words pleased the supreme sovereign.

Thus, Macella scribbled away as the meeting droned on. The Grand Vizier, Grand Mage, and Grand Treasurer made their daily reports. Macella tried not to wince as Grand Treasurer Theomund wheezed and coughed his way through updates on the kingdom's finances. She noticed Queen Annika watching the old man with a smirk playing at the corner of her full, pink lips. Her sharp blue gaze was eager. Macella could practically see the young queen calculating how many days Theomund might yet live. It was evident Annika had plans for his position.

Next, King Khari asked Aithan to update the council on the kingdom's safety. Macella listened carefully, knowing much of his report would need to be veiled or hidden entirely. Kōsaten's citizens needn't know too much of the dangers stalking their world. Macella had once been blissfully ignorant of death deities and hellspawn. Of course, everyone was aware that the Aegises closed rifts between their world and the others, but their understanding was abstract. Few truly understood how frequently the rifts appeared or what horrors emerged when they did.

"As you all are aware, hell has been restless of late," Aithan explained, his deep voice somber. "We've just witnessed the shortest cold season on record. Since then, I and each of the other Aegises have sensed rifts at steady and above average rates. I believe something dangerous is brewing."

The council murmured amongst themselves. This was not the first discussion of these matters, but, as yet, no solutions had been raised. Aithan was in regular communication with the seven Aegises who patrolled the kingdom. He'd told Macella how each of them reported closing more rifts and dispatching more demons than in previous seasons.

"What of the efforts to fill out your ranks?" Lord Anwir demanded, silencing the side conversations. "The kingdom is short two Aegises. We have temporarily allowed the recruitment roles to remain vacant, but we cannot allow this indefinitely."

King Khari smiled, cutting her eyes toward Macella knowingly. "While your point is valid,

Lord Anwir, our need for new recruits is negligible. Thanks to the improvements we have made to Aegis training in Smoketown, we have more healthy, well-trained soldiers who can attempt the transformations. We even anticipate gaining stronger soldiers for our army, as those neophytes unsuitable for transformation are still quite impressive."

Macella forced herself to keep writing and to maintain her placid facial expression. Inside, though, she felt a stab of guilt and grief. King Khari was clearly taunting her, reveling in the Crown's triumph. The king had been furious when Macella's anonymous writings, as the Shield's Scribe, had alerted the general populace to the abhorrent treatment that Aegis recruits endured. Because of the widespread success of Macella's Aegis stories, public opinion was so strongly in favor of the Aegises that the Crown had no choice but to make changes to appease them. Now it seemed that Macella's victory had become another triumph for the king.

"Macella," King Khari said, jolting Macella from her thoughts. "Be sure to note this for our next bulletin. My people will be so pleased to hear of our successful reform efforts. I hope that the Shield's Scribe also hears of it and lauds it in a future story for those feckless society papers that so love to print their scribblings."

"Of course, your grace," Macella replied, studiously avoiding the many eyes upon her by bending her head over the desk and writing furiously.

Macella had always dreamed of having her stories read and loved by the masses. She'd been surprised when the society papers had printed her Aegis tales and even more surprised when they became so widely beloved that readers clamored for more. The society papers printed her stories as quickly as she could write them, and the more that they published, the more public sentiment toward Aegiskind shifted. Macella had been pleased that her work helped people to recognize the true heroism of the Aegises but hadn't bargained on the Crown ever discovering her true identity.

Now, she teetered on the edge of a blade. Officially, she was the Royal Scribe. She was still allowed her other writings for the society papers, under the thinly veiled threat of punishment should those writings displease the Crown. Now it sounded as though she would have to somehow praise the improvements in Smoketown, while trying not to encourage more parents to sacrifice their children to its wretchedness. Macella felt her earlier anxiety and sadness threatening to overtake her again.

"Pardon my insistence, your grace." Lord Anwir cleared his throat, reclaiming the general attention of the room. "While we might not need additional recruits, tradition dictates that we maintain a consortium of thirteen Aegises. This is the deal Khalid brokered with the gods to maintain balance."

Macella risked a look around to gauge the council's reactions. Mostly, they were looking between the king and Aithan for a response. Unfortunately, Queen Annika's ice blue eyes were locked on Macella. Macella quickly turned her attention to Aithan and the king, not wanting to give the young queen a reaction.

"As supreme sovereign for nearly a century, I am well aware of Khalid's valiant work," King Khari drawled lazily, her voice laced with menace.

Lord Anwir heard the king's displeasure and quickly amended his words. "Since the Crown has so impressively diminished the need for recruits, we have a unique opportunity to resolve two challenges with one effort. When the Aegis ranks are full once more, we can allocate two additional Aegises to the order of shields. With the increase in rifts, this could better secure the kingdom's safety."

King Khari sat back, her expression contemplative. "Have you any update from Smoketown, Lord Protector?"

"Our commanders report extraordinary improvements since the start of the cold season," Aithan replied. "They anticipate advancing several new candidates by the start of the harvesting season."

Macella focused on her notes, calculating the timeline Aithan laid out. It was currently the planting season—no, the *warm* season. She'd learned that calling it the planting season betrayed her poor roots—only farmers and day workers used that terminology. Funny that the wealthy had no problem with using "harvesting" season. Obviously, they were used to reaping what they did not sow.

Queen Awa's eyes flicked toward Macella and then quickly away. Macella knew what the eldest queen was thinking—how many new Aegises could there be? As their first ally at court, Queen Awa knew the secret of Macella and Aithan's parentage. She was one of the few people living who knew that Macella had undergone the dark gods' scrutiny and succeeded in gaining Hades's favor, thereby making her one of the Thirteen.

"Ensure they know that it's a matter of urgency," King Khari commanded, now smiling at Lord Anwir. "The Grand Vizier is the first of this council to offer a viable solution for restoring the balance of dark and light. Would that you were all so useful."

King Khari's ochre eyes lingered on Queen Awa as she spoke. Both Macella and Aithan had noticed that the long-standing animosity between the king and her first spouse had grown increasingly hostile since the cold season. King Khari's rash execution of Shamira, the previous Protector of the Crown and

Queen Awa's secret beloved, had apparently been the final affront. It seemed but a matter of time before one of them took drastic action.

As if wishing to lean into the tension of the moment, King Khari shifted the conversation to another contentious topic. "What news from the north?"

The room fell completely silent, aside from Lord Theomund's coughing. Macella's pen slowed. She would have to frame these next notes carefully.

"My initial parley with the lairds of the region demonstrated their willingness to find common ground," Queen Awa began, her voice a sonorous tenor. Most everyone in the room unconsciously leaned toward her, listening intently. She so rarely spoke that people always paid close attention when she did.

"The common ground is that I am their sovereign," King Khari snapped. "Their voice is represented in this chamber by Queen Awa of Highview, my eldest spouse. Highview is one of the wealthiest cities in all of Kōsaten. The north should be honored with their favorable position in the kingdom. Instead, they plot treason."

"Highview prospers, my king, but some parts of the region remain among the poorest in the kingdom," Queen Awa persisted, her face a haughty mask. "Cities like Newburg and Shively are filled with families struggling to survive. They need to see that the Crown understands their plight and intends to aid them."

Macella could sometimes forget her long-ago life in Shively—so far was it from her life in the capital. She remembered how hard her adopted family had worked just to afford the barest necessities. The people in her village would hear tales of the rich families in Highview and

Belknap, but though those cities were within their region, they seemed as fanciful as stories of Pleasure Ridge Park and Kōsaten Keep. It was strange to hear royals discussing her people's welfare.

"Bah!" King Khari scoffed, flouncing back in her chair crossly. "Perhaps Queen Awa has lost touch with the interests of her home region. Mayhap she's tarried at court too long to truly represent her people."

This time, even Lord Theomund was silent. The king's words hung in the air, icy stalactites of tension and hatred. The council members all seemed to have found very interesting spots on the walls to study. All but King Khari and Queen Awa, who glared unflinchingly at one another, and Queen Annika, who watched the standoff with poorly suppressed merriment.

The moment stretched on for an uncomfortable length of time. Eventually, Lord Theomund couldn't help but break into a fresh coughing fit. So intense was this attack, that the Grand Mage summoned a servant to fetch the Grand Treasurer a draught from her apothecary. Several more servants rushed in to attend to the old man until the draught was procured. Several minutes passed before Lord Theomund had settled back into quieter hacks and snuffles.

During the general clamor of Lord Theomund's coughing fit, Macella noticed something odd. Everyone was watching or assisting the Grand Treasurer, but Macella happened to glance around. Monarch Meztli drew Macella's attention because they were unnaturally still and not attending to the tumult at all. As Macella watched, Monarch Meztli's eyes went distant. The black of their irises and pupils lightened until there was only whiteness visible.

Macella should've been alarmed, but she felt oddly calm. Her shoulders relaxed involuntarily. The tense atmosphere of but a few minutes prior began to melt away. The room grew quiet as everyone resettled themselves. Macella saw King Khari glance sharply at Monarch Meztli. Following the king's gaze, Macella saw that Monarch Meztli looked as inscrutable as ever, their black eyes perfectly normal.

Finally, King Khari broke the silence. "Macella, please strike my last comment from the record. I am afraid it might be misinterpreted as a slight to my dear wife."

Macella attempted to conceal her start of surprise at the sound of her name. Her voice was slightly breathier than usual as she replied. "Of course, your grace."

"Thank you for your continued diplomatic efforts, my queen." King Khari's voice dripped with sarcasm as she smiled coldly at Queen Awa. "The Lord Protector and I are currently considering additional ambassadorial actions—but we will discuss that further when our ideas are more solidified. Let us adjourn for the day. Lord Theomund is weary and in need of rest."

The abrupt conclusion to the meeting did not surprise Macella. Most interactions with the Crown concluded at King Khari's momentary whim. Macella imagined that the king had amused herself at Queen Awa's expense as much as she dared for one day. Now, she would return to her solitary scheming for the remainder of the morning.

The room filled with the rustle of papers and fine fabrics as each of the council members gathered themselves and left the chamber. As Macella collected her writing instruments, she noticed King Khari pull Grand Mage Kiama aside for a brief, whispered exchange. She looked away before the king could catch her watching them.

Her desk wobbled as Queen Annika brushed by with a bit more force than necessary. The queen extended an apologetic hand, steadying the desk.

She blinked her wide blue eyes at Macella. "I beg your pardon, dear, I didn't even notice you there—I thought you'd already left the chamber." Queen Annika's voice trilled with false sincerity. "I assumed you'd hurried back to your rooms to rest yourself for a spell. You really do look exhausted."

Macella bared her teeth in what she hoped would pass as a tired smile. She inclined her head in acknowledgment, not trusting herself with a verbal response. The young queen's returning smile was triumphant. She seemed to truly relish any opportunity to get under Macella's skin. Satisfied, the queen turned away and moved toward the chamber's large doors.

Macella saw Queen Annika touch King Khari's arm, standing on tiptoe to whisper into her ear. The king smiled, running a hand lightly down the young queen's back. As Annika departed, King Khari turned her sharp ochre eyes on Macella. Macella quickly looked down, pretending to be arranging her notes. King Khari turned to leave.

As Aithan made to follow, the king held up a hand to stop him. Her eyes assessed Macella shrewdly, her mouth curling into a smirk. This time Macella stared back, willing her face to remain bland. The moment stretched, neither of them looking away.

At last, King Khari laughed and looked at Aithan. "Dear Macella seems a bit unlike herself today," she said flippantly. "I am afraid I have kept you from her too much of late. Captain Drudo and the rest of the Royal Guard can handle matters for a few hours. Take the day to yourselves and report to my chambers after supper."

With that, Khari strolled from the room, the doors clicking loudly closed behind her, leaving Macella to puzzle over her intentions and the insinuations beneath her words. Again, she felt a jolt of exhausted anger at the constant calculations necessary for survival at court. As much as she loved words, Macella missed when they actually carried their surface meanings.

"The king is not wrong," Aithan said, moving to stand before her. "Your spirit is heavy today."

Macella looked up into Aithan's amber orange eyes. She could not deny that Finley's letter had disquieted her, nor that she was exceedingly weary of court politics. She knew she must do her duty and yet she grieved that she had so little time to feel her emotions—to be her true self.

"We will find some reprieve," Aithan murmured, cupping her face gently in his big, calloused hands. "We have worked tirelessly for some time under challenging conditions. We deserve respite—you especially."

I cannot know how tiresome it must be to constantly mask your true nature. I am working on a solution. Give me but a bit more time.

Aithan's voice in her mind was earnest and reassuring. Macella knew that this life was no easier for him than it was for her. She sighed heavily, then squared her shoulders. She could endure, as long as they were together.

"What should we do with our unexpected holiday?" she asked, mustering a smile.

"The king has been so gracious, surely we must make the most of her generosity."

(5) "I have an idea," Aithan replied, his gaze falling to her lips. He traced his hands from her face to her neck, then slowly along her arms.

Macella's breath caught in her throat. "Do not keep me in suspense. What do you propose?"

"Propose?" Aithan smiled, taking her hands in his. He inclined his head, bringing his mouth close to hers. His breath was warm against her slightly parted lips.

Macella held her breath, lifting her face toward his in anticipation. Instead of kissing her, Aithan moved his mouth over her cheek and down the side of her neck, his lips hovering an inch from her skin. Still holding her hands, he slowly sank to one knee.

Macella felt her heart stutter. Aithan gazed up at her, his amber eyes burning with desire. Her stomach clenched hard as he released her hands before sliding his over her hips, his rough skin rasping against the silk of her skirt.

"I propose we remember who we are," Aithan replied, his voice a low rumble. "I propose we use this time to relax and reconnect."

He slipped his hands beneath her skirts, trailing his hands lightly up her legs. Macella shivered, though her skin had grown hot. Aithan's gaze smoldered as he watched her face, savoring her reaction to his touch. Warmth throbbed between her legs.

"Drudo's fantasizing has given me several ideas," Aithan continued, sliding his hands from her thighs, over her hips, and around to cradle her ass. "Since I have the privilege of acting on his desires, I should take full advantage of the opportunity."

Macella felt his strong fingers nimbly untying the laces of her panties. He tucked them into his pocket, smiling up at her wickedly. Then, gripping her ass firmly, he rose and lifted her onto the table. Hooking a leg of the nearest chair with his foot, he pulled it to him, and sat down between her thighs. Running his fingers over her skin, he pushed her skirts up to her hips.

"This is by far the most interesting thing to ever happen at this table," Aithan told her. He ran a hand up her bodice, gently guiding her to lie back. "And, certainly, the most delicious."

Macella felt Aithan's lips on her inner thigh. Scooting closer, he lifted her legs to rest on his shoulders, then brushed his lips up her leg until he reached the juncture of her thighs. Her vagina clenched as he inhaled deeply, then exhaled a low groan.

"I misspoke," he whispered, his breath against the sensitive skin of her vulva making her shiver. "You are the most delicious thing to ever grace this entire castle."

And then his mouth found her clitoris. Macella gasped as he sucked gently, sending tendrils of sensation through her torso. Aithan gripped her hips tightly, holding her in place as he explored her crevice with his tongue. He hummed with satisfaction, and Macella felt the vibration of his lips against her labia. She arched her back and cried out, entwining her fingers in his silky silver hair.

"You are so much more exquisite than Drudo could imagine," Aithan murmured. "You are divine."

His tongue traced slow circles on her clit. Macella moaned and squirmed against the polished wood of the table. Aithan held her steady, increasing the pressure of his tongue and pulling her closer. Macella cried out, moving her hips in time with the incredible rhythm of his tongue.

"You somehow taste even better than you smell," Aithan said as he carefully slid a finger inside of her. "And, gods, don't get me started on how you *feel*."

His finger moved within her, massaging that spot inside of her that was directly tied to the bundle of nerves he was manipulating with his tongue. Deliberately, in slow increments, Aithan moved his tongue faster, pressing still more firmly. With one hand, he held her still, while his other hand worked in tandem with his mouth, coaxing her toward her climax. Macella felt a quiver spreading through her torso.

She was moaning louder now, unable and unwilling to stifle her pleasure. She could feel Aithan's arousal in her mind, their connection stronger, as always, when they made love. He relished her reactions, reveled in making her moan. Macella cried out again, and Aithan groaned, the buzz of his lips awakening an electric current deep in her belly. Sensing her orgasm building, Aithan worked his tongue and finger relentlessly, his strong grip allowing her no escape from the unbearable pleasure.

And then she was falling over the edge into an ocean of stars. Her throaty cries echoed through the chamber. Her body racked with tremors.

Aithan stood, and Macella's thighs slipped from his shoulders. With one hand, Aithan guided her to wrap her legs around his waist, while his other hand unbuttoned his trousers.

Macella's orgasm had just begun to ebb when she felt Aithan's steely cock push inside her.

"Gods," he groaned, his grip spasming on her thigh as he thrust into her again. "Fuck, you are divine."

Macella replied by moaning loudly and lifting her hips eagerly to meet him. The buzz in her belly intensified at the immaculate agony of Aithan's cock plunging inside of her, filling her as only he could. With nothing else within reach, Macella grasped at the soft fabric of Aithan's tunic. She clenched it in her fist, using it to pull him closer as she wrapped her legs more tightly around his waist.

Aithan growled and moved faster, his strokes deep and urgent. Macella felt a weightless bliss begin to radiate from deep in her core. She moaned in wordless yearning, each thrust pushing her closer to an inevitable eruption.

Aithan slid his arms beneath her, pulling her into a tight embrace. Macella wrapped her arms around his neck, and then they were moving as one. His strong arms guided her as she matched his strokes. His lips were on her collarbone, her ear, the swell of her breasts above her bodice. Macella clung to him, the sounds of his pleasure mingling with her own as the throbbing at her center built to an almost painful ecstasy of sensation.

"Macella," Aithan whispered, and she came apart in his arms.

Chapter Three

It wasn't clear how much time had passed before the world finally returned, but eventually, Macella found herself blinking up at the intricate chandeliers of the small council chamber. Aithan smiled down at her. He'd found a towel and bowl of water.

"You are truly something, Lord Protector," Macella told him, smiling as he helped her from the table.

Aithan kissed her slowly in reply, his embrace a gentler mirror of the frenzied final minutes of their lovemaking. After a few long moments, he reluctantly pulled away. He bent and carefully rubbed between her thighs with the warm towel.

"We should probably allow the servants to come in and complete their chores." Aithan grinned. "I suppose we are fortunate they didn't interrupt us. Perhaps they suspected we needed a private moment."

Macella rolled her eyes, but she couldn't deny that her mood had lifted significantly. "The entire keep knew we were having a private moment, and you love it, you rake. So, what shall we do with ourselves now?"

I have an idea, Aithan thought at her. *Follow my lead.*

Aithan held her close as they left the council chamber. Macella tried not to blush at the furtive glances they attracted from the nearest soldiers and servants. Members of the Royal Guard saluted as Aithan passed, but she was certain they were suppressing grins. She smiled to herself, shrugging inwardly. She'd had good sex, and she'd given everyone something to smile about—win-win.

"Queen Annika was right," Aithan said, slightly louder than necessary. "You should lie down and rest awhile."

Macella quirked an eyebrow at him, before remembering she was supposed to be following his lead. "I suppose I could use a nap now."

Aithan smirked at that. *As if I could tire you out that easily.*

Aloud, Aithan continued. "I'll train in the gardens awhile and then procure our lunch. Since we are free to dine together today, I thought it would be nice to eat alone in our chambers."

Macella faked a yawn. "That sounds perfect."

In reality, Macella was far more wound up than she was tired. The sex had been a spectacular release, but she was still full of tumult. She needed to channel her frustrations into something positive before they got the best of her. She'd already made the mistake of allowing Annika and Khari a glimpse of her true emotions today.

They made their way to their rooms, repeating the same conversation beats whenever within earshot of other people. Macella was sure that, within minutes, anyone who might be interested would know their alleged plans for the morning. One thing they could count on in Kōsaten Keep was the rapid spread of gossip.

Once inside their rooms, Macella gave Aithan a skeptical look. *I'm not at all tired.*

Aithan wrapped his arms around her, brushing his lips against her ear. When he whispered, his warm breath sent a delicious chill down Macella's spine. She shivered.

"I have been thinking of ways to restore some of what you have lost," he murmured.

"Today is the perfect opportunity to test one of my ideas."

Aithan grinned roguishly but refused to give Macella any further information. He instructed her to change into more casual attire. As Macella slipped into a soft tunic, leggings, and boots, Aithan closed the curtains around their bed. He nodded at the bed, then looked her over and nodded again.

"Perfect," he said. "Now disappear and follow me."

Macella gaped at him. She couldn't remember the last time she'd used her gift of invisibility. They'd been so busy learning their new roles and navigating court politics, they hadn't yet tested the effectiveness of that particular skill within the castle. They were still unsure of the extent of the Crown's gifts. For all they knew, King Khari might be able to penetrate Hades's cloaking.

I am almost certain this will work, Aithan insisted. *Trust me.*

He reached for her, and she took his hand without hesitation. Macella trusted Aithan unequivocally. Smiling, she summoned her inner flames, pleased at how quickly they responded despite her infrequent practice of late.

Epanofório. As soon as she thought the word, the black flames dancing over her skin shimmered and grew translucent. Though she could still see her body and the hazy onyx flames, she knew that she was invisible to everyone else.

It's still so odd. I can feel your hand in mine and yet you're completely transparent. Aithan shook his head, his eyes fixed vaguely on the air where Macella's face should be. For a moment, his grin turned rakish. *I can smell you very clearly, however. You smell like a stream, a crackling fire, an evening breeze, and good pussy. Very, very good pussy.*

Macella's breath hitched in her chest. Aithan had said those words to her on the night they'd met. She had been so inexperienced and afraid, and so excited simultaneously. On some level, she'd known even then that her life was about to change forever.

Aithan squeezed her hand before letting it drop. He turned toward the door of their apartments, beckoning for her to follow. He opened the door, quickly scanning the corridor before stepping out.

"Stay close," he whispered.

Macella touched him lightly on his broad back, assuring him that she was right behind him. Aithan lingered by the door, his hand resting on the knob. Macella knew he was listening intently for something.

When the rustle of quick, light footsteps sounded nearby, Aithan closed the door with elaborate care. As it clicked shut, a young woman rounded the corner. Her arms were full of linen. She was attempting to balance the mound of cloth on one side so that she could free a hand to tuck a loose lock of brown hair back under her servant's cap. She started a little when she saw Aithan.

"Lucy," he said, giving the young woman a warm smile. "I hoped I'd see you."

Lucy blushed furiously, her spattering of freckles standing out against the pink tint of her pale cheeks. Though Lucy was one of the servants that most frequently tended to their rooms and needs, she never seemed to grow used to interacting with the Protector of the Crown. Macella had noticed the young woman reading the scribe's stories in the society papers. Lucy was clearly a bit starstruck by Aithan of Auburndale.

"Lady Macella is very tired this morning and is taking a much-needed nap. I don't want her disturbed for the next few hours," Aithan explained, his voice both gentle and assertive.

"Can you make sure no one enters our rooms until I return?"

Macella saw the blush crawling up Lucy's neck and knew that the servants had indeed been discussing their vigorous activity in the small council chamber. Embarrassed by the knowledge of what had allegedly tired Macella out, Lucy couldn't even make eye contact with Aithan. She nodded, made a quick bow, and scurried away.

Macella was beginning to understand Aithan's plan as he led her through a nearby corridor to King Khari's lavish quarters. He nodded at the knights guarding the outer doors into Khari's foyer and then at another guard outside the king's study. They all saluted and let him pass. None of them noticed Macella trailing behind their high commander. Thus far, her invisibility seemed to be working.

King Khari sat at a grand mahogany desk, poring over a large tome. Captain Drudo stood behind the king. He smirked when he saw Aithan enter the room but then quickly schooled his expression into blankness. Obviously, the captain had also heard about Macella and Aithan's post-meeting activities.

The king looked up at Aithan. Unlike Drudo, King Khari did not bother hiding her mirth.

She leered, her ochre eyes dancing with amusement. "Lady Macella is quite tired out, I hear."

Macella's heart stopped for a moment at the sound of her own name. Nervously, she touched her star charm, but it hadn't changed temperature. The king wasn't looking at Macella, hadn't even glanced at the space where she stood a few feet behind Aithan. Could it be that her invisibility actually worked on the king? Aithan was watching Khari carefully as well, tensely awaiting the moment she noticed her Royal Scribe.

"She is resting a bit, your grace," Aithan lied smoothly. "I am busying myself with a bit of training, but we are looking forward to dining together. We are grateful for the extra time you've granted us."

The king spread her hands magnanimously. "You both serve me well. I want you to be happy."

No one lied more smoothly than King Khari. She didn't care about anyone's happiness but her own. Her sly grin made Macella's skin crawl. It didn't reach her cold ochre eyes.

Aithan bowed. "I only stopped to confirm that all was well before I left this wing of the keep. I will return after supper, if that still pleases the king."

King Khari waved her hand indifferently, already turning back to her book. "You're dismissed."

Macella held her breath as Aithan led her out of the king's study, across the foyer, and past the outer doors. She followed him through the corridors, until they exited into the west gardens. The air and sunlight immediately made Macella feel better. It was harder to feel trapped outside under the open sky.

She exhaled loudly, releasing the air she'd been holding in since they left the king's presence. "She couldn't see me," she marveled. "The king is not immune to my gifts."

Aithan smiled. *I suspected as much, but I am glad to have it confirmed. I imagine it's something to do with your unique nature.*

Soon, Aithan led her onto the Aegis training grounds the Crown had prepared for the previous cold season. Much like the training fields she'd seen in Duànzào, the course featured all manner of obstacles, alongside targets, straw figures, and sparring grounds. Aithan stopped at the latter.

"I thought you might like to run through some drills and then, perhaps, spar," he explained, limiting the movement of his lips as he did so. "Since no one can see you, you've no need to hold back. To anyone watching, it will look as though I'm simply drilling alone."

Macella felt a warm surge of love for her kind, beautiful man. Though it was such a simple gesture, it felt utterly profound. He had thought of a way to allow her the release of using her full strength and gifts after many months of hiding her true Aegis nature.

It is nothing. I am honestly surprised that we did not think of it sooner.

(6) The modest tenor of Aithan's thoughts filled Macella with another surge of love and gratitude. She flung her arms around him. He nearly stumbled—unable to see her and anticipate such impulsive movements. She felt a laugh rumbling in his chest.

"We must still behave as if there are eyes on *me* though they cannot see you," Aithan murmured. "I should not hug you in return, but it has never been so difficult to control my arms."

Macella released him, laughing breathily. She thought, *I adore you*, and Aithan smiled her favorite, crinkle-eyed smile. The worries of the morning suddenly seemed small and distant.

Soon, Aithan was walking her through a series of drills. He could not see her to offer feedback, but he was an excellent teacher and modeled each movement perfectly. Using her muscles freely, using her special gifts, along with her full strength and speed—it was all exhilarating. She felt lighter, as if the weight of her secrets had been a physical burden. This was the outlet she'd craved.

Sparring was even better. It gave Macella the rare chance to truly push herself. She felt as if she were finally stretching after being caged for months. Her daggers felt warm and solid in her hands, though they remained invisible like anything else in her possession whenever she disappeared. She twirled them instinctively, testing their familiar weight. They felt right. *She* felt right.

Macella couldn't help but think of their days wandering the kingdom. Aithan had taught her to better wield her dagger, and then, once they'd uncovered the true depths of their Aegisborn powers, he'd trained her intensively. They'd spent their days traveling, sparring, and making love, and Macella had never been so happy in all her life.

As then, it took everything Macella had to keep up with Aithan, despite her invisibility. His other senses were as strong as he was. Since Macella could not throw her daggers for risk of them being seen, she lost the advantage of long-range attacks and was, instead, forced into close combat. Whenever she neared for a strike, Aithan was ready, smelling or hearing her despite her moving in near silence.

"I am going to need that sword you promised me," Macella grumbled after the third time she yielded with the tip of his blade pointed at her throat.

Aithan chuckled, remembering his long-ago pledge of getting her a sword of her own when they reached the capital. Of course, they didn't know then that she was Aegisborn. She'd only had one ordinary dagger, and her gifts were nascent or not yet emerged. Once she crossed through the veil, endured Hades's trials, and emerged as her fullest self, both her body and her weapons had changed. She was different now and would need a sword befitting a warrior.

I would die before breaking a promise to you, Aithan told her, as he had said and proven many times. *You will have a blade worthy of you.*

Before Macella could reply, her stomach growled loudly, catching them both by surprise. "I believe I've worked up an appetite."

"You've had a vigorous morning," Aithan replied, covering his mouth to hide his smile from any unseen onlookers. "Let us adjourn our training for today. I must tend to another matter—it will take but a few minutes. I will find Lucy and send her to fetch our lunch and meet you back in our chambers."

They returned to the castle, Macella, at least, feeling better than she had in months.

They parted ways at the corridor to the royal living quarters, Aithan turning toward the kitchens. Macella continued toward their rooms, finding it strange and a bit exciting to move invisibly through the halls of the keep.

It was not as easy as she might've expected. Being both transparent and corporeal meant having to be extremely careful. The castle was a busy place. Macella had to maintain constant awareness of her surroundings to avoid colliding with people and objects.

Nearing their apartments, she was forced to hastily slip into a side corridor, narrowly avoiding a servant pushing a dish-laden cart. As she waited for it to pass, she caught movement from the corner of her eye. It seemed the little corridor led to some sort of hidden alcove. It was dim and full of shadow, and Macella could not immediately determine what had drawn her eye. She took a few silent steps toward the concealed nook.

(7) A flicker of light danced on the wall. Someone in the alcove had a candle. Macella crept closer.

"You've served me long and you have served me well. I believe I can risk trusting you with delicate matters. Am I correct?"

Macella froze. She knew that voice. It was the unmistakably dangerous tenor of King Khari.

"It is my duty and my honor to serve the Crown, your grace."

Macella could not help but draw nearer to the hushed voices. She knew she recognized the other speaker's voice, but they were so quiet that she couldn't quite place them. Had Macella been an ordinary human, she would not have heard the whispered conversation at all from this distance.

"You alerted me to your suspicions of Kiho's treacherous intentions after they stole from our stores of brimstone but did not question my decision to let matters play out," King Khari went on. "While I do not know how that little experiment will culminate, it has made me think on my reign."

Macella's heart sped up. She'd met the Aegis, Kiho, after they'd stolen that brimstone. They'd been using it to summon rifts in a foolish attempt to raise a demon army against the Crown. Aithan and Macella had stopped them, hoping to forestall a war, but it seemed the king might've learned of their treasonous plans anyway.

Macella inched forward, hoping to catch a glimpse of Khari's informant. She saw that the corridor bent slightly, obscuring the alcove from view. From the main passage, it would appear that the little hallway ended at a stone wall. Past the bend, Macella could see now that it was Grand Mage Kiama standing with the king.

"There are so few truly loyal people among us," King Khari mused. "I am the king, the supreme sovereign, and yet I have so few I can trust. The nobles make false promises in exchange for power. My youngest spouses try to manipulate me, while my eldest plots to destroy me. Even the Aegises, bound to me by the gods themselves, conspire to depose me."

King Khari paused for a long moment. Kiama waited silently, giving nothing away.

Macella held her breath.

"Perhaps I need warriors bound to me by blood as well as magic," the king said finally. "I could protect Kōsaten for another century or more, but not like this. I need more true allies. Strong, powerful allies."

Again, the king paused. The air was perfectly still. Macella and Kiama waited.

"Have you ever seen an Aegis as remarkable as Aithan of Auburndale?" King Khari asked suddenly.

Macella barely got her hand to her mouth in time to smother a gasp. Her mind spun at the sudden shift in the conversation. Whatever she'd expected the king to say next, it hadn't involved Aithan.

Kiama and Khari's heads turned toward Macella in unison. She shrank back, forgetting that they could not see her. Or at least, she hoped they couldn't. It had seemed like her gift worked against King Khari that morning, but now she wasn't so sure. A king blessed by the gods and the most powerful mage in the kingdom might be able to see what others could not. Macella held perfectly still.

"He is exceptional, your grace," Grand Mage Kiama answered, turning her attention back to the king. "Each year our tests and examinations reveal that he outpaces his peers in every possible area and each year he exceeds his own previous records."

"He is exceptional, indeed," King Khari agreed. "Do your tests show anything else unique about him?"

The Grand Mage hesitated. Macella knew Kiama had to be wondering what the king already knew and what she wanted to hear. Macella wondered the same.

Finally, Kiama decided on her answer. "His genetic makeup is different from the others. It is unlike anyone's I have ever seen. I have yet to discover why."

Macella choked back another gasp. She'd known that the king was aware of Aithan's heritage but had not considered the Grand Mage might have her own suspicions. How would King Khari react?

To Macella's surprise, the king smiled. "Do you suspect it is because he is a crossbreed born of an impossible Aegis-human union?"

Grand Mage Kiama nodded, her face carefully blank. "I suspect it is because he is a crossbreed born of just such an unlawful union."

King Khari tilted her head at the Grand Mage. "I notice you say *unlawful* rather than *impossible*."

"We both know that it is possible." Kiama shrugged. "Dangerous and requiring a great deal of magic, but possible."

The king and the Grand Mage stared at one another for several long breaths. Macella felt it—the line they were toeing. Could they trust each other? By admitting her suspicions about Aegisborn, Kiama had stepped over a precipice. Would King Khari follow?

The king's voice was resolute and cold when she finally spoke. "I would have an Aegis army as loyal as you and as exceptional as Aithan of Auburndale. Many of the Thirteen are nearing the end of their usefulness. I wish to replace them with better."

The pieces came together for Macella even before the king took Kiama's hand and pulled her close. The Grand Mage, significantly taller than the king, bent until their heads nearly touched. The king's voice was barely a whisper when she spoke again, but Macella's Aegisborn hearing still picked up her words.

"You will help me replace them with my progeny—Aegisborn of my own flesh and blood."

Chapter Four

━━━━━◆◇◆◇◆━━━━━

...Honestly, Finley, as much as I enjoy reading the scribe's tales, I'm not sure they could do you justice. Whoever the scribe is, they surely must have heard of your exploits during their research into Aegiskind. Thus, they likely do not include you in their tales because they simply lack the words to adequately describe one as otherworldly as you.

I am pleased to hear that the young recruits are continuing to improve. As you know, the king is eager to see your ranks full again. She often comments on the Lord Protector's strength and skill. I even once overheard her grace say she would love to have a full Thirteen <u>just like him</u>. Of course, I'm partial to Aithan, considering he and I are such uniquely kindred souls...

Macella sighed and reread her latest letter to Finley for perhaps the dozenth time. It was so challenging to relay important information while concealing her true meaning from the prying eyes that all correspondence at court passed through. She wanted to alert Finley to King Khari's plan of creating Aegisborn, but there was no safe way to tell them in writing. She'd have to hope they got the gist, and she'd fill in the details when they met again. Regardless of the challenges of conveying secrets, Macella found that she enjoyed keeping up regular correspondence with her growing list of loved ones.

Mostly, she exchanged letters with Zahra and Finley, plus the occasional note from her family or the society papers. At first, she'd thought it simply an extravagance that servants retrieved and delivered all mail to the castle's inhabitants. However, she'd learned soon enough that it was much more calculated—another method for control. King Khari would know of every word coming in or out of Kōsaten Keep.

Macella smiled to herself. She was sure Khari enjoyed the awestruck letters from Macella's family in Shively. Had her letters not borne the royal seal, her parents probably would never have believed that their wayward child had not only survived on her own in the world, but that she now lived a life of luxury at court. Their typically sporadic correspondence had become much more regular since they'd learned of Macella's rise in status. Her siblings wanted to hear all about the clothes and food and parties, while her parents coveted the generous sums of money and parcels of gifts she sent. Writing home gave Macella a chance to lavish praise on the Crown and all the castle's extravagances—a chance that she utilized strategically. She'd learned quickly that flattery could take one far in Pleasure Ridge Park.

Macella's imagined that when her adoptive parents had accepted the charge of an orphan, they had not realized the arrangement would prove so advantageous. They'd undoubtedly been frightened of the cold-eyed Aegis who offered them money to take her in and had agreed out of fear more than altruism. Of course, even then, they'd already had a large family on a small income, so the money had definitely been a strong incentive. The coin Shamira paid would've seemed like a small fortune. They certainly could not have expected Macella to be the source of even greater riches.

While her family had never been loving, they had kept her alive. That was no small feat in the harsh Shively terrain, situated in the hottest region of Kōsaten, where food rarely grew, and money was scarce. Were it not for the demand for precious magical plants native to Shively, her hometown would have died long ago. Despite those obstacles, her adopted parents had fed and sheltered her until she was ready to strike out on her own.

So, Macella didn't let it bother her that they'd never shown much interest in her before—had never made her feel as though she truly belonged to them. She did not begrudge them their little requests now that she had so much to spare. She wrote her mother dutifully, sent money and gifts for them all, and then dismissed her family from her mind.

Her correspondence with Zahra and Finley was far more enjoyable. It was odd to find so many people in the world who seemed to accept and understand her. Aithan of Auburndale's love had disarmed and surprised her, but Zahra's and Finley's love had been somehow more shocking—two people who had no need for her, yet chose her as family. She'd never had so many people she cared for so genuinely, so many people who truly cared for her. And that was without even considering the allies they'd found at court, like Queen Awa, Captain Drudo, and Lynn, the castle's head tailor.

Sheriff Zahra Shelby had been charming from the moment they'd met, back when Macella and Aithan had followed a rift to the sheriff's town. Contrariwise, Macella's first meeting with Finley had culminated in her first and only real battle. Her daggers had left bloody gashes on Finley's long, graceful legs and, improbably, she'd left a positive impression on their heart. They'd spent the cold season getting better acquainted and, to her surprise, when the other Aegises left the capital to return to their duties, Finley had demanded that Macella write to them. Since then, seldom a week passed without a long letter to and from Duànzào.

Finley's natural aloof elegance translated well to letters, filling pages and pages with their dry humor, scathing observations, and scandalous stories—which they wanted Macella to incorporate into the scribe's tales for the society papers. Between the humorous anecdotes, they exchanged lines of coded messages like the one Macella was trying her best to convey in her latest letter. She didn't know exactly how the Duànzào Aegises would react to King Khari's plan of having her own Aegisborn army, but she knew they'd agree the king must be stopped.

Aithan had been grim when Macella relayed the conversation she'd overheard between King Khari and the Grand Mage. He and the other Aegises were accustomed to being subjected to extensive tests and having a variety of specimens taken from them every cold season. Though he'd never thought much of it, he had begun to suspect something was amiss in recent months.

"I assumed the Protector of the Crown, as the only Aegis stationed at court, was subjected to the tests year-round," he explained wearily. "I should have recognized that the king was taking a greater interest in me specifically."

Macella and Aithan had been considering appropriate countermeasures but had yet to determine a viable plan. Stealing or destroying the Aegis samples would make it difficult for the Grand Mage to use them for ill, but it would be impossible to get away with. Attempting to ally with Kiama was too risky—they had no clue where the woman's true allegiances lay. Fortunately, the king was incredibly busy at present and, thus, unlikely to attempt to enact her plans immediately. They had time to figure out a solution.

"Be sure to give Finley my love and tell them I know they stole my new braided leather sword belt," Aithan declared, strolling into the room.

Macella laughed as Aithan stooped to kiss her forehead. "They will only insist that it suits them better. But I'll add your message tomorrow when I finish my letter."

"Of course," Aithan smirked, pulling his formal sword belt from his wardrobe. "By tomorrow, you will have lots more interesting gossip to share. The Crown is making much ado about this evening's festivities."

King Khari had invited several influential nobles from the north to visit Kōsaten Keep. While a diplomatic effort, the invitation was also a political tactic. King Khari would want to show off her wealth and prowess so that the nobles would return home a bit more afraid of the Crown's power.

That evening, the Crown would hold a private dinner with the northern guests, which Macella was relieved not to be invited to. Unfortunately, she *was* expected to attend the subsequent ball in the northerners' honor. The event was mandatory for all of the castle's regular inhabitants and a few wealthy guests from nearby estates.

"I will return as soon as I am able," Aithan told her, kissing her again before slipping from the room as quickly as he'd entered.

With tensions high between the Crown and the north, Aithan was taking extra precautions to ensure the monarchs' safety. He'd spent all morning increasing and monitoring the castle's security, making adjustments as visitors arrived throughout the day. While Macella would be free to enjoy the ball, the Lord Protector would be on high alert.

"Not that I expect to find much enjoyment in it," Macella complained to the empty room.

While she'd hated the endless etiquette lessons the Crown had required her to take, Macella had to admit that they'd eased some of her anxiety about interacting at court. She knew the customs now, knew how to behave at events like tonight's ball. She didn't think it would be terrible, but she found all the pomp and circumstance exhausting. She did not relish the self-important small talk she would have to endure, nor the care she would have to take not to offend. At such social events one could meet useful allies or make dangerous enemies.

Macella didn't have long to wallow in her apprehensions. A brisk knock on the door gave her a moment's preparation before the high tailor came bustling in. As always, a handful of assistants followed her, carrying all manner of bags, baskets, and baubles.

"Good, you're all clean and ready," Lynn remarked, ushering Macella into the dressing chamber. One assistant took Macella's dressing gown while the others scurried to unpack their materials.

"You always say that." Macella grinned, stepping onto the box positioned before the room's huge mirror. "Do your other charges need you to bathe them as well as dress them?"

Lynn barked a laugh. The sound was rusty, as if rarely used. Macella loved to coax signs of mirth out of the no-nonsense tailor. Lynn was one of the few people at court Macella had both liked and trusted immediately.

"You would be surprised," Lynn retorted, circling Macella and looking her over with a practiced eye. "Now stop distracting me and let me work."

Macella smothered a smile and went obediently silent. She let Lynn and the assistants move her this way and that, adjusting fabrics and applying creams and powders. As usual, the long process was worthwhile in the end.

Macella smiled at her reflection. "You are a true artist, Lynn. You have outdone yourself yet again."

The older woman made a dismissive sound, flapping a hand at Macella impatiently. She fussed over the dress's hem, concealing her face. Macella knew that meant she was pleased.

After Lynn bustled out, her assistants hurrying behind her, Macella looked at her reflection again. She hadn't been lying; Lynn had truly outdone herself. But then, every ensemble the tailor had put together for Macella had been more amazing than the last.

This time, her sleeveless dress featured a corset bodice and a skirt shaped like a mermaid's tail. The lace overlay had strategic cut outs on the sides. It accentuated Macella's curves, the advantageously arranged black lace over red satin giving her even more of an hourglass shape than usual. A thigh-high split offered a glimpse of her leg. Though Lynn's assistants had put jewels in her ears and hair, her own familiar star charm rested in the hollow of her throat, cool against her skin. With her black and silver curls piled atop her head, a few loose locks framing her face, Macella thought she looked almost regal.

A knock at the outer chamber door startled her out of her reverie. Quickly, she made sure her daggers were concealed in her thigh holsters, adjusting them so they weren't noticeable beneath her dress. Taking one final look at her reflection, Macella left the dressing room to answer the door. It was probably a servant sent to fetch her to the party. Aithan must be too busy to leave his post.

When Macella opened the door, however, she was surprised to see Captain Drudo. He looked even more handsome than usual, attired for the occasion in his garnet and gold dress uniform. It complemented the gold highlights in his hair and the golden flecks in his warm, dark eyes.

Drudo's eyes went quickly from warm to hot as he took Macella in. She felt herself flush as his gaze raked over her hungrily before he caught himself and lowered his eyes.

He made an uncharacteristically stiff bow. "Lady Macella, I—I apologize for the intrusion," Drudo stammered, speaking too quickly.

"It's no intrusion." Macella smiled, adjusting her hair needlessly and pretending not to notice his discomfort.

The captain took a deep breath before meeting her gaze. "The Lord Protector asked that I escort you to the ballroom, with his apologies. With so many guests tonight, he cannot stray far from the Crown."

"Of course," Macella replied, moving to take Drudo's arm. "I expected he would be needed, but I had no notion I'd get the pleasure of your company in his stead."

Captain Drudo took her arm, covering her hand with his. He'd regained most of his normal, charming demeanor, though he was still avoiding looking at her directly for long. He led her through the corridor, chatting amiably the entire way.

The grand ballroom was lavishly decorated for the occasion. Candles flickered in gold chandeliers, their light glinting off the Crown's garnet and gold banners. Immaculately dressed servants wove through the crowd with goblets of fine wine and trays of delicacies.

As Captain Drudo led Macella through the throng of elegant guests, he regaled her with amusing anecdotes about them all. His racy humor distracted Macella from the uncomfortable number of eyes that followed them through the ballroom. One man stopped and stared so openly that he nearly collided with a passing server.

"That is Lord Koroibos," Drudo murmured, his eyes dancing with glee despite his smooth expression. "He has proposed marriage to at least a dozen eligible persons of noble birth, yet he remains single. He has the hygiene habits of a bunyip with the intelligence to match."

Macella snorted a laugh, hiding it behind her hand. "What is a bunyip?"

"A disgusting water spirit that favors lounging in swamps and devouring human flesh," the captain replied. "They even have Koroibos's bulging eyes."

Macella glanced back at the man, who was still gaping at them, and burst into a fit of giggles. Drudo found them a prime spot from which to observe the festivities. Soon, he'd acquired Macella a drink, and she was laughing into her goblet at his continued commentary on the gathered nobles.

Finally, a herald announced the arrival of the Crown. The grand doors were thrown open and the monarchs appeared. They would move to the center of the parquet and open the ball with the first dance, after which the rest of the gathered gentry could take to the floor.

King Khari led the way with Queen Annika on her arm. The king was attired entirely in garnet and gold, from her surcoat to her trousers. Queen Annika was in her element, clearly pleased to be escorted by the king and have all attention on them. She looked immaculate in a gown the exact same shade of blue as her wide eyes. Her silver and sapphire crown nested in an interwoven pile of braids atop her head. The rest of her thick hair fell in golden waves down her back.

Behind them, Monarch Meztli and Queen Awa were the picture of regality. Meztli wore a tunic, surcoat, and skirt in shades of topaz and turquoise. Their long black hair was parted so that it fell over one eye, with their crown of gold and quetzal feathers contrasting beautifully against it. Awa's white dress had oversized puffed sleeves and a massive, layered skirt. Her head dress was made of intricately knotted fabrics, her slim silver crown nestled in its folds.

The Crown positioned themselves in the center of the ballroom floor. As the musicians began to play and the monarchs started to dance, Macella shifted her attention back to the doors. Aithan of Auburndale had entered discreetly behind the Crown and was already scanning the room, assessing threats, and planning contingencies.

Macella's heart lurched. He was exceedingly beautiful in black and crimson, his golden skin glowing in the firelight. His crimson-tipped silver hair fell around his shoulders, half of it tied away from his face so that all could see his gorgeous cheekbones, smoldering amber eyes, and full lips.

Aithan's eyes snapped to hers, no doubt hearing the admiration radiating from her mind. His chest lifted with a sharp intake of breath. Macella watched him take her in, his eyes traveling the length of her body. Her skin warmed under the heat of his gaze.

(8) *Macella, I do not have sufficient language to describe how you look tonight. It is entirely unfair. How am I to do my job with you looking this way?*

Macella blew him a kiss. Aithan pressed a hand to his heart in response, before tearing his attention away and resuming his vigilant watch. Macella looked back to the Crown, who were finishing their dance to enthusiastic applause.

"Lady Macella, may I have this dance?" Captain Drudo bowed and offered a hand.

Macella took his hand. "Of course, Captain."

She let Drudo lead her through the crowd. They must have made a striking pair—the dashing young knight and the unknown beauty, freshly elevated in rank. Heads turned and the crowd parted as they passed. Though the captain's demeanor was collected and unconcerned, Macella could still sense his pleasure.

His hand rested lightly on the hollow of her back as he led her onto the parquet. Macella could feel Aithan watching them, as he had been since he entered the ballroom. She could feel his longing, even as part of his mind remained vigilant, scanning the room for threats. He wanted it to be his hand on her back, a little lower than strictly decent, holding her a bit closer than the dance required.

Macella and Drudo stepped onto the floor, stopping to bow deeply to the Crown. King Khari did an almost-comical double take before slowly looking Macella over. She could feel the king's gaze—and Queen Annika's glare—following her as she and Drudo took their place in the dance.

Captain Drudo proved to be an excellent dancer. His arms were strong, but his touch gentle. He whisked Macella around the floor, leading her through the steps with confident ease.

"I am the envy of everyone in this room right now." Drudo grinned. "I am not accustomed to being an object of envy. Is this how the high commander feels every day? What a lucky, lucky man."

Macella laughed, the intake of breath bringing her a whiff of Captain Drudo's scent. He smelled of bergamot and sandalwood, a pleasant aroma Macella had never really noticed before. It was certainly not as attractive as Aithan's sweet smokiness, but was agreeable, nonetheless.

When the set ended, Macella was surprised to find King Khari approaching. She could do nothing but consent when the king asked for the next two dances. As they moved to the center of the floor, Macella met Aithan's gaze again. He grinned ruefully at her, shaking his head.

"I might have Drudo flogged for taking your first dance." King Khari chuckled, her ochre eyes alight with interest. "The most beautiful woman in the room obviously owes her first dance to the king."

She fixed Macella with a predatory gaze, her grip tight on Macella's waist. Macella had rarely been so near the king. The monarch radiated an intense, powerful energy that set her nerves on edge. She took a steadying breath, unintentionally taking in the king's scent. Pomegranate and vanilla laced with something darker—like metal and ash.

"You flatter me, your grace," Macella demurred. "You did indeed have the first dance of the most beautiful woman in the room. Her grace, Queen Annika, looks exceptionally lovely this evening."

King Khari glanced briefly toward the spot where Queen Annika danced sulkily with Monarch Meztli. The young queen had obviously been displeased by the king's second choice of dancing partner. Macella was torn between being vindictively smug about Annika's jealousy and worrying that she would regret this amusement later.

"Yes, she is a lovely creature," King Khari agreed, her attention intently focused on Macella. "But no one can deny your beauty and elegance, my dear."

Macella lowered her eyes. "Thank you, your grace."

The king twirled Macella, her fingers grazing the bare skin of Macella's arm as she pulled her back into an embrace. The watching nobles gasped and applauded when King Khari dipped her low, holding Macella tightly around the waist. The king's face was mere inches from hers, a mischievous smile playing at the corners of her mouth.

"Tell me about your home in Shively," King Khari commanded, whisking Macella upright.

Macella obeyed, describing her large family and their small home. As they danced through a second song, the king prodded her to talk of her upbringing. It was strange discussing her humble beginnings with someone who had lived most of the last century in an enormous castle with people catering to her every whim and desire.

Politeness required the king choose a new partner for the next dance, but she made Macella promise that they would dance again before the evening was over. Relieved, Macella started to leave the parquet, only to be accosted by several other requests for her hand. Unsure how to escape, she let herself be led back onto the dance floor.

Chapter Five

The night passed in a blur of partners, awkward conversation, and the occasional pleasurable interaction. When Drudo left Macella at the door to her apartments, she was exhausted and eagerly anticipating being off of her feet.

Lucy was waiting to help her undress. Macella gave the young woman a grateful smile. She stood before the long mirror of the dressing room, marveling one last time at Lynn's handiwork. As Lucy unlaced her bodice, Macella pulled the pins from her hair, sighing contentedly at the relief of freeing her curls from their careful updo.

"I can handle it from here, Lucy." Aithan's voice was a low rumble as he stepped into the dressing room.

(9) Macella met his gaze in the mirror. His amber eyes burned with desire, full of wicked promises. It was clear that anticipation had been building all evening, while he forced himself to remain stoic and vigilant. Now, his face showed every bit of his lascivious intent. Suddenly, Macella wasn't tired at all.

Lucy bowed, blushed, and hurried from the room. Aithan moved to take the vacated place behind Macella. She saw that he'd removed his outer layers of clothing, now wearing only his shirt and trousers, his feet bare. He trailed his hand down her neck to the bare skin of her upper back, stopping where Lucy had left off with the laces. Macella shivered, despite the warmth that followed his touch.

"All night, I've listened to covetous and lustful minds," Aithan murmured, tugging lightly at the laces of her bodice. "I have seen elaborate fantasies played out as they watched you dance or, even more vividly, when they were lucky enough to snag your hand. With you in their arms, on the receiving end of that sweet, dimpled smile of yours, and close enough to smell your delicious scent—their minds were positively indecent."

Aithan leaned down and pressed his face against her curls. He exhaled a warm breath against the back of her neck, making her shiver again. Slowly, he snaked an arm around her middle, sliding his hand deliberately between her breasts, before gently wrapping his fingers around her throat. Macella arched into his touch, nipples stiffening and heart racing as warmth spread between her thighs. The hand at her throat tightened the slightest bit, the other still occupied in loosening her bodice.

"I am not a jealous man, but tonight was a trial of my patience," Aithan continued, his mouth near her ear, eyes still locked on hers in the mirror. "Nearly everyone in the room was dreaming of doing exactly what I'm doing now, and yet I could not even draw near you. I could not proclaim to the greedy throng that the most exquisite beauty in all of Kōsaten is *mine*."

The last word came out as a low growl that sent a thrill of excitement through Macella's core. Her breath caught as her stomach filled with butterflies. Lips parted and chest heaving, she watched him watch her. His desire saturated his thoughts, loud and unashamed.

Aithan leaned closer, his lips brushing her ear. She felt his arousal, rock hard against her lower back. His fingers tugged the laces of her bodice more urgently.

"I want to remind you that you are mine," he whispered. "I want to remind you over and over again."

Macella gasped, her stomach clenching in anticipation. Aithan held her gaze in the mirror, his lips grazing her neck before moving back to her ear. Her heart tried to escape her chest, hammering against her tight, aching breasts. Suddenly, her bodice felt much too tight. She wanted it off.

"May I show you, my love?" Aithan implored, his voice husky and raw. "Can I fuck you right here in front of this mirror? Can I eat your pussy from behind and then fuck you until you cannot stand?"

Macella's breasts spilled free as her bodice loosened. Aithan's gaze flicked away from her face and then back, the fire in his eyes intensifying. His erection pressed into her back, twitching with urgency.

"And when you cannot stand any longer, can I carry you to our bed and fuck you some more?"

Aithan let the laces of her bodice fall. Carefully, he slid her dress down, lowering to his knees as he pushed it past her hips and down to her feet. Macella stepped out of the dress, letting Aithan set it aside. He knelt behind her, his eyes on hers in the mirror. She nodded, unable to speak, her breath caught in her throat.

Aithan planted kisses along the curve of her ass. When he reached the center, he brought up his hands to grip both cheeks and gently spread her thighs. Macella leaned forward, bracing herself with a hand on either side of the mirror.

Then she felt Aithan's tongue sliding over the sensitive skin between her ass and vagina. She found her voice then, letting out an agonized moan. Aithan trailed his tongue back and forth over that spot a few times before dipping his tongue inside of her. He hummed in pleasure, the buzz of his lips rippling across her skin.

Macella's arms trembled, her hands tensed against the stone wall. Aithan's tongue flicked against her clit, and she cried out. Her hips spasmed, but his firm grip held her in place. He began tracing slow circles from her clit to just past her pussy and back, again and again, teasing that tender spot maddeningly.

The buzz was spreading to Macella's belly, filling her with a glittery anticipation. She gasped and let out another throaty cry. Aithan increased the pressure, ratcheting up the intensity to nigh unbearable levels.

And then the glittery sensation exploded, filling Macella's abdomen with fireworks. Hips bucking, she released a wordless cry. Around her, the room melted away, leaving her suspended in a soundless sea of bliss.

Moments later, Aithan's tongue was replaced by the hard press of his cock. He thrust into her, and Macella thought she might cum again immediately, so exquisite was the sensation of his steely girth plunging deep inside of her, hitting the perfect, most tender spot. Aithan groaned, eliciting an answering moan. This was the moment they'd been craving all evening.

Aithan thrust again, lingering at the end of each stroke, savoring the depth of their union. Macella panted, both reveling in the fullness and yearning for the pounding intensity she knew he could unleash. He clutched her hips, holding her tight against him. Macella made a sound between a purr and a whimper.

Aithan held her gaze in the mirror as he eased slowly back. When he thrust forward again, *hard*, she threw her head back in ecstasy. His fingers twined in her hair, pushing her head forward so that she was again looking at their reflection.

"Watch," he ordered.

Then, with a growl, he gave her the intensity she wanted, plunging into her again and again, hard and fast and deep. Macella's cries of pleasure filled the chamber, growing louder with each thrust. Her arms trembled and her legs shook, and she wanted more and more and more.

"Whose are you?" Aithan demanded. "Who does this good pussy belong to?"

Macella's legs threatened to give out completely. Her stomach clenched hard, her hips jerking spasmodically. She moaned, throwing her hips back in time with his rhythmic thrusts.

"It's yours," she panted. "I am yours."

"Good girl," Aithan growled.

And Macella fell over the edge.

Her legs did, in fact, give out. As promised, Aithan caught her and scooped her into his arms. He carried her from the dressing chamber and laid her gently on the bed before spreading her legs and positioning himself on top of her.

"I want to look at you," he told her, slipping inside her again. Running his fingers lightly over her cheek and across her parted lips, he leaned down to give her a slow, lingering kiss.

He propped himself up so that he could look into her face. One hand cupped her ass as he moved slowly in and out of her, his eyes never leaving hers. Macella held his gaze, biting her lip. She reached up to wrap her arms around his broad back.

"You are so beautiful, my love," Aithan whispered. "You will always be the most beautiful woman in the world to me."

Macella whimpered. She felt as though she would burst. Every fiber of her being was alight. She felt beautiful and powerful and so very loved.

"You are mine," Aithan vowed. "You are mine and I am yours. For all of this life and every other if the gods will it. And if they do not will it, I will still make it so."

This time, he lingered in their lovemaking, painstakingly slow, savoring her, relishing the satisfaction of finally fulfilling his desires.

Afterward, he held her in his arms, his lips pressed against her hair. Macella drifted on the residual euphoria. Her body felt light and pleasantly heavy simultaneously. She had to admit that, on the whole, the evening had been more enjoyable than she'd expected.

"You will have much of interest to tell Finley about tonight's festivities, after all," Aithan teased with a low chuckle. "Tell them that I believe you actually may have surpassed their record for most hearts broken in a single night."

Macella smiled sleepily. "I will tell them no such thing. That is one battle in which I have no desire of engaging Finley."

A laugh rumbled in Aithan's chest. Macella loved that sound. She fell asleep listening to the soothing cadence of his heartbeat.

The next day, Macella found herself with a free hour after the midday meal. The Crown's occupation with their esteemed guests had given Macella an unexpected respite from their demands. She decided to spend her leisure time in one of her favorite places in the castle, the library, poring over the old tomes, searching for any mention of Aegises. She'd done this often, visiting the vast castle library during her spare hours, hoping to learn all there was to know about her kind. Unsurprisingly, little had been documented aside from the well-known story of Khalid's brokering with the gods and a list of every Aegis that had ever served.

Today, Macella gave the timelines more careful study. Each of Kōsaten's six sovereigns were recorded in order, accompanied by a list of all the Aegises who'd served them. Some names were marked with an X, indicating an Aegis had perished during a given monarch's reign. Those who had served as Protector of the Crown were marked with stars.

Macella saw that none of the preceding ruler's Aegises remained in King Khari's service. Shamira had said that any Aegises who served Queen Rhiannon, and thereby might have known about Aithan's birth, somehow died either prior to or very early in Khari's reign. Only Shamira was allowed to live on after Khari's ascension to the blessed throne. Disgraced and degraded under Queen Rhiannon, Shamira had been the one to tell Khari the secret of the Aegisborn, giving the then-aspiring king useful leverage against the incumbent queen. When she'd defeated Queen Rhiannon and claimed the blessed throne, King Khari had rewarded Shamira by appointing her Protector of the Crown. Now, Shamira was dead, Aithan was Protector of the Crown, and the truth felt dangerously close to being revealed.

How many living souls knew of Aithan's parentage? Macella counted to herself: King Khari, Grand Mage Kiama, Queen Awa, Finley, Kai, Diya, Aithan, and Macella. Eight people—at least. While King Khari and Grand Mage Kiama didn't also know of Macella's Aegisborn nature, it still felt as though far too many people did. Word would eventually spread.

Macella's eyes lingered on Queen Rhiannon's pages. There, marked with an X, was her father's name. *Matthias of The Highlands.* She hadn't even known from whence her father hailed. Macella had no memory of their brief life together, had only spoken to him once, long after his death. That had been a far-too-fleeting meeting beyond the veil before she'd faced the dark gods' trials. She knew so little of her parents, of her own formative years. She and Aithan had been stripped of those memories—Aithan so that he could not betray the truth, Macella so that she would be protected from it.

She wondered which of the marked names belonged to Aithan's Aegis parent. That mystery might never be solved. Everyone who might've known their identity was long dead. And though Macella could communicate with the dead, she'd never managed to call a particular spirit. Hades had allowed Matthias to come to her as a favor. Each of the other three dead people she'd spoken to—the child recruit Tuwile, the mage Anwansi, and Shamira—had all died recently and had interacted with Macella not long before their deaths. They'd each had a reason of their own for seeking her out and had come to her of their own accord. Even Shamira, the only one to linger, came and went seemingly at whim rather than Macella's desire.

"Kali has granted me leave to remain in this realm until I complete my quest," Shamira told Macella when they'd last spoke. "She is generous in matters of righteous vengeance."

Ever eager to learn about her kind and their relationship to the gods, Macella had pressed for more information. Even in death, Shamira retained the taciturn nature of most Aegises. It seemed to take her a long time to decide what to say.

"Kali Aegises are considered fierce and bloodthirsty because those traits are attributed to Kali herself," Shamira said finally. "But she is so much more than that. She was created to restore balance when no other god could. She was vicious because she had to be to save us all. Kali is a protector. And so, she will allow me to be the same."

"You will not find what you seek in those volumes."

A voice startled Macella back to the present. She'd been so preoccupied with her own thoughts that she hadn't even noticed her star charm growing cooler against her throat. She looked up from the old books to find Grand Mage Kiama looking down at her intently. Her pale gray eyes were hawk-like.

Macella hadn't heard the woman approach. Looking around in confusion, she noticed that the library was eerily silent. Though the nearest door was ajar, she heard none of the usual hallway bustle. She narrowed her eyes at the Grand Mage.

Kiama smiled. "I wanted to speak to you in private. It's only a temporary engulfment spell."

Macella's unease grew. She'd rarely spoken to the Grand Mage during her time at the castle and certainly never alone. Had Kiama seen through her invisibility? Did she know Macella had overheard her secret conversation with the king?

"The mages' records are much more detailed and reliable, and even they don't contain the answers you seek," Kiama continued calmly. "I have searched them quite thoroughly."

Macella decided that silence was the best course of action. If the Grand Mage wanted something out of Macella, she was going to have to work for it. Hopefully, she would thereby reveal her own hand.

Kiama smiled as if she knew exactly what Macella was thinking. The older woman had come to this conversation prepared. She would choose her words carefully.

"I know of his mother," Kiama said, the abrupt shift surprising Macella again. "Every mage has heard of her prowess. Maia of Kosmosdale was highly renowned. Everyone expected she'd eventually become Grand Mage. Instead, she disappeared."

Macella's silence was now stunned rather than calculated. She'd come to the library searching for answers and here was the Grand Mage casually speaking of Aithan's mother. What was the woman after?

"Based on the timeline, his other parent must have served King Omari and probably for a short while under Queen Rhiannon," Grand Mage Kiama concluded. "But that only narrows it down so much."

Macella kept her eyes locked on Kiama's, giving away nothing. They were at the crux of the matter now. The Grand Mage's next words would be dangerous. Macella was sure of it.

Kiama leaned forward, resting her hands near Macella's on the table. Surreptitiously, Macella inched her hands away. When she'd touched the seer, Aisling, she'd triggered the sorcerer's foresight. Anwansi, the only other mage she'd spent much time around, had detected Macella's strangeness when he shook her hand. She wouldn't allow Kiama to touch her if she could help it. The Grand Mage knew too much already.

Despite the engulfment spell, Kiama dropped her voice. "I do not know or care whether Aithan of Auburndale knows of his true nature as an Aegis-human crossbreed. I need to know which Aegis fathered him, and Aithan is the only one who can provide that information. I need you to pass my request along to him discreetly."

Macella's mind spun. So, Kiama figured they knew Aithan was a crossbreed, but not that King Khari had demanded the Grand Mage make more like him. Taking a chance, Macella decided to tell a partial truth.

"Aithan doesn't know who his parents are," she said flatly. "He cannot recall his life before Smoketown."

Kiama waved a dismissive hand. "Of course, he cannot. That is how memory spells work. I can reverse the enchantment, if he will allow me. But only on the condition that he tell me the name of his Aegis parent afterward."

Macella noted that the Grand Mage didn't mention the king or the task she'd been given. Perhaps Kiama needed the identity of Aithan's parent to fulfill Khari's request. The Grand Mage knew better than to disappoint the king, so she'd decided it was worth the risk to reveal one secret to uncover another.

Kiama seemed to take Macella's pause as a denial, because her voice was sharper as she continued. "I am offering him something no one else can. Only a powerful mage can unlock the part of his mind where those memories hide. Does he not want that part of his life back?"

Macella remembered when Matthias told her he'd had Meng Po erase her memories of him. It'd been a precaution meant to protect her, but Macella resented that her past had been stolen from her without her consent. She knew Aithan felt the same.

"What will he have to do?" she asked.

Kiama smiled. "I will prepare a draught to immobilize him and lower the protections around his mind. Then you will have to administer another concoction and wait. That is all."

Macella lifted an eyebrow. "That's all?"

Grand Mage Kiama sighed, her broad shoulders drooping slightly. "The memories will not all return at once, but the first to come will be the most intense. They will be the best and the worst of his experiences."

"So, he'll very likely have to relive serious trauma while already in a weakened physical and mental state," Macella conjectured.

Again, crossbreed.

A hazy, terrible memory flooded into Macella's mind. *Burning alive. She was engulfed in flames, screaming as her flesh melted and blackened.*

She forced her mind back to the present. "Will he remember the trials?"

Kiama shook her head. "I believe that a mage was used to suppress his early memories. If I am correct, I can reverse such a spell. But when Meng Po removes memories, they cannot be recovered. Her soup of forgetfulness frees Aegises of the burden of recalling their time in the Otherworlds. Those memories are gone forever."

Macella felt a mixture of relief and disappointment. Blessedly, Aithan would not be forced to relive the horrors of the Aegis trials. However, if Grand Mage Kiama was right, then Macella had no chance of ever recovering her own childhood memories.

"Anything else?" she forced herself to ask.

"It will be painful," Kiama replied hesitantly. "Physically and mentally. His mental defenses will fight back. There is a small but terrible chance that they will win."

"What happens if his mind fights back and it wins?" Macella demanded, already knowing the answer.

"It will break, with him trapped inside," Kiama said simply. "He will break. He will lose himself."

Macella shivered. *He will break.* Even as she replayed the words in her mind, she knew they were true, and that the possibility was more likely than the Grand

Mage would admit. And still she knew that Aithan would go through with it. Because that's what Macella would do, given the same opportunity.

Chapter Six

Aithan took nearly a fortnight to consider it. He did not have time enough to try the experiment sooner, as the Crown and their guests required his constant attention. However, as the northerners' visit drew to a close, the time came for him to make a decision.

Macella knew he would try to recover the memories. She'd known even as they discussed and deliberated during their brief moments alone over those two weeks. Soon after Aithan agreed to Kiama's terms, they found two vials hidden in their morning breadbasket. One held a milky liquid, the other a thick, swirling, crimson smoke. When the northern guests departed and King Khari shut herself in her chambers not to be disturbed, Macella and Aithan knew the opportunity had come to attempt the Grand Mage's procedure.

Macella sat beside Aithan on the bed, gripping the vials so tightly that her hands shook.

Aithan reached for her, covering her hands with his. He looked into her eyes, his forehead wrinkled with concern. "If you do not want me to do this, I will not," Aithan told her, not for the first time. "My future with you is far more important than a past I cannot recall."

Blinking her eyes against tears, Macella heaved a sigh. "Of course, I do not want you to endanger yourself. But this is not my choice. I would never rob you of your choice. And, if the opportunity were mine, I know I would try. I cannot fault you for doing the same."

"I will not break," Aithan promised her, cupping her cheek in one of his big hands. "I will not lose myself. And, if I do, you will be right here to lead me back."

They had agreed that Macella would monitor his mind, staying alert for any foul play by the Grand Mage. They weren't sure if Macella would be able to help, but at least she would know what was happening. And neither of them would have to face this alone.

"I will always find my way back to you," Aithan vowed.

He kissed her then, his lips gentle and sweet. Macella returned the kiss hungrily, desperate to muffle the sob rising in her throat. Finally, Aithan pulled away, taking the draught from her hand. In a swift movement, he uncorked the vial and downed its contents.

Macella watched him lie back against the pillows and close his eyes. The Grand Mage had said the effects would come on quickly. Macella prepared the second vial, her gaze obsessively flicking between her hands and her Aegis lying on the bed.

In a few moments, Aithan was breathing deeply. Macella touched his arm. He didn't move. She lifted his arm an inch off the bed. When she released it, it flopped back to the bed heavily. Beneath his eyelids, his eyes had begun to move rapidly back and forth.

Then Aithan's breath hitched, his face contorting in pain. A sharp hiss of air burst through his pursed lips. His hands curled into fists. Though he didn't change positions, his entire body had grown rigid. Macella knew his mind was fighting against the potion's attempts to lower its defenses.

Leaning over him, she held the second vial under his nose. When she uncorked it, thick red smoke poured out. Aithan's eyes snapped open as the smoke rushed into his nostrils, mouth, eyes, and ears. The whites and pupils of his eyes were replaced with a dull crimson glow.

Aithan's body convulsed. He grunted in pain, the muscles in his arms bulging, his veins standing out scarlet against his golden skin. His mouth opened in a soundless scream, full of the thick smoke. It looked disturbingly like his mouth was full of blood.

Macella felt like her heart was ripping in two. She felt helpless, watching him suffer. She laid down next to him, resting her chin in the hollow of his neck so that she could speak directly into his ear. She draped an arm over his chest, holding him close.

"I'm right here, love," she whispered. "I am right here with you."

Macella gasped as her mind flooded with emotion. Pain and fear, sadness and joy, and expansive love all vied for prominence. She felt herself in two places simultaneously. She could feel Aithan's skin hot against hers, could feel the soft bedding beneath them.

(10) But she could also sense things that weren't in their room: an evening breeze over a cool stream, a roaring bonfire, peppermint and vanilla, the whinny of a horse, and the clatter of wagon wheels on uneven terrain.

Finally, a clear vision began to unfold. She/Aithan sat at a small wooden table, looking down at a pastry decorated prettily with wildflowers. A candle nestled in the center of the bouquet.

"Make a wish," a throaty, musical voice told him.

The voice filled Aithan's chest with a sense of love and safety. He looked up into the beautiful face of his mother, Maia. She had his same golden skin and high cheekbones, and an open, familiar face framed by long auburn waves. Her light gray eyes danced with mirth.

"Hurry before it melts onto the pastry," said another voice, this one a low tenor.

Aithan turned his head the other way. Macella held her breath as she saw the moment through his eyes.

"I'm so glad you're home, Mama," Aithan said in his sweet, child's voice.

Another beautiful woman looked down at him. She had lovely dark brown skin, angular features, full lips, and a slender frame. Tall and thin, she was sharp and muscular everywhere Maia appeared soft and curvy. Most striking, however, were her orange eyes and crimson-tipped silver hair.

She was an Aegis.

"I would never miss your nameday, my love," the Aegis told him, a smile softening her severe features.

"And what am I, yesterday's droppings?" Maia demanded, poking Aithan in the ribs. "You're not glad I'm home?"

Aithan giggled. "You're always home, Mommy, but Mama has to go fight monsters and see the queen sometimes. I'm glad you both are here."

Aithan blew out the candle, wishing that his moms could be at home with him forever. It was always better when they were all together. Mommy worried so much when Mama was away. She tried to hide it, but Aithan knew anyway. He still heard her thoughts sometimes, even though she used her magic to shield her mind.

Mommy laughed her noisy, happy laugh and kissed his forehead with a loud smack. "We are so grateful for you, mijo."

"I have something for you," his mama said, holding out a small parcel.

Aithan took it, feeling like nothing could possibly make this day better. He opened it carefully, ignoring the way his mothers giggled about his meticulous nature. When he'd finally removed the wrapping—completely intact—a small bracelet fell into his palm. Its leather band was worn soft, stitched with letters spelling a name Aithan didn't know.

"Who is Gabriel?" Aithan asked, looking up at his mama.

"That was my birth name," she explained, smiling softly. "My grandmother gave me that bracelet before she died, and I went to live in Smoketown. It is the only thing I've saved from my childhood."

Aithan turned the bracelet over in his small hands. He saw that the clasp was a silver eight-pointed star. The charm was cool to the touch.

"Abuelita said it would protect me," his mama continued. "It will do the same for you."

"Why did abuelita put your old name on it?" Aithan asked, rubbing a finger over the star charm.

"She didn't live to see my twelfth nameday, so she never learned my true gender," his mama explained. "I did not yet know my identity for sure myself—not like you always have, mijo. I was so young when I lost her. With all of my roughhousing, strong will, and love of swordplay, she didn't suspect I was really more of a Gabriela."

The part of Macella's mind that remained in the present processed this information. Like some women, Gabriela had been born with a penis. In Kōsaten, children were raised agender, declaring their true gender identity on their twelfth nameday—though many of them knew long before that day. Aithan's mama might've known earlier, but not early enough to tell her only family. She had lost her grandmother, had been sent to Smoketown, and had become an Aegis blessed by Lucifer, before eventually falling in love with a mage and having a miraculous, impossible child.

(11) The edges of the memory began to blur. Macella felt a deep foreboding. In the present, her star charm flashed briefly cold, an echo of long-ago danger. She was absolutely certain that she'd just experienced Aithan's last good memory. And now it was being pushed away to make room for something bigger. For the worst memory of them all.

Macella/Aithan jerked awake at the tinkle of bells. His body was out of the bed and halfway to the door before his mind caught up. Mommy had made him practice this so many times that it had become muscle memory.

But Aithan knew instinctively that this wasn't practice. The air felt wrong. The night was too quiet. Where were his mothers?

A sudden explosion broke the eerie silence. Aithan jumped, remembered what he was supposed to do. He ran to his closet and opened the hidden hatch beneath the false clothes basket. He pulled the door shut behind him and crawled into the tunnel his mothers had made.

Another chorus of explosions. Aithan trembled. He was supposed to keep crawling all the way and wait for his mothers to come and find him at the other end. But there had never been explosions before. Where were his mothers?

"Gabriela of Edgewood, Queen Rhiannon demands an audience," came a booming voice from outside.

Footsteps on the floor overhead, followed by a low, familiar voice. "She needn't have sent you all this way to retrieve me. I would have responded to a written summons."

"She does not want only you, sister," another voice called. It had a cold, angry edge to it. "She thought you might need persuasion to bring your pets along."

"My pets?" Gabriela's voice was harder than before. "What did Queen Rhiannon tell you? What do you believe I've done?"

"It is not for us to know," answered the first voice. "It is for us to serve. Your service has been compromised. You are to drink this draught and relinquish your weapon. Anyone with you is to do the same. There should be a mage and a child."

"They are not here," Gabriela replied coolly. "I will send for them when we reach the capital if the queen still wishes it. I am prepared to relinquish my sword and come with you now."

Then Aithan heard the most terrible sound he had ever heard. His mama was screaming. Mama never screamed. She was always quiet, even when she was angry. Mommy would yell and say words they told Aithan he wasn't supposed to use, but Mama never raised her voice. She was screaming now, though. She was screaming and screaming like she might never stop.

Aithan knew he was supposed to be crawling. Mommy might already be at the other end of the tunnel waiting for him. But he couldn't move. He could not even breathe. His mind was filled with his mama's pain.

He hadn't meant to find her mind with his own. That just happened sometimes with his mothers. Aithan was still learning how to control the things he could do.

But now he wished—with the tiny fraction of his brain that still held the capacity to think—that he had learned control sooner. He wished he knew how to shut off the connection. He wished he could shut off everything. He wished he could die.

Every inch of his body felt as if it was being pierced with hot needles. The pain was worse than anything he'd ever imagined. It was so blindingly terrible that Aithan couldn't even scream with his mama. Every fiber of his being was consumed with the horrible shredding, burning, grinding pain.

Then, miraculously, it stopped. Aithan's body sagged as he gasped for air. He was sobbing raggedly and was vaguely aware that he had wet himself. For a moment, he hardly knew who or where he was.

No, Maia, RUN. Get our boy and get out of here now.

Aithan felt his mama pushing the thought toward another mind. He couldn't find Mommy's mind though. She must already be far away from the house. On her way to the other end of the tunnel to get him.

Aithan knew he should crawl as fast as he could. He desperately wanted to reach the safety of Mommy's arms. But he couldn't. His body refused to move. The pain had been too much. The lines between his brain and body must have burned away. He no longer had control of his muscles.

"Alessia, enough," the first voice snapped.

"Her traps nearly maimed Shamira," the angry woman spat back. Distantly, Aithan understood that she was the voice that had called him and his mommy pets. "And she's obviously lying."

The first person sighed heavily, but before they could speak again, another voice interrupted. "The house is empty."

"Where are they?" the angry woman demanded.

Then the terrible pain returned. His mama began to shriek. Dark spots clouded Aithan's vision, the world narrowing around him. Gratefully, he slipped into unconsciousness.

(12) When he awoke, he was lying on the rough floor of a rickety cart, the faint scent of vanilla on the breeze that brushed his skin. Speaking of skin, his felt feverishly hot, except for the spot where the clasp of his bracelet rested against his wrist. The silver star felt icy cold.

A woman with silver hair tipped in cerulean sat nearby. Even with the hood of her cloak obscuring her face, Aithan could see the nasty bruise stretching across her cheek beneath one swollen, orange eye. Her head and arms were heavily bandaged.

Aithan blinked dully at her. His mouth felt dry and tasted coppery. He must have bitten his tongue.

"The others will find her. They found the child after you said the house was clear."

"Hmmph."

Aithan pushed himself up to a sitting position and turned his head toward the voices. Two more silver and cerulean-haired people sat behind the horses, talking quietly. The landscape around them was frighteningly unfamiliar.

"Where's my mama?" Aithan croaked. "Where's my mommy?"

The bandaged woman only stared at him, her face blank and impassive. Maybe she hadn't heard him. His throat was extremely dry, his voice papery thin.

Aithan looked around helplessly, his eyes burning with unshed tears as he again took in his strange surroundings. His mothers would never let anyone take him away. If he was here without them, that meant something very, very bad had happened to them. All of their planning and practicing hadn't saved them. His mothers' worst fears had come true.

Aithan didn't want to think about that, because when he thought about the explosions and the screams and the tunnel, his throat felt tight, and he couldn't get enough air. It already felt like his heart was beating too fast and he couldn't remember the breathing exercises Mommy taught him to do when his feelings got too big.

The bandaged woman was still watching him. Her lips twitched almost imperceptibly, and then her orange eyes flicked deliberately past him. Aithan followed her gaze to something he'd overlooked at first. A shape covered in a blanket. A shape roughly the size of a woman.

Some part of him had known from the moment he'd regained consciousness. The scent of vanilla. Mama always smelled like vanilla.

The only good thing was there was no peppermint. Mommy wasn't here. She had escaped. She might be okay. Even though he would never see her again.

Aithan let the tears roll down his face, but he did not make a sound. He scooted across the rough wooden floor until he was beside the covered body of his mama. He curled against it, breathing in her sweet vanilla smell.

He took all his big feelings and buried them deep inside, building walls around them, brick by brick. He took the indescribable, life-altering pain, melted it down, and formed it into a shield. As the endless clatter of wagon wheels marked the passing days, Aithan of Auburndale buried all of the sad, vulnerable parts of himself—hid them so deeply not even he would be able to find them again. He lay shivering beneath a too-big cloak that someone had put over him and made himself into stone. He made himself ready for all the terrible things he knew lay ahead.

Aithan of Auburndale laid beside his dead mother and let himself cry for the very last time.

Back in the present, Macella's cheeks were wet with tears, her own mixed with those running down Aithan's cheeks. Her mind was abruptly ejected from Aithan's consciousness with a force she had not experienced since the first time he had made her practice her gifts on him. Reeling, she opened her eyes and lifted her head from the crook of Aithan's neck.

Then she clamped a hand over her mouth to stifle a scream.

Trails of tears and blood streamed down Aithan's cheeks. His eyes had gone from crimson to completely white and utterly blank. His jaw was clenched so tightly that the veins of his temples bulged.

His body convulsed and a trickle of blood dripped from his nose. A sound between a growl and a whimper escaped his lips. His body jerked again.

"Aithan, come back now," Macella whispered, panic sapping the energy from her voice. "I am right here. Come back to me."

Aithan's only response was another convulsion, another pained growl. Macella sat up, struggling until she pulled him into her arms. She cradled him to her, not caring that his bloody tears stained her face, chest, and arms. She kissed the top of his head, his temples, his wet cheeks. She stroked his hair, his face, ran her hands over his neck and arms.

Aithan's fists loosened, then clenched again. He sucked in a sharp breath, his nostrils flaring. Macella could feel his pulse, hard and fast.

"Come back to me, Aithan of Auburndale, son of Maia of Kosmosdale and Gabriela of Edgewood," Macella pleaded, her lips against his ear. "Son of Lucifer. Protector of the Crown. Love of my life."

Aithan took another deep breath, his fists loosening again. Macella held him tighter, feeling his body relax infinitesimally. Without realizing it, she had begun to rock gently, still rhythmically stroking his hair.

"You are the only home I have ever known. You are my Fate, my partner in this life and every other, gods willing. And if the gods do not will it, I will still make it so," Macella hissed fiercely. "We are far from finished with our journey. Come back to me. Come home."

Another deep breath. And another. Another.

Aithan's jaw unclenched. The veins in his temples receded. Slowly, his blank eyes darkened.

He blinked once, twice. After a third blink, his orange pupils had reappeared.

Finally, his eyes met hers. His gaze was clear. He reached up and touched her face, his fingertips coming away bloody.

"You led me back," Aithan said softly. "I knew you would."

With a sound that was half laugh, half sob, Macella hugged him. She slid down in the bed, fitting herself against him, relief and exhaustion washing over her. Aithan held her close and kissed the top of her head.

"The rulers of this kingdom have committed unspeakable atrocities against our families, our people," Aithan said after a long silence. "We cannot allow it to continue. Nor can we allow it to go unpunished."

Macella heard the hard edge in his voice, remembered the silent child who lay beside the corpse of his murdered mother. No, they could not allow the tyranny to continue. They would have righteous vengeance.

Chapter Seven

※

Dearest Finley,

Please accept my sincerest apologies for my unusual slowness in replying to your last letter. The weeks since the northern dignitaries' visit have seen some changes to my routine. Her grace, King Khari, sees benefit in my being more involved at court. She believes engaging more with persons of rank will inform my work as Royal Scribe, while also improving my mind and manners.

Thus, her grace has kept my daily itinerary full of meals and social visits with the resident nobles here at Kōsaten Keep. I have even begun to accompany the Crown on official engagements beyond the castle walls in Pleasure Ridge Park and the estates nearest the city. I very much enjoy these outings, as I still miss the days

Aithan and I spent wandering the kingdom. I am grateful that spending so much more time with the Crown allows me to see the Lord Protector more often...

Macella hurried to finish her letter to Finley before the inevitable chime of a royal summons. She hoped her annoyance and distaste had not bled too much into her carefully chosen words. It certainly wouldn't do for her to show her true sentiments about her newfound popularity.

Apparently, the northern dignitaries had raved about the ball and had been delighted to learn that Macella hailed from Shively. They hadn't been aware that someone from one of the poorest cities in their region held such a favored position at court. As such, King Khari had decided that it would be advantageous to place Macella in more prominence.

Thus, Macella had spent the last few weeks more immersed in court happenings than ever. She dined with members of the Crown at least once a day. Each afternoon, she joined one of the monarchs and their entourages for a social visit. With King Khari, that often meant listening to her talk, while sitting uneasily alongside dignitaries and sycophants. Disconcertingly, however, Khari frequently asked Macella for her opinions, forcing her to fumble through the awkwardness of speaking before those wealthier and better educated than herself. On these occasions, Macella was reminded of why she preferred writing to speaking.

Seeing King Khari's interest, Queen Annika insisted upon Macella's company whenever possible, despite the obvious fact that neither of them enjoyed these visits. Macella would sit in the young queen's parlor with all her rich, silly, vapid associates and count the minutes until she could escape. For her part, Queen Annika hardly spoke to Macella unless she could offer some thinly veiled criticism.

Unlike their young spouse, Monarch Meztli preferred the outdoors to stuffy parlors. Macella actually enjoyed accompanying them and their small coterie on walks and hunting trips in the castle's woods, or for swims in its many lakes and ponds. They seldom talked much. Macella soon decided that her appointments with Meztli were the least taxing and most rejuvenating of her new demands.

She also enjoyed her time with Queen Awa. They typically spent their afternoon visits outside on the grounds as well. Macella would ride Cinnamon while the elder queen rode one of the Crown's many elegant mounts. She favored a lovely white Camarillo with a sweet temper and sad black eyes. Together, she and Macella would ride toward the far-flung edges of the castle's estate.

They used these rides to talk privately. Though a knight and a servant followed at a respectful distance, Macella and Queen Awa were relatively alone and could often speak honestly, which was a rare gift. Soon, Macella had informed Awa of Khari's plans for her own Aegisborn and of Grand Mage Kiama's subsequent efforts to discover Aithan's Aegis parent.

That day, they'd stopped at the western edge of the castle's lands, on a hill overlooking a lush valley. Their security detail stood a ways off, and the servant had left to gather water for the horses. Macella and Awa stood together atop the hill while their mounts grazed nearby.

"I suppose there would not be records of just how a mage can facilitate an Aegis birth," Queen Awa mused. "Anyone with that knowledge would keep it close. Kiama is an exceptional mage, but she will need time to discover this magic."

Queen Awa stared silently at the valley beyond the castle walls. Macella followed her gaze. She got the sense that she and Aithan were not the keep's only inhabitants yearning for freedom from its confines. She could not imagine living within these walls for decades, growing increasingly distant from those around her. Queen Awa must have been far more miserable than she let show.

"What I cannot determine," the queen continued as if without pause, "is who Khari intends to carry her crossbreed offspring."

Macella looked up sharply. "Would she not do it herself?"

Queen Awa surprised Macella with a hoarse laugh. "Never. Khari is far too selfish for the restrictions of childbearing—or motherhood for that matter. I suppose Annika would be all too happy to serve as surrogate."

Macella could envision the beautiful young queen grown rounder with pregnancy, smugly carrying the king's child. Oh, how Annika would exult in the triumph. She would finally be more precious to Khari than everyone else. And if Khari was honest with Annika about the child's true nature, she'd be even more unbearable. She would surely love to taunt Macella with the fact that she would be ostensibly carrying Aithan's child. Macella clenched her fists.

"There was a time when I would have happily borne as many children as Khari wished," Queen Awa admitted wistfully. "There was a time when I believed she truly loved me. That was before I knew that she loves no one but herself."

"She is a fool," came a hard, low voice.

Macella and Awa spun toward the sound. Macella's daggers were in her hands before she realized she'd reached for them. Quickly, she sheathed them again.

"Very smooth," Shamira deadpanned. "You totally pass for a regular human."

Macella scowled at the dead woman. "Must you always appear from thin air? My heart nearly leapt from my chest."

"I am a shade," Shamira replied, shrugging. "Appearing from thin air and frightening people is in our nature."

(13) Queen Awa laughed her throaty laugh, and then Shamira had no attention to spare for Macella. She glided closer to the queen. Though she appeared solid enough, when she reached for the queen's hand, hers went translucent and passed through the other woman's flesh. Awa shivered and wrapped her arms around herself. The two women exchanged a look of such longing that Macella had to look away.

"Khari is a fool," Shamira repeated. "I loved you from the beginning. When Khari brought you to the keep, I knew that I would do everything in my power to remain Protector of the Crown, just to be near you."

Queen Awa's eyes brimmed with tears. "You are also a fool then. For a decade, I ignored you entirely, too enamored was I with the king to see anyone else. Then I spent the next thirty years letting my hurt become rage. And all that time you waited."

Shamira shrugged again. "What did I have but time?"

"Time I wasted," Awa spat. "Because I was too oblivious, then too angry, then too afraid to do anything with it."

The queen swallowed hard, pressing her eyes tightly shut. Despite her efforts to stifle them, tears spilled down her cheeks. Shamira stood before her, one hand hovering helplessly near her cheek.

Queen Awa opened dark, shining eyes. "I wasted it all."

In bits and pieces, Macella had learned some of the story of the elder queen and the Protector of the Crown. Shamira had served for all of Khari's reign, meaning she'd known Awa for nearly a century. It had taken the elder queen most of that time to realize that Shamira always stood on the side of Khari nearest to Awa, or that she made sure no one else took out the Camarillo on the days the elder queen liked to ride. Once, when Queen Awa had been away from the castle for a number of weeks, she'd returned to find fresh flowers and lit candles on her private altar—someone had tended it for her in her absence, a kindness she thought no one in the castle would even think to bestow.

Books with pages held by wildflower bookmarks appeared on Queen Awa's tables. Awa responded by choosing her favorite passages, marking the pages with feathers or bits of fabric, and leaving them for Shamira to find. Still, they did not speak to one another any more frequently than they ever had. If their fingers brushed when the Lady Protector handed the queen her mail or a goblet of wine, it was merely by accident. They never declared their love, never acted on it. Queen Awa had been terrified to even acknowledge it, knowing how King Khari would use Shamira against her if she ever suspected their attachment.

Then King Khari impulsively executed Shamira in an unnecessary display of power and their nascent love story was cut short. Now they regretted the missed touches, the chances not taken. They were only able to profess their love now that it was too late. Soon, Shamira would be forced to pass from the mortal realm and their story would truly end.

"How long can you stay today?" Macella asked, hoping she'd be able to make herself scarce and give the star-crossed lovers some time alone.

Shamira shrugged. "Time is different now. I am here and then I am not and then I am again. To me, it is like the blink of an eye, but then I notice you've all changed clothes, or the gardens have grown noticeably, and I realize I have been gone a day, a week, a fortnight. And each time I go away, it is a little harder to return, a bit more difficult to stay."

"Time eludes us yet again," Queen Awa intoned sadly, her eyes still swimming with tears. "I should be thanking the gods for my gift allowing us even this brief borrowed time together, but I am cursing them for taking you from me so soon."

"Do you think, perhaps, your love is what allows you to see Shamira?" Macella ventured.

Queen Awa let out a surprised laugh, wiping away her tears. "You are a writer, indeed, Lady Macella. Such a fanciful imagination."

Macella huffed indignantly, drawing another laugh from the elder queen. Shamira smirked, enjoying Awa's mirth. Macella put her hands on her hips and gave them a stern look. She wasn't truly upset, but rather glad she was able to cheer them up a bit.

"When the gods blessed us and bestowed gifts upon us, they manifested in various ways," Queen Awa explained. "None of us knew what to expect. Nor do we know the extent of one another's abilities."

"You don't know what supernatural gifts the other monarchs possess?" Macella asked incredulously.

Awa lifted her shoulders delicately. "I have suspicions, but we rarely speak of it. As you know, we do not particularly trust each other."

"That's an understatement," Macella agreed. "So, the gods gifted you with communion with the dead?"

Awa paused. "I believe they enhanced many of our attributes, besides our health. That they amplified what was already inside each of us. My people have always revered our ancestors. We pray for their guidance and keep altars of remembrance."

"Thus, you can now fully communicate with loved ones who have passed from this life," Macella inferred.

"Precisely," Queen Awa replied, her eyes on Shamira again. "I have not had many uses for my gift in the last century, and far too many of those occasions were melancholic. I did not fully appreciate it before now."

Macella's heart ached as she again looked away from the intensity of Awa and Shamira's longing. She promised herself that she would touch Aithan at every opportunity. She would tell him how much she loved him every single day. When they crossed the veil into the Otherworlds, they would go without regret. They would know that they had cherished every moment of their time together in the living realm.

"We cannot allow Khari to make children only to build her own army," Shamira said, bringing Macella back to the present. "It may take Kiama some time to accomplish, but she will eventually succeed unless we ensure she does not."

For a quarter of an hour, the three women discussed possible actions. Each idea seemed more implausible than the last. There didn't seem to be a way to stop the king without outright bloodshed or that wouldn't end in a death sentence for all of them.

"We must delay them. We need more time." Macella sighed in frustration. "Eventually, our plans for deposing the king will come to fruition. We just have to thwart Kiama's efforts until then."

"That is exactly what we will do," Queen Awa exclaimed, clearly struck with an idea. Eyes alight with excitement, she outlined a dangerous and foolhardy plan.

"Absolutely not," Aithan said, when Macella later shared the idea with him.

He had fallen into bed with a grateful sigh after another long night attending to King Khari. Macella had been in his company for much of the late afternoon and evening following her outing with the elder queen, but there had been no opportunity to even think in his direction. She'd been far too busy juggling conversations with various nobles, while Aithan had been completely absorbed in his own duties.

Now, she rolled onto her side to look at him. Even in profile, she could see the displeasure in his expression. His jaw was clenched tight, his lips pressed into a thin line. Macella sighed, propping herself up on an elbow so she could look fully into his face.

"Aithan—" she began.

"It is too dangerous," he snapped, cutting her off. "I will not risk your life."

Macella's eyes narrowed, her chin lifting in defiance. It had been quite some time since Aithan of Auburndale had seen her stubborn side. She was prepared to carry her point. She would force him to see reason.

"Our task requires risks, and those risks are worth it because our purpose is honorable and true," Macella said hotly, determinedly talking over him when he tried to interrupt. "It is the best plan we have. Or would you like to see more like us in her grace's service?"

"Of course, I would not," Aithan conceded in exasperation. "But—"

No buts, Macella thought sternly. *You know this is our best option. If I destroy the Aegis samples, it will set Kiama back—perchance long enough for us to devise a more permanent solution. We cannot delay much longer in deciding whether to tell her what we learned of your Aegis mother. This will distract her.*

Aithan was silent, his expression grim.

Macella sat up, leaning over him so that he could not avoid her gaze. *I will not let her make a mockery of what we are. I will not let her expand her cruelty to another generation. I will not let her enslave your offspring.*

Aithan's expression grew stricken. "They would not truly be my—"

"I know," Macella amended quickly. "I did not mean that. I just meant that I cannot stand by and allow such villainy to go unchallenged. I *will* not. It is not in my nature, just as it is not in yours."

"I can do it then," Aithan argued. "I know the keep better than you do."

Macella sighed. They'd been over this already. The Aegis samples were kept in the refrigerated undercroft below the mages' annex. The storeroom was magically chilled to maintain the freshness of the specimens, which could be ruined by even a slight increase in temperature. As such, the undercroft had been well-warded against fire. A torch would instantly extinguish before passing over the threshold. No flame could be kindled inside its walls.

No *earthly* flame. The undercroft had not, however, been warded against hellfire. That meant that Macella only had to get inside for a few minutes—long enough for her onyx flames to warm the samples. By the time the mages began work the following day, the undercroft would be back at its regular temperature. After that, it could take weeks or even months of failed experiments before anyone suspected the specimens were the problem. Even then, there would be no way of knowing what had ruined them.

Macella flopped back down beside Aithan, bringing her lips to his ear. "I can move through the castle unseen. You cannot. And though I do not know the keep so well as you, I will have Shamira to guide me."

Aithan heaved another sigh. "Macella, we do not even know what rules govern Shamira's comings and goings. We cannot rely on her presence."

"If she does not appear on the designated night, I will not attempt it," Macella promised. "It is not as if I wish to put myself in danger."

"I am not certain that's true," Aithan grumbled.

Macella could tell she had won. She draped an arm across Aithan's chest and snuggled closer to his warmth. He pressed his face into her hair, humming thoughtfully. Macella waited.

"If Shamira does not appear that night, you will not attempt it," Aithan said in a tone that brooked no argument. "If Khari does not visit Annika's chambers that night, you will not attempt it. If the Grand Mage appears suspicious, you will not attempt it. If anything at all seems out of the ordinary that day: *You. Will. Not. Attempt. It.*"

Macella laughed, relenting. "You have my word."

"Good," Aithan murmured, wrapping his arms around her. "You have always kept your word and I trust you always will."

Macella remembered the promise she'd made to herself that afternoon. She lifted up to look into Aithan's face again. Carefully, she kissed each of his eyes, his forehead, and, finally, his lips. She rested her forehead against his and closed her eyes in silent prayer.

"I love you with all of my being, Aithan of Auburndale. You are *mine*," Macella whispered fiercely, feeling Aithan's answering flare of pride at her claim. "I want to spend many, many more years with you. I promise that I will do everything I can to earn us those years together. And I would die before breaking a promise to you."

Chapter Eight

Despite her bravado, Macella felt herself growing increasingly nervous as the time to enact their plan drew nearer. There wasn't much she could do to prepare, so Macella only obsessively reviewed the plan in her mind over the four days before King Khari's weekly visit to Queen Annika's chambers. The time passed incredibly slowly and far too quickly in turns.

Soon, the day arrived. It was all Macella could do to sit through her engagements with the Crown. More than once, she failed to hear her name called, so lost was she in her anxious thoughts. As planned, Queen Awa sent Macella away from their afternoon visit early, since neither of them could stand to attempt idle conversation. Macella gratefully returned to the solitude of her chambers.

While Macella escaped the Crown early, Aithan remained, carefully observing every aspect of the monarchs' comings and goings with even more intensity than usual. Macella knew that he was watching for the slightest indication of danger or suspicion. He was doing all in his power to ensure the day went perfectly, so that the Crown would have no possible reason to deviate from their schedules—especially King Khari and Queen Annika.

Macella felt a pang of guilt. She knew that Aithan was worried sick about her and that he nevertheless would not stand in her way. She believed that this was the best course of action, but she still hated to cause him anxiety.

There's no time to wallow in guilt, she told herself sternly.

Time was their greatest gift. It was something so many people deserved more of—people like her parents, Aithan's parents, Shamira and Awa. Macella would make the most of the time they'd been given. She'd honor them all by stopping King Khari.

She sat down and wrote awhile, not worrying about whether her ramblings made sense, just allowing space for the cacophony of thoughts in her mind to have their say. Then she took a long bath, forcing herself to be still and present. Her shoulders and the knot in her stomach gradually loosened a little. By the time she wrapped herself in a warm towel, she felt much more at peace, and knew exactly how she would spend the evening.

Later, after the servants had come and gone as requested, Macella oiled her skin, looking thoughtfully around the dressing chamber. Her eyes fell on white cloth, and she smiled to herself. She picked up Aithan's shirt, which he'd tossed hastily aside when he last dressed. She pressed her face into the fabric, inhaling the faint traces of his sweet, smoky scent.

Macella slipped the shirt over her head. It was much too large and fell to her mid-thigh. She rolled the sleeves, so they didn't cover her hands. The thin cotton was soft against her skin. Her reflection in the long mirror was flattering—her skin glowed, her wild curls were a sexy mess, and the thin fabric of the oversized shirt showed just enough to make him want to see more.

(14) The click of the outer chamber door opening and closing softly announced Aithan's arrival. Macella poured a chalice of wine. When he reached the door of the dressing chamber, she met him with a kiss, handing him the wine. He pulled her into a tight embrace, took a long drink from the cup, then kissed the top of Macella's head.

"This is quite nice," he murmured into her hair.

"I'm just getting started," she replied, pulling free and grinning up at him. "You are due for a carefree evening, and I intend to give it to you."

Aithan quirked an eyebrow as she took his hand but let her lead him through the dressing room and into the bathing chamber. The massive clawfoot tub was filled with steaming water, filling the room with the hazy scent of flowers. Candlelight flickered off of the chamber's intricate pattern of mosaic tiles.

"These last weeks, I have observed your daily duties," Macella continued, dropping to her knees to remove Aithan's boots. "You spend every moment tending to others' needs. The Crown's constant demands, the incessant questions from the knights and servants, and a million other details to track, and yet you are always calm and know exactly what to do."

Aithan gave a dismissive hum, though he was smiling. He was humble to a fault. Macella kissed him again, taking his chalice and setting it atop a table beside the tub. She tugged his shirt over his head and tossed it aside.

"Though my shirt looks very good on you," Aithan said, leaning back to look her over, "I would not mind if we threw it on the floor as well."

He laid a hand on Macella's waist and pulled her close. Giving her a slow kiss, he ran his hand over her hip and down her thigh. Her breath caught and warmth flooded her body as his fingers caught the hem of her borrowed shirt and began to slide the fabric upward. Macella stroked the soft silver hair on his chest, leaning into the kiss. Then she gently pushed him away.

"Not yet," she teased.

With an unwilling grunt, Aithan released her. Macella grinned impishly as she unbuttoned and lowered his trousers. She wasn't surprised by his waiting erection. Looking up at him mischievously, she trailed her tongue around the tip of his cock. He inhaled sharply.

"Not yet," she repeated, this time addressing his erection.

Macella gave the tip of Aithan's penis a playful kiss before standing. She took his hand and led him to the tub. The surface of the steaming water had been sprinkled with petals of lavender and rose.

Aithan scowled at her. "You promised a carefree evening, not one of torment."

Macella laughed. "Forgive me, Lord Protector. I assure you your patience will be rewarded. Now get in."

With a longsuffering sigh, Aithan stepped into the bath, then lowered himself gracefully into the hot water. He sighed as he leaned his head back against the tub's edge. Macella smiled down at him expectantly.

"Fine, this is pleasant," Aithan begrudgingly allowed.

Smirking, Macella handed him his wine. As he sipped contentedly, she seated herself near his head. Using a basin and pitcher, she rinsed his long waves. She loved how the water darkened his tresses from silver and crimson to a steely gray and wine red. Aithan hummed quietly as she washed his hair, soothingly kneading his scalp.

"I did not remember it before, but I have always loved having my hair washed," Aithan mused dreamily.

Macella looked at his face. His eyes were closed, the candlelight making his golden skin glow. His face was serene, though his voice was wistful.

"Before you, no one had washed my hair for me since I was a child," Aithan continued. "But Maia used to. And she sang as she did it."

In his mind's eye, Macella saw Maia's face smiling down at him as Aithan remembered the feel of his mother's hands in his hair. Maia's own auburn waves fell in a curtain around them. They brushed Aithan's face, smelling of peppermint.

"Duérmete, mi niño, duérmete, mi sol," Maia sang in Aithan's memory.

Aithan finished aloud. "Duérmete pedazo de mi corazón."

Macella felt a twinge of bittersweet longing. Whether it was Aithan's emotions or her own, she wasn't entirely sure. Probably both.

"I have heard that lullaby before," Macella realized. "You sing it sometimes as I fall asleep. I do not know the language."

"I don't think I do either," Aithan confessed. "I know it is one of the ancient ones—it was passed down in my mother's family. Gabriela used words and short phrases, terms of endearment mostly, but Maia knew entire songs and stories. She had a knack for languages, and she studied that one extensively so that she could pass Gabriela's heritage on to me. She sang that one all the time. Maia was always singing. She had a terrible voice, but Gabriela and I didn't mind."

Macella rinsed the soap from Aithan's hair, letting him relive the pleasant memories. The past weeks had seen many such episodes, as his unlocked past gradually returned to him. After that first, worst memory, the rest had mostly been good. There were a few more horrors from his time with Queen Rhiannon, but he'd soon been sent to Smoketown. Only his life until that point had been suppressed, meaning his memories thereafter had always been intact.

And so, the pieces that were returning to him were from a joyful childhood in a cozy home with mothers who'd loved him and one another fiercely. Macella knew that recovering the memory of that love had made the effort totally worth the risk. She was happy that Aithan had regained some of what had been taken from him. He deserved that and so much more.

Aithan caught one of her hands and brought it to his lips. His amber eyes were on her, like melted caramel in the low light. Macella shivered, the intensity of his gaze having its customary effect on her body.

"Do not give up hope," he said, pressing her hand. "The Grand Mage is not all-knowing. We may yet find a way to restore your past as well."

Macella shook her head, grinning ruefully. She kissed Aithan's forehead, then turned away to gather a sponge and sweet-smelling soap. She knew that the Grand Mage was right about memories taken by Meng Po—they were gone forever, into the void of the goddess's Broth of Oblivion. Still, she certainly didn't begrudge Aithan his recovered past.

"I am enjoying the gift of your memories and that is enough," Macella said. She moved her stool to a spot beside the tub. "But, perhaps, let us not think about your mothers during this next part."

Aithan chuckled as Macella began to wash his arms and chest. She could feel him relaxing further as she worked the sponge against his skin, massaging his muscles. When she leaned across the tub, she felt Aithan press a kiss against her shoulder.

"You are too good to me," he murmured with a contented hum. "Some days I still find it difficult to believe that this is my life."

(15) Aithan obediently lifted and turned as Macella directed, letting her wash his arms, back and legs. The chest and sleeves of her borrowed shirt were soaked

and clinging to her skin, the thin white fabric leaving little to the imagination. Aithan watched her moving around the tub, his eyes lingering on her breasts and hips. Macella could feel the arousal returning to his mind. Her nipples stiffened in response, straining against the wet fabric.

Macella knelt, running the sponge over the taught ridges of Aithan's abdomen beneath the water. She met his gaze as she moved the sponge lower. He drew in a sharp breath when she grazed his growing erection.

Macella let the sponge float away, taking up the bar of sweet soap instead. She lowered it into the water, rubbing her hands against it until she'd worked up a slick lather. Carefully, she took Aithan's rigid cock in her hands and began to work the soap along the length of his shaft. She ran her hands rhythmically from base to tip, squeezing gently as she stroked him.

Aithan let out a low moan, a tremor passing through his body. Macella again lifted her gaze to his face. Eyes closed, lips parted, his wet hair clinging to his golden skin—he was utterly beautiful in his pleasure. Macella relished it, watching his face as she increased the speed and pressure of her hands. His hips rocked slightly in time with her rhythmic strokes and Macella imagined herself on top of him, burying him inside of her, moving her hips in time with his.

Aithan's eyes snapped open, his burning gaze holding hers. Before she could react, he had plucked her from her kneeling position beside the tub and pulled her into the water on top of him. After a flurry of movement and laughter, Macella finally managed to position herself astride his hips.

"You've gotten me all wet!" she exclaimed, trying to sound indignant.

"I am about to get you much wetter," Aithan growled, sitting up.

Water sloshed over the tub's sides to splash against the tile floor. Aithan wrapped an arm around Macella's waist, using his free hand to cup her breast. He lowered his head and took her nipple between his lips, sucking it into his mouth through her soaked shirt. Macella moaned, the pressure of Aithan's tongue teasing at her nipple sending spasms through her stomach. She entwined her fingers in his hair, pressing his head to her breast eagerly.

Beneath the water's surface, she felt Aithan sponging the soap from his cock before positioning it against her. With exaggerated slowness, Macella lowered herself onto him. His arm tightened spasmodically around her waist. His mouth found her collarbone and then her neck, his breath warm against her wet skin. She moaned again, tugging gently at his hair. He growled in response, guiding her up and down his shaft.

Macella freed her hands from Aithan's hair and braced them against the tub on either side of his head, forcing him to lean back. Using the tub for leverage, Macella worked her hips, arching and releasing her lower back, sliding his throbbing cock in and out of her pussy, reveling in the feel of him inside of her.

"Gods," Aithan gasped. Leaning his head against the tub's edge, he watched her ride him, his eyes devouring her and hands clutching her ass.

Still moving slowly, Macella leaned forward. She kissed him, catching his bottom lip between her teeth. Then, steadily sliding up and down his cock, she trailed her tongue along his neck, stopping with her lips at his ear.

"You feel so good," she purred. "Why do you always feel *so fucking good*?"

Macella punctuated each word with a sharp release of her hips. Aithan shuddered, his hands clenching against the supple flesh of her ass. Macella's heart raced, warmth spreading through her torso. He really did feel incredible inside of her. He always did.

Her pussy clenched involuntarily, and she moaned against Aithan's neck, then bit him gently, savoring the taste of his skin. As always, he consumed her senses—the sweet woodsmoke scent of him, the timbre of his low growls and moans, and, gods, the velvety hardness of him inside of her. She would never be able to get enough of Aithan of Auburndale.

"Macella, you are driving me mad." Aithan's voice was husky and choked. "I am not sure how much more of this I can stand."

"Don't hold back," Macella panted, moving faster. "Please."

Aithan groaned, his grip tightening. With another shudder, he pressed her down hard, lifting his hips to drive himself as deep as possible. Macella cried out, using the leverage of her hold on the tub's edge to match his thrust.

Then Aithan was in control, guiding her hips, plunging inside her. His moans echoed hers, filling the tiled bathing chamber with a hollow chorus of pleasure.

He came with his arms wrapped around her, holding her tightly against his chest. His breath was ragged against her neck.

"Macella, my love, my life," Aithan whispered. "Mi amor, mi vida."

As they lay in bed afterward, Aithan humming that old lullaby, Macella thought about the task ahead of her. This would be their first direct attack on King Khari. It was up to her to complete the mission undetected, so that their tenuous peace might remain unbroken.

"You know that my fear is not a slight against you," Aithan murmured, breaking off his song. "I know that you can do this. You are brave and smart and extremely well-trained, if I do say so myself."

"I know," Macella replied, smiling in the semidarkness. And she did know. He always believed in her.

"It is just that I cannot bear the thought of Khari hurting you," Aithan said, his voice pained. "Knowing that I would be powerless to lift a hand against her—"

"I know," Macella replied, running her fingers through the soft hair on his chest. "You will not have to endure that because I am not going to be caught."

"I know." Aithan sighed. "I know."

Macella was surprised that either of them could sleep, but she found herself waking a few hours later beside a still sleeping Aithan. Momentarily panicked, Macella looked to the glimpse of sky beyond the window. She exhaled in relief. Not yet time.

She rose and slipped from the room. In the dressing chamber, she put on trousers and soft boots, and pulled her curls into a tight bun. Her heart hammered in her chest, but she couldn't tell if it was from nerves or exhilaration.

When she returned to the bedchamber, Aithan and Shamira were waiting for her. Of course, Aithan did not realize Shamira was present until Macella acknowledged her. Macella thought she saw a flash of disappointment cross Aithan's features. She knew part of him had hoped Shamira would not come, so that they would have to call off the plan.

"Be careful," Aithan commanded, holding her face in his hands. "If you are not back by the hour of Erebus, I will come looking."

He crushed her to him and kissed her hard. Macella hoped he couldn't feel her heart attempting to pound free of her chest. She let herself cling to him for a long minute before forcing herself to pull away.

"See you soon," she whispered, then she ignited her onyx flames and vanished.

Chapter Nine

In Aithan's mind, she watched a wall panel slide open of its own volition (16). In reality, Macella had released the hidden latch and opened the concealed door to the Crown's secret passageways. She and Shamira slipped into the darkness. Macella closed the wall panel behind them, pausing to let her eyes adjust.

She didn't dare light a torch, for fear of it being noticed through some crack or crevice. Fortunately, the dead did not need light to see. Shamira led her through the narrow corridors swiftly, somehow emitting a faint otherworldly aura for Macella to follow through the darkness.

Before long, they stopped before a stretch of wall no different than any other they'd passed. Macella pressed her ear against it. She could hear muffled snores.

Shamira stepped through the wall, leaving Macella alone in the pitch dark. Macella counted slowly, matching her breathing to her count. Shamira returned just after Macella reached thirty-seven. She nodded, before disappearing through the wall again.

As quietly as she could, Macella felt for the hidden latch. It clicked faintly when she pressed it, but the panel itself was silent as she slid it open. Aithan had visited each of these hidden doors over the past few days, testing their functionality and oiling their mechanisms. As always, he'd done a meticulous job.

A few guttering candles cast dim light on the large and lavish chamber. Macella left the panel slightly ajar, not wanting to risk the click of the latch, then moved swiftly and silently over the lush carpeting. The centerpiece of the room was a huge four-poster bed hung with gauzy blue curtains.

Queen Annika and King Khari were asleep, tangled in the luxurious satin bedclothes. Annika looked like a fairy tale princess, lying on her back with her golden hair spread across her pillows. Her surprisingly loud snores ruined the illusion a bit, however.

King Khari seemed oblivious to the snores, her face buried deep in the blankets and pillows. She lay on her stomach with one of her arms dangling off the bed. A handsbreadth from her trailing fingertips, her trousers lay in an untidy heap.

Macella crept to the bedside, pausing every few seconds to check the sleeping monarchs for any sign of disturbance. Annika snored on. Khari remained as still as a corpse. Macella inhaled a shaky breath.

"I will watch them. You get the keys already," Shamira hissed impatiently. "If I was corporeal, I would have had them and been back in the passage already."

Macella jumped, stifling a yelp. She'd forgotten Shamira was even in the room. She glared at the dead woman, her chest heaving.

"What? Are you going to kill me again?" Shamira demanded. "If you don't get those damn keys soon, I might well die of boredom."

Macella scowled, dropping into a crouch beside the king's discarded pants. Slowly, she reached into one pocket. Her fingers found cool iron. She pulled the keys free, trying not to let them jingle.

King Khari's fingers twitched, close enough for her to touch Macella if she only reached out a bit. The king stirred, her hand brushing closer. Macella stayed very still.

The king fidgeted a bit more before settling again. Macella stood slowly, backing away a few steps. She stuffed the keys into her own pocket before hurrying back to the passageway. As the hidden door slid shut with a faint click, Queen Annika's snores abruptly ceased.

Not allowing herself to worry about the young queen, Macella hurried after Shamira, who was already disappearing around a curve in the passageway. This time, their journey seemed to take much longer. The secret passage twisted and turned and bent back on itself intricately as they navigated to the mages' annex.

Finally, just when Macella thought the claustrophobia was going to overwhelm her, Shamira stopped. The panel she directed Macella to opened behind a tapestry. They paused to listen before stepping out into the corridor. It seemed cavernous and bright compared to the tight, dark passageway.

Macella had seldom seen this part of the castle. Aside from a perfunctory tour and a brief accidental visit while searching for the library, she'd had no reason to venture near the mages' wing. If Shamira had not been leading her, she would no doubt be wasting precious time getting lost.

The halls of the annex were silent. When the corridor split in three directions, Shamira explained that the left path led to the mages' bedchambers, while the path forward would lead to their laboratories, menagerie, and conservatory. They turned right, toward the storerooms.

Shamira led Macella past several identical doors before stopping. "This will lead to the undercroft. It is always locked."

(17) Macella fished the keys from her pocket, holding them aloft so Shamira could point out the one she needed. Taking a deep breath, Macella unlocked and opened the door before Shamira could grow impatient. Stone stairs descended into darkness; however, Macella could make out a faint bluish glow somewhere below.

She didn't let herself hesitate. Bracing one hand on the cool stone wall, she padded quickly down the stairs. Her circuitous journey through the hidden passageways had taken more time than she'd hoped. It must've been nearing the hour of Khonshu. They had to hurry.

The blue light grew brighter as they drew closer. Soon Macella saw that a huge, round door lay ahead, emitting the glow she'd followed. She shivered as she neared it, the temperature dropping notably with each step she took.

"It will be locked as well," Shamira said, pointing to a different key on the king's massive keyring.

Macella unlocked the door. It opened with a hiss and a blast of icy air. The vaultlike room beyond held rows and rows of glass cases, steel shelves, and massive cabinets. Shamira and Macella split up in search of the Aegis samples.

They found two opposite shelves of glass cases filled with vials, bottles, and boxes. All were labeled with an Aegis's name followed by a sequence of numbers and letters. Some of the specimens had to be hundreds of years old. How were they thus preserved and for what purpose? Macella read the names—she'd seen them all in the library's ledgers, but this somehow made them seem more real. Dozens of Aegises had reported to Kōsaten Keep year after year, where they were subjected annually to the mages' experiments and had all manner of bodily fluids and tissues taken for gods only knew what reason.

Had other sovereigns planned to crossbreed like Khari? Or had they perhaps even more nefarious intentions? Macella did not want to think about the many terrible possibilities. Instead, she focused on her translucent flames. They flared brighter, still invisible to any outside observer. Well, any living observer. Shamira seemed to have no trouble seeing through Macella's cloaking.

"Hurry," Shamira barked, her voice strained.

Macella's looked around sharply. "Shamira? What is the matter?"

Shamira didn't answer. She probably hadn't even heard Macella's question. Shamira had vanished.

Macella was alone in the undercroft.

She tried not to panic. Perhaps Shamira would return. Macella needed to do her job here and she needed to do it quickly. She would worry about the next step when she had to. Right now, she had to heat the samples.

Macella stretched her arms to either side. Her fingertips brushed against the cases, onyx flames licking at the glass. She walked up and down the row slowly, lifting and lowering her arms, letting her flames warm the air around the shelves. She counted to herself as she walked, focusing only on the next number and her flames.

After nearly half an hour, she decided the damage was done. Shamira had not returned. Macella would have to find her way on her own. It was well into the hour of Khonshu now. If she did not return soon, Aithan would risk himself by coming in search of her.

Pulse pounding in her ears, Macella left the cold room, locking the glowing door behind her. At the top of the stone stairs into the undercroft, Macella locked the second door. Another step completed. Now to get out of the mages' wing.

Macella walked past the row of identical doors. When she reached the juncture, she was sure she knew which path would lead her back to the main corridor and the hidden door behind the tapestry.

But as she turned to go, a flicker of flame and a shifting shadow caught her attention. Straining her ears, Macella could detect hushed, angry voices from the mages' sleeping quarters. Before she realized it, she was moving stealthily toward the voices and candlelight.

"This is inappropriate, even for you," hissed a woman's voice. Grand Mage Kiama.

"I am only doing my duty to the Crown," an oily voice replied.

Macella crept closer. She knew that false politeness, that honeyed condescension. The Grand Vizier, Lord Anwir.

"You are doing your duty to Queen Annika," Kiama corrected him bitterly. "And whatever she's put you up to will not bode well for the other monarchs, I'm sure."

"Grand Mage, her grace is giving you the benefit of the doubt," Lord Anwir contended breezily. "When she learned that an Aegis had stolen brimstone from the castle stores, she knew that they had to have had help. Very few people in the keep have access to those stores. Only the Grand Mage and the Crown, actually."

"She is accusing me of treason?" Kiama challenged. "She believes I assisted the Aegis thief?"

"Her grace is not sure, which is why she has sent me to have this conversation with you—as a courtesy," Lord Anwir answered patronizingly.

There was a long pause. Macella imagined the two council members sizing one another up. The Grand Mage's expression would be unreadable, but the Grand Vizier would be smirking. Macella wasn't sure how she felt about Kiama, but she knew without a doubt that Anwir was a snake.

"If her grace could be sure of your loyalty to the Crown, she sees no need to take her concerns to the king," Lord Anwir's tone was casual. "Can she count on your loyalty, Grand Mage?"

Another long pause. Macella tensed, unsure what Kiama's next move would be. She already had secret doings with the king. Now she'd be in bed with Annika as well. At some point, those two parties would have conflicting interests and the Grand Mage would be in a tight spot.

"Of course, Lord Anwir," Kiama said finally. "How can I satisfactorily demonstrate my loyalty to my queen?"

"You will have an opportunity to prove yourself soon. Her grace trusts that when that moment arises, you will not let her down," Lord Anwir's voice sounded closer.

He must have been moving to leave, his work complete. Macella hurried back down the corridor, not wanting to risk bumping into the Grand Vizier in the narrow hall. She retraced her steps and escaped into the open space of the main corridor.

Macella had reached the tapestry before she stopped to think. Her heart sank. She had to get the keys back into King Khari's pocket before the king awoke. That was the aspect of this plan they had been unable to predict. The king sometimes slept the entire night with the young queen, other times she stayed only a short while before returning to her own quarters, usually to her study to pore over her papers and schemes.

That meant that every moment Macella spent wandering the castle was another moment closer to Khari potentially discovering the missing keys. There was no way she would be able to find her way back through the hidden passageways to Queen Annika's bedchamber. For that matter, she'd be lucky to find her way through these corridors to her own apartments.

But that was the safer wager, so Macella set off in search of her familiar halls. Fate must have been smiling on her that night, because the route turned out to be much more intuitive and significantly faster than the labyrinth of the hidden passage. She reached her own door mere minutes before the hour of Erebus.

She used Khari's skeleton key to let herself inside. Aithan sprang to his feet as she shut the door behind her and sagged against it. His nostrils flared before his expression shifted from anxiety to relief.

He smiled, his eyes on the door just above Macella's head. "I was just about to come for you," he exhaled. "Why are you coming through this door and not the hidden panel? What's happened?"

Macella let herself materialize as she pushed away from the door. There was no time to rest. The task was not done.

"You must lead me back to Annika's bedchamber immediately," Macella said, brushing past Aithan and into their bedroom.

She was opening the hidden panel when Aithan caught up to her. He took her hand, squeezing it gently as he passed ahead of her into the dark passageway. *Tell me on the way*, he thought, as she slid the panel shut behind them.

So, she showed him the memory of the undercroft and Shamira's sudden disappearance, and of her making her way through the castle alone. Then she relayed the whispered conversation between the Grand Mage and Grand Vizier. It was a wonder that Aithan could take in her adventures while navigating the intricate passageway in the pitch dark, but somehow, he did. Macella kept one hand on his back or arm, not wanting to be left alone in this maze. She didn't want to have to traverse the castle on her own again tonight.

When they stopped at the panel to Queen Annika's chamber, Macella felt a stab of panic. Neither she nor Aithan could move through solid walls. There was no way to confirm that Annika and Khari were asleep without opening the panel. If they were awake, they would notice the hole appearing in the wall. Even if she went invisible, Aithan would have a hard time explaining himself.

I'll go first, Aithan thought at her.

Macella gripped his arm, shaking her head vehemently in the dark. *You cannot come at all. There is too great a risk you'll be seen.*

They both knew she was right, but she could feel the tension rolling off of Aithan in waves. Macella had no time to waste. Igniting her translucent flames, she found the latch and slid the panel open the tiniest bit. When she pressed her eye to the crack, she could see a sliver of the bed, but not enough to determine whether it was occupied.

Holding her breath, she inched the panel open farther. Now she could see King Khari, asleep on her side, facing away from the paneled wall. The room was quiet. Had Queen Annika shifted into a position that quelled her snoring? Macella slid the door open a bit more.

The queen was not in bed.

Macella inhaled sharply, waiting for the queen to cry out or to appear before the panel and discover them. She waited for a full ten count before exhaling that breath. King Khari hadn't moved. Queen Annika hadn't appeared.

Macella had to take the risk and simply hope that Fate was still on her side. She slid the panel wide enough to slip through. This time, she didn't hesitate, hurrying to the bedside and dropping to the floor beside King Khari's trousers. Clutching them tightly to minimize any noise, she shoved the keys into the king's pocket.

She was halfway across the room when she saw flickering candlelight coming closer. Macella ran for the panel as King Khari stirred in the bed behind her.

The king lifted her head. "Annie?" she called groggily.

"I'm here," Queen Annika answered, stepping into the bedchamber. "Just needed the privy."

As Macella slid the panel closed, the young queen set her candle on her bedside table. Her head turned toward the panel wall just as the latch clicked.

Aithan and Macella held very still, hardly breathing. This time, Macella couldn't even make herself count. She stood in the cloying darkness and waited to be discovered.

An eternity passed. Macella stayed pressed to Aithan's side, both of their bodies coiled and ready to react. She could feel her hands trembling, so she clenched them into fists, her fingernails digging into her palms. She hardly noticed the pain, until Aithan's warm, rough hand wrapped around hers and gently coaxed her fingers loose.

After another endless stretch of time, they heard voices from the bedchamber. Macella held her breath and listened. Aithan shifted slightly to stand in front of her.

Muffled voices. Laughter. Silence. A gasp. A moan. A cry of pleasure. The sounds of lovemaking.

Macella nearly collapsed. Relief turned her muscles gelatinous, and she leaned heavily into Aithan. He wrapped an arm around her, letting out a slow exhale.

When they emerged back into their own bedchamber, Macella was hit by a wave of exhaustion. If she never saw the inside of that secret passageway again, it would be far too soon.

She shed her clothes and climbed into bed, Aithan slipping in behind her. The moment he wrapped his arm around her, she felt the knot that had been in her stomach all night finally began to loosen. She slept like the dead that night.

Over the next few days, her jittery energy began to settle. Their days continued as normal. She dined in company with the Crown, sat in small council meetings with the Grand Mage and Grand Vizier. No one seemed any more suspicious than usual. Macella let herself hope they'd gotten away with their espionage. The castle was calm.

Then Queen Annika made her move.

Chapter Ten

Dearest Finley,

I confess, I do not even know where to begin...

The small council had gathered for a regular meeting. (18) Macella sat in her usual place, taking notes of the proceedings. Aithan stood at attention behind the king's seat. Captain Drudo stood behind the other monarchs, alternating between attending to the conversation and sneaking surreptitious glances at Macella. The Grand Treasurer coughed and wheezed. All seemed normal.

"I believe returning the dignitaries' visit with a good faith journey north is a prudent step," King Khari said, finishing another discussion of the unrest in the northern region. "It would do them good to see the Crown, in all our glory, and to hear from their representative, Queen Awa."

Queen Awa nodded stiffly in acknowledgment. They'd been discussing a tour of the kingdom for some time now, as a centennial celebration of King Khari's reign. Aithan had been instrumental in the plan, considering it a way of getting out of the confines of the capital. Macella had been looking forward to the possibility.

"We will continue planning the visit then," King Khari stated, moving as if to rise. "If no one has anything further, we will adjourn for the day."

"My king," Queen Annika's high voice interrupted the shuffle of papers and chairs. "I do have one matter to bring forth, and I'm afraid it is of great import. It may impact our plans to journey north."

Everyone stopped moving, resettling into their seats. King Khari raised an eyebrow as she sat back to consider her young queen. Macella felt a stone settle in her stomach, accompanied by a shiver of foreboding.

"By all means, bring forward your concern," King Khari said coolly. "The floor is yours."

Aithan's eyes snapped to Macella. *If you must flee, use the hidden door behind the far column. I will buy you time and come for you as soon as I'm able.*

Macella nodded slightly. Her hands were fisted in her lap, itching to go for her daggers. She watched Queen Annika, who looked around at the gathered faces solemnly, though her bright blue eyes danced with suppressed glee. This would be bad. Very bad. Macella was certain of it.

"I am afraid that I have uncovered some very troubling information," Queen Annika began, her voice quaking with feigned sadness. "I have learned that someone stole from our store of brimstone, your grace."

Khari regarded her wife with a calculated calm. "Yes."

Queen Annika faltered, clearly unsettled by the king's noncommittal response. Nobody looked the least bit surprised, aside from Lord Theomund, whose shocked gasp turned into another coughing fit. Everyone ignored him.

From her position, Macella could see all the monarchs' faces clearly, but only the backs of the other council members. She wished she could see the Grand Mage's expression. Had she failed to prove her loyalty to Queen Annika? Was the queen going to accuse her of treason in front of the entire council?

"Yes, well," Queen Annika continued, no longer bothering to pretend reluctance. "It seems the perpetrator had help. From a trusted member of this council, I am sorry to say."

The room went utterly silent. Macella saw Aithan's hand slide toward his sword belt. Across the room, Captain Drudo already rested a hand on the pommel of his sword. If Kiama attempted to attack or escape after the queen made her accusation, the Royal Guard would act quickly.

"That is a heavy accusation, my love," King Khari cautioned, her tone icy. "That would mean someone I trust has committed treason. Their life would be forfeit."

The silence was tense—a water skin grown too full, ready to burst. Annika lowered her gaze, shaking her head regretfully. When she lifted her gaze again, her eyes locked with Macella's. There was a dangerous gleam in their cobalt depths. Macella's stomach tightened with anxiety.

"I know, my love, and it hurts me to have to do this," Queen Annika replied somberly, heaving a heavy sigh. "But I cannot allow you to be mocked by their duplicitous behavior."

Queen Annika paused. She licked her lips in a nervous gesture unlike her normal arrogant calm. Whether she was intentionally drawing out the moment, or if she was uneasy about what she was about to do, Macella couldn't tell.

Finally, she took a deep breath and squared her shoulders. "Your grace, the thief was aided by our lady wife, Queen Awa."

There was stunned silence, followed by a chorus of questions and exclamations. Queen Awa did not move. She only stared at the king, her face impassive. King Khari looked from the elder queen to the young queen, her expression unreadable.

"What evidence do you have of her involvement?" The king might've been asking what was on the dinner menu, so casual was her voice. Her eyes, however, were piercingly cold and intense.

"I have witnesses, my king," Queen Annika declared resolutely. "It was Lord Anwir who aroused my suspicions, and the Grand Mage has confirmed it."

The king slowly turned her head to look at her Grand Vizier and Grand Mage. Even from behind, Macella could see Lord Anwir's simpering posture, his head lowered deferentially. Conversely, Grand Mage Kiama's head was high, her back ramrod straight.

"When we discussed this matter, Lady Kiama, you made no mention of the queen." King Khari's voice was dangerously low now.

The Grand Mage would have to tread carefully. Here was the moment Lord Anwir had meant. This is when she would prove her loyalty to Queen Annika. Macella imagined that, were Kiama to deny Annika's accusation, it would be the Grand Mage executed for treason when all was said and done.

"I am sorry, your grace," Grand Mage Kiama apologized. "I was loath to make such an allegation against the queen without absolute certainty of her guilt."

Khari narrowed her eyes. "And you are now absolutely certain that my eldest spouse, my beloved wife, Queen Awa, has committed an act of treason by providing brimstone to an insurgent with the intention of using it to wage war against the Crown?"

Kiama did not hesitate. "I am certain, your grace."

Macella was suddenly very afraid for Queen Awa. King Khari had been tiring of her wife for a very long time. Their mutual hatred was a poorly kept secret. This could be the king's chance to finally rid herself of her unwanted spouse.

"Clear the council chamber," King Khari commanded. "I would like to speak to Queen Awa alone."

For a moment, no one moved. In an instant, everything had changed, and it seemed that the council members were still trying to catch up. Macella realized she was still clenching her fists, her nails digging deeply into the flesh of her palms. She forced her grip to loosen.

"Out!" King Khari roared. "All of you! Out! *Now!*"

Macella jumped to her feet, along with everyone else in the room aside from Awa and Khari. The elder queen caught Macella staring. She shook her head at the concern on Macella's face. Almost imperceptibly, Awa tilted her head toward the door. Macella did not have to be able to read human minds to know the queen was telling her to leave and stay out of this.

As the council members neared the door, Khari called out again. "Do not go far. I will summon you when I have come to a decision."

No one seemed to know what to do once the chamber's doors closed behind them. They spent a few minutes milling aimlessly about the corridor before people began to drift away. Queen Annika announced that she, Lord Anwir, and Grand Mage Kiama would wait in her parlor and have some refreshments. Monarch Meztli asked Lord Theomund to join them in their sitting room to await the king's summons, and the Grand Treasurer gratefully accepted.

Macella politely declined Meztli's invitation to join them, preferring to stay near Aithan. For his part, Aithan was busy with Captain Drudo, undoubtedly preparing for whatever might come of the king and queen's private conference. Macella paced, her mind spinning. Defeating King Khari would already be extraordinarily difficult. What would happen without Queen Awa among their allies?

To Macella's great surprise, they were not left long in suspense. The king summoned them back only half an hour later. As she retook her place, Macella tried to catch Queen Awa's attention, but the queen was staring at her hands and did not look up. Macella's heart sank.

King Khari leaned back in her seat, steepling her fingers beneath her chin. The room waited, everyone watching the king. Everyone except Queen Awa, who kept her gaze on her hands clasped delicately in her lap.

King Khari let the expectant hush stretch a long while before she spoke. Finally, she took a breath, clearly preparing for a speech. Macella leaned forward, her heart in her throat.

(19) "This has been a difficult day, indeed," King Khari began soberly. "I am very grateful for the honesty and dedication of my dear Annika. But it pains me that my beloved Awa has felt driven to such measures. I blame myself for not being a better spouse. We loved one another so much once, and I have let that love wither. Now my wife sees me as her enemy. She has committed a crime, and I must punish her, but I could never harm or disgrace my queen, no matter the offense. Hurting her would hurt me much worse. I cannot."

Macella knew the king's words were hollow and false. Yet, there was a glimmer of truth hidden amongst the lies. King Khari was an exceedingly proud woman. If she publicly proclaimed Queen Awa a traitor and executed her, it would reflect poorly on her reign. She would look weak, unable to even govern her own household.

And, of course, there was the unrest in the north. The king could not afford to appear vulnerable when seeds of rebellion were already taking root. Furthermore, Queen Awa hailed from the very seat of the insurrection. Executing her would practically be a declaration of war.

Macella had no knowledge of Queen Awa's involvement with Kiho's plot. Perhaps she *had* helped them steal brimstone. Or perhaps King Khari and the elder queen had come to some other agreement. What could the king have possibly said to Awa to convince her to take the blame?

King Khari cleared her throat. "And yet, I can no longer trust my queen. I cannot rule alongside one who would seek to depose me. Nor can I remain married to such a person."

Macella could not help but glance at Queen Annika. The young queen was practically beaming, though she was attempting to maintain a solemn expression. Macella swallowed against a wave of disgust.

"Queen Awa and I have discussed our options and have agreed upon a course of action that will be best for us both and that will spare our honor." King Khari smiled, her eyes still cold. "Queen Awa is understandably weary of life at court. A century is quite a long time, after all. She will renounce the throne and return to Highview to age gracefully and live out her days among her people."

Queen Awa still did not raise her gaze. Macella wondered if the elder queen was relieved that she would finally escape this place, would finally be free of Khari. Perhaps she would find love or companionship, and even peace, once she made a new life for herself in her homeland.

King Khari continued, smiling wider still. "We will escort the queen home on our centennial visit to the north. There, I will announce my intention to take a new spouse from the region, ensuring the people of the north see that their king values them. They will be able to feel confident that they have a representative on the Crown who understands their plight and will advocate for them."

Queen Annika's serious expression was no longer forced. Her cheeks pinkened and her lips turned down in a pout. She'd gone from suppressed mirth to simmering rage in a matter of seconds. Clearly, she hadn't thought the king would think of taking a new spouse so soon. Macella felt a twinge of spiteful pleasure. At least the young queen's victory was bittersweet.

"I have decided that I will not announce my choice publicly until the centennial celebration," King Khari proclaimed, a sly smile spreading across her face. "However, I wish for my small council to share in my joy."

Aithan's head snapped up, his eyes flashing crimson. His expression was strange—confused, unsure, afraid. He met Macella's gaze and the despair she saw there stopped her heart. Her star charm went icy cold.

"It is my intention to court Lady Macella of Shively," King Khari announced.

Part 2
Predator or Protector, One Must Choose

The balance of life and death requires that thirteen Aegises protect the realm. One, the strongest, is stationed at court to protect the Crown. Two, the newest, travel the kingdom recruiting children to become their eventual replacements. Three, the wisest, remain in Duànzào as teachers and trainers. Seven, the bravest, patrol the kingdom, sealing rifts and destroying demons. These thirteen are a siblinghood of heroes, united to protect us, united under the Crown.

To make optimal use of their superior strength, senses, and speed, Aegises undergo years of rigorous combat training. Every Aegis trains with the sword, but many come to prefer other artillery, such as axes, spears, and maces. Of course, in the hands of these elite warriors anything can become a deadly weapon.

While all of Kōsaten's Aegises are skilled combatants, several are renowned for their fighting prowess. There are none so graceful as Finley of Fairdale with their spear, nor so formidable as Valen of Valley Station with his axes. And, of course, there are none as versatile—as talented, valiant, and lethal—as Aithan of Auburndale, Protector of the Crown.

Kōsaten's Aegises are bound by honor, blood, and magic to protect and maintain balance in our realm. From childhood, these great warriors forgo family and friendship to train for their noble calling. Forged in hellfire, claimed by the dark gods, and bound to the Crown, Aegises have but this one purpose. Their Fates are intertwined with that of Kōsaten and its supreme sovereign. It is an unbreakable bond.

-From *Stories of Shields and Shadows* by S.S. (The Shield's Scribe)

Chapter Eleven

King Khari's announcement was met with stunned silence from all except the Grand Vizier. Ever ready to say what the moment required, Lord Anwir heartily congratulated the king on a fine choice, before complimenting Macella on the great honor of procuring the king's affections. Later, Macella would wonder whether Lord Anwir had known of the king's intentions in advance, or if he simply acted his part so well.

Macella could not move, could hardly think. The sense of spiteful pleasure she'd had at Annika's backfiring scheme was long gone. She couldn't even enjoy the young queen's now livid expression. She felt sick.

Queen Annika's face was flushed and pinched, her eyes brimming with tears. Macella might've felt a bit sorry for the spoiled little fool, if she had any room for concerns beyond her own. It was obvious the young queen had never been so thoroughly thwarted.

Macella looked helplessly around the room. Captain Drudo watched her sympathetically, his handsome face tight with concern. Queen Awa's head remained lowered. Monarch Meztli stared at a spot on the far wall, their black eyes sad. Conversely, Queen Annika's eyes were locked on Macella. If looks could kill, Macella would be brutally murdered.

King Khari looked for all the world like the cat who'd caught the canary. She gazed around the room, seeming to find great delight in each of the varied reactions to her announcement. When she looked at Macella, she smiled magnanimously. Behind her, Aithan's face was a vacant mask, his mind as closed as his expression.

"There is much to be done," King Khari proclaimed, clapping her hands.

Macella jumped at the sound, earning another grin from the king. She felt very, very close to falling apart. There seemed to be a vise tightening around her lungs. Her eyes darted around the room frantically, searching for she knew not what. She just wanted to escape this room, this castle, this nightmare. She wanted to crawl out of her own skin. She couldn't breathe.

Monarch Meztli's dark gaze caught Macella's attention. They lifted their eyebrows, tilting their head slightly. It was a question—they were asking for permission. Blinking back tears, Macella gave a stiff nod. At that moment, any offer of help felt miraculous.

Meztli's eyes went white. Immediately, Macella felt calmer, the tightness in her chest loosening. She drew in a ragged breath, grateful that her lungs were working again. Her heart slowed and she was able to subdue the tears that had been threatening to fall.

"Captain Drudo, please escort Queen Awa to her rooms, where she is to remain under constant guard until I say otherwise," King Khari commanded. "She is to have no visitors aside from her handservant to tend to her comfort. The two are not to be left alone at any time. She is not to be spoken to unless absolutely necessary. Am I clear?"

"Yes, my king," Captain Drudo struck his fist against his chest in salute before helping Queen Awa from her seat and leading her from the chamber. The elder queen never lifted her head.

"The rest of you are dismissed," King Khari said, waving them away. "Lady Macella, Lord Protector, a word."

The other council members filed from the room. Lord Anwir supported Queen Annika on one arm, the young queen trembling with rage. Grand Mage

Kiama was the last to depart, giving Macella a long, assessing glance before the huge doors closed behind her.

"Join me, both of you," King Khari said, pouring herself a goblet of wine from her personal pitcher. She poured two more goblets and set them at the places to either side of her.

Aithan sat stiffly, his eyes on the far wall. Macella moved dazedly to sit opposite him.

King Khari looked between them, smiling. "To our union," she declared, lifting her goblet.

Aithan didn't bother touching his cup. Macella, however, downed half her goblet in a single drink. Khari chuckled and took a long sip from her own cup.

"Alright, I can see you're upset, and I understand," the king acquiesced, lifting her hands in a placating gesture. "Do me the courtesy of hearing my explanation before you condemn me, at least."

Aithan finally looked at Macella. His mask slipped for just a moment, and she could see the anguish beneath his hard exterior. Then he raised his goblet to his lips and drained it. When he sat the cup down again, the fleeting emotion was gone, the blank mask returned.

"First of all, I assure you I have no intention of parting the two of you," King Khari began. "On the contrary, I expect you to continue exactly as you are. Our marriage is simply to be a mutually beneficial business arrangement."

The king leaned forward, covering one of Macella's hands with her own. Macella tried not to recoil.

The king looked at her earnestly. "You represent the people. Whether as the scribe or the rose of the revelry, you make a lasting impression. You will help me win back the north and solidify my rule for another century," Khari proclaimed. "And all that time, you will get to spend with Aithan of Auburndale. As my spouse, you'll be granted long life, like your beloved. I can give you the gift of multiple lifetimes with your soulmate."

Macella looked into Aithan's tense, beautiful face. She wanted nothing more than to live as many lifetimes as possible with him. She, of course, could do that without the Crown's help, but being Khari's spouse would give her the cover needed to hide her Aegisborn gift of unnaturally long life.

King Khari pressed her hand. "I mean it when I say I do not wish to part you from one another. As long as you fulfill your royal duties, our relationship can be as intimate or as distant as you desire."

The king paused, tracing her fingers lightly across Macella's wrist and over the back of her hand. Macella's skin crawled. Aithan clenched his jaw.

"While I know we would both enjoy it immensely, I will not require you to engage in a romantic or sexual relationship with me," King Khari promised. "I do not require that of any of my spouses, and I do not deny them their paramours if they wish to take them."

The king sat back, releasing Macella's hand. She looked between Macella and Aithan again for a long moment.

Her expression grew dark. "You have until our northern journey to decide," King Khari said coldly. "I need to know whether or not to begin searching for another suitable match in the region."

Macella swallowed hard, forcing herself to speak. "And if I were to decline your kind offer?"

The king's smile was cold. "I am not a monster, Macella. You have every right to say no. Of course, I would be so heartbroken that I could not endure you remaining at court. We would escort you back to Shively to live among your kin."

Macella saw a muscle twitch in Aithan's jaw. Her palm had begun to bleed where her fingernails dug into it, her fist clenched in her lap. The calm Monarch Meztli had granted her was gone, replaced by a bottomless dread.

"We would acquire you a fine home of your own and set you a monthly allowance to supplement your earnings as the scribe and help ensure that your work continues to please us," King Khari continued. "And the Protector of the Crown would return to court to fulfill his duties. For the remainder of his life, as his most honorable position requires."

Both Macella and Aithan gaped at the king in horror. King Khari smiled back at them as if they'd come to the conclusion of a pleasant conversation. She pushed back her chair and stood, adjusting her crown with unnecessary pomp.

"Now, Lord Protector, I believe we have much to discuss regarding how we will handle this situation with my soon-to-be ex-queen," King Khari declared. "Let us retire to my study."

With that, she swept from the room, leaving Aithan no choice but to follow in her wake. He gave Macella a last, tortured look before striding after the king.

Macella sat alone in the empty chamber for a long time, not trusting her legs to carry her back to their apartments, nor her brain to guide her safely there. The servants came in and tidied up, no one disturbing her as she stared vacantly at the polished wood table. She might've sat there all day, were it not for Lucy eventually appearing to tell her that she'd laid out lunch.

Lucy took one look at Macella's face and, without a word, took her arm and led her from the room. Back in their apartments, she settled Macella on the sitting room couch and made her a cup of tea. Mechanically, Macella drank the tea and nibbled at the cheese and cold meat Lucy had brought for her midday meal.

She wasn't sure when she'd begun to cry. One moment she was sipping her tea and the next she was choking on loud, hiccupping sobs. By then, it was too late to stop the flood. She wept helplessly, feeling the day's misery settling deep into her bones.

"Oh, Lady Macella," Lucy fretted anxiously. "Oh, there now, none of that."

The young woman handed Macella a handkerchief, then patted her face with a cool towel that smelled of lavender. The kindness made Macella cry harder.

"I'll take care of her, Lucy. You clear up," a brisk voice instructed.

Lucy bowed gratefully and gathered up the remnants of Macella's barely touched lunch. The high tailor, Lynn, draped a blanket around Macella's shoulders and sat beside her on the couch. To Macella's surprise, the typically stern woman opened her arms, gathering Macella into a warm embrace. After a few minutes, Lynn guided Macella to lie down and rest her head in her lap. The high tailor stroked her hair while she cried herself out.

"I've been instructed to expand your wardrobe significantly with a number of exceptionally fine pieces," Lynn told her finally. "I am supposed to be fitting you for those items right now, but I know your measurements well enough. I just thought you might need the company, seeing as the king has the Aegis holed up in her study."

"Thank you," Macella whispered hoarsely.

"You are going to have yourself a nice long nap," Lynn proclaimed, placing a pillow beneath Macella's head, and standing up. "I am going to get a cold compress for your eyes, so that the swelling is down some by the time the king summons you to dinner."

Macella didn't resist, letting the older woman tuck the blanket around her. She was tired and afraid, and sleep sounded like a welcome escape. Lynn soon acquired a cold towel, which she settled over Macella's closed eyes. She sat beside Macella awhile, a silent but comforting presence, as Macella let exhaustion overtake her.

"The gods have marked you for something," the high tailor said quietly, as Macella drifted into a restless doze. "Anyone with sense can see how brightly you burn. Though it might be dark today, nothing can hide that fire. Everything is going to work out just as it should."

(20) Soon, Lynn left her to her nap. However, as tired as she was, Macella couldn't seem to find true sleep. She drifted somewhere between waking and dreaming, her anxiety thrumming through her subconscious. Disconnected images swirled through her mind, hazy and indistinct.

Slowly, the images began to take form. Macella was in her chambers at court but also somewhere dry and hot and thick with smoke. The smoke filled the sitting room, distorting the familiar shapes of the furniture into something more sinister. Macella moved through the smoke, her anxiety just as thick as the haze around her.

"Macella of Shively, born of Matthias and Lenora, magic and suffering. Macella, orphan abomination, blood of Hades."

The ancient, terrible boom of Hades's voice overwhelmed her, seemingly coming from every direction at once. Macella's heart raced, her skin growing hot. When she looked down at herself, she saw that she was engulfed in flames. Her skin bubbled and blackened, melting into the burning fabric of her dress. She opened her mouth to scream.

Wwwwhhhhoooooooooo bbbbeeeeccckkkkonnnsss uuuusssssss?

Instead of her own voice, a guttural hissing growl burst from Macella's mouth. She remembered that voice, though she'd only ever heard it in her mind. It was the voice of a brucha, a wolfish beast with footlong poisonous quills. Macella sensed the hellspawn behind her. She snapped her mouth shut, spinning around. She saw nothing but indistinct shapes moving in the smoke, drawing nearer.

Macella reached for her daggers, but they turned to serpents in her hands. Startled, she tossed them away, only to find her hands covered in thick, dark liquid. It dripped from her fingertips, warm as blood.

When Macella looked up again, a small figure sat on the floor, obscured by the fog. It was a child with shaggy hair and a malnourished frame. When he lifted his head to look at her, his eye sockets were empty pits. She recognized him then—it was Tuwile, the first dead person who had ever come to her. As Macella watched, a giant crow landed on the child's head and, to her abject horror, began to peck at the empty holes where his eyes should've been. The same dark liquid that covered Macella's hands started to stream from his eye sockets. The serpents slithered toward the boy, hissing menacingly.

Tuwile's hollow eyes stared blindly in Macella's direction. When he spoke, it was in a harsh rasp unlike the childish voice she remembered. Dark liquid oozed from his mouth as he asked her the same question he'd asked her long ago in Smoketown.

"Are you going to help us all?"

Macella started toward him, meaning to protect him from the vicious reptiles and vile bird. When she stepped forward, however, the serpents turned on her, striking at her reaching hands. Though their bites missed, they spat more of the dark liquid at her. It sizzled against her skin.

Macella wiped her hands on her dress, backing hastily away from the hissing serpents. Though the liquid left streaks and stains on the fabric, her hands still remained covered in it. She left a trail of black splatters in her wake as she retreated.

Then her back hit something solid. Macella turned to face the obstacle.

A pale face loomed inches from her own.

Macella screamed. The woman shrieked. Smoke swirled around them, chunks of ash and embers of flame whirling inside.

Macella tried to back away, but her feet seemed rooted to the spot. Behind her, hisses and growls echoed from the fog. Before her, the ghostly face loomed, but now it looked more familiar. Flaming red hair floated around it, contrasting sharply with its pale skin and white eyes.

"*Darkness, gathers. Trouble brews,*" the face whispered, the sound somehow loud in Macella's ears, as all-encompassing as the swirling smoke. "*Predator or Protector, one must choose.*"

"Aisling?" Macella croaked, her throat thick with ash.

"*Baptized in blood, forged in flame. Stars align, prophets proclaim,*" the face replied.

Macella knew those words. They were a prophecy from Aisling, an oracle she and Aithan had met during their travels. Aisling had foretold their Fate—their love, the looming threat of warfare between realms, and Macella and Aithan at the center. Children of both worlds, crossbreeds, destined to love one another and to defend their realm.

"*A shield. A scribe. A sword. A pen,*" the Aisling-thing hissed. "*Against hell's fury. Against our end.*"

Macella looked down at her hands. In one, she found parchment. The other held a pen. And now she knew the nature of the dark liquid dripping from her palms. It was ink.

Macella looked up and was startled to see a different face staring back at her. She gasped before realizing she now stood before a looking glass. Her eyes in the reflection were in their hellform, completely black from rim to rim. Her skin was coated in onyx flames, but now she was completely unburnt.

And atop her gleaming black and silver curls sat a crown.

Macella jerked awake, bolting upright, and reaching instinctively for her daggers. The room was empty, the lessening light indicating several hours had passed while she slept. The air was hot and smelled of smoke.

Then Macella noticed the blanket was on fire. Her onyx flames blazed over her skin, singeing the fabric. Macella willed them away as she sheathed her daggers and doused the blanket with a nearby pitcher of water. She took several deep breaths, calming her racing heart.

Once she felt more composed, she made her way to the bathing chamber. It was nearing the dinner hour, and she needed to refresh and dress herself. She would have to behave as normally as possible over the meal among the Crown's entourage.

In the tiled chamber, Macella splashed water on her flushed face. She patted her skin with a soft towel, staring at her reflection in the looking glass. The image of herself adorned with a silver and onyx crown flashed through her mind.

"A shield. A scribe. A sword. A pen," she whispered to herself. "Against hell's fury. Against our end."

Macella let her eyes slip into their hellform, glowing onyx, the whites completely disappeared. She could feel her flames simmering just beneath her skin. She felt calm. And strong. This is who she truly was—marked by Hades, chosen by Fate.

"Stars align, prophets proclaim," Macella told her reflection, her voice steady and sure.

Chapter Twelve

When Lucy returned to help her dress, Macella was composed. She chose a simple but flattering evening gown of shimmering gold fabric that clung to her curves. She let her curls do as they wished, which meant flying full, free, and wild, and falling over her eyes. As an afterthought, she added a jeweled hair clip on one side to hold her curls behind her ear. The gold and garnet trinket was a gift from the king. Macella figured Khari would approve of the accessory and, now more than ever, she knew she needed to stay in the king's good graces.

(21) When she entered the Crown's intimate dining hall, a fair few heads turned her way. To Macella's surprise, Queen Annika was in attendance, but Monarch Meztli and Queen Awa were notably absent. Lord Anwir sat near the young queen at the opposite end of the table from King Khari. Aithan stood behind the king's chair, a somber, silent shadow.

"Lady Macella!" King Khari exclaimed as she, too, strode into the hall. "You look lovely. I must have you seated at my side."

The gathered nobles had risen as the king entered and now shifted awkwardly to clear a spot for Macella. She bowed and took the seat, ignoring the put-out expression of the man who'd given up his place. Though she could feel the daggers Queen Annika was glaring at her, she kept her attention on the king.

"If I knew how well you'd wear that hairclip, I might've gifted you more," King Khari murmured as they sat down. "I shall shower you with such baubles during our courtship."

Macella swallowed hard against bile but forced her face into a pleasant expression. "As always, your grace, you are too generous."

Behind the king, Aithan was completely unmoving, but Macella knew he was listening intently and had heard their exchange, despite their lowered voices. Her heart ached. Of course, Aithan knew that Macella despised the king. Still, he had to stand by and watch the sovereign play her dangerous games with the one thing he'd dared to love and call his own. The unfairness of it all made Macella want to burst into flames.

Instead, she turned away from King Khari and apologized to her neighbor—the nobleman who'd lost his coveted position beside the king. Unfortunately, turning meant it was harder to ignore Queen Annika's glares. Despite Lord Anwir's officious attentions, the young queen seemed determined to spend the evening stewing in her anger. With Aithan's simmering rage on one side and Annika's open hostility on the other, the air of the room felt charged with lightning.

Apparently, however, only Macella could feel the tension. King Khari was merry and loquacious. She talked loudly and laughed louder still, drinking deeply from her goblet at every pause. The other guests mimicked the king's mood. Macella wondered how many of them had heard about the morning's events. She was sure at least some had—after all, secrets were currency in Kōsaten Keep.

Over dinner, she was able to feign interest in the conversation, making the proper sounds at the appropriate moments. Often, she found King Khari watching her with assessing eyes. Macella returned the king's gaze unflinchingly.

She could not, however, catch the eye of Aithan of Auburndale. He stood stiffly at his post, purposely avoiding Macella's gaze, his mind guarded and impenetrable. She decided to give him his space to process as he saw fit. They would talk soon enough.

The meal went smoothly until the final course. Macella was nodding encouragingly at the noble beside her, who was boring her immensely with a description of planned renovations to his large estate, when she felt a searing, ripping sensation she hadn't felt in quite some time.

A rift!

She fixed her eyes on her lap, knowing they'd changed. Luckily, several of the dinner guests had cried out in alarm, gesturing at Aithan. In his prominent place behind the king, the reaction of his eyes was more noticeable.

"Do not be alarmed everyone," King Khari reassured her guests. "The Lord Protector has sensed a disturbance, but you are in no immediate danger. There has never been a rift within the castle walls. This is the safest place you can be."

Macella begged to differ, but she, of course, kept that opinion to herself. She willed her eyes back to their normal state. When she looked up, Aithan's eyes were back to their customary orange hue.

"Lord Protector, how close is the rift you've detected?" the king asked.

"Within the city limits of Pleasure Ridge Park, but far from the keep," Aithan replied. "In the Bardo."

To Macella's surprise, the king smiled gleefully. The Bardo was the most densely populated area in all of Pleasure Ridge Park—poverty-stricken and crime ridden, full of desperate souls doing whatever it took to survive. If any demons escaped into those overcrowded streets, they would have plenty of humans to prey upon.

"You will have to excuse us," King Khari apologized, rising. "The Lord Protector and I must attend to this matter immediately. Please stay and finish your dessert."

The king hastened from the room, calling for servants to ready a carriage and to gather her cloak and riding boots. Aithan sent for several members of the Royal Guard, instructing them to prepare for the king's departure. No longer hungry, Macella started to excuse herself from the table, when King Khari swept back into the room.

"Lady Macella, hurry to your chambers and dress for our outing," the king commanded. "Bailey, help Macella into something dark and comfortable and ensure she has a lightweight cloak."

Aithan's head snapped toward the king, his expression darkening. He quickly recovered himself, however, his face returning to the blank mask he'd worn since the small council meeting. Queen Annika's mouth popped open, but she somehow managed to hold her tongue.

Macella bowed and left quickly to dress. She hadn't gone far when she heard quick, light footsteps behind her. Sighing, she braced herself and turned to face the young queen.

"Run ahead, Bailey, and lay out Macella's clothes," Annika spat at the servant lingering nearby.

Bailey did as they were told, leaving the two women alone in the corridor. Macella willed her face into a blank mask as the queen stepped closer.

She looked angrily up at Macella, her ice blue eyes narrowed. "You must be very pleased with yourself," Queen Annika hissed, her voice dripping with venom. "You have certainly slithered your way up the ranks."

Macella almost laughed. After months and months of polite insults and sweetly spoken slights, they were finally going to cease pretending. After the day she'd had, she was in no mood to back down.

"You are mistaken, your grace," Macella shot back. "It is you who must be pleased. This is your doing, as much as King Khari's. Was it worth it? Is supplanting Queen Awa as satisfying as you'd hoped?"

Annika blanched, then reddened, clearly surprised Macella would dare speak so plainly. For her part, Macella worried she might've been too rash, but she refused to let it show. Curling her lips in a sneer, she returned the young queen's glare fiercely.

"I am the queen," Annika snapped, stepping nearly toe-to-toe with Macella. "You are a disgusting little upstart, a mongrel-fucking whore from a stinking, disease-ridden hovel. And I will still be on the throne when you are back in the sewer where you belong."

This time, Macella did laugh. It felt good to laugh right in the queen's smug little face.

Macella leaned toward her, one eyebrow raised. "Was it *you* King Khari wanted at her side tonight?" she asked quietly. "Did she ask *you* to come along for her adventure this evening? Is it *you* she cannot seem to keep away from? Or is it the disgusting, mongrel-fucking little upstart from the sewer?"

Queen Annika flushed, her mouth opening and closing soundlessly. Macella knew she would probably regret this later, but right now it felt good to show her true feelings for a change.

She smiled at the queen's floundering and leaned so close their noses nearly touched. "I would take care, if I were in your position," Macella purred, lacing her voice with menace. "Thus far, I have not tried to attract the king. But if I feel like Aithan or I are in danger, I will do what I must to secure our safety—even if that means giving King Khari the attention she so desperately wants from me."

Macella leaned further forward, placing her face beside the young queen's. She brought her lips to Annika's ear. The queen trembled with rage, the anger practically rolling off her skin. Macella felt a surge of vicious triumph.

"And then we will see which of us sits the throne and which is discarded in the gutter," she whispered.

With that, she spun on her heel and stalked toward her rooms, her back ramrod straight and her head held high. She could feel Annika watching her march away. Macella did not look back.

Soon, she found herself inside one of the Crown's smaller, lighter carriages. It was more opulent than anything on wheels had any right to be, but Macella had grown used to the frivolous luxuries of court life. Four knights of the Royal Guard flanked the carriage on horseback, while Aithan sat astride Jade, calling out orders in his gravelly rumble. He led their procession from the keep, through the bailey, and out of one of the smaller gates of the castle's outer wall.

Macella was grateful to find King Khari too interested in adventure to talk much. The king leaned from the window, shouting questions to Aithan, and watching the darkening city pass by. Macella stared out at the capital city, still unused to its people and geography. After a while, the state of the surrounding buildings began to decline. Vibrant thoroughfares were replaced by crumbling facades and dilapidated storefronts. The people they passed were often dressed in rags, filthy, thin, and malnourished.

"Take shelter!" Aithan bellowed as they passed through the Bardo. If you value your safety or your sanity, you will not linger in these streets after dark tonight!"

Most folks fled at the very sight of the Protector of the Crown. Those that remained quickly followed suit when they heard his words. They knew that having the Crown's Aegis in their neglected neighborhood at night could only portend danger.

The Royal Guard members made sure any stragglers moved along as the procession reached the heart of the Bardo. Aithan stopped, his eyes going fully crimson. He sniffed the air as the group waited in silent suspense. Macella could feel the rift burning somewhere near, could feel the presence of something otherworldly in their midst.

"The rift is close by, and has most likely already been crossed," Aithan predicted. "We used to sense rifts weeks in advance—we'd feel the tiny tears long before they grew into a full breach. Now it seems they sometimes grow so quickly we have very little warning."

"Another indication that something is awry," King Khari replied thoughtfully. "Now that dear Annika has revealed the secret of the theft of brimstone from our stores, I can tell you that I believe the perpetrator might have used it to upset the delicate balance of the realms."

Macella bristled, wondering if the king would have ever told Aithan about Kiho's thievery were it not for Annika's announcement. Surely the Protector of the Crown should be privy to such obvious threats to the Crown's safety. What else was the king keeping from him?

(22) *Kill her. Slay the king. She will never expect it. A dagger to the eye should suffice.*

Macella jumped, the hairs at the nape of her neck standing on end. Her star charm grew icy. There had been an unfamiliar whisper in her mind. It sounded much like her own voice, aside from the eerie undertone.

The king frowned, her eyes narrowing. Aithan unsheathed his sword, his eyes going crimson again. Macella could feel something foreign in the air. The sun had nearly reached the horizon. In this area of the city, the buildings crowded against each other, cold and ominous. The glow of the sunset hardly penetrated the shadows.

"Stay in the carriage," Aithan ordered. "Knights of the Royal Guard, lower your eyes and do not believe your own thoughts. Light your torches and surround the king. Do not let your flames go out!"

Slay the king. Blame demons. No one will ever know, and you will be free of her. Slit her throat and live free with your Aegis.

Guard your mind, Macella, Aithan thought at her. His mental voice cut through the fog she hadn't realized was engulfing her thoughts.

Quickly, she walled off her mind, shutting out every voice but her own.

"What is it, Aegis?" King Khari hissed. "I can sense it prodding at my mind's defenses. What manner of demon plagues us?"

Aithan drew Jade nearer the carriage, his voice pitched low. "Nalusa Falaya. Shadow demons from the forests of hell. Their only purpose is to corrupt humans into evil deeds."

"I heard it in my mind," Macella admitted quietly. "Can it actually force people to do those things?"

"Not unless it p—" Aithan started to explain, but a scream and the clash of metal interrupted him mid-sentence.

Before the king or Macella could ask, Aithan had leapt from Jade's back and sprinted to where Sir Griselda and Sir Igor tussled on the ground. Their horses backed away toward the carriage, rearing up on their hind legs and whinnying frightfully. Macella gasped as she watched Sir Griselda bring her sword down hard toward Sir Igor's face. He rolled away moments before her blade struck the cobblestones.

The knights' torches lay dying against the uneven ground. In their guttering light, Macella thought she saw shadowy figures moving along the edges of their little circle of illumination. Was it simply her imagination or was that a long-fingered hand reaching toward Sir Kamau?

Aithan had reached the scuffling knights and disarmed Sir Griselda, who continued to struggle violently against him. Sir Igor climbed to his feet, trying to yell over Sir Griselda's enraged screams to explain what had happened.

"She slumped forward on her horse, and when I came to check if she was hurt, she attacked me!"

Sir Igor sounded more frightened than angry about his comrade's sudden burst of violence. Macella couldn't hear Aithan's reply, but she saw Sir Igor approach him cautiously. When Sir Igor was near enough, Aithan freed one of Sir Griselda's arms. Sir Igor caught the flailing limb and struggled to hold it steady.

Suddenly, Sir Kamau's torch extinguished, increasing the shadows around them. Only Sir Quirino's torch and the carriage's lanterns remained. The sun had all but gone.

Then Aithan's sword blazed with crimson flames, scattering the worst of the shadows. Macella saw Sir Kamau frantically reigniting his torch. Sir Igor had managed to take hold of Sir Griselda's hand and seemed to be removing something from it. The big woman slumped backward, falling against Aithan.

"Reignite torches and close ranks," Aithan commanded. "Keep your torches alight and stay tight against the carriage."

He set Sir Griselda on her feet. She swayed a bit, confusion clouding her features. Then her training kicked in and she moved swiftly to follow Aithan's orders. Moments later, all four knights had drawn their weapons and surrounded the carriage, their torches held high above their heads. Aithan stalked around their circle of light, his sword still ablaze with crimson flames. Everyone waited in tense silence, watching the shadows.

Sir Igor disappeared, too quickly for him to cry out. His torch flew from his hand, rolling away over the cobblestones. Macella and King Khari leaned from their window to see the knight on his back on the ground, attempting to scoot away from the carriage. Long, shadowy hands clutched at his feet, dragging him forward. Miraculously, Sir Igor had managed to hold onto his sword. He slashed at the hands now holding his legs.

The blade passed through them as if they were made of smoke.

Then Aithan was there, his flaming sword actually severing the grasping hands, which fell to the rocky ground, shattering into wisps of smoke. Brimstone spilled from the blunted shadow arms as an earsplitting shriek shattered the silence. Sir Igor scrambled to his feet, chest heaving.

A monstrous crunching sound filled the carriage, rattling the frame. Macella reached for her daggers, reminding herself to move with human speed. She hesitated, realizing that her blades would likely do nothing unless she ignited them, which she couldn't do in the king's presence. Luckily, King Khari acted quickly. Just as a dark shape began to squeeze through the jagged hole it had ripped in the carriage floor, Khari wrenched the lantern from the wall and slammed it through the opening. The shadow dissolved into brimstone, its death shriek tearing through the night.

The horses pulling the carriage took fright, pulling them several yards before Carter, the driver, could rein them in. Macella leaned out of the window to see a mass of shadowy figures now revealed behind them, having taken refuge from the light by hiding beneath the carriage.

Aithan's burning blade sliced through them with ease. Brimstone and screeches filled the night. Crimson-eyed, Aithan left his knights to guard the king as he sprinted down the road, slaying Nalusa Falaya as he went. Their screeching reverberated through the silent streets. Macella imagined the inhabitants of the Bardo huddling in their homes, glad they'd heeded the Aegis's warning. She watched him go, wishing she were running beside him. He was so fast that soon the glow of his sword had vanished.

Macella leaned back from the window to see King Khari dousing the carriage floor with water. Macella hadn't even noticed that it'd caught fire.

The king smiled at her, heaving a loud exhale. "I believe I could use a moment outside of this blasted contraption," King Khari declared. "Shall we stretch our legs?"

Macella joined the king as she climbed from the carriage to stand near her Royal Guard. It was indeed nice to be out of the confined space for a few minutes. She looked in the direction Aithan had gone, hoping he'd found and sealed the rift those terrible shadow creatures had come through.

King Khari circled the carriage, inspecting the damage. Macella saw her produce a vial from the folds of her cloak, using it to gather the lingering brimstone. Two members of the guard followed her closely, torches aloft. The other two knights stared into the darkness beyond their illuminated circle of safety, watching the perimeter. Suddenly, Macella's star charm went cold again.

She saw it just as the king straightened from a crouch, corking the vial of brimstone. A clawed hand stretched from the shadows, creeping toward the preoccupied monarch. Instinctively, Macella drew her daggers, her onyx flames coming, unbidden, to engulf the blades. She caught herself before throwing them, fighting against her impulses.

For a terrible moment, the king was turning toward her, and she had only an instant to retract her flames. None of the knights had looked in her direction during her momentary lapse, but Khari had sensed her movement. Macella's breath caught in her throat as she willed away the onyx fire, praying her secret was still safe.

Chapter Thirteen

Aithan reappeared suddenly, distracting everyone, passing close enough to her that Macella felt the heat of his hellfire. He sprung at the king, effortlessly vaulting her as he brought his flaming sword down to behead the shadow demon still creeping nearer.

The king gasped, then let out an exhilarated whoop. "Now, was that not a lovely way to blow off some steam?" Khari exclaimed. "The only better release than a good fight is a good fuck."

King Khari clapped Aithan on the shoulder. Aithan nodded curtly, wiping his sword clean before sheathing it. Macella wondered if slaying the Nalusa Falaya had truly given him any release. She was buzzing with energy, her hands itching for her daggers, her muscles coiled and wanting to strike. Holding herself back during the battle had been difficult, and her body seemed reluctant to suppress the adrenaline coursing through her Aegis blood.

"The rift is closed, and the demons slain, your grace," Aithan reported.

"Splendid! Very well done, Lord Protector," King Khari praised. "Well done, indeed. Now, I believe I'm in need of a bit more release. Which is why I was delighted that this little adventure would bring us to the Bardo. It's a lovely excuse to visit my favorite pleasure house."

Aithan and Macella turned surprised faces to the king.

She grinned wickedly back at them, clearly pleased with herself. "I have not been to such a place since you began your service as Protector of the Crown," the king said to Aithan. "I am afraid you will have to become acquainted with my particular preferences. I believe I will be frequenting this establishment regularly for the foreseeable future."

"Of course, my king," Aithan replied, bowing stiffly. "Sir Kamau can escort Lady Macella back to the castle on horseback and we can continue on."

King Khari smirked. "Why do you think I invited Macella along? I believe this experience will allow us all to nurture our budding relationship."

Macella looked from Aithan to the king. While Aithan was stoic and tight-jawed, King Khari was almost jovial. She wasn't sure what the goal was here, but she was no stranger to brothels. She wondered if King Khari knew that Macella had been working in one when she and Aithan met.

"I am honored by your invitation, your grace," Macella said. "May I ask how a visit to a brothel will benefit our relationship?"

King Khari laughed heartily. "It amuses me how you manage to question me without insolence."

The king took Macella's arm and led her back toward the waiting carriage, gesturing for Aithan to follow. The knights fell into step on either side of them, guarding the periphery. The starless night sky stretched above them, heavy and silent.

"As I explained this morning, I do not require intimacy from my spouses," King Khari continued. "Queen Awa and I could not resist each other at one time, but it has been many years since we've touched. Monarch Meztli is a remarkably pleasant companion, but they do not experience physical desire. Annika is quite vigorous, but she is displeased with me at present. Thus, I must find my satisfaction elsewhere."

Macella nodded. "I see. So, the Lord Protector must learn the geography and operations of your preferred haunts in order to ensure your safety. What, then, is my purpose?"

"You are coming along to enjoy yourself," King Khari answered, grinning. "And, perhaps, to make Aithan of Auburndale enjoy himself. I am quickly growing weary of his melancholy expression. Carter, to Wildfell."

The king waved to the driver, then sprang lightly up the carriage steps, leaving Macella to consider her words. She turned toward Aithan, but he had moved away to direct his knights. Macella sighed and began to climb the steps when a warm, rough hand caught hers, helping her into the carriage. Then he was gone, mounting Jade, and leading their little procession up the cobbled lane.

It took but a few minutes to reach their destination. The building was nondescript, but noticeably better kept than the surrounding structures. Aithan sent several knights to sweep the area, then went inside the building.

"Do not judge it by its exterior," King Khari warned. "This is the finest pleasure house in all of Kōsaten."

"I know better than to judge anything by its appearance, your grace," Macella replied. "I have learned that much during my time at court."

King Khari guffawed. "Oh, Macella, you are a delight. How could I not make you my choice when the gods so obviously sent you to my doorstep?"

Macella was spared an answer by Aithan's return, the other knights just behind him. She and the king alighted from the carriage. A pair of stable hands appeared to take charge of the horses.

As their group approached the building, the front door opened, spilling dim light, a sultry aroma, and soft music out into the night. A tall shape stood silhouetted in the doorway.

"Brontë, you are as fetching as ever," King Khari beamed, opening her arms.

Brontë was indeed striking. Tall and svelte, their imposing form was adorned in elaborate silk and lush velvet and topped with an ornate feathered headdress. Their face was heavily made up, each feature embellished with striking colors and bold lines.

"We are so honored to have you join us tonight, your grace," they purred. "It has been far too long since you paid us the compliment. Come in, come in! I have prepared the perfect combination of tasty morsels for you."

King Khari was all smiles. "I apologize, my dear. Running a kingdom does keep one busy. I'd like a room with a semiprivate adjoining chamber for my protector and our companion here."

The king gestured at Aithan and Macella in turn. Brontë turned their attention to the pair, then theatrically clutched at their chest. Their heavy-lidded eyes widened with exaggerated surprise, and they smiled widely, almost wolfishly.

"You brought your own tasty morsels! That one there is a full meal," Brontë exclaimed, giving Aithan a once over, before examining Macella. "My word, where do you find such beauties?"

"There are also benefits to running a kingdom," King Khari replied with a wink.

Brontë snapped their long fingers and called directions to various attendants as they ushered the group into the building's dim interior. Aithan ordered Sir Igor and Sir Kamau to remain outside on guard, one at each entrance, and then followed Macella and King Khari inside. The remaining knights flanked their small party, their eyes scanning the room, hands on the hilts of their swords. Their group had barely passed the threshold before a server had furnished them with chilled wine and cool damp towels with which to refresh themselves. Macella gratefully sipped the cold liquid and patted her face and neck with the sweetly scented cloth.

(23) She was surprised to see they'd stepped into a single large, cavernous space with high ceilings and smooth stone walls. There were archways around the perimeter, some hung with curtains or doors, others open to reveal the lush bedchambers within. Many of the open archways were in use, their occupants in various stages of sexual exploration. Macella's cheeks warmed.

The room was mostly dominated by a rounded center space furnished with massive cushions and hung with veiled chandeliers. Patrons lounged on the cushions, drinking, smoking, and cavorting. A quartet of musicians played on a raised dais, their bard crooning in a lilting, sultry alto. Most striking, though, were the performers suspended above the room. They moved gracefully through impressive body contortions, looking as Macella imagined faeries or angels might.

Toward the back of the space, there stood a structure made of two crossed beams of sturdy wood. A nude man was bound to it, his arms and legs spread to match the structure. Despite the gag in his mouth, Macella could still hear the moans and cries of pleasure he emitted as a burly man flayed and caressed him with a cat o' nine tails.

Their group slowed as a pair of performers wearing only shimmering body paint somersaulted past them. The one painted rich turquoise with sparkling gold accents landed in a handstand and then lowered herself onto her back with her feet in the air. The other, painted violet and silver, flipped to land gracefully atop the soles of the first performer's feet. She lifted one leg, grasping it and pulling it high until it touched her head. Macella gasped. She'd never seen such a display of balance and flexibility.

The woman straightened again, moving her arms like snakes as she did so. The pair parted their legs until their inner thighs touched in a split. They looked like reflections in a pond, one an inverted replica of the other. As their group moved on, Macella watched over her shoulder to see the pair meet face-to-face on the ground, their legs still splayed in a full split. Then the women pressed their lips together in a slow kiss.

Brontë led them around the massive space toward a back corner that featured fewer doorways. Macella watched a woman climb a swath of silk, wrapping it around her otherwise naked body as she made her way nearer and nearer the vaulted ceiling. When she reached the top, she suddenly dropped, the silk unrolling as she fell. Before she reached the ground, she caught herself in a graceful swan dive and ended upside down, her legs wrapped in the silk, one bent and the other extended in an elegant pose. Without thinking, Macella laughed with delight, clapping her hands together.

Aithan and King Khari both turned to her at the same time. For a moment, Aithan's face softened at the sight of her obvious enjoyment.

The king smiled openly, appearing pleased with Macella's reaction. "The finest pleasure house in all of Kōsaten," she repeated, preening.

Brontë led them down a side corridor and into a smaller chamber. It was richly furnished, with soft cushions and plush rugs on the floor and intricate tapestries covering the walls. Above them a woman hung, bound by ropes tied in elaborate knots. She maneuvered in and out of her bonds, contorting her near-naked body into impossible positions. Two doors at the opposite end of the chamber were open to reveal lovely rooms furnished with large, lushly laden beds.

Before them, a line of half-dressed sex workers of all descriptions stood, giving King Khari timid, eager glances. They bowed in unison. The king grinned, moving to examine them. Macella watched her inspect an extremely pretty young man with wide, green eyes and full, pink lips.

"Tasty morsels, indeed," King Khari remarked. "You."

She pointed to the pretty young man. Then she moved down the line, eventually selecting a round, dark-skinned woman with short, tight curls, and a willowy brunette with red-brown skin. Meanwhile, Aithan inspected the rest of the space, before positioning Sir Griselda in the corridor and Sir Quirino beside the door to the king's room.

"You have done your due diligence, Lord Protector," King Khari said as she allowed her escorts to lead her to one of the adjacent bedchambers. "The Royal Guard can handle matters for a while. That room there is for you and Lady Macella."

"With respect, your grace, the Bardo can be a dangerous place—" Aithan began, but Khari cut him off.

"That is an order, Lord Protector," she commanded sternly. "You will take a few hours with your beloved, or I will take her into *my* room. Is that clear?"

Aithan nodded curtly, his mouth a thin, hard line. "Yes, my king."

"When I emerge from these pleasurable exertions, I expect your mood to be significantly improved," King Khari added, eyes narrowed. "Otherwise, I will be extremely displeased, and it will ruin what is shaping up to be an extraordinary night. Do not ruin my night, Aegis."

"Yes, my king," Aithan said again, hitting his closed fist against his chest.

King Khari swept from the room, whispering something that made her companions giggle. Macella watched her go.

When she turned to look for Aithan, he was already stepping out into the corridor. Assuming he was going to check in with the knights at the entrances before following the king's command to leave them to do the guarding, Macella wandered into the chamber designated for their use. Behind her, Brontë, the other courtesans, and the rope performer slipped from the room, leaving it empty and silent, but for the distant sound of the musicians playing, and laughter from the king's chamber.

Their chamber smelled of lavender and honey. Candles flickered in ornate sconces on each wall, bathing the room in a soft glow. There was a painted screen concealing an archway that led to the adjoining chamber, from whence Macella could hear the low murmur of King Khari's voice. Aithan would have quick access to the king should trouble arise.

Macella removed her cloak before crossing to the bed and climbing onto the pile of luxurious fabrics. Aithan returned as she was removing her boots. His expression was still grim as he closed the door behind him.

Sighing, he dropped onto a cushion against the wall. "Sir Griselda is serving as runner, rotating through all three posts and maintaining communication," Aithan said. "I have instructed her to alert me at the slightest concern, so I cannot promise you we won't be interrupted."

Macella rose and crossed to him, dropping to her knees in front of the cushion. She placed a hand on his arm, forcing him to look at her. When he did, his orange eyes were dark with suppressed emotion.

"I don't care," Macella said quietly. "Will you please stop shutting me out? I am going through this difficult thing, just as you are."

Aithan sighed again, his shoulders drooping. "I know. It is not that I wish to shut you out. I am just ashamed of my thoughts at present. You would have no patience for the pity party I've ceaselessly indulged in all day."

"Why don't you let me decide how much patience I have?" Macella countered. "I will tell you when I've had enough. And at present, I've had quite enough of dealing with this shitty situation without you."

Aithan ran a hand through his hair, taking a deep breath. As he exhaled, Macella felt the defenses around his mind lower. Immediately, she was awash in a wave of emotion—anger, helplessness, fear, but mostly guilt.

"I brought you to court," he choked out, his voice tight. "That decision outed you as the scribe, led to my battle with Shamira, resulted in my becoming Protector of the Crown, and now this. Had I left you at Zahra's estate or even established you in a boarding house in Clifton for the cold season—far enough to be safe but near enough that I might visit you—all of this would've been avoided."

Macella barked a laugh. Aithan's head snapped up in surprise. His bewildered expression made her laugh harder still.

"You utter fool," she scolded. "What in my character would lead you to believe I would've allowed you to leave me anywhere?"

Aithan groaned, raking his hand through his hair again, his frustration apparent. "You don't understand!"

Macella jumped at the vehemence of the outburst.

Aithan raised his hands apologetically, his expression repentant. "I am so sorry," he whispered. *You do not understand because there is something I have not told you, that I must. During the small council meeting, right before Khari's announcement, I was focused intently on her because I was preparing for whatever danger might follow her words. And right before she spoke...Macella, I saw her mind.*

It was Macella's turn to be bewildered. She leaned forward, dropping her voice to hardly a whisper. "That's not possible. You've never been able to hear the Crown."

"I know," Aithan replied just as quietly. "But I did today, just for a moment. And what I saw was dangerous. Her plans for you are elaborate, Macella."

Aithan took both of her hands in his, placing his forehead against hers. To Macella's heartache, a tear rolled down his cheek. He let out a ragged breath.

"She will never, ever let you go," he rasped. "Once she has you, you will never escape her again. Not while you live."

Chapter Fourteen

A chill raced down Macella's spine. She had never heard his voice so haunted. Correction: she'd only heard him sound this haunted once before, when he described his childhood in Smoketown. If that was the scale by which to measure King Khari's plans for Macella, then the king's mind was dark indeed.

"She wishes to possess you, to collect you," Aithan went on. "She covets your beauty and cleverness just as she covets my speed and strength. You are a treasure she must have to prove her prowess. Even now, it may be too late for you to escape her."

Aithan buried his head in his hands. Macella was silent for a long moment. She had no doubt the king was capable of the blackest deeds. She had no wish to be bound to such a woman, nor did she relish being longer bound to Kōsaten Keep. It was stressful enough serving her current role at court; being queen would be immeasurably worse.

And yet, this is where Fate had led her. She remembered her restless dream from that afternoon. She could almost feel the warm ink dripping from her hands and the weight of the crown atop her head.

"*A shield. A scribe. A sword. A pen,*" the Aisling-thing had hissed. "*Against hell's fury. Against our end.*"

"Do you remember the night we met?" Macella mused, squeezing Aithan's hands. "That old brothel was a far cry from this one."

"Of course, I remember," he replied. "It was the night my life truly began."

Macella stood and kissed his forehead, before snuggling into his lap. He gathered her into his arms and pressed his face against her curls. Macella felt some of the tension melt from his posture.

"Do you recall the promise you made me that night?" Macella asked, already knowing the answer. "Your memory is so exact. You repeat it—I won't get it right."

Aithan sighed against her hair, but dutifully repeated that long-ago promise. "I vow to protect you as best I can. I will never tell you a falsehood, even if the truth is painful. I will never hinder you or your Fate. You are not bound to me. You are always free."

"You were wrong about me not being bound to you, but you have nevertheless kept those promises. You will not break them now," Macella told him, her voice low but firm. "I cannot do this without you. If you are not with me, it will hinder my Fate, which you promised me you would never do. Is this the day you go back on your word?"

Aithan lifted her chin so he could look into her eyes. "Never."

"We will figure this out," Macella said earnestly, holding his gaze. "I am not afraid. I know who I am truly bound to. And I trust that, together, we will always find our way."

Aithan crushed his mouth against hers. Relief spread through her body, easing some of the anxiety she'd been holding inside all day. Macella knew that she was a survivor and would always do what she must to fulfill her Fate, but she had no desire to continue this journey without Aithan of Auburndale at her side.

Macella pulled back to study Aithan's face. "Our bond can never be broken or weakened, no matter the machinations of human kings. I am yours and you are mine, remember? For all of this life and every other if the gods will it. And if they do not will it, I will still make it so."

Aithan pressed his forehead to hers again, his arms tightening around her. "The list of obstacles in our path seems to grow longer each day. I have faith in us, in you. But I am still afraid. I do not fear any torment humankind can fathom. I am not afraid of death. But I am terrified at the thought of you coming to harm. I've already lost the only other people I have ever loved."

Macella closed her eyes, breathing in his familiar sweet, smoky scent. If she were unable to smell that scent ever again—if it slowly faded from the bedclothes as, each day, she woke up alone—she would be utterly destroyed. A sharp ache throbbed in her chest, a whisper of the fragment of her soul that would leave this realm with Aithan of Auburndale.

"This afternoon, Tuwile and Aisling visited my dreams," Macella said, conjuring the hazy memory so that Aithan could see. "They reminded me that this is what I was destined to do, what *we* were destined to do. It is why we were baptized in blood and forged in flame. It is our purpose, love. We must see this through."

"You are so very brave, Macella," Aithan whispered. "I will seek to be half as brave as you. We will conquer these obstacles, come what may."

"We will, because we must," Macella agreed. "Come what may."

She paused to kiss him again, long and slow. He returned the kiss eagerly, his tongue exploring her mouth. She shivered, her stomach clenching.

Macella broke the kiss and looked intently into her Aegis's amber orange eyes. "We will because we are the only ones who can," she whispered, following her words with another quick, soft kiss. "But not tonight. It has been an exceedingly long and arduous day. I think we've earned a few hours of mindless enjoyment."

Aithan chuckled. "Is that what you call our lovemaking now? Mindless?"

"You are so contrary today," Macella huffed with pretended exasperation. "Mayhap I will go next door."

"Not funny," Aithan growled, biting playfully at her neck.

Macella squealed and squirmed free of his arms. She stood just out of reach and lifted her head imperiously. Then she glared down her nose at him. "Is that how you treat your future queen?" she demanded. "I should have your head."

Aithan shook his head at her playfulness. "You are incorrigible. Forgive me, your grace. I did not realize you had already accepted the king's hand."

"Perhaps I will, perhaps I won't, but I do not think you should risk earning my displeasure," she warned. "You should be begging me for mercy."

(24) Aithan stood to tower over her, close enough that she could feel the heat of his skin. He leaned his head toward her, stopping with his lips a breath from hers. Then he dropped to one knee before her, his face near the juncture of her thighs. He inhaled deeply before lowering his head in deference. Macella shivered.

"I beg you to allow me to make up for my impertinence," Aithan implored, his voice low and husky. He lifted his head, pinning her with his fiery gaze. "Allow me to fuck you like a queen deserves to be fucked."

Macella's pussy clenched. She was suddenly very warm. Now that he had lowered the defenses around his mind, Aithan's thoughts were loud and laced with the many emotions he'd been suppressing all day. Now they'd coalesced into pure, desperate desire. Macella's own need had flared quickly, making her hungry to feel his hands, his mouth, his body on hers. They needed to claim each other, to reconnect physically now that they'd unburdened their hearts. King Khari had been right about the need for a release.

At the thought of the king, Macella noticed a new sound. A chorus of moans and cries now drifted from the adjoining chamber. King Khari's night was apparently still going well. Macella's heart sped up.

"May I, your grace?" Aithan murmured, running his hands up her legs to rest on her thighs. "May I fuck you like a queen should be fucked?"

Macella's breath caught in her throat as warmth pooled in her belly. "How should a queen be fucked?"

"Reverently," Aithan answered, his voice a low purr. "A queen should be fucked like it's worship, as if every touch is an expression of veneration and gratitude."

Macella licked her lips. "Show me."

Aithan hid his smile with another respectful bow. "As you wish, my queen."

Ever so slowly and gently, he slid her leggings down so that she could step out of them. Still on his knees, he genuflected before her, his forehead resting against her toes. Then, he carefully planted a kiss on top of each foot. More slowly still, he trailed his fingers lightly up her legs as he kissed his way up her shins, and over her knees to linger on her thighs.

Macella shivered, her legs growing weak. Aithan continued rubbing kisses over her thighs, working nearer and nearer their apex. His breath was warm against her skin, spreading electricity everywhere it touched. Desire, intense and insatiable, coursed through her body.

Aithan pressed a kiss against her mound through the silk of her panties. Macella shuddered, anticipation sending tendrils of excitement through her core. Her vagina clenched again as Aithan gently pushed her panties to the side enough so that he could run his tongue over her clit.

Macella made a sound between a gasp and a whimper as his tongue traced a path up her center, humming against the sensitive flesh of her clit. She tangled her hands into his hair, feeling unsteady on her feet. Her body was abuzz, a powder keg of sensation.

Aithan gripped her hips, spreading her with his fingers, holding her steady as he worked his tongue against her clit, humming every so often in appreciation. Macella's legs trembled as the tingling in her abdomen became a frenzied buzzing. Were it not for Aithan's strong hands, her unsteady legs would've surely buckled.

When she thought she couldn't remain upright for another moment, Aithan guided her forward as he settled on the thick carpet, leaning back onto the cushion. To the relief of Macella's wobbling legs, he guided her to kneel on the cushion, straddling his face. Then he really went to work.

He held her firmly, still gripping her hips. Macella moaned, throwing her head back in ecstasy. She rocked her hips, riding the rhythmic undulations of his tongue. The buzzing at her core built to its sparkling apex.

Cum for me, my queen, Aithan purred in her mind. *Your humble servant wishes to taste your pleasure on his tongue.*

"Gods," Macella gasped, her hips bucking. "Gods, Aithan! I—"

Coherent thought dissolved, and she could only cry out wordlessly as the orgasm took hold. The buzzing exploded in an all-encompassing shower of blazing stars. Tremors racked her body as Aithan clutched her hips, allowing her no escape as he took her clitoris into his mouth and gently sucked, focusing his skillful tongue on that one spot, the epicenter of her bliss.

Macella arched her back and buried her hands in her own hair, losing herself completely in another, more expansive, wave of rapture. Her throaty cries echoed through the chamber. She did not care about being heard. All she cared about was Aithan's tongue on her clit and that moment of exquisite release.

When she finally slumped forward onto the cushion, slipping ungraciously from Aithan's face, she felt wrung out. The day's trials had been thrust from her mind, replaced by a euphoric satisfaction. Both her mind and body felt lighter, her muscles soft and gelatinous.

She opened her eyes to see Aithan grinning lazily up at her, still seated on the floor. He sat up, licking his lips, and whisked his shirt over his head. He used it to wipe away any lingering wetness on his face, his amber eyes burning with need.

"Is my queen satisfied?" Aithan asked, a wicked smile tugging at his lips.

Macella pushed herself upright, despite her shaky arms. Looking into his beautiful face, hearing the longing in his mind, she felt her desire building again. She suddenly needed him inside of her, needed to be as close to him as physically possible, recommitting and reconnecting. Their bodies would speak the promises of their hearts.

"I am very pleased, but not satisfied," Macella answered, her voice hoarse. She stood and removed her tunic, but before she could do more, Aithan stood and took her hands.

"Queens do not undress themselves," he murmured, bringing her hands to his lips, and pressing a soft kiss on each knuckle. "And loyal servants do not leave their queen unsatisfied."

Aithan spun her slowly. Carefully, he unlaced the ribbons of her bodice. As he did so, he traced kisses down her spine, starting at the nape of her neck. The bodice fell to the floor and Aithan's nimble, calloused fingers moved on to the laces of her panties.

As he dropped them atop her discarded bodice, Aithan kissed the tender spot in the curve of her lower back, circling the hollow there with the tip of his tongue. He stood, trailing his tongue back up her spine. Macella shivered, her heart racing, as he licked the place where her neck and shoulder met. When he bit down and sucked at her skin, she let out a moan, her hips rolling involuntarily. She leaned against him, savoring the feel of the bare skin of his chest against her back. He was all hardness—muscled arms and torso and the stiff bulge of his erection straining against the fabric of his pants.

Macella whirled to face him, wrapping her arms around his neck, and pressing her body tightly against his. Aithan growled, his mouth finding hers hungrily. His hands roamed over her back, the curve of her ass, and her hips. She moaned into his mouth, grinding against him, feeling his hands clench against her flesh in response.

She didn't realize they'd been moving until she felt her back meet the smooth stone wall. Aithan kissed her deeply, his tongue circling hers, as he unbuttoned his pants. He stepped free of them and returned his hands to her ass. Lifting her as if she weighed nothing, he pressed her into the wall, his mouth exploring her neck, her collarbone, the swell of her breasts.

Macella wrapped her legs around his waist, her hands in his hair, as he took her nipple between his teeth and flicked his tongue against it. She moaned again, louder, her breathing ragged with yearning. Frantically, she freed a hand from his hair and snaked it between their bodies until she found his cock. She positioned it against her quivering, waiting warmth.

"Please," she gasped into his ear.

Obediently, ravenously, Aithan plunged inside of her, filling her completely and perfectly, just as she needed him to. Macella moaned his name again and again as he thrust into her over and over. Each stroke hit that spot deep in her gut that made her feel weightless and infinite and raw and wild. She clawed at his back, begging him for more, needing every bit of him, wanting nothing more in this life than to be joined with him forever.

"Macella," Aithan breathed against her neck. "Oh, Macella, my love, my hell goddess."

And then the world dissolved into a glittering mass of colors and sensation.

When they rejoined the king and Royal Guard a few hours later, Khari looked them over with a lecherous smile. Her ochre eyes glittered mischievously.

"That is much better," King Khari pronounced, her gaze lingering on Macella. "My ears did not deceive me then. A good night has been had by all."

It was nearly the hour of Nyx by the time they left Wildfell. The king was quiet on the journey back to the keep. Macella could hardly stay awake, but in such close proximity to Khari, she refused to doze. She was relieved when the king dismissed them immediately, citing her own desire for sleep, and she and Aithan retreated to their quarters.

Macella could not wait to be alone in the dark with Aithan, their bodies entwined, reveling in the quiet and closeness. Maybe they would talk until they fell asleep or, perhaps, they'd simply be still, not needing to fill the silence, just enjoying the gift of being together. To her surprise, though, a servant awaited them at the door to their chambers, two envelopes in his hand.

"Lord Protector, urgent news from Duànzào," the servant said. "Lady Macella, you've a letter from The Forge as well."

The servant bowed and excused himself as Aithan opened his letter and skimmed it quickly. Macella held hers with tense fingers, waiting for him to finish. When he did, he looked at her with a solemn expression. She already knew what he would say, even before the words formed in his mind. She'd known what news that letter must hold since she saw the servant waiting up for them at such a late hour.

"We have a new sibling," Aithan said. "Our number is again thirteen."

Dearest, darling Macella,

You may cease your weeping and gnashing of teeth, as your dull existence shall soon be again brightened by my presence. I have the pleasurable duty of escorting our newest sibling to Pleasure Ridge Park for his presentation to the Crown. Prepare yourself to divulge all of the juiciest court gossip and to lose all of your admirers to my charms.

All My Love,

Finley of Fairdale

Chapter Fifteen

Finley's imminent arrival in Pleasure Ridge Park could not have been better timed. Macella needed something to look forward to in the weeks after King Khari announced their intended courtship. While the king seemed to enjoy the tense atmosphere she'd created, few others did.

Queen Annika sulked and scowled, though she didn't attempt to confront Macella directly again. On the rare occasions when she was permitted to leave her chambers, Queen Awa spoke only when required. While she'd never spoken much, Awa's words had always carried weight. Now her responses were flat and lacking conviction. And though Monarch Meztli had always been as quiet as the elder queen, their silence now carried an air of melancholy. It seemed as though the castle held a collective breath, awaiting the next move in the dangerous game that trapped them all.

It had taken several days for Aithan to show Macella the glimpses he'd caught of Khari's mind. When he had reluctantly done so, she was struck not by what she saw, but by the peculiarity of those thoughts. Macella had never seen a mind like the king's. The images in it were somehow darker, sharper, colder than the other minds she had accessed. It felt harsh and foreign, somehow inhuman—nothing like the Aegis minds Macella knew firsthand or the human minds Aithan had reflected to her from his thoughts. King Khari's mind felt more like that of the brucha, the lamia, and the ancient sleeping demons Macella had sensed during Kiho's attempted mutiny.

"Why is it like that?" Macella had whispered, shivering beside Aithan, despite the warmth of their bodies and the bedclothes.

Aithan had pulled her tighter against him, humming thoughtfully. "I do not know. Hers is unlike any mind I've ever glimpsed. Perhaps the gods' gifts, her bindings to us and the Chosen, and a century of power have corrupted what was already a cruel and cunning soul."

Macella shivered again. She could practically feel the cold clamminess of the king's mind clinging to her skin. She replayed the images Aithan had shown her. Macella seated on a throne beside King Khari. Macella in the king's bed. Macella on the king's arm. Macella round and glowing, carrying the king's crossbreed offspring. Macella at the king's side, looking out over a new Aegis army, the former Aegises dead at their feet.

"Now do you see why I do not want you in her clutches?" Aithan had asked in that haunted voice Macella so disliked. "I cannot protect you from her. It sickens me."

"I know, love," Macella had soothed him. "I had no doubt that your reasoning was sound. But we have little choice in the matter."

They had debated the issue regularly, but they both knew it was a moot point. Macella would accept King Khari's hand. When the alternative to marrying the king was to part from Aithan of Auburndale forever, the choice had been made for her. There was no danger known to gods or men that could frighten Macella from his side.

"Hey," Macella had whispered, cradling his strong jaw in her hand. "I will never be hers. I am my beloved's, and my beloved is mine. Wherever you go, there go I."

Aithan lowered his mouth to hers and kissed her, his smoky sweetness consuming her senses as always. Macella sighed against his lips. She knew that this love was the only true binding that could ever hold her, because she wished to be held. She wanted to spend the rest of her nights wrapped in Aithan of Auburndale's arms.

"I have not been to very many marriage ceremonies in my life," Aithan said huskily, pulling away. "But I have heard those words spoken during the few I've attended. Are you offering me your hand?"

"Well, I've never much considered marriage, let alone taking multiple spouses, as some in Kōsaten do," Macella giggled, before growing more somber. "I would not have our bond made into a farce, as my marriage to the king will be."

Aithan hummed thoughtfully, his lips pressed to Macella's temple. Her inevitable betrothal to King Khari was a constant dark cloud over their heads. Sometimes, she wondered if it was her Fate all along to marry the king. Perhaps it was how she would help save the kingdom from war. As queen, she would have more influence and access to information and, with Aithan as Protector of the Crown, they could be in the perfect position to change Kōsaten for the better. And if that indeed meant destroying King Khari, then they'd be perfectly positioned for that feat as well.

If they wanted to learn the king's weaknesses, Macella was likely their best chance. Aithan hadn't been able to penetrate Khari's mind again since the unexpected moment during that tumultuous small council meeting. He dared not try too hard, fearing the king would sense the attempt as she had when the Nalusa Falaya had attacked. If she ever suspected Aithan even dared to attempt to read her thoughts, she would certainly put him to death. Or worse.

Macella pondered these things for the millionth time as she sat in the small council chamber a fortnight later. The days had been repetitive, with the king and Aithan planning the centennial tour and Awa's retirement from the monarchy, and most everyone else too tense, angry, or melancholy, to make for enjoyable or entertaining company. Macella found herself thanking the gods that she had Finley's visit to look forward to.

She smiled at the thought. Finley and the new Aegis should arrive at court within the next few weeks. Macella knew she could count on Finley for a dramatic and sympathetic reaction to the news of her pending courtship with the king. Their visit would also disrupt the monotony, as King Khari had initiated arrangements for a ball on the occasion, featuring a demonstration of the Aegis's skills.

Macella remembered when Aithan and Shamira had been forced into a similar display during the cold season. It was the event that had changed their entire way of life and had started their intimacy with the Crown. And it ended with Shamira being executed.

Macella looked across the chamber to Queen Awa's empty chair. In a brash, thoughtless spectacle, King Khari had murdered the queen's true love. And now Awa was being dethroned, punished for a crime she may not have committed, and exiled to live amongst virtual strangers. The elder queen had lived nearly a hundred years in Pleasure Ridge Park. The family and friends that she grew up among were long dead. What would the rest of her life be like without her love for Shamira or her hatred of King Khari?

Macella wished she could talk to Awa, even for a few minutes. She was burning with questions—the most pressing of which was what had Khari said to convince Awa to take blame and lose her crown? Several times, Macella had considered using invisibility and the secret passages to reach Queen Awa's chambers, but it seemed an unnecessary risk. The queen was under constant guard, and not allowed to be alone with anyone aside from the king. Even if Macella could reach her undetected, what difference would it make?

Awa and Khari's feud was always going to end with one of them dethroned. It really didn't matter when and under what pretense it occurred. Knowing the elder queen's reasoning would not change the fact that she would soon be gone and Macella would be forced into her place.

Macella felt eyes on her. She raised her gaze to see Captain Drudo staring. He gave her a wink, and she could not help but smile in return. She exhaled, bringing her thoughts back to the present. The members of the small council were discussing tedious governing matters that she needn't note down. Macella almost wished for some more interesting topic to arise—a wish she regretted mere moments later.

"Your grace," Lord Anwir began, clearing his throat. "I have received news from the north that is quite concerning."

(25) The room went silent. Queen Awa's empty seat seemed especially conspicuous all of a sudden. Lord Theomund stifled his coughing in a handkerchief. King Khari went still as a serpent, her eyes narrowing.

Lord Anwir cleared his throat again, looking uncharacteristically flustered. "One of the northern noblemen who visited us wrote to update me on their deliberations," the Grand Vizier continued. "It seems that, without our friends' knowledge, the other northern lords sent envoys to the south, east, and west, in addition to the capital. They were hoping to garner support for regional sovereignty."

A muscle in King Khari's temple twitched. She spoke through clenched teeth. "And did they gain any supporters?"

"The southern and eastern regions definitively declined," Lord Anwir replied hesitantly, pointedly avoiding Queen Annika's panicky gaze. "However, the western lords expressed...mild interest."

The king slowly turned her head toward the young queen. Annika's cheeks reddened. She bit her lip and tossed Lord Anwir an angry look.

King Khari leaned forward, never taking her attention off of Queen Annika. Her voice was low and cold when she spoke again. "And why would the westerners ever consider such a thing? After all, our alliance with the Lord of Edgewood is still quite new. His daughter, Annika, has sat upon the blessed throne but a few years. It is practically still our honeymoon."

Queen Annika went from red to white, her eyes wide and shining with unshed tears. King Khari cocked her head, her lip curling. It was chilling how swiftly she could pivot from debonaire to deadly.

"Our friends are not aware of the westerners' precise reasoning," Lord Anwir hedged. "However, they heard that the Lord of Edgewood was quite vocal about his concerns for his daughter's happiness in marriage."

The temperature in the chamber seemed to plummet. King Khari's icy gaze remained fixed on Queen Annika. The young queen stared back, her cherubic face ghostly pale, her lower lip trembling.

"Now why would the queen's father be concerned about that?" King Khari mused quietly. "My wife is an excellent correspondent, so he surely receives regular updates on her good fortune and well-being. My dear, have you any insight into this matter?"

"I-I don't know," Queen Annika stammered, her voice wobbly. "Perhaps my last few letters have been a bit grave. I've been so upset about Queen Awa, and all that."

The young queen cut her eyes toward Macella. Macella stared back, her expression smooth. She could imagine exactly what kinds of letters Annika had written of late. Surely, she would not be foolish enough to reveal Queen Awa's treason and pending retirement, but Macella would not be surprised if she'd at least hinted at her displeasure with the king. Perhaps she had complained of being neglected for a paramour of inferior birth.

"Well, I am sure when you next write home, you will set your father at ease," King Khari said breezily, despite the implicit threat in her tone. "I believe we will adjourn, and you can go to your chambers to begin your letter now."

King Khari pushed her chair back sharply, the legs scraping the floor with an ugly sound that sliced through the silence. Everyone scrambled to their feet respectfully, except Queen Annika, who sat frozen with dismay. The king stalked from the room, leaving a chill in her wake.

"Lord Protector, Lord Anwir, my study, now!" she bellowed over her shoulder as she passed out of the chamber's huge doors.

Aithan and the Grand Vizier followed King Khari, leaving the rest of the small council in awkward silence. Tears coursed down Queen Annika's cheeks, and she swayed a little as she climbed stiffly to her feet. Captain Drudo took her arm, murmuring quiet apologies for the presumption, and guided her out of the chamber.

Once the young queen had departed, the stupor over the room lifted slightly—enough that the remaining council members let out a collective sigh of relief. Macella nodded goodbye to the Grand Mage and Grand Treasurer as she started from the chamber.

"Lady Macella," Monarch Meztli's low voice slowed her steps.

The middle monarch joined Macella at the door, taking her arm. They had spent more time together in the weeks since Awa's confinement, since they both missed her company, and both wished to avoid Khari and Annika as much as possible. It was hard to say Macella and Meztli were friends, considering Meztli was so quiet and inscrutable, but they enjoyed one another's company and that was a rare gift at court.

"Would you join me after midday meal for a long walk on the grounds?" Monarch Meztli asked. "I imagine that your Aithan will be busy with my lady wife for much of the day. That being so, I thought you might, like me, relish some fresh air and exercise. The energy in the keep is oppressive."

Macella wondered just how keenly the monarch felt the emotions of others. She knew that they could manipulate other people's feelings and that they were incredibly empathic, but how did that impact the monarch's own psyche? It must have been awful absorbing all the tension of late.

"I would love to," Macella replied, giving their arm a gentle squeeze. "That is exactly what I need. I shall be ready in an hour."

Thus, only a little over an hour later, Macella and Monarch Meztli wandered the vast castle grounds. In all of her time at Kōsaten Keep, Macella had not yet explored all the estate had to offer. There were forests and hills, streams and lakes, carefully kept gardens and wild fields. If she kept the castle at her back, she could almost pretend she was far from court, wandering the expanse of the kingdom.

(26) Eventually, Macella and Meztli settled beside a sparkling pond amid a copse of blossoming magnolia trees. They found a spot near the pond's edge and buried their feet in the soft, sandy soil. Enveloped in the scents of the encircling trees, they watched flying insects and small animals flitting about in the warm afternoon sun. Macella closed her eyes and lifted her face to let the dappled shadows dance over her skin. She sighed contentedly.

"Thank you," Monarch Meztli said quietly, as if not wanting to disrupt the peacefulness of the moment. "I have missed Awa's calming presence of late, and you've been so willing to give me more of your time."

Macella smiled, her eyes still closed. "You have done the same for me. I, too, have missed the company of her grace, Queen Awa."

"I do not mean to imply that you are only useful as a surrogate for Awa," Monarch Meztli amended. "You have been a pleasant addition to our party here at court. You are always so full of love. It is refreshing."

Macella glanced over at the middle monarch. Their profile was striking—sharp cheekbones, aquiline nose, chiseled jaw, and bronze skin that practically glowed in the sunlight. Today, they'd gathered their waist-length shiny black hair into two long braids. Macella had to admit that King Khari had a knack for finding beautiful spouses.

"May I ask you a personal question? About your...gift?" she asked hesitatingly, hoping she wasn't crossing a line.

To her relief, Monarch Meztli's lips quirked into a smile. "My dear, it seems we will be espoused soon enough. When you marry the king, you will marry us all. It is only right that we get to know one another. Ask whatever you wish."

Macella had thought about this in the last weeks, wondering about the bindings that kept the Crown united. Mostly, she'd worried about the magic's requirements and how her Aegisborn nature would react to the gifts bestowed by the gods of light. Would it work? Would her secrets be laid bare? Would she survive it?

She pushed those concerns aside, thinking instead about what she wanted to ask Meztli. She gazed back at the pond where a large teal toad had emerged from the water to sit atop a drifting log. It trumpeted its arrival with a throaty croak. Macella smiled.

"That is precisely what I mean," Monarch Meztli remarked, smiling at the toad as well. "Few others here appreciate the natural wonders as we do. But you reacted to that little toad with love and joy."

Macella tilted her head, considering. "There was not much in the way of natural beauty in Shively. Only the hardiest plants and animals could survive the harsh terrain. While some of the rarest and most dangerous magical plants thrive there, aside from that, it is quite barren. I suppose that has helped me to appreciate lands such as these."

The middle monarch nodded. "Yes, that is probably true. But it is also simply your nature to find the good."

Macella fought not to shrug off the compliment. "Perhaps. I guess you are a good judge of character, since your gift requires you to sense and shape others' emotions."

"Indeed," Monarch Meztli agreed.

"Does it affect your own emotions?" Macella asked finally. "Is it taxing?"

The middle monarch was quiet for a long moment. They watched the toad, their head tilted in consideration. Finally, they nodded.

"You know how you are enjoying the sun on your skin? But there are also times when the sun can be too hot and cause you discomfort? Or in its absence, the cold can chafe your skin, and make you wretchedly uncomfortable?" Monarch Meztli spread their hands, watching the shadows drift across their palms. "Emotions affect me in a similar way. I feel the changes in 'emotional temperature' acutely, and the variations in groups of people sometimes feel quite overwhelming. But I can adjust the temperatures of others. If I use my gift, I can stoke the fire when someone's feelings are too cold or wave a fan when they're too hot. Metaphorically speaking, of course."

Macella considered their words. She imagined walking through life, constantly buffeted by erratic weather changes. Even in the most intimate of groups, there would still be plenty of emotional variation. It was no wonder Meztli had such a small entourage, or why they drank their way through small council meetings and recreational gatherings.

"Well," Macella said, placing a tentative hand on their arm. "I am glad to provide pleasant temperatures when I can."

Monarch Meztli placed their hand over Macella's, sighing quietly. The two sat that way for a long while, watching the toad catch flying insects with its long black tongue. A light breeze cooled the afternoon air, wafting the scent of magnolia blooms.

"I do not believe Queen Awa is guilty of treason," Meztli began, breaking the companionable silence. "But the king is very persuasive. If Awa is willing to accept blame, then the alternative was much, much worse."

Macella shifted positions, pulling her hand free and burying it in the sandy soil. She had wanted to know Meztli's thoughts on the situation but had thought it too dangerous a question to ask. Was the middle monarch so very intuitive or had it simply been on both their minds?

"That was also my assessment," Macella answered carefully. "I do hope that it turns out to be in Queen Awa's best interest."

"It's the only choice she had," came a voice from behind them.

Macella jumped, her head whipping around. Monarch Meztli started as well but only stared at Macella. She quickly realized why.

Shamira stood in the grass, looking somehow fainter in the bright sunlight. She moved to Macella's side and sat on the ground beside her. On her other side, Monarch Meztli studied Macella's face with concern.

"Sorry," Macella apologized hastily. "I thought I heard something."

Meztli glanced around before looking back at Macella. Then they turned their attention back to the pond. Macella forced her breathing to slow. She cut an annoyed look at Shamira.

"My apologies," Shamira said, rolling her eyes. "It is not a precise science, teleporting around a castle in a realm you are no longer fully tethered to."

Macella gazed at the water, thinking of what to say. "It seems a long time since we saw her last."

Meztli nodded. "Time is strange when you age as slowly as we do. Even so, the days have seemed unusually long these last few weeks."

"I know," Shamira said, also answering Macella's unspoken question. "I have been away a long time. Awa told me. I am sorry I left you in that undercroft. It could not be helped. I am losing my grasp on this realm. Even with Kali's permission, it is difficult for me to linger. I no longer belong in the lands of the living. My quest isn't enough to hold me here. Were it not for Awa, I don't think I would've returned at all."

A pang of sadness throbbed in Macella's chest. Soon, Awa would lose Shamira for good. And Shamira might be forced to depart before getting the vengeance she so deserved. It was deeply unfair.

Macella felt a hand on hers, which she'd unconsciously clenched in the rocky soil. When she looked into Monarch Meztli's black eyes, she saw that they had grown sorrowful. They pressed her hand lightly.

"Do not grieve too deeply for Awa," Meztli told her. "No matter the circumstances, she will be happier when she is free of this place. There is nothing here for her any longer."

Monarch Meztli paused, cocking their head in Macella's direction. For a moment, Macella thought they were looking past her at Shamira. How sensitive was their gift? Could they sense the dead woman's feelings?

Meztli's voice was low when they spoke again. "She does not know that I know, but there was someone Awa loved. And they loved her very much. I had hoped the two would discover one another's feelings, but alas, it was not to be. Now that person is gone, and Awa's temperature feels different—so different than over the last few years. I hope that when she settles back among her people, she might recover some of the Awa I have grown to love."

Beside her, Shamira let out a strangled sob. Macella ached to put her arms around the woman but knew she could not. Instead, she pulled her knees to her chest and wrapped her arms around them. Chin on her knees, she watched the toad, apparently finished with its lunch, hop back into the pond.

"I hope she does," Shamira whispered. "I hope she finds someone to love her as she deserves to be loved. Someone who will be everything I never could have been, someone who will be all Khari refused to be."

"I hope so too," Macella replied to both of them.

Shamira stood abruptly. "I will return to her now. I know not how much time I have left. I simply came to tell you that Awa is very sorry that you must take her place. The king promised that, if Awa did not step down and return to Highview, she would make her alleged treason public. Then, in a false show of mercy, she would keep Awa confined in luxurious accommodations in the keep, rather than executing or imprisoning her. Awa would still be dethroned and stripped of her gifts from the gods of light, but she'd be forced to live out her final years under lock and key, allowed no visitors but the king. She has received a glimpse of that life in the weeks since Annika's accusation. She hopes you don't begrudge her the chance to live a few decades free of Khari's control."

Even if Macella had been able to respond, she wasn't given the chance. Shamira had vanished, leaving her to ponder these new revelations. Macella was grateful to be with Monarch Meztli, who was always satisfied to sit in silence and simply enjoy the day. They stayed by the little pond a long while, watching the shifting sun glint on its surface, but Macella's mind was still whirring when they finally returned to the keep and parted ways.

Chapter Sixteen

───✦───

Macella had barely related the events of the afternoon to Aithan, who had finally escaped the king, before they were both summoned to the king's study. She felt his annoyance rising as they made their way through the corridor. Aithan had told Macella that King Khari was in perhaps the foulest mood he'd yet seen and had spent the afternoon ranting and scheming in turns.

(27) When Macella and Aithan stepped into the king's study, they were surprised to find that she was not alone. A plump, pale woman in only a corset and panties was bent over the desk, her wrists bound behind her back. Her golden hair fell across the wood in shiny waves, a few strands sticking to her sweaty forehead.

"Come in and close the door," King Khari snapped when they tried to back out of the room.

Jaw tight, Aithan closed the door. Macella tried not to look at the red marks on the white skin of the woman's ample bottom. Unfortunately, she didn't know where to place her gaze. She couldn't look at King Khari, who wore only trousers and a binder, and held a wide leather whip.

"You will not speak or move until I say," the king commanded the woman, giving her ass a sharp strike with the whip. "Tell me that you understand."

"I understand, your grace," the woman panted.

Macella couldn't help but look at the king. She exuded a sensual, simmering rage that made her somehow both entrancing and frightening. Her ochre eyes blazed, and there was a sheen of sweat on her golden-brown skin. And goodness was there plenty of skin exposed—her toned arms, much of her chest, and chiseled midriff completely uncovered. Macella had to admit that the king was quite the physical specimen.

Macella jumped a little as King Khari hit the woman with the whip again, then rubbed the spot lightly with her free hand. The woman whimpered and bit her lip. The king ran her hand over the woman's ass slowly, her eyes locked on Macella.

"Good girl," Khari said, delivering a sharp smack with her bare hand.

Aithan and Macella stood silently as the king moved unhurriedly behind the desk. She patted at her face and neck with a towel and took a long drink from a chalice. Finally, she rounded to the front of the desk and leaned back against it. Despite her casual stance, the hand still gripping the whip shook slightly.

"We are setting off on our northern journey in one month," King Khari stated flatly. "Based on the latest from the north and the new unrest in the west, we cannot afford to wait for the harvesting season as we'd initially planned."

Macella could practically hear the king's teeth grinding as she mentioned the western region. Clearly, King Khari's fury at Queen Annika had not yet diminished. Macella now understood the purpose of the pale, plump, flaxen-haired woman. She wondered if Khari had sent a messenger to Wildfell requesting a sex worker who resembled the young queen or if she already had the woman on standby for occasions such as this. Perhaps she had Awa and Meztli look-alikes on retainer as well. The thought almost made Macella laugh aloud.

"I detest traveling during the hot season," King Khari complained, her expression darkening. "But it cannot be helped. Thus, you have one month to make your decision. Either we are announcing our courtship during the northern visit, or we will be leaving you there when our visit is done."

Macella felt Aithan tense beside her. She swallowed hard, trying to keep her face neutral. She reminded herself that there was no reason to get upset. The decision was made. Yes, they'd thought they had more time, but time would make no difference. She would never be ready to commit to the king, even if she had years to consider it. But she would do what she must.

"Thank you, your grace," Macella replied, her voice steadier than she'd expected. "But you need not be in suspense any longer. We have already made our decision."

You do not have to do this now. Aithan's mental voice was strained and sorrowful.

It is as good a time as any. She will appreciate having her power recognized on a day such as this.

King Khari lifted an eyebrow. "By all means, put me out of my misery. If the news is good, I can look forward to having at least one queen who does not plague me, and if it is bad, I can punish Annie for it for the rest of the night."

The king gestured at the bound woman, who obediently had not moved so much as an inch during their conversation. Macella internally confirmed her earlier suspicion as to the woman's purpose—an obedient Annika surrogate. What would the young queen say if she saw this display?

"I am honored to accept your offer, my king," Macella said, lowering her gaze and bowing so the king wouldn't see the fear in her eyes. "I only hope that I can live up to the distinction you've bestowed upon me."

"My dear, this is wonderful news!" King Khari exclaimed, brightening. "I am ashamed now to be seen in this state. I would embrace you, but I am not properly attired. You have greatly improved my mood."

The king looked genuinely joyful and even a bit abashed as she looked down at her sparse clothing. Her binder covered little more than her small breasts and her trousers hung low on her hips, revealing the sharp lines of oblique muscles that led to her pelvic bone. Macella and Aithan bowed, keeping their eyes on the ground.

"Go, enjoy your evening," Khari laughed, waving them away. "We will discuss this more when I am decent."

As they slipped from the room, the king turned back to "Annie" with a devilish grin. Just before the door closed, Macella heard another sharp smack, followed by the king's low voice. Her words sent a thrill through Macella's core.

"You are a lucky, lucky girl," Khari murmured. "I am going to make you cum until you cry."

Back in their chambers, Aithan dropped heavily onto the sitting room sofa. Macella poured two goblets of wine before joining him. They drank in silence for a while, each lost in their own thoughts.

"Do you think Khari will immediately task Brontë with recruiting a Macella doppelgänger?" Macella wondered aloud, after she'd finished her goblet of wine in a few gulps.

Aithan frowned at her and drained his own goblet. "She probably already has one. I doubt she was waiting for your consent to begin indulging in fantasies about you."

"I'm sure you're right," Macella agreed with a weary laugh. "At least my substitute won't be getting a spanking anytime soon."

"I am very tempted to spank the original," Aithan replied, his orange eyes narrowed. "Maybe a little punishment would do you good."

"For what crime?" Macella demanded, ignoring the little thrill that shot through her belly at his words and look.

"Obstinance. Impatience. Reckless endangerment," Aithan deadpanned. "You have no regard for your own well-being."

Macella huffed indignantly. "I have the highest regard for my well-being and yours too. You know that agreeing to the king's proposal is our only option. I chose to do so at a time when it would elevate us even more in King Khari's eyes. Proving myself amenable when Annika is showing herself to be intractable is a smart move."

Aithan ran a hand through his hair, pushing it out of his face. "Even so, I hate it. I hate this farce. I hate having you in such danger. I hate the way Khari looked at you tonight—the way she's been looking at you lately, as if you are already hers. I have never in my life thought about murder as often as I have over the past few weeks."

"Hmmm," Macella hummed thoughtfully. "You have had your decisions and desires overruled a lot of late. And today, I took your last option for resistance by accepting the king's offer sooner than I had to. I am so sorry."

Aithan shook his head. "You don't need to apologize. I—"

(28) Macella pressed a finger against his lips, silencing him. When she was sure he wouldn't try to finish his sentence, she stood and stepped out of her boots. Keeping her eyes on him, she stripped off clothes until she stood in only her corset and panties.

"Punish me," she said, climbing back onto the sofa and laying across his lap.

Aithan hesitated. Macella could feel his indecision. She knew he had no desire to actually hurt her. But she also knew that she could trust him to find the line between pleasure and pain.

It would please me to surrender myself to you. I trust you.

Macella felt Aithan's cock stir against her belly. He ran his hand lightly over her ass. She shuddered and squirmed, her breath quickening in anticipation.

Aithan's hand struck her left buttocks, swift and sharp. She gasped and squirmed again. A tingling began between her legs.

"Be still," Aithan commanded, rubbing the spot he'd just smacked. "What will you say if you wish for me to stop?"

Macella craned her neck to look back at him, a mischievous grin spreading across her face. "Khari."

Aithan growled and smacked her right buttocks. "You are going to pay for that."

He unlaced her panties and ran his hand over her bare ass. Macella gasped and buried her face in the sofa. She squirmed again, her vagina clenching eagerly.

"I told you to be still," Aithan chided, delivering another quick slap. "And lift your face from the cushion. I want to hear you enjoy every moment of what I am going to do to you."

Obediently, Macella turned her head and rested it on her folded arms. Her breath was coming fast now, and it took every bit of her willpower to keep her hips still. And the hard press of Aithan's cock against her belly was certainly not helping.

"That's right," Aithan purred, his hand rubbing maddening circles over her ass. "Be a good girl and I might let you cum before I fuck you."

Macella let out an involuntary squeak and focused all of her energy on keeping her hips motionless. Her pussy was already throbbing, and he'd hardly done a thing. The anticipation was unbearably arousing.

Smack. Aithan's hand struck her ass with serpentine speed. And just as her body processed the sting, the sensation was heightened into something different by the warm caress of his calloused palm. Macella whimpered.

"Do you want to cum?" Aithan asked, his voice low and husky.

Macella fought a shudder. Aithan's hand traced lower, moving along the underside of her ass toward the juncture of her thighs. He alternated between a teasing, light circle, and a firm, massaging grip. Her pussy made wet, squishy sounds as he kneaded one cheek and then the other. Macella could not help but grind her hips in rapturous frustration.

Smack. Smack. She moaned and shuddered as Aithan stroked away the sting from the two sudden slaps he'd just delivered.

"I asked you, do you want to cum," Aithan growled. "The answer is *yes, please, Lord Protector.*"

"Yes, please, Lord Protector," Macella panted, the pulsing between her legs growing to a nigh unendurable level.

Smack. Macella moaned.

"I also told you to be still, did I not?" Aithan asked.

"Yes, Lord Protector," Macella whispered.

Smack. She thought she might die soon if he did not touch her, did not press his fingers to her clit, did not slip his fingers inside of her and relieve the insistent, delicious, agonizing throbbing. Aithan's erection twitched against her belly, undoubtedly responding to the desperate tenor of her thoughts. His hand still moved over her ass, petting, and massaging in turns.

"Four more and you had better not move," Aithan commanded. "Count."

Smack. Aithan's hand against her skin, elicited a stinging, thrilling sensation. Then those infuriatingly gentle circles. Macella willed her lower body to remain immobile.

"One," she panted.

The waiting was maddening. She could not decide if knowing that she had three licks left helped or if it made the anticipation worse. She could think of nothing but the next moment of stinging pleasure.

Smack. Aithan's hand struck again. Then he was rubbing, chasing away the ache, his fingers slipping teasingly close to the place where her thighs met. Macella wondered if he could feel the heat of her arousal radiating from the spot.

"Two," she gasped.

Smack. And the gentle, tantalizing caress.

"Three." Her voice trembled between a moan and a whimper.

Aithan slid his hand over the backs of her thighs. Macella moaned louder, fighting to remain stationary. Time stretched into an endless expanse of desire. Just when she thought she would lose all control—

Smack. Aithan delivered a final, sharp slap, and then his fingers were between her legs, and all Macella could do was surrender. The exquisiteness of her suffering until that moment amplified her pleasure at his touch.

"Four," Macella cried out.

"Good girl," Aithan purred. "You may cum now."

His fingers moved nimbly, manipulating her wetness, rubbing her clit, faster and faster, pressing the place that seemed to resonate in her very core. Macella felt tingling heat spreading through her belly. Her hips bucked, her throaty cries of ecstasy matching the tempo of his fingers.

In an embarrassingly short amount of time, Macella felt herself boiling over. She came hard and fast, her body racked with shudders. She cried out Aithan's name, gripping the sofa cushion for support, feeling as if his fingers were the only things keeping her tethered as gravity dissolved around her.

Then his fingers were gone, and he lifted her into a kneeling position. As she caught her breath, Aithan slipped swiftly out of his clothes. He sat down again, leaning back and spreading his arms over the back of the sofa.

"Ride me," he growled.

Macella shivered, her need reigniting immediately. She moved to straddle him. Aithan didn't move, but his eyes devoured her as she positioned his cock against her and slowly lowered herself onto it. They gasped in unison.

"Show me that this good pussy is mine," Aithan said, his eyes smoldering amber. "Show me that you are mine."

"Yes, Lord Protector," Macella breathed.

She let her hips make up for lost time, eager after her restricted movement during her punishment. She took him deep inside her, grinding against him to force him deeper still. She felt full and weightless and wild.

"You have very, very good pussy, don't you, Macella?" Aithan purred, his gaze burning. "I want to hear you say it."

Macella's hips spasmed, his words thrilling through her torso. "I have good pussy."

Aithan's arm suddenly left the back of the couch, and Macella felt the sting of his palm against her ass. She arched her back and cried out. Warmth spread across her skin.

"Do not undervalue my beloved," Aithan chastised. "You do not simply have good pussy. You have very, very good pussy. Say it."

"I have very, very good pussy, Lord Protector," Macella whimpered.

She moved steadily up and down his shaft, lingering at the bottom to feel him fill her entirely, hitting that spot in her belly that made her feel ethereal. She wasn't sure how much more she could take. Submitting to him had aroused her in new ways, making all of her nerve endings buzz, the possibility of an explosion growing closer each moment.

"You'd better not cum yet," Aithan warned, gripping her ass with one hand. "Not until you convince me that your spectacular pussy is mine, this amazing ass is mine, every inch of your perfect fucking body is mine. Your heart is mine."

Macella moaned, fighting the rising hum in her core. Letting him control her, allowing him to drive her to the very edge, only to delay her orgasm—it filled her with a wanton excitement. She placed her hands on his shoulders for leverage, moving faster up and down his shaft.

"Good girl. That's my good girl," Aithan groaned, his grip on her ass tightening. "This cock is yours. My body is yours. My heart is yours."

As if he could not help himself, he brought his other hand down to clench her ass, pressing her forcefully down as he drove his hips upward. The sudden thrust nearly pushed her over the edge, but she held back. She wanted to end this right, to complete the experience properly.

"Please, Lord Protector," Macella begged. "Please may I cum?"

Aithan growled, jerking upright, and burying his face in her neck. He bit the delicate skin where her neck and shoulder met as he pressed her down onto his cock. Macella let out a desperate whimper.

"Cum for me," he whispered.

Then he leaned back against the sofa, planting his feet more firmly on the floor. Before Macella could reply, he was driving his hips upward as he pushed hers down, thrusting into her fast and deep. She leaned into him, pressing her face into his hair, the swell of her breasts above her corset spilling into his face.

Macella felt his tongue against her skin, working between the fabric and her flesh to find a nipple. He teased at it, licking and flicking his tongue, all the while thrusting into her, driving deep, igniting her frenzied nerve endings.

And then Macella was trembling, hips bucking, burying her cries in his hair, his neck, the sofa back. Aithan followed her over the edge, clutching her tight as his cock swelled and released, and he came deep inside of her. Macella shuddered and shook and finally slumped against him. Aithan held her close, gradually slowing his breathing and relaxing into the hazy afterglow of their lovemaking.

"Are you alright, love?" he whispered after they'd sat a while in that position, not moving or speaking.

Macella lifted her head. "I am quite alright. My rear end may be a bit tender tomorrow, but it's not a bad tenderness. I kind of like it."

Aithan chuckled and kissed her collarbone. "Well, I think we should ring for dinner and a hot bath. When we are all fed and cleaned, I will rub some soothing oil on that delectable rear end."

"That sounds perfect." Macella smiled.

She kissed him again, savoring the taste she so loved. He squeezed her in his strong arms, filling her with a sense of safety and stability. She broke the kiss and placed her forehead against his.

"This is real," she whispered. "We are real. Khari cannot change that."

Chapter Seventeen

A few days later, Finley and the new Aegis arrived with the dawn. Lucy brought Macella and Aithan the news, along with an invitation to the presentation to the Crown after breakfast. Macella couldn't stop smiling as she dressed and prepared for the day. While they broke their fast, she caught Aithan watching her with amusement. She grinned back, practically dancing in her seat.

"It pleases me that you love Finley so," Aithan said, his eyes warm amber. "You have been so good for them. They've always been secretly kind beneath their detached demeanor. You have brought out the best in them—as you have done for me."

Macella shrugged. "I am not sure about that, but I am grateful for their friendship. I've never had such a relationship with any of my siblings. Some of the younger ones were sweet, especially little Lotta, but none of them understood me. Finley does."

Aithan's face clouded over, and Macella knew he was thinking of her birth parents. Surely in the lost memories of them, Macella had been more loved and valued than her adopted family had ever made her feel. Maybe if the world had been different and her parents hadn't had to hide themselves, she would have had close siblings.

"Hurry! The presentation will start soon," Macella urged, standing and twirling to distract him from that sad train of thought. "How do I look?"

"Radiant," Aithan replied.

He took her arm and soon they were settled in the throne room. Aithan and Captain Drudo stood at either end of the Crown's dais. Other members of the Royal Guard stood at attention around the room. The Grand Mage and Grand Vizier watched the proceedings from their places below the dais. Macella sat at a writing stand near the herald, keeping a record of the proceedings.

The grand double doors opened to admit the newly arrived Aegises. Macella's heart lifted as Finley sauntered into the throne room. They wore a fine jade jacket, embroidered white tunic, and russet trousers. Their gleaming silver hair hung loose around their shoulders, the emerald ends as lush as the rich satin of their surcoat.

Their orange eyes found Macella as they kneeled before the Crown. They winked and covertly blew her a kiss before straightening to look at the monarchs. Unsurprisingly, the Crown appeared captivated. For the first time since the disastrous small council meeting, King Khari wasn't scowling, and Queen Annika wasn't sulking. Monarch Meztli looked almost interested, and even Queen Awa was watching Finley, instead of staring blankly into some middle distance as she'd frequently done of late.

"I present to you, Finley of Fairdale, one of the three Aegis elders of Kōsaten, newly arrived at the palace, your graces," announced the herald.

"Finley of Fairdale, child of Apophis, the Crown is pleased to receive you," King Khari greeted, her gaze intent on the lovely Aegis.

Finley stood, bowing their head to each of the rulers in turn. "Thank you, your grace. And you Queen Awa, Monarch Meztli, and Queen Annika. It is my honor to be in your presence once more."

Their voice was as velvety as Macella remembered, the husky tones lulling, inviting listeners to lean forward and catch each word. A smirk played about their lips, though their face remained impassive. Macella imagined that Finley knew exactly the effect they had on most people.

"My rulers, allow me to present the newest addition to our ranks," Finley announced, gesturing smoothly with their hands as they spoke. "This is Jacan of Prestonia, son of Apophis."

Macella had been so busy watching Finley that she'd forgotten to examine the Aegis who'd entered the chamber behind them. It said a lot about Finley's allure, because Jacan of Prestonia was certainly noticeable. He was tall, like Aithan, though more leanly muscled, with sandy brown skin, and the hellfire orange eyes of all Aegises. A string of tattooed jade symbols circled his bald head, glowing ever so faintly with a hint of magic.

Though she couldn't be certain of his age, Jacan was obviously young. Macella knew that his age was no indicator of his skill—Aegises did not get to be children for much of their long lives. It had been less than a year since the Crown had improved conditions for Aegis recruits. That meant Jacan of Prestonia had spent the majority of his life starved, abused, and suffering.

He was clad in worn armor that had clearly been mended and shined for this occasion. Of course, as a new Aegis, he had not yet had the time and means to acquire a proper wardrobe. Macella knew Lynn's tailors would soon be hard at work fitting him for his dress uniform and other attire for his stay at court. She made a mental note to befriend the young Aegis—she knew what it was like to go from abject poverty to obscene opulence. It could be jarring.

Jacan of Prestonia dropped to one knee, his head bowed. King Khari turned her attention to the neophyte, assessing him shrewdly. The other members of the Crown studied the young Aegis with varying degrees of interest.

"Rise, Jacan of Prestonia," the king commanded. "Let us look upon our newest warrior."

Macella noticed Finley tap their foot several times, obviously signaling the young Aegis to stand. Jacan stood and lifted his head. He bowed to each of the monarchs in turn.

"Thank you, your graces, for the opportunity to serve," Jacan said.

"You have survived insurmountable challenges to be here today," King Khari replied, rising to stand. "You have demonstrated superior will, strength, intelligence, and resilience. The Crown thanks you for all you have endured for your kingdom, and all you will do to protect it over the many years of life in front of you."

Jacan watched King Khari closely as she spoke. When she'd finished, he bowed his head in humble acknowledgment. When he again lifted his gaze, the king beckoned him closer to the dais.

(29) Grand Mage Kiama came forward, carrying a leather pouch. Macella leaned forward eagerly. She'd never seen an Aegis presented to the Crown for the first time. Aithan had told her what to expect, but she was still keen to see it firsthand. She watched as the herald unrolled a tied parchment. As Jacan and Kiama drew nearer to the dais, the herald stepped forward and began to read.

"For thousands of years, Kōsaten was a desolate battleground. The kingdom is an in-between place whither the veil between the world of the living and dead has always been thin. These thin places threaten to tear, allowing untold dangers to cross into our realm, intent on destruction. In this land of gods and monsters, humanity stood little chance of survival. When the first human mage, Khalid, was born, he devoted his life to making Kōsaten safe for human habitation.

"After much negotiation with the gods of both light and darkness, Khalid succeeded. The gods of light were weary of war, while the darker gods saw an opportunity for gain. In exchange for their power and favor, the death deities would receive the souls of all those mighty warriors recruited into the line of the Aegis. The Aegis shields us, carrying the weight of our world and the power of the gods on their shoulders. Only the Aegises stand between our kingdom and complete desolation.

"Only the very best survive the training, transformations, and trials. These survivors are no longer our children. They know the unknowable and can do the unimaginable. They've looked into the fires of hell, into the face of fear. No matter their appearance when they began, they leave The Forge with the telltale wisdom silver hair and hellfire orange eyes that mark the Aegis.

"To keep the dark deities and their offspring in check, however, the gods of light created the Chosen—three beings of immense power and mystery, of whom we only hear whispers. And all of these great beings—Aegis and Chosen alike—are bound to the Crown."

King Khari glanced at Macella with a catlike grin. Those words—it was a story everyone knew, but the words were *hers*. Macella had written them for a society paper as the scribe. Aithan told her that the origin of the Aegis was always shared during these presentations. Apparently, the king had added an extra touch for Macella's benefit.

King Khari descended the steps to stand before the young, much taller Aegis. Jacan immediately dropped to a knee once more. Grand Mage Kiama tipped her pouch, pouring a circle of dark earth around them. When the circle was complete, the Grand Mage lifted her hands, extending one toward the king and the other toward the kneeling Aegis. Her gray eyes went white.

"Jacan of Prestonia," King Khari boomed, her voice reverberating with power. "You have been chosen by Apophis to maintain balance in the realm as agreed upon by the gods and promised to King Khalid of Kōsaten."

The temperature in the room seemed to drop suddenly. King Khari placed a hand atop Jacan's head. Grand Mage Kiama produced a vial, uncorked it, and released a cloud of thick, inky smoke. Again, she circled the pair, the brimstone trailing behind her.

"From this day until your last, you will protect the kingdom of Kōsaten, serving the sovereign upon the blessed throne," King Khari decreed, as the circle of smoke wafted around them. "From this day until your last, you are bound to Kōsaten. As it thrives, so shall you, and if it dies, you shall sacrifice your final breath to revive it. By the will of the gods and of your supreme sovereign, King Khari of Kōsaten."

Macella took a steadying breath. She felt a sudden wave of sadness, watching the beautiful young man swear his life away. Distantly, she registered Finley tapping their foot.

"From this day until my last," Jacan swore, his voice steady and emotionless.

Macella shivered. She could feel the pull of magic in the air. She glanced to where Aithan stood, watching the proceedings with his typical stoic reserve. Many years ago, he'd been similarly bound to Kōsaten and to King Khari after Lucifer claimed and blessed him. So many bindings, so many lifelong choices made for him. Macella realized she was perhaps the first choice he'd made for himself—the only thing he'd ever freely chosen to bind himself to.

Aithan's eyes met hers, bright and warm. She saw the love and loyalty there, felt it enveloping her as surely as the brimstone enveloped the king and the new Aegis. He had chosen her, and she had chosen him and that was a bond that needed no magical ritual to ratify.

The brimstone sank to the floor, where it sought out the dark earth. When the two substances met, they ignited into a ring of fire. The flames blazed jade, reaching high enough to obscure the two forms within, before abruptly extinguishing. The air in the throne room warmed again as Grand Mage Kiama's eyes shifted back to their normal gray.

King Khari lifted her hand from the young Aegis's head. "Stand and serve, Jacan of Prestonia."

From the corner of her eye, Macella saw Finley tap their foot again. Jacan stood to face the king. Despite his greater height, the king still seemed to tower over him somehow. Her ochre eyes seemed to glow, an aura of power coating her skin.

Jacan saluted the king with a fist to his chest. From their places, Finley and Aithan mimicked the movement. When Jacan spoke, they joined him, reciting their oath in unison.

"I am the tower that withstands the tempest.

I am the bolt that bars hell's gates.

I am the flame that repels the shadows.

I am the harbinger of Fate.

I am the hunter that predators fear.

I am the blade that fells the beast.

I am the guardian that keeps vigil.

I am the shield that protects the peace."

The king touched her fist to her chest. Then she smiled and shook Jacan's hand heartily. She spoke to him less formally for a few minutes, turning on the charm easily, as Macella had seen her do many times. Finally, she dismissed them all, encouraging Finley and Jacan to rest and enjoy the castle's amenities as they recovered from their journey.

As soon as the Crown and Royal Guard had left the chamber, Macella threw her arms around Finley with a girlish squeal. Finley staggered back a step, laughing their throaty laugh. The sound was like music, and they smelled of honey and hazelnut. Macella breathed them in, squeezing them tightly. They patted her gingerly on her back.

"Well, obviously your time at court has not refined your manners," they quipped, before hugging her back tightly. "I suppose I can't blame you. I would be thrilled to see me too."

Macella stepped away, smiling so widely it hurt. She turned to the young Aegis, extending her hand in greeting. To her surprise, he dropped to one knee, pressing his forehead against the back of her hand.

"I'm sorry," he said, releasing her and standing quickly. "It's just...I know who you are. We haven't stopped telling the story of the Saviors of Smoketown—the Lucifer Aegis and his beautiful companion. You changed everything. You saved us."

Are you going to help us all? Anwansi thinks you will.

The memory of Tuwile's words flashed through Macella's mind. Tuwile had come to her after she'd witnessed the horrors of Smoketown. It had been too late to help him—he'd already been dead when she met him. But she had done her best to help the others.

"I used the gifts the gods gave me to serve others, as Fate intended," Macella replied. "I only wish I could have done more."

Jacan had been watching her lips closely. When she finished, he looked incredulous. He leaned toward her, turning his head to one side, and touching a spot behind his ear. Up close, Macella could see that the tattoos on his scalp partially concealed a jagged scar over most of one side of his head. As a matter of fact, his body was riddled with scars, more than Macella had ever seen on a single person.

"I lost my hearing when I was four or five," Jacan explained. "One of the soldiers made a wager that I could stand on one foot on broken glass for three minutes without losing my balance."

Inadvertently, Macella glimpsed the memory in the young Aegis's mind. She wasn't used to having any minds around that she could access aside from Aithan's, so the suddenness of the imagery surprised her. The pain and fear permeating the memory made her sick.

"When I fell onto the glass, he broke another bottle over my head and beat me until I lost consciousness," Jacan continued. "His name was Grizzle."

Macella gasped. She'd first met Grizzle in the aftermath of him making a similar wager. She'd protected the child he'd been terrorizing and pressed her dagger to the soldier's throat. The second time she encountered Grizzle, she had slit his throat with the same dagger.

"You saved us," Jacan repeated earnestly, taking her hand in both of his and squeezing.

Macella's eyes pricked with tears. She flung her arms around the young Aegis and hugged him tightly, breathing in his faint scent of saffron and sandalwood. He blushed furiously and hugged her back.

"It's like she's starved for affection," Finley drawled from behind them. "Aithan of Auburndale, are you neglecting my dear sister?"

"You know Macella does not love by halves," Aithan replied.

Macella released Jacan and spun to glare at the other two Aegises. They were both watching her with the same lovingly amused smirks. She couldn't even hold her glare, looking at two of her favorite people in the world. Aithan was right; she certainly didn't love by halves.

Over the next few days, Macella enjoyed a lightness she had not felt in some time. She spent every possible moment talking and laughing with Finley. As she'd predicted, they reacted with dramatic sympathy to her intended courtship. They hung on every word of her stories about hers and Aithan's adventures thus far at court. It was a relief to unburden herself to a trusted friend.

All four Aegises passed a fair amount of time together as a group in easy camaraderie—though, of course, Jacan did not know of Macella's Aegisborn nature. The young Aegis seemed as delighted as she was to spend leisure time with other Aegises. Their kind were largely solitary warriors, but when they formed bonds, they were strong. And the four Aegises were quickly solidifying that bond.

They were beginning to feel like something Macella had never truly had. A family.

Chapter Eighteen

Over the next few days, the Crown included the visiting Aegises in their social events, showcasing them to the wealthy nobles and touting their might. However, the real display would take place at the upcoming ball. The keep was bustling with preparations for the festivities.

Macella was relieved when, a few days prior to the ball, King Khari decided that she needed a private dinner with her spouses. The king probably wanted the four monarchs to have a conversation about their future without any other listening ears around—and before the castle was filled with new guests and schemes. Macella was sure the king had plenty of thinly veiled threats to deliver. Thus, the Aegises had an evening off from the demands of court life. They would have a quiet dinner and enjoy a few hours free from the Crown's scrutiny.

"It is going to be so delightful to have a dinner to ourselves," Finley called from the chaise where they lounged. "I could not possibly endure another meal with all those preening sycophants or that infantile queen."

"Imagine spending hours with her every day," Macella called back from her dressing room where she was readying herself for the evening. "I much prefer the preening sycophants."

"Gods, what an absolute nightmare!" Finley exclaimed. They made their voice high and childish when they spoke again. "My king, these Aegises make such lovely pets, do they not? My love, doesn't Macella look tired and poor and not at all prettier than me? My one and only, did you notice my luscious breasts spilling from my dress the last twenty times I contrived to lean toward you?"

Macella snorted a laugh, reentering the sitting room. "You are terrible, but I don't disagree. Tonight will be a pleasant break. And I am thrilled to dress down."

Finley sat up and looked her over with a dismayed expression. "No, no, no. Absolutely not."

To Macella's surprise, Finley sprang to their feet and was at her side in two graceful strides. Before she could respond, they were steering her back toward her dressing chamber.

"You are not wearing a tunic and leggings tonight," Finley proclaimed, throwing open Macella's wardrobe. "I see you but rarely, so every day with me is an *occasion*, dearest."

Macella harumphed and crossed her arms. "You have seen me plenty done up during this visit and there's still the ball ahead! This may be the only evening we have away from the Crown's prying eyes. Why can I not be comfortable?"

Finley made a dismissive sound and began rummaging through Macella's clothes. They examined several dresses with an appraising eye and then returned them to the wardrobe. Finally, they pulled out a simple, lightweight dress in pale blue. It had a soft cotton bodice with a gauzy lace overlay and wide neckline that showed off Macella's collarbone and shoulders. It was actually one of her favorites, but she had only worn it once—on an outing to a nearby estate with the Crown. When he saw her, Aithan had told her she looked like a sky goddess. When she'd quipped that she was more of a hell goddess, he'd grinned and said that hell must have a sky.

"You can be comfortable and fabulous simultaneously." Finley smiled, holding the dress out. "You know that I love beautiful things and yet see so little beauty, confined to Duànzào as I am. Indulge me."

"Fine," Macella huffed, rolling her eyes.

Even as she pouted, she was pleased. She wouldn't deny Finley any pleasure that was within her power to provide. She took the dress from them and stomped over to stand before the long looking glass. She held it up to her body and couldn't deny that she liked the color against her skin.

"Hurry and change! I want a nice, long ride on the grounds before our intimate little evening party," Finley said as they sauntered from the room wearing a satisfied grin.

Macella shook her head ruefully. Finley was the one insisting on the fancy costume change and now *they* were rushing *her*? It was annoying and adorably endearing. She smiled and shimmied out of her tunic and leggings, amazed by the stab of love she felt for the lovely Apophis Aegis. This is what it must be like to have a close relationship with one's siblings.

(30) The sun was growing low in the sky when Macella and Finley emerged from the castle. A cart and horse awaited them, as requested. Finley took the reins, urging the horse into an easy trot. They talked freely, enjoying the gentle evening breeze. The grounds were in full bloom and the air was sweet with the perfume of flowers.

"We're going to have to come up with a signal for when I want you to read my thoughts," Finley declared. "It's going to be so delicious to gossip about people right in front of them. It's going to make the ball even more fun!"

"You're incorrigible," Macella replied.

"You love it," Finley countered, tossing their shimmering silver hair and giving her a saucy wink. "Our mental conversations are going to be so much more entertaining than whatever you and Aithan talk about."

Macella rolled her eyes, but she couldn't help smiling. Finley knew who she truly was and accepted her as if it was perfectly normal to communicate telepathically with your Aegis-human crossbreed friend. And Macella loved them for it.

Before long, they were far from the keep, traveling a winding path along the edge of a stretch of woods. As usual, Macella marveled at how much land the Crown possessed, and how well they kept it tended and protected. She could live a hundred years at the keep and never discover all of the beauties and secrets of these lands.

You may get the chance to find out, she reminded herself wryly. As queen, she could easily expect to pass the next century in Pleasure Ridge Park. Macella's stomach knotted at the thought. She still couldn't really envision her life as queen, even knowing how false and ornamental her reign would be. Most of all, she hated the thought of being trapped here, bound to King Khari.

Macella shook off the wave of sadness. She'd made the only choice she could. She wasn't going to waste a minute of Finley's visit grieving things she could not change.

Just as she refocused her attention on Finley, she sensed another presence. The cart rounded a bend and slowed. Aithan stood beside Jade, watching them approach. Finley drew the cart up beside him, ignoring Macella's questioning look.

Macella had quickly learned to block out the thoughts of the visiting Aegises. She wanted to respect their privacy—not to mention that Finley's thoughts were often of exploits that made her blush. Now, though, she risked a peek at her companion's mind. Finley, however, was thinking very loudly and determinedly about the details of a surcoat they'd commissioned.

"Aithan of Auburndale, what a pleasant surprise," Finley drawled in a voice that was entirely unsurprised.

They alighted from the cart gracefully and helped Macella down, taking her by the waist and swinging her around before setting her down. When she was on the ground, Finley squeezed her hand, looking at her with shining eyes. Macella started to ask them what was going on, but they planted a quick, chaste kiss on her lips.

"I wish to explore alone for a bit," Finley declared, giving Macella's hand to Aithan. "I will catch up with you two later."

They bounded lightly away before Macella could protest. She turned to Aithan with an accusatory expression. He was watching her carefully, but she couldn't read his mood. Or his thoughts. Macella realized he'd closed his mind to her.

"What are you two up to?" she demanded, narrowing her eyes.

Aithan smiled but didn't answer. Instead, he removed a long parcel from Jade's saddlebag and tucked it under his arm, then led Macella toward the trees. Curiously, she looked him over. He didn't appear as he had when they'd parted early that afternoon—her to Finley's chambers in the Aegis quarters, him to King Khari's study. Then, he'd been dressed in court finery as normal, looking every bit the high commander.

Now, he appeared far more relaxed, though no less beautiful. He'd partially tied back his shiny silver hair so that it was out of his face, but still hung about his shoulders. The crimson tips were stark against the thin white cotton of his shirt. He wore black trousers and black boots, his sword sheathed in a simple holster rather than the more ornate piece he wore most days.

The trees thinned to reveal a small clearing beside a trickling stream. It reminded Macella of the places where they'd liked to make camp during their travels. They would find a clearing like this one, quiet and complete with everything they needed. Aithan had trained her in combat, often ending their days with an evening sparring session. Afterward, they'd use the stream to rinse their clothing and bathe—Macella rinsing his hair and watching the water cascade over the muscles of his back. When they'd finished bathing, they'd lie on blankets in the warm evening breeze, Aithan using a soft cloth to massage her sore muscles as he patted her dry. Then they would make love and fall asleep beneath the stars.

"That is what I hoped you would be reminded of," Aithan said, stirring her from her thoughts.

"Those are easily my fondest memories," Macella nodded. "We lived as we chose, committed only to fighting demons and loving one another."

Aithan smiled, placing the long parcel in her hands. "It is serendipitous that you mention choices. That is what I hoped to discuss with you."

Carefully, Macella loosened the string securing the parcel. With Aithan's help, she removed the wrapping to reveal a gleaming sword. It felt perfectly weighted in her hands as she gave it a tentative twirl. The hilt was inlaid with three obsidian jewels and engraved with an elegant letter M.

"It was forged in hellfire in Duànzào, the only place in Kōsaten where that can be done, and only by and for an Aegis," Aithan explained. "I commissioned Finley to craft it for you. I promised you that I would obtain a sword worthy of you."

Macella's heart lurched. She hadn't realized how much she wanted to be acknowledged as an Aegis, to feel as though she belonged among the warriors she cared so much for. Instead, she'd had to hide her nature from almost everyone. The few other Aegises who knew the truth hadn't been very accepting. Adding insult to injury, she'd had to constantly suppress her instincts since they'd taken up residence in the capital.

Now, she was holding her own Duànzào forged sword. Her dearest friend and sibling had fashioned it for her with their own hands. And the love of her life had commissioned it for her to uphold a passing promise he'd made during those early training days.

"It's perfect," she whispered, looking up at Aithan through eyes blurred by tears. "Thank you."

(31) "I promised," Aithan answered, his eyes soft. "And I would like to make you another promise."

Macella blinked back tears as Aithan gently set her sword aside and took her hands into his. Her heart rate spiked as he looked intently into her eyes. His gaze was warm and full of love, and as Macella stared back, the walls around his mind began to dissolve. Everything crystalized then. Her heart swelled.

"I have had very few opportunities in my life to choose for myself," Aithan said softly. "But I thank the gods that those few choices led me to fall in love with you. You are the one thing I choose to be bound to of my own free will. Ours is the only bond that is true."

Aithan brought both of her hands to his lips, his eyes never leaving hers. He kissed her knuckles, and she shivered, butterflies flooding her stomach. Aithan pressed their clasped hands to his heart. Macella felt the reassuring rhythm of his heartbeat, steady and strong.

"Macella, I promise you my sword, my heart, and my hand," he vowed. "I choose to bind myself to you by all the laws of gods and man. Will you be my wife?"

Time slowed around them. Macella could see every mote of dust dancing in the sunlight streaming through the trees. She could hear her heart pounding out a rapid counter to Aithan's steady drum. Her breath caught in her throat.

She had never much considered marriage. She certainly didn't believe that she and Aithan needed to marry to legitimize the unbreakable bond between them. However, since King Khari had announced Macella as her intended, she'd realized that she loathed the thought of taking marriage vows lightly. Now, the person she truly loved was giving her back the power to choose.

"Yes," Macella whispered. "Yes, of course, you fool."

And then they were kissing, and time was stretching into long, lazy rivulets of sweetly scented breeze. Aithan held her close, his arms warm and strong around her. This was it. This was the way she wanted to spend the rest of her life.

"Shall we?" Finley's melodic voice broke the stillness.

Macella and Aithan pulled apart. Finley strode into the clearing, carrying a satchel and wearing a pleased grin. They also carried what looked like a sizable tree stump as if it weighed nothing at all.

"Impeccable timing, as always." Aithan smiled.

"I assume she accepted?" Finley teased, lifting their eyebrows.

Macella put her hands on her hips, giving both Aegises a mock glare. Finley only grinned wider, placing the tree stump on the ground and beginning to unpack the satchel they carried. Aithan took her hand again as Finley straightened and beamed at them both.

"As an Aegis, I am endowed by the Crown and bound by honor to uphold and enforce the laws of Kōsaten," Finley proclaimed. "Thus, it is my great pleasure to preside over this union today."

Macella gasped. She looked from Finley's radiant face to Aithan's loving smile to the items arranged on the tree stump. She could feel the tears spilling down her face.

She shook her head, laughingly wiping them away. "I love you both so much," she sniffed.

"I know this might not be ideal, but I did not wish for your first wedding to be a farce," Aithan said, staring intently into Macella's eyes. "You deserve to marry for love, surrounded by people who love you, happy and unafraid."

Macella pressed her fingers to his lips, smiling brightly through her tears. "It's *perfect*."

Aithan's answering smile was luminous. "I did not want Khari to take the magic of this experience from you, but we must keep our union private for now. It would displease the king to have attention diverted from her grand plans. We'll tell her later—much later."

Finley swelled with pride. "Ah, the triumph of well-laid plans coming to fruition."

Aithan rolled his eyes. "Yes, you've done a beautiful job planning this all alone over these many months."

"I suppose you helped a bit," Finley admitted. "Now hush and let me perform my duties."

"Gods forbid I interfere with your performance," Aithan muttered.

Finley ignored him. They uncorked a bottle and, walking around Aithan and Macella, poured water on the ground in each of the four cardinal directions. Wetting their fingers from the same bottle, they pressed their fingertips to the spot between Macella's brows, repeating the gesture for Aithan.

"We ask the blessings of the gods and ancestors on this union," Finley intoned solemnly. "We call upon the ancestors in love and gratitude. Lenora, we thank you. Maia, we thank you. Matthias, we thank you. Gabriela, we thank you."

Macella thought her heart might burst. She was surrounded by the love of her chosen family and the spirits of her ancestors. She'd been validated as an Aegis, treated as a sister, chosen as a wife. Here beneath the setting sun, amid the trees, and in the company of her sibling and her soulmate, she felt whole.

"We honor the gods, the ancestors, the land and the sky, and ask that your sacred bond be abundant and grow stronger through the changing seasons,"

Finley continued. "There shall never again exist loneliness in your world because you share an inseparable life until your days come to a rest."

Finley produced a gleaming silver dagger. Carefully, they cut Macella's and then Aithan's palm, guiding the two to squeeze a trickle of blood into a silver goblet of dark wine. Finley then bound their bleeding hands together, slowly winding a white ribbon around them in an intricate pattern.

"Aithan of Auburndale." Finley smiled, gesturing for Aithan to speak.

Aithan's amber eyes burned as he held Macella's gaze. "I shall not seek to change you in any way. I shall respect you, your beliefs, your people, and your ways as I respect myself. I am my beloved's, and my beloved is mine. Wherever you go, there go I."

"Macella of Shively," Finley prompted.

Macella swallowed hard, wanting her voice to come out clear and strong. "I shall not seek to change you in any way. I shall respect you, your beliefs, your people, and your ways as I respect myself. I am my beloved's, and my beloved is mine. Wherever you go, there go I."

In succession, Finley added ingredients to the silver goblet. "A squeeze of lemon to represent the disappointments you will inevitably face. A sip of vinegar for the bitterness you must overcome in fights and trying times. A pinch of cayenne to bring spice and passion to the relationship. A spoonful of honey to represent the joy you will share throughout it all."

With their free hands, Macella and Aithan took the goblet in turns, drinking until they'd drained it completely. When they finished, they kissed, mixing the many flavors on their tongues.

Finley took their bound hands and held them between their own. "Repeat after me," Finley commanded. "You are blood of my blood, and bone of my bone. I give you my body, that we two might be one. I give you my spirit, until our life shall be done."

In unison, Macella and Aithan repeated the words as had so many before them. As during Jacan's presentation ceremony, Macella felt a pull of magic, though this was far softer, more natural. It felt as though the trees, the setting sun, the whispering breeze, and scurrying creatures had all lent their spirits to the forging of this union.

"You are two separate bodies, yet there is only one life that is set before you. While your union might grow as you both choose, it can never shrink or fade. From this day until your last, you are bound to one another in the eyes of gods and men," Finley pronounced.

Macella had not seen Aithan light up so fully as this since the day she confessed that she loved him. As soon as Finley removed the ceremonial ribbon, Aithan pulled her into his arms and crushed his mouth to hers. Macella melted into him, kissing him back with all she had.

"I love you, my husband," she whispered fiercely when they stopped to catch their breath.

"Macella, my hell goddess, mi vida, mi corazón," Aithan whispered back. "My wife. I love you always."

Chapter Nineteen

When Macella, Aithan, and Finley returned to the keep, dinner was waiting for them in the Aegis dining hall. The room had not been in use since the cold season, but it had clearly been refreshed for Finley and Jacan's arrival. At least, that's what Macella thought initially. As the evening progressed, however, she began to think Aithan and Finley had ensured it received special attention that day.

The chandeliers filled the room with warm candlelight that glimmered off the stained-glass windows and were enhanced by floating candle centerpieces on the long tables. Bouquets of fresh flowers lent their sweet scent to the air. The tables were covered in pristine crimson cloths and set with fine crystal and silver.

"Why are there so many places set?" Macella asked, taking in the lovely décor.

"We are not the only ones excited for an evening away from the Crown." Aithan shrugged, taking her hand, and leading her to a central seat.

Soon, Finley and Jacan were seated with them, and goblets of wine were being drained amid loud laughter and boisterous conversation. Servants laid the table with more food than necessary, but when Macella mentioned it, Aithan only slung an arm around her shoulders, planted a kiss on her temple, and smiled. Finley was animatedly signing and orally recounting a comical story about Jacan's inexperienced mishaps during their journey to the capital, while Jacan adamantly refuted the more embarrassing details. Since he'd never left Smoketown after his recruitment as a toddler, everything on the journey had been new to the young Aegis. Macella, who had known some hand signs already and had picked up more during Jacan's visit, joined eagerly, though clumsily, in the simultaneously signed and spoken conversation, defending Jacan against Finley's biting wit.

Meanwhile, their party slowly grew in number. Captain Drudo was the first to join them, slipping naturally into the noisy exchange. Macella saw Finley eyeing the handsome knight, and she didn't need to read their mind to know that Drudo was in trouble. Aithan kissed her temple again, chuckling under his breath, obviously sharing Macella's musings.

Sir Griselda and Sir Kamau arrived together, saluting their commander before piling their plates high with food and finding places at the long table. Sir Quirino and Sir Igor soon joined them, followed by several other knights of the Royal Guard. Macella saw Finley catch Lucy's hand as she refilled their goblet, and soon she'd been convinced to sit with them and pour herself a drink.

The high tailor, Lynn, came looking for Jacan to take his measurements for formalwear. When she'd finished, Finley engaged her in conversation, and Macella could see them turning on the charm. Soon enough, the high tailor had taken a seat and was hotly debating the merits of current fashion trends.

(32) Macella wasn't sure how it happened, but at some point, the intimate evening meal transformed into a party. Jacan produced a lute and plucked a familiar tune. Sir Griselda accompanied him on a polished wooden fife. Then, Sir Kamau joined in with a fiddle and a few of the knights cleared away the extra tables, dancing and singing along to the bawdy melody.

When the improvised band began a slower ballad, Aithan pulled Macella onto the makeshift dance floor. He held her close, whisking her around the room to the whistles and catcalls of the others. Finley joined the musicians, crooning the story of a warrior who'd crossed the veil to challenge the gods for the return of his lost love.

"You have made me so happy," Aithan whispered into her hair. "I never dreamed I could be this happy."

Macella leaned her head against his chest, breathing him in, relishing the pure bliss of the present moment. This was the absolute truth. This was the purpose. This was the meaning of it all.

"I love you, Aithan of Auburndale," Macella said, lifting her head to look into his eyes. "I love you with all that I have, all that I am, and all that I ever will be."

He kissed her slowly, eliciting more raucous cheers that Macella hardly heard. She felt giddy, drunk on love and happiness as much as wine. Her feet hardly seemed to touch the floor as Aithan whirled her about, holding her close and whispering his devotion and joy.

When the next song began, Sir Igor cut in to ask for a dance, and Aithan smilingly went to dance with Finley. Macella saw that Lucy and several of the other knights had joined the dancers as well. It all filled her with a lightness she'd never felt at one of the Crown's balls. These people were here because they wished to be. They were relaxed and genuinely enjoying themselves, without even realizing that they were the perfect wedding gift, that they were adding to Macella and Aithan's joy.

Macella blinked back tears. She could not ever have imagined having such a celebration. She'd been to many parties during her time at court, but none that felt like this. She had never hosted nor been given a party, having never had enough friends to warrant music and dancing. Tonight, she'd been given so much. She would hold this memory tightly forever.

Macella felt herself being watched. She looked around to see Aithan and Finley dancing nearby, beaming at her. Of course. This had been their doing. They had planned every aspect of the occasion. This covert wedding reception was completely premeditated, though even the guests didn't realize it.

When the song ended, Macella started toward the scheming pair of Aegises. However, she was distracted by another arrival before reaching them. She saw from Aithan's and Finley's expressions that this late visitor had not been included in their careful plans.

Monarch Meztli drifted into the room with their customary quiet dignity.

"Your grace!" Macella bowed, genuinely pleased to see the middle monarch. "How did you find your way to this part of the castle and our unsanctioned festivities? I thought your royal spouses would keep you all evening."

Monarch Meztli smiled softly, letting Macella lead them to a nearby seat. "The gods decided to spare me tonight."

"I am glad you could join us," Macella said honestly. "It was supposed to be a quiet dinner for four, but then the instruments appeared, and it was like a siren's song."

Monarch Meztli laughed with her as she gestured around the room at the revelers. Captain Drudo was blushing as he danced a reel with Finley. Jacan's lute and Sir Griselda's fife filled the chamber with a spirited tune. Sir Kamau had taken a break from his fiddle to dance with Lucy. Even Lynn had somehow been coaxed into dancing with Aithan, though she was trying valiantly to maintain a stern expression.

"It was not the music that called to me," Monarch Meztli said. "The joy was impossible for me to ignore."

Macella nodded. "I would have sent for you had I known you were free. Might we expect any other members of the Crown to honor us with their presence?"

The middle monarch gave Macella a sidelong glance. Despite her polite tone, she knew that Meztli saw through the courtesy. Macella would rather eat glass than have this perfect evening interrupted by King Khari or Queen Annika.

"Queen Awa has been escorted back to her chambers, and Queen Annika convinced the king to give her a private audience," Monarch Meztli reassured her. "I am sure they will be occupied for some time. They have much to discuss."

Macella sighed in relief. "I almost admire the young queen's tenacity. She is very adept at getting her own way."

"Annika's most prominent characteristic is her skill at manipulating perception," Monarch Meztli said flatly. "People look at her and see the sweet young innocent or even the jealous, foolish brat. All the while, though, she is deceiving your senses, hiding her true nature."

Macella felt a little of the warmth leave the room. "And what is her true nature?"

Monarch Meztli shrugged delicately, spreading their hands. "I haven't the slightest idea. But enough of that talk. I know I cannot monopolize your time tonight. You are quite in demand."

Macella might've pushed for more information, but Captain Drudo was approaching, smiling his winning smile. Pressing Monarch Meztli's hand, Macella rose to meet her friend.

The captain bowed grandly and extended his hand. "Finally, you are disengaged!" he exclaimed dramatically. "May I claim a dance?"

Macella danced with every guest at their impromptu celebration, laughing herself breathless. Whether Sir Kamau and Jacan played a lively jig or Finley crooned a sultry ballad over Sir Griselda's mournful fife, Macella was moving, flying across the floor with the knights, twirling gracefully with Finley, or, best of all, swaying in the circle of Aithan's strong arms.

It was after the hour of Ix Chel when the revelry finally began to wane. Monarch Meztli kissed each of Macella's cheeks warmly before gliding from the room. They'd watched the evening's activity in a seemingly contented silence. Aside from short conversations with Macella or Aithan and calling for their goblet to be refilled, they had not mingled much. After the initial surprise of an unexpected monarch among them, the guests had relaxed and left Meztli to their peaceful voyeurism.

After Monarch Meztli departed, it wasn't long before others began to drift away. Flexing his fingers, Jacan declared himself exhausted, and tromped off toward the Aegis quarters. A few drunken knights were next to depart, leaning on one another for support. Soon, nearly everyone had gone.

"I will not join you for breakfast in the morning, darling," Finley announced, blowing Macella a kiss as they rose to leave. "I am planning to have a lively, late night. Perhaps, if I'm lucky, it'll carry over into a long, lazy morning. Captain, escort me to my room?"

Captain Drudo's face went crimson, but he stood to follow, kissing Macella's hand and saluting Aithan before following Finley from the room.

When the dining hall was empty save for the two of them, Aithan stood and stretched, extending a hand to Macella. She took it, still feeling wide awake and far from ready for the night to end. Her Aegis grinned knowingly and led her from the room.

Instead of moving in the direction of their chambers, he led her outside. There, they found Cinnamon and Jade saddled and ready, laden with suspiciously bulky saddlebags.

Macella shook her head and hiked up her skirt. "It seems you thought of absolutely everything," she said, kissing the corner of Aithan's mouth, which quirked into a smile.

"I have been thinking about this night for quite a while," he replied, helping her onto Cinnamon's back.

"Did the evening match your vision?" Macella asked, grinning up at the starry night sky.

"It was far better than I could have planned," Aithan said, patting Jade affectionately. "Though my one regret is that I could not arrange for Zahra to be here."

Macella had thought of Zahra Shelby that evening as well. With her mischievous wit and lively personality, she would've been a perfect addition to their party. Zahra had been the first friend that Aithan and Macella had made. She'd fought monsters at their side and taken many a pleasurable tumble in their bed. But Zahra was both the sheriff and vicereine of Shelby Park and couldn't simply leave her duties to galivant in the capital at a whim. Besides, while Zahra was exceptional, she was still human and vulnerable. Macella and Aithan had agreed never to give the Crown reason to target their dear friend and lover.

Macella patted Cinnamon who, along with Jade, had been a gift from Zahra—a reminder of her lovely, mismatched eyes. "She was with us in spirit. And we will celebrate heartily with her when we see her next."

Aithan nodded, then gave her a sidelong glance. "I thought we would return to the meadow where we married. Shall we race?"

Instead of answering, Macella tapped her heels against Cinnamon's flank, urging him into a gallop. Aithan and Jade were right behind them. Macella laughed breathlessly, the wind whipping her curls. She couldn't number how many times she and Aithan had raced this way back when they'd traveled the kingdom. It seemed like ages since they'd been this carefree.

Cinnamon and Jade were remarkably fast and intelligent horses. Macella thought they, too, seemed delighted to be flying through the night air. The poor things hadn't had as many chances to run full out since they'd taken up residence at Kōsaten Keep. It hardly took any time at all for them to find themselves back at their little clearing.

They settled the horses near the stream to drink and graze. Aithan spread a blanket near the stump Finley had left, then placed two goblets and a flask on the stump. He poured them both a drink, then raised his goblet in a toast.

"To our union," he proclaimed.

(33) Macella clicked her cup against his and then downed the wine. Aithan pulled her to him and kissed her hard. His mouth tasted of wine and his own sweet smoky essence. Macella slid her tongue into his mouth, molding her body to his. Aithan tossed his goblet aside and buried both of his hands in her hair. She moaned against his lips.

He slid his hands to her back, finding the laces of her bodice. She lifted her arms and let him pull the dress over her head. Then his hands were on her bare skin, and she felt heat spreading, growing from the places he touched. Macella unbuttoned his shirt and slid it off his broad shoulders, running her hands greedily over the chiseled muscles of his arms.

Her binder and his trousers were next to go, then their underwear, and then they were pressed skin to skin, nerve endings alive and buzzing. Aithan trailed kisses down Macella's neck and across her throat. She threw her head back and gazed up at the bright constellations of stars above them.

Aithan kneaded her ass, pressing her to him, his cock hard against her stomach. Macella felt electric and alive. She stood on tiptoes and wrapped her arms around his neck, pressing her mouth hungrily against his once more. Aithan groaned and lifted her from the ground. Macella wrapped her legs around his waist, kissing him frantically as he lowered her onto the blanket.

The stars seemed to glow brighter overhead as Aithan kissed his way from her mouth to her neck to her breasts. He buried his face in them, nuzzling the tender flesh and sending shivers through her at the scratchy sensation of his stubble against her sensitive skin. Taking a nipple into his mouth, he ran his hand down her side and over her hip to clutch her ass. Macella arched her back, leaning into the incredible sensation of his mouth on her skin.

Aithan licked a path from one nipple to the other, lingering to draw slow circles with his tongue, sucking and biting in turns. Macella moaned loudly into the warm night air, watching the stars pulse seemingly in rhythm with her cries of pleasure. Aithan hummed his satisfaction and Macella felt the vibration of his lips buzz across her skin, spreading through her torso, and settling in a warm pool in her belly. She tangled her fingers into his hair, squirming against him, feeling the answering throb of his erection against her leg.

"It is maddening how alluring you are," Aithan said gruffly. "I want to take my time and relish you tonight, the night you became my wife. But I want to be inside you so fucking badly."

Macella shuddered. She also wanted both of those things in equal measure. "How about you split the difference and relish me quickly?"

Aithan chuckled, shifting position so that he could trail kisses down her belly. Macella's breathing hitched, the butterflies in her stomach suddenly swooping in unison. The muscles in her vagina clenched hard. She writhed against the blanket, barely feeling it against her back. All of her senses seemed focused on the progress of Aithan's mouth.

"As you wish, wife," he replied with a wicked smile.

Then he was feasting on her, kissing her folds, licking every crevice, sucking gently on her clit. Macella arched her back, clutching at Aithan's hair, the blanket, the soft grass. She panted as her stomach filled with a glittering sensation as vibrant as the stars above. Aithan did not relent, his mouth moving hungrily, greedily, desperately as he hummed with pleasure.

Macella felt the frenzied, glittery, buzzing in her torso reach a fever pitch. Then the world seemed to invert, and she was falling into the multitude of stars. She cried out hoarsely, enveloped in the fire and majesty of their celestial bodies.

Before she could recover, Aithan's mouth was on her neck, kissing and biting, and then he was inside of her, filling her, pushing her orgasm to another level. Macella clutched at the hard muscles of his back, her thighs clamped tightly around his waist, her hips moving in time with his deep rhythmic thrusts. He moaned against her neck, sending a shiver zipping across her skin, igniting every nerve ending in its path.

Vaguely, Macella thought to herself, *this is my husband, my forever love, mine, mine, mine.*

Aithan groaned. He ran his hands up her arms, pulling them over her head and intertwining their fingers. "Tell me," he whispered, and Macella knew exactly what he meant.

"You're mine," she said, tightening her legs around him. "You're *mine*, my husband."

Aithan growled as though her words had unleashed him, moving faster, harder, and deeper as they lost themselves in one another. Macella clung to him as Aithan plunged into her over and over. Time disappeared and there was nothing but their union, their love, and the endless sea of stars around them.

Afterward, they lay on their backs, staring up at the night sky. Macella nestled against Aithan's shoulder feeling completely at peace. She couldn't wait to write about all of this in her hidden journal. She wanted to store up all the love and joy of the night. She would draw on it for strength against the obstacles ahead.

"Do you have any idea how incredible you are, Macella?" Aithan asked quietly, his voice breaking the comfortable silence.

Macella exhaled a laugh. "Tonight, of all nights, after you've given me the most perfect day of my life, you're calling *me* incredible?"

"Incredible day for an incredible woman," Aithan replied with a smile in his voice. "When we met, you ignored the well-meaning warnings from the other women, ignored your own fear, and gave me a chance. You confidently walked out of that brothel with me and stepped into the unknown. And you have never once looked back, no matter what challenges we've faced. You accepted my hand this evening, knowing our lives will likely never get easier, fearlessly stepping into the unknown once again. Incredible."

"You've led me to adventure, purpose, and the greatest love I've ever known," Macella answered. "I know this is where I am supposed to be. And it is where I want to be, no matter the difficulty."

Aithan pulled her onto his chest, wrapping her in his arms. He kissed the top of her head, burying his face in her curls. Macella sighed contentedly.

"Incredible," he repeated.

They made love again, slower this time. Under the stars with only the trees for company, Macella felt at home. She felt safe and free.

She had no idea that in a matter of days, she'd be reminded just how far they were from freedom and safety.

Chapter Twenty

The day of the ball soon arrived, bringing with it a bustle of activity and excitement. The oppressive mood that had plagued the Crown lately had finally lifted—likely because King Khari and Queen Annika were compatible in their love of ostentatious display. Macella assumed that Monarch Meztli felt better because their spouses did, and that Queen Awa would just be happy to be out of her confinement.

Nobody was more excited than Finley, however. According to the high tailor, they'd worried her half to death about their attire. As Lynn helped Macella into her ball gown, she listened sympathetically to the details of the many lengthy conversations the older woman had had with Finley. Despite her purported annoyance, Macella could tell the high tailor had a begrudging respect for the stylish Aegis. It was probably rare that she got an opportunity to bicker with someone with such good taste and ideas.

Macella, on the other hand, was happy to let Lynn make all of her fashion decisions. The high tailor was talented and creative, and she'd never failed to make Macella look stunning. Unsurprisingly, she'd had concocted the perfect ensemble for the evening.

Macella gazed at her reflection, feeling absolutely glamorous. Lynn had turned her into some kind of shimmering, ethereal nymph. The high tailor stood behind her wearing a satisfied grin.

"I know I say this every time," Macella whispered, "but you are truly a sorcerer. Every time I think you cannot possibly create anything more beautiful, you outdo yourself again."

Macella wore a sleeveless, floor-length gown made of hundreds of tiny, iridescent silver beads. The weight of the beads made the fabric cling to her frame, shifting subtly whenever she moved. Depending on how the light struck it, the dress gleamed shades of blush, turquoise, and lavender.

Lynn's assistants had pinned Macella's glossy silver and onyx curls to one side, securing them with jeweled silver combs. They'd painted her lids with glittery silver dust and lined her eyes with kohl. Even her lips shone with sparkly silver gloss. At her throat, she wore a wide necklace of moonstones on delicate silver chains. The iridescent gemstones shimmered and shifted colors in the light, accentuated by the matching moonstone bracelets circling her wrists.

"You look lovely," Lynn said matter-of-factly. "But you'd look beautiful in a grain sack."

Before Macella could thank her, Lynn herded her assistants out of the room. Macella heard the high tailor giving directions for final adjustments to the Crown's attire as the apprentices scurried behind her into the corridor, where music and voices mingled in the air with the rich scents of the impending feast. Guests from all of the neighboring cities had been arriving throughout the day to supplement the collection of nobles already residing at court.

When Finley arrived to escort Macella to the ball, her mouth fell open at the sight of them. Finley always possessed an otherworldly beauty, but they rarely had the opportunity or occasion to dress up. They'd clearly decided to make the most of this chance.

Their shiny silver hair fell around their shoulders, the sleek emerald ends blending into the satin of their surcoat. Their hair was pinned behind one ear, which was adorned with a gold cuff and a dangling jade earring. The jewel of their earring matched another they wore in a lace choker necklace around their pale throat. Their fingers were covered in scaly gold claws attached by delicate golden chains to a set of gold bracelets.

Beneath their emerald surcoat, Finley wore a lightweight black blouse with an elaborate, ruffled collar, and a long black tunic that rustled around their knees. A wide belt with a large gold and emerald clasp cinched and accentuated their small waist while black tights and boots completed the look. Finley's glossed lips turned up in a smile when they saw Macella's reaction.

"I know. Aren't I breathtaking?" they preened, batting their long lashes. Shimmery gold paint dusted their eyelids and traced their dancing orange eyes.

Macella laughed. "You are absolutely stunning, of course."

"Of course," Finley agreed, taking her hand, and twirling her around. She caught a whiff of their lovely honey and hazelnut scent and marveled at how anyone could be so naturally alluring. "And you look positively delicious! Honestly, if I'd met you before Aithan did, you'd probably be my wife by now."

"As if you could settle down," Macella retorted, rolling her eyes. "But thank you. I am flattered."

"I never said we'd be monogamous." Finley grinned. "But I would have snatched you right up. And I am smarter than Aithan, so I would've married you as soon as possible. Gods just look at you!"

Finley twirled her again, more slowly this time. Macella struck a few dramatic poses, eliciting Finley's warm, throaty chuckle. They kissed her hand, and took her arm, leading her into the corridor.

"Queen Annika is going to be furious," Finley said, sounding absolutely delighted by the prospect. "There is no way she'll be the center of attention with us in the room."

Macella giggled. She had thought the same thing but had felt petty for it. Finley's honest cattiness was one of the many things she loved about them. She felt a pang of loss knowing that their visit to the capital would soon end.

"I should be more charitable. I do feel sorry for the poor thing. All of this opulence and yet she still reeks of desperation," Finley added, obviously enjoying themself.

Macella covered her nose to stifle her snort of laughter. "Oh, Finley, I love that I can be my authentic self around you."

"The feeling is mutual, darling," Finley purred.

(34) When they entered the ballroom, it was as if they were bathed in a spotlight. Finley glided through the crowd, looking bored, aloof, and effortlessly beautiful. Macella knew that underneath that smooth expression, they were having a wonderful time. She tried to look as composed as they did but was sure she failed. The opalescent beads of her dress and her moonstone jewelry caught the light, making her shimmer angelically in a rainbow of soft colors. Contrastingly, Finley's black and emerald ensemble and gold claws gave them a darkly sexy allure.

"Lady Macella, Finley of Fairdale, you both look exquisite." Captain Drudo approached and bowed deeply, his dark eyes raking over them each in turn. "May I fetch you a drink?"

"Please do," Finley drawled, fixing their mischievous gaze on the captain. "I like my drinks like I like my lovers—dark, deep, and surprisingly sweet. Something that I can sip slowly and savor."

A deep blush spread across Drudo's face, and he stammered something nonsensical before turning to Macella. She wasn't used to seeing the young captain so flustered. She tried to hide her amused smile.

"That would be lovely, captain," she said. "I'll have the same."

Captain Drudo bowed and hurried away, leaving them to the crowd's stares and whispers. Nobles Macella had met during her time at court greeted her ostentatiously, eager to introduce her and Finley to their friends. While Macella was only as polite as the moment required, Finley had a bawdy, coy, or enchanting comment for everyone. By the time Drudo returned with their drinks, they were practically holding court, a throng of nobles clustered around them, vying for attention. Somehow, Finley showed every individual just enough interest to keep them engaged, but not enough to be sure which of the admirers they preferred.

After a while, Macella began to wish the Crown would make their entrance so the dancing could commence, and she could escape the inane chatter. She never would have talked to so many people, and for so long, had she attended the ball without her outgoing sibling. But when she watched Finley mesmerizing the gathered gentry, relishing in the role of the rose of the revelry, she did not so much mind the social demands.

"I have heard much about Macella of Shively." An unfamiliar noble took her hand, bowing, and kissed it. "It is a pleasure to finally meet you."

When he straightened, Macella saw that he was pale and plump, with thick blond waves, and bright blue eyes. Though his face was pleasant enough, she immediately disliked him.

She inclined her head. "I am afraid you have me at a disadvantage," she replied. "I have not had the honor of learning of you through any mutual acquaintances."

The man smiled, though it did not reach his ocean eyes. "Of course. I am Lord Kasper of Edgewood. I've only arrived today, but we will have plenty of time to get to know one another. My cousin has invited me for a lengthy stay at court."

Macella forced her smile to remain in place. "How fortunate for us all. Am I correct in deducing, then, that you are a relative of her grace, Queen Annika?"

"Guilty," Lord Kasper gave her an oily grin. "My cousin has certainly understated your beauty. You simply must save me a dance."

Macella felt her lip attempting to curl in disgust. Instead, she inclined her head again. "You flatter me, Lord Kasper."

"Flattery? Yes, I'll have some of that," Finley interrupted, ignoring their crowd of suitors, and sidling closer to Macella. "Has your cousin ever mentioned a gorgeous Aegis with flawless skin and cheekbones to die for?"

Luckily for Lord Kasper, the grand doors opened, and a herald announced the arrival of the Crown. King Khari escorted Queen Awa, who looked cold and distant in a sleek white gown, her bald head bare aside from her slim silver crown. Intricate patterns of silver paint crisscrossed her scalp, the design continuing onto her face in a mask-like shape around her downturned eyes.

The king wore a variation of her typical garnet and gold finery. Her garnet blouse was embroidered with golden adders. Its plunging neckline showed her glowing skin and the swell of her small, pert breasts. Her surcoat swept along the polished floor, its rich silk brocade whispering against the stone.

Monarch Meztli wore a patterned skirt of teal and bronze, beneath a teal tunic and bronze surcoat. Their lustrous black hair hung down their back in a thick braid. On their arm, Queen Annika looked miffed and lovely, her mass of blond waves falling freely, held out of her face with sapphire encrusted combs. Her gown had a massive skirt constructed of layers and layers of blue satin and gold tulle. Her pale shoulders were bare, and the low neckline of her bodice emphasized her full, firm breasts.

As the Crown began to dance, the guests vied for positions around the perimeter of the parquet. Finley gave the monarchs an uninterested glance, before excusing themself and slipping away in search of more wine. King Khari noticed the movement and her eyes found Macella. The king gave her an appreciative smile and inclined her head.

Macella tried not to squirm as many of the guests followed the king's gaze and gawked at her anew. She felt Queen Annika's glare, saw Lord Kasper observing the interaction from across the parquet. Perhaps she should've gone for more wine as well.

A hand rested on the small of her back. She relaxed, feeling a familiar warmth at her side. She looked up to see Aithan gazing down at her, his expression awestruck.

"You look angelic, little hell goddess," he murmured. "But none of the people looking at you right now are thinking pious thoughts."

"Well, we cannot expect everyone to worship me as you do," Macella teased.

Aithan smiled her favorite crinkle-eyed smile, trailing his hand lightly down her arm and intertwining their fingers. He was as resplendent as ever in his black and crimson dress uniform. Even so, Macella couldn't help but think about how much more enjoyable it had been to dance freely in their casual attire with a handful of friends and a makeshift band accompanying them. Aithan squeezed her hand in quiet agreement.

When the first dance ended and other couples began to crowd the parquet, King Khari moved immediately in Macella's direction. Aithan had slipped away to tend to his duties, leaving her with a promise to return to her side as soon as possible. As the king approached, Macella resignedly pasted a pleasant expression on her face.

(35) "As your escort, I claim your first dance," Finley declared, appearing at her side once more and taking her hand.

Macella started in surprise, having been too focused on the king to notice the other Aegis's silent approach. For her part, King Khari had been halted in her progress by Queen Annika, who had beelined for the king the moment she'd seen her royal wife's trajectory. With a tight smile, Khari bowed to her young queen and took her hand.

Finley proudly led Macella to a prominent position near the Crown, giving each monarch a polite bow as they passed. They patted their hair, discreetly tapping their temple at Macella as they found their spot in the dance. She knew it was an invitation to read their mind.

Everyone is watching us, just as they should be, Finley thought triumphantly. *Let's give them a show!*

Though she was much less excited about the many eyes on them, Macella couldn't resist Finley's infectious joy. When the music began, they twirled and turned her around the floor with such grace and gusto that few eyes followed any of the other dancers. With Finley's otherworldly loveliness and Macella's elegant beauty, the two were far too striking to ignore.

"The young queen is about to shit a shisa." Finley chortled, dipping Macella low, before pulling her into another fluid turn about the floor.

"What is a—" Macella began.

"Oh, it's a lion-dog hybrid creature that can ward away evil spirits or contain good ones," Finley answered lightly. "Do they not have that saying in the north?"

Macella giggled, catching a glimpse of Annika's sour expression. "Perhaps, but not in Shively. I quite like it though."

By the time the dance had ended, Macella felt as if she'd glided over every inch of the parquet and captured every eye in the room. Finley bowed grandly and slipped back into the crowd, ignoring the suitors that rushed forward to claim a dance. They certainly knew how to leave their audience wanting more.

"Lady Macella, your king will not be thwarted again," King Khari stated, appearing at Macella's side, bowing, and extending her hand.

Macella bowed and took the offered hand. She'd known that she could not avoid the king for long. She could feel the many eyes watching as Khari led her back onto the parquet. She looked around, wondering if the rest of the Crown had new partners. Unsurprisingly, Queen Annika was nearby with her cousin, Lord Kasper. They shared the same self-important, dissatisfied expression.

Monarch Meztli and Queen Awa were partnered for a second time. Macella wondered if this was a nice break from isolation for the elder queen, or if it was just as lonely in this room full of potential enemies and allies. Aithan had explained that Queen Awa had only been permitted to attend for appearance's sake and that she was under strict watch, only allowed to interact with the Crown and a choice few others, and never to be out of the king's sight.

"How is it that you manage to look more enchanting on every occasion?" King Khari asked, interrupting Macella's musings.

"As always, you flatter me, your grace," Macella replied politely. "The Crown employees the finest tailors and beauticians in the kingdom, and the high tailor is unmatched in her skill and creativity. I am simply a canvas for their artistry."

King Khari laughed heartily and shook her head. "Those same artists dress us all, and yet no other person in this room even comes close to rivaling your magnificence."

"My king, you are too charming for your own good," Macella demurred.

She looked away from the king and locked eyes with Queen Annika, who was close enough to overhear King Khari's compliment. The naked hatred on the young queen's face assured Macella that she'd felt the king's words as an insult to herself. Somehow, Macella knew it would not be the king who suffered Queen Annika's wrath. She wondered if Khari had intended to be overheard. Considering the two monarchs had been at odds of late, Macella wouldn't be surprised at the vindictiveness.

"I simply speak the truth, my dear. Though I will allow that Finley of Fairdale is looking remarkable as well," King Khari replied. "They certainly add some excitement to the festivities."

Macella couldn't help but smile. "That they do."

"I have been thinking that I am not yet ready to part with their company," King Khari said smoothly, twirling Macella into a lift, and then pulling her back into an embrace. "I plan to invite them to join us for our centennial tour north. With the Lord Protector's assistance, Finley can train young Jacan on life in the field, and then both Aegises can depart for their own duties on our return journey. What do you think?"

Macella tried not to look too excited by the prospect. "I think that is a lovely idea. And I am sure Finley, Aithan, and Jacan will all agree."

King Khari shrugged dismissively. "I am sure they will do their duty as I command it. But will it please you, my dear?"

Macella felt herself flush at the implication. Clearly, King Khari had noted her partiality for Finley and meant this extension of their visit as a gift for Macella. As much as she hated to accept anything from Khari for fear of what such "gifts" would truly cost long-term, she could not deny that this was precisely what she'd wanted. Hadn't she just been lamenting that their visit was close to its end?

"It would please me greatly, your grace," Macella admitted, lowering her eyes deferentially. "Thank you for the kindness."

King Khari beamed, her grip on Macella tightening slightly. "It pleases me to make you happy. You only have to ask for what you want, and I will grant it to you. Please keep that in mind in future. If you are to be my queen, you must grow used to having your desires met."

Macella did not know how to answer. The thought of being queen made her queasy. And she would never grow comfortable asking favors of King Khari, no matter how much the king pretended at kindness. She reminded herself that Khari was the most dangerous creature in Kōsaten. Glancing around at the other members of the Crown, it was easy to imagine that the king had made them similar promises, only to break those vows or use them to manipulate her spouses into bending to her will. Macella would not be fooled by compliments and false pledges.

"I desire very little, your grace," she answered carefully. "My life has already far exceeded the expectations anyone had for me or any I dared imagine for myself. How could I ask for more?"

King Khari laughed again. "You will learn. I always desire more. And I always get what I desire."

Macella shuddered inwardly at the possessive note in the king's voice and knew that Khari was already counting her among those acquired desires. The sliver of gratitude she'd felt for the king's invitation to Finley shriveled and died. She would never belong to this despicable woman, would not let the Aegises and the kingdom remain in her possession.

"When one is accustomed to getting everything one wants, possessions can lose their value," Macella countered. "How can you ever be satisfied with what you have?"

One corner of the king's mouth lifted in an amused half-smile. "It is quite simple, my lady. I will be satisfied when I have everything."

When the dance ended, Macella dodged her waiting suitors and went in search of Finley, eager to tell them of her conversation with the king. She saw Aithan speaking with members of the Royal Guard, and Captain Drudo leading Queen Awa to her seat on the raised dais. Jacan looked extremely uncomfortable surrounded by a group of chattering nobles.

"Okay?" Macella signed, widening her eyes in concern.

"Please kill me," Jacan discreetly signed back with a pained smile.

Macella snickered and mouthed *sorry* before continuing through the crowd. Finally, she spotted Finley in a dim alcove on the outskirts of the ballroom. They were leaning toward a pretty brunette, who stood against the wall staring raptly into their eyes, and looking as though she might swoon. Finley lifted their hand, tracing along the woman's jawline with one golden claw. The woman actually swayed a little, and Finley placed a hand on her waist to steady her, which didn't seem to help at all. Macella decided that their conversation could wait.

She found herself on the dance floor again sooner than she'd hoped. It felt like she danced with practically every noble in the keep. When she thought she couldn't stand one more pompous, fumbling fool, Aithan caught her eye from across the room.

You'll be free of them soon, he thought at her. *King Khari has just asked that Finley and Jacan prepare to exhibit.*

Moments later, King Khari called for refreshments and the guests took their seats. A parade of servants appeared with pitchers of wine and cider, and trays of assorted finger foods. Macella, Grand Mage Kiama, Grand Vizier Anwir, and a few distinguished visitors joined the Crown's table on the raised dais. To her chagrin, Macella was seated beside the king. She gratefully accepted a goblet of wine.

"For your entertainment and edification, the Crown presents an exhibition of might from our newest and one of our eldest Aegises," announced the herald, gesturing to the parquet. "Finley of Fairdale and Jacan of Prestonia!"

Macella leaned forward as the two Aegises took their places. They'd changed out of their finery and into leather armor. Finley lazily twirled their spear, looking aloof and unamused. Jacan gripped the wooden staff of a frightening-looking morning star. The iron spikes on the weapon's head were longer than Macella's fingers.

At King Khari's command, the two Aegises began to spar. Though Finley was clearly superior to Jacan in skill, the neophyte was resilient and put forth a respectable effort. He utilized his long reach to his advantage, forcing Finley to demonstrate their impressive agility as they gracefully evaded every strike. Still, Finley bested Jacan several times before they fought to a draw. The watching nobles gasped and exclaimed amongst themselves.

"My love," Queen Annika's high, sweet voice rose above the murmurs. "Do you not think it would be comforting to see how the Lord Protector fares against these impressive warriors?"

King Khari regarded the young queen coldly. "Why would that be necessary to my comfort, my queen?"

Hesitantly, Queen Annika leaned toward the king and placed a hand on her arm. King Khari looked from the hand to the young queen's ample bosom and, finally, her face. Her expression softened slightly.

"You are never frightened, my king, but I'm afraid I am not as brave. And, well, you surely recall what happened with Shamira." Queen Annika went on, lowering her voice. "We thought she was the strongest, but we were mistaken. How do we know this new Aegis and the graceful teacher Aegis do not exceed Aithan of Auburndale's skillset?"

King Khari sat back, studying Finley and Jacan contemplatively. Macella suppressed the annoyance and anxiety growing in her chest. She focused her attention on the parquet, afraid of what her face would show if she looked at Annika. The last time the young queen made such a suggestion, Shamira had been executed and Aithan had been appointed to her position. Would the king choose to risk Aithan's life once again to satisfy her queen's whim?

"A friendly exhibition might be entertaining," King Khari conceded. "Lord Protector, you wouldn't mind sparring with your comrades to assuage the queen's fears, would you?"

"Not at all, your grace," Aithan replied dryly. "The queen's comfort is my top priority."

Casually, he shrugged off his surcoat before pulling his tunic over his head to reveal the leather jerkin beneath. It seemed the Lord Protector had prepared for the possibility of a fight. Aithan moved to the parquet, drawing his sword. Finley and Jacan exchanged a glance, and Finley gestured for Jacan to take the first turn. Jacan drew his morning star again.

"I do not wish to endure two additional matches," King Khari declared, her voice laced with boredom. "The Lord Protector will face both opponents simultaneously. Begin."

The three Aegises fell smoothly into fighting stances, Finley drawing their spear. Macella's heart pounded hard against her ribcage. She was certain Aithan could best the other two Aegises. Her real concern was the battle's consequences. Would the punishment for the loser be execution? Was she witnessing the final minutes of life for one of the few people in the world that she loved?

Chapter Twenty-One

The match began, a blur of fast strikes and smooth evasions. As Macella had expected, Aithan held his own admirably. No matter how the other two Aegises attacked him, neither could land a blow, even when they advanced simultaneously. Aithan's speed and agility were simply unmatched. He dodged and parried almost effortlessly, again and again succeeding in disarming them or pressing his sword to his opponents' throats and hearts.

It did not take long for Queen Annika to grow bored. She called for more cider, distracted the others on the dais with inane chatter, and finally sighed heavily several times before King Khari decided to acknowledge her. Macella could see that the king was growing impatient with her young queen.

"My love, is the demonstration you requested not to your liking?" King Khari inquired politely, her ochre eyes cold.

"Well, it is clear that the Lord Protector is quite superior," Queen Annika said, tilting her head innocently. "But I wonder if his opponents are fighting quite as hard as they can. I am sure that they do not wish to injure one another. I believe that our Lord Protector is quite good friends with the pretty one."

Macella glared at Queen Annika, unable to hide her anger any longer. She could hardly stop herself from launching at the young queen and wrapping her hands around the vindictive snollygoster's pale throat. Instead, she clenched her fists in her lap, and focused on steadying her breathing.

"If it will wrap this up and soothe your worries, my love, then we will make sure they show their true capabilities," King Khari declared, a hint of irritation creeping into her tone. "Meztli, would you motivate Finley and Jacan, please?"

The star charm against her throat went cold, making Macella inhale sharply. She wasn't sure what was coming, but she knew it was not going to improve the situation. She caught Monarch Meztli's eye for just a moment, but it was long enough to confirm her fears. Their black eyes were full of apology.

(36) Then they turned their attention back to the battle. Their eyes went white. Macella tensed.

Finley's face suddenly went red, twisting into a mask of hatred Macella had never seen. Jacan wore a similar expression, his teeth bared at Aithan. With a roar, he charged at Aithan with renewed vigor. Finley sprung forward as well, their spear aimed for Aithan's heart.

Meztli's using their gift! This is no longer an exhibition, Macella thought frantically at Aithan.

Whether he'd identified the source of the change, Aithan had clearly already noticed the violent shift. His eyes had taken on a crimson glow. He took a defensive posture, his muscles coiled and his expression tight.

Finley sprang forward, twirling their spear from hand to hand before flicking the blunt end at Aithan's head. It grazed Aithan's ear as he parried it with his sword, then immediately caught the descending shaft of Jacan's morning star with his free hand. The young Aegis had brought it down hard with both hands, and Aithan's bicep bulged as he held the weapon at bay.

Finley swung their spear at Aithan's calves, sweeping his feet from beneath him. With the added weight of Jacan's morning star, Aithan couldn't regain his balance. Adapting quickly, he leaned into the fall, abruptly yanking the morning star down with him. Surprised by the sudden reversal of resistance, Jacan stumbled into Finley, knocking them both to the ground.

Aithan rolled and leapt back to his feet with his sword raised. The other Aegises were up almost as quickly, even more enraged than they'd been before.

Finley's spear pulsed with emerald light. They charged Aithan, spear aimed at his chest. Just as they reached Aithan, who was preparing to counter the attack, they dropped low and slid past him, gliding over the parquet on their knees. They were past him before he could turn, and he couldn't quite dodge the jab they took at his side. Macella saw him grimace as the sharp tip of the spear pierced his jerkin.

Aithan did not have a moment to react to the pain, because Jacan was stalking toward him again, and Finley was circling like a feline predator. Aithan went on the offensive, pushing Jacan back with swift sword strikes that the younger Aegis could barely manage to block in time. When Finley lunged forward again, Aithan spun back-to-back with Jacan, placing him in the path of the spear instead. Finley narrowly missed the young Aegis, before course correcting and resetting their stance.

Aithan meanwhile pivoted back around Jacan, bringing his free arm up at a right angle and slamming the back of his fist into the neophyte's face with audible force. Blood flew from Jacan's nose, and he staggered back. Aithan ducked under Jacan's arm, wrapping his own arm around the young man's chest. Before Jacan could recover his balance, Aithan lifted him and slammed him down hard. Jacan's back and head hit the parquet with a reverberating thump.

Then Finley and Aithan were clashing, the sound of colliding steel echoing through the ballroom, the two Aegises locked in a dangerous, deadly, and oddly beautiful dance. For a few minutes they seemed evenly matched, then Aithan spun beneath their crossed weapons, his sword scraping along the length of Finley's spear. He hooked an arm around their neck, but before he could complete the hold, Finley dropped to the ground, one leg extended gracefully. Finley planted their spear against the ground and used the leverage to lift themself and kick Aithan in the chest with one foot, and squarely in the mouth with the other, forcing him back.

As Aithan steadied himself, Finley put as much space between them as possible. They obviously knew they couldn't win a battle of brute strength. They couldn't allow Aithan close enough to grab them again. Aithan wiped blood from his lips as they circled one another, sizing each other up.

"Oh!" Queen Annika exclaimed, opening an ornate hand fan to shield her face. "As much as I desire the assurance that Aithan of Auburndale can defend us, I do not think I can watch such a violent display!"

Macella clenched her teeth but could not look away from the battle to glare at the manipulative young queen. She leaned forward, watching as Aithan deflected Finley's spear and spun to deliver a brutal elbow strike that sent the lighter Aegis sprawling. Back on his feet, Jacan roared and leapt forward, his morning star arcing down toward Aithan's head.

(37) Macella's star charm turned to ice. Time seemed to slow as she realized that something was terribly wrong. Instead of moving to evade or counter Jacan's attack, Aithan hesitated. Macella saw his eyes widen and felt a sudden panicked confusion emanating from his mind.

Move, Aithan! Macella pushed her thought into Aithan's mind, imbuing it with the force of compulsion. He took a stuttering sideways step, obviously still disoriented. The spiked iron head of Jacan's morning star passed inches from his face before slamming into his shoulder with a sickening crack.

Macella's strangled scream was lost in the noise of gasps and cries from the watching guests and Aithan's hissing growl of pain. Instinctually, Aithan switched his sword from his dominant hand and leaned backward into the momentum of the blow, kicking Jacan squarely in the gut as he fell. The morning star was jerked free as Jacan keeled over, and Aithan hit the ground hard, rolling into a crouch with his sword extended at his side, steadying him. Blood spread across his jerkin, the leather torn where the spikes had pierced it.

My senses are lost to me. Macella could hear the strain in her Aegis's mental voice. She prodded his mind, trying to understand what was plaguing him. He felt her searching and opened his mind more fully, showing her what he saw.

Or more accurately, what he could not see. Through Aithan's eyes, the world was white, as if blanketed in dense fog. The sounds of his audience and opponents were but a muffled staticky hum. He was engulfed in a bubble of absolute nothingness.

Macella fled from the awful blankness, her eyes darting frantically around the room. What was happening to Aithan? She saw Monarch Meztli's white eyes. Could they do such a thing?

Though he couldn't seem to hear or see, Aithan could definitely feel. He was carefully compartmentalizing the pain, but Macella could feel it searing hotly through his dislocated, lacerated shoulder. Her eyes snapped back to the parquet where both Finley and Jacan were advancing on Aithan again, their glowing emerald eyes still full of rage. Aithan remained crouched, his right arm hanging uselessly at his side. Finley twirled their spear menacingly, stalking around Aithan to approach from the opposite side. Aithan's head turned to follow them, perhaps using his sense of smell since he could not see his opponents.

I am your eyes. Macella clenched her fists and focused on reflecting a clear picture of the battle into Aithan's mind. Aithan stood slowly, cocking his head, and gripping his sword with his good hand. The Protector of the Crown raised his sword and slid into a fighting stance.

Finley and Jacan attacked at the same moment, Jacan's morning star again aimed for Aithan's head, while Finley's spear swooped toward his legs. Aithan leapt over the spear, swinging his sword to knock the morning star away. He landed lightly and spun toward Jacan, dropping at the last moment to sweep the young Aegis's legs. The pull of the deflected morning star threw Jacan even more off balance and he fell backward to the floor. His head hit the parquet again with frightening force.

Finley jabbed their spear at Aithan, and anyone but Macella likely thought they lost their balance when it jerked abruptly off course. Only she'd seen the flare of crimson in Aithan's sightless eyes as he used his telekinesis to make up for his missing arm, pushing the spear aside with his mind. Finley stumbled toward Aithan, who shot to his feet, forcibly driving the crown of his head under Finley's chin.

The crack of the impact seemed to echo through the ballroom. Finley staggered drunkenly before collapsing to one knee. They tried to stand but swayed sharply and fell over instead. Weakly, they managed to roll onto one side, and Macella could see that their eyes still glowed emerald with rage, but try as they might to rise, the blow had been too much. Meztli's influence could only go so far—it was clear that the fight was over for Finley.

Aithan stepped cautiously backward, his sword still raised. Neither of the other Aegises were back on their feet. Aithan slipped his sword into its holster. In a swift motion, he grabbed his right wrist with his left hand, pulled his injured arm high, bent the elbow, and jerked the arm down behind his head. The crowd gasped and squealed at the sharp pop of bone snapping into place.

Jacan stood slowly. Aithan grimaced and drew his sword again, still holding his injured arm against his side. Macella dared a quick glance away from the match to see the Crown's reactions. Queen Awa's hands were clenched in her lap, her eyes fixed on the fight. Monarch Meztli's blank eyes were turned in the same direction. Queen Annika still hid behind her fan, while King Khari leaned forward with eager interest.

Macella's eyes narrowed. Queen Annika was not the squeamish sort. She hadn't looked away from the vicious battle between Aithan and Shamira, nor had she seemed at all disconcerted while watching the latter be executed. Why would she orchestrate this mêlée only to miss the part she would most enjoy? She would certainly never pass on an opportunity to witness Macella in distress.

It hit Macella then—the only logical explanation. It was so obvious. Annika was behind Aithan's sudden sensory deprivation.

Annika's most prominent characteristic is her skill at manipulating perception, Monarch Meztli had said. *People look at her and see the sweet young innocent or even the jealous, foolish brat. All the while, though, she is deceiving your senses, hiding her true nature.*

That was Annika's gift. And she was using it now to hurt Aithan. Maybe Annika thought that, if Aithan were killed, Macella would have no reason to marry King Khari. Or maybe the young queen just hoped to cause Aithan, and thereby Macella, as much pain as possible. Regardless, Annika was Aithan's true opponent in this battle.

Macella would be damned if she'd let that bitch win.

She turned her attention back to the parquet, focusing on Jacan's advance toward Aithan. Aithan's skin looked ashen, and his jerkin was slick with blood.

Macella could feel her own blood boiling. She fought to keep her onyx flames at bay.

Land a blow to his head, she thought at Aithan. *I'll do the rest.*

Jacan swung his morning star, targeting Aithan's injured arm. Aithan sidestepped the blow. Jacan tried again, and again Aithan dodged the blow. Then, suddenly, he surged forward, aiming the pommel of his sword at the young Aegis's head.

SLEEP.

Macella channeled all of her rage and anxiety into pushing the command into Jacan's mind. Jacan stumbled, his eyes rolling back into his head. He dropped his morning star and collapsed.

The guests erupted in applause. Aithan sheathed his sword. He stepped over the prone Aegises to face the dais.

Eyes on Queen Annika, he bowed deeply. "Is my queen satisfied?" he asked, his polite tone belying the fury in his orange eyes.

Annika lowered her fan. Macella felt Aithan's senses flood back in a rush. His eyes snapped to hers, and Macella was filled with a mutual surge of emotion. They had survived again due to their secret, unique gifts. Their Fates did not end in this ballroom. Not this day.

Macella saw with satisfaction that Queen Annika held her closed fan in a clenched, trembling fist. She nodded stiffly, her mouth a thin, hard line.

The king smiled widely, standing, and clapping her hands. The crowd joined her for another round of uproarious applause.

"Well done, Lord Protector," King Khari praised when the cheers had quieted. "You truly impress your rulers. My spouses and I may rest easily tonight and every night. We know beyond a doubt that we can entrust our safety to you."

Aithan hit his fist against his chest, only grimacing a little at the jolt to his injuries. Queen Annika looked as if she'd bitten a lemon, but she remained silent. She even managed to clap lightly with the other guests.

"Fetch the medical mages, quickly," King Khari commanded. "More wine for everyone! Let the meal commence with a toast to our mighty warriors! Musicians, a lively tune!"

With that, the festivities recommenced. Aithan, Finley, and Jacan were led or carried from the chamber by a group of medical mages. The guests moved freely around the room, talking, eating, dancing, and drinking with renewed vigor. It made Macella want to scream with rage or collapse into bed from exhaustion. For them, that battle was a spectacle, an edgy entertainment, not the fight for survival it had been for the Aegises. It was disgusting.

"Go on. Go to him." King Khari's voice interrupted Macella's brooding.

"Your grace?" she replied, smoothing her expression.

King Khari smiled knowingly and waved her away. "You've done your duty this evening. You may be excused."

"Thank you, your grace," Macella replied gratefully.

She stood to leave, but then thought better of it. Turning back, she caught Queen Annika's eye, briefly letting her rage show on her face. Then she quickly rearranged her expression into a warm smile and bowed low to the king. Trailing her fingers over the king's wrist, Macella took her hand and kissed it.

"Thank you for a lovely evening, my king," Macella said, glancing up at Khari through her lashes.

Surprised, King Khari held Macella's hand for an extra moment, her gaze intense. Macella straightened slowly, inviting Khari's eyes to trace her curves as she stood above the seated sovereign. Gently, she pulled her hand away. King Khari's eyes followed as Macella ran her hands over her waist and hips, pretending to smooth nonexistent creases from her dress.

"The pleasure has been all mine," the king answered, her ochre eyes still intently studying Macella.

Without bothering to spare Queen Annika another glance, Macella left the ballroom, certain that there were many eyes watching her go.

When she reached their chambers, she found all three Aegises within. The medical mages appeared to be finishing up their ministrations. Jacan sprawled on the sitting room sofa, grimacing as he sipped from a steaming mug. A mage busied herself nearby, gathering up bandages and vials.

"How are you feeling?" Macella signed, looking him over anxiously.

"I have been beaten much worse," Jacan answered ruefully, signing sluggishly with one hand. "The mages healed most of my injuries right up, and this henbane is taking away the pain of those that remain. My head feels nice and fuzzy. This stuff works fast. It tastes like kappa ass though."

Macella laughed and shook her head. Jacan raised his mug in salute. She left him to it, eager to check on Finley and Aithan. She found them both in the bedchamber, lying in the huge bed. A second mage was gathering up empty vials and clean bandages. He nodded to Macella as he and the other mage left.

Aithan and Finley appeared to be sipping the same elixir as Jacan, and based on their identical looks of disgust, they agreed with the young Aegis's assessment of its taste. Aithan was propped against a mound of pillows, his hair falling loose around his face. He was shirtless, allowing Macella to take in the medical dressing covering his shoulder and side. Despite the spike of worry that she felt at the sight of the bandages, his color had returned to normal, and he smiled softly when he saw her.

"Are you alright?" she asked uselessly, crossing the room to stand at his bedside. "I mean, does it hurt?"

"It's horrible," Finley replied dramatically.

They lay stretched out on Macella's side of the bed, their hair spread artfully around them, gleaming silver against the crimson linens. They had one arm draped over their eyes.

Peeking from beneath their sleeve, they sighed heavily and affected a sultry pout. "I was absolutely exquisite tonight, and yet I had to leave the party at intermission because of some kuja with an inferiority complex," Finley complained. "It is painfully unfair."

Macella shook her head and turned her attention back to Aithan. "Before I engage in the foolish conversation our sibling has started, are you gravely wounded?"

Aithan took her hand, brushing his lips lightly over her knuckles. "I am fine. The wounds will heal rapidly. I'll be back to full functionality in a week. Were my injuries less severe, they'd already be gone."

He cast a sidelong glance at Finley, who heaved another dramatic sigh. They uncovered their face and propped themself up on their elbows. A frown marred their lovely features.

"What in the absolute fuck was that?" Finley demanded. "I felt completely out of control. It was—"

They broke off, shuddering delicately. Macella felt a wave of revulsion. To be manipulated that way—practically puppeted—was a deeply upsetting violation. Fiercely independent, Finley obviously felt the same way.

"It was Monarch Meztli," Macella explained. "Their gift from the gods allows them to influence emotion. Khari made them use it."

Finley scowled. "Oh, I heard Queen Annika quite clearly. I know it was ultimately her doing."

For a moment, Macella saw her own hatred of the young queen reflected clearly on Finley's pretty face. Then they sighed and collapsed onto their back once more. Their expression shifted back into elegant boredom.

"I will have my revenge on the young queen," they said coolly. "But Aithan of Auburndale cannot rightfully hold a grudge against me. I was but a powerless pawn of the monarchy."

"Aren't we all?" Aithan muttered bitterly.

"No," Macella said, squaring her shoulders defiantly. "They believe we are playing their game. By the time they realize we've been rewriting the rules, they will have already lost."

Finley uttered a low laugh. "It is adorable how sincere you are. I really could marry you."

"Get in line," Macella quipped, rolling her eyes. "And stop laughing at me. I am quite serious. We will be the victors. We simply have to trust Fate."

"When I'm back in Duànzào with Diya and Kai, I'm going to miss all of this plucky determination," Finley drawled. "I wish I could take you with me."

Macella smiled brightly, remembering King Khari's offer. "It is you who will be coming with me! The king wants you and Jacan to join the centennial tour."

Finley sat up quickly, their eyes wide with excitement. Macella relayed her ballroom conversation with the king. The news seemed to perk Aithan up a bit.

He kissed Macella's hand again, grinning at his sibling. Though they tried to look aloof, she could tell that Finley was thrilled by the invitation.

"Well, it's the least the king can do, considering how she sabotaged my ball," they sniffed.

"*Your* ball?" Macella laughed.

Finley ignored her. "Every noble who hosts us on our way will have to throw lavish parties to honor the Crown. I am going to be the rose of every revelry!"

The thought seemed to cheer them up completely. Finley leapt to their feet and waltzed about the room. They grabbed Macella and twirled her until she dizzily escaped and collapsed onto the bed. Exhaustion washed over her in a sudden rush.

"Pardon me, my lady," a small voice interrupted.

Macella sat up and found Lucy hovering near the bedroom door. "What can I do for you, Lucy?"

"Finley of Fairdale, Lady Bronwyn is asking for you." Lucy blushed. "I told her you were probably resting on account of your injuries, but she's quite insistent that you requested to see her tonight."

Finley grinned widely. "Thank you, Lucy. Could you have someone show her to my room and tell her I will be with her momentarily?"

Lucy bowed and scurried away.

Finley patted their hair and pinched their cheeks, peering into a looking glass on a side table. They turned back to Macella and Aithan and gave an exaggerated bow. "This evening may yet be salvaged," they said with a wink. "Good night, darlings. I will drop young Jacan back at his chambers. Get some rest, Aithan of Auburndale. I *am* sorry about your side."

They blew a kiss and drifted from the room. Moments later, Macella heard the outer chamber door click shut behind them. She started to undress. Then, thinking better of it, she left the room to bolt the chamber door. She needed at least the illusion of security tonight.

Aithan gave her a long look when she returned but made no comment. He watched Macella as she slipped from her dress and freed her curls. She washed her face, cleaned her teeth, and pulled on a gown, feeling the weight of the day's events settling into her bones.

Then Aithan opened his good arm to her, and she climbed into bed, and curled against him. He held her close, burying his face in the crown of her head. Macella rested her head against his chest and listened to his heartbeat. It was as steady as ever.

For the first time all evening, Macella felt safe. She fell asleep to the familiar music of her husband's heart.

Part 3
A Shield, A Scribe, A Sword, A Pen

What a heavy calling it is—the call to rule. How can one person bear the responsibility of such vast power and control? What selflessness is required to give all of yourself to the benefit of others, to take the burdens of a people as your own and act always to advance their best interests? Blessed is the kingdom of Kōsaten, for we shall always have leaders willing to fight for our progress, peace, and prosperity.

But who is this Macella of Shively? Some know her as the daughter of poor herb harvesters. Others claim she's a headstrong, idealistic dreamer who never quite fit in. Still others say she's a whore turned wanderer, who took up with an Aegis after her first night of work.

Dear readers, I can tell you who she is. She is all of those things and none of them. Most importantly, she is someone who has known hunger and cold, loss and desperation, poverty and oppression. And she will make it her mission to ensure <u>ALL</u> of Kōsaten's citizens live free of such hardships.

-Anonymous Source, Society Paper Exclusive, Hot Season, Year of the Serpent

Chapter Twenty-Two

Dearest Zahra,

Please accept my apologies for any delays in correspondence. Hopefully, my last letter reached you in enough time to alert you of our departure for the north. I wish that we were on our way to Shelby Park or that we would at least pass near enough that I could slip away and pay you a visit. As lovely as this journey with the Crown is proving to be, I must admit that I am less than thrilled about our destination. I anticipate little pleasure in being among my kin...

Macella sighed as she sealed her letter and handed it to the waiting servant. Even when they were not near a town, someone was always ready to ride ahead or venture back to the nearest village to post letters and purchase whatever the Crown demanded. There was so much correspondence—letters to and from Kōsaten Keep, announcements to local nobles warning of their impending arrival, and the many missives to allies across the kingdom that King Khari always seemed to be writing.

Macella had done her best to prepare her family to receive a visit from the king. She didn't know how to soften the shock of her imminent engagement announcement. Even more worrisome was her utter loss as to how she'd explain her relationship with Aithan. While polyamory was perfectly normal, polyamory between a lowborn woman, an Aegis, and a king was atypical, to say the least.

Macella honestly couldn't decide which they would find more shocking: her engagement to the king or her intimacy with an Aegis. She wondered how much of the scribe's work they'd read and if it had influenced them as it had others in the kingdom. If they were as uninformed and close-minded as they'd been when she'd left home, it would be Aithan of Auburndale that most concerned them.

Macella did not care whether they approved or not, but she wanted to spare Aithan any unkindness from her family. And, as much as she hated to admit it, she found herself a bit embarrassed. Aithan had never seen her among her kin, had never seen the conditions from whence she'd come. She knew she shouldn't be ashamed of her modest roots but that only made her feel more ashamed of herself for feeling ashamed.

"Ugh!" Macella flopped against the seat cushions, exasperated with herself.

The servant had long since left with her letter to Zahra, and she was still sitting in her stuffy carriage ruminating on her worries. The convoy plodded steadily along, but it would be at least two days before they reached another sizable township where they would honor the local nobility with their company.

"Knock, knock," a welcome voice drawled.

Macella sat up and saw Finley's lovely face peering in her carriage window. They looked especially striking atop a gorgeous chestnut horse, their silver hair streaming behind them in the breeze.

Macella smiled widely, immediately grateful for her good fortune in having Finley along on this journey. "I could not be more delighted to see you!" she exclaimed. "Are you free to train?"

Finley gave her a long-suffering look. "There are so many delightful things about me, and you choose to use me for my teaching abilities. I do plenty of training when confined to Smoketown and Duànzào, you know? Out here, we could actually be doing *fun* things."

"Training with me is fun, and you know it," Macella retorted. "We gossip the entire time, and you get to show off."

Finley rolled their eyes. "That nervous little stableboy is bringing Cinnamon around for you as we speak. Get dressed."

Macella smiled again and set about getting ready. The best parts of her days were often spent with Finley, training and talking. Sometimes, she'd accompany them as they prepared Jacan for the nomadic life of the shields—the Aegises who patrolled the kingdom in search of rifts in the veil between worlds. Since Macella had no formal Aegis training, these lessons were incredibly useful to her, despite Finley's apparent boredom. Even with restraining herself to human speed during combat training alongside Jacan, she felt her sword-wielding skills improving rapidly.

Other times, she and Finley wandered deep into the countryside alone. There, far from prying eyes, Macella would train full out, exploring the limits of her Aegis speed and strength, as well as her gifts of invisibility and telepathy. To her surprise, she discovered that she was more than a match for Finley, especially since she could peek into their mind and anticipate their next move. Finley grumbled about unfair advantages, but Macella knew they enjoyed the added challenge. Plus, they loved the way Macella marveled at their expert workmanship on her new sword.

Now, Macella dressed quickly, relishing the feel of her daggers on her thighs and the weight of her sword on her back. As much as the nobility praised her appearance when prancing around ballrooms in elaborate gowns, Macella felt much more herself while in trousers and wielding steel. She leapt from her carriage without bothering to ask the driver to stop and was galloping away astride Cinnamon before the old servant could fuss at her for it.

Don't be late for dinner. Khari has a lot to say today.

Macella glanced back, spotting Aithan watching her from his position beside the king's carriage. She could feel his longing to escape with her but knew he would stay behind. Ensuring the Crown's safety while traversing the kingdom was an all-consuming task. Though he had done everything he could to plan a safe route and prepare his knights for all eventualities, there was still always much to be done.

The weeks since the ball had passed in a blur of preparations. Traveling with the Crown was absolutely nothing like traveling with Aithan had been. Every servant in the keep had worked around the clock to prepare the Crown's massive caravan. Macella had never seen such arrangements. There were entire wagons of food and drink, carriages dedicated to individual wardrobes, and humongous carts where fresh horses rested, so that the convoy only ever had to stop when it pleased the king. They seldom slept on the road since, as Finley had predicted, every lord, lady, and laird on their path eagerly hosted them, throwing lavish parties in their honor.

Even camping in the countryside was elegant in the Crown's company. Macella had been given her own massive carriage for the journey, equipped with every possible luxury. The plush seats extended and reclined for comfortable sleeping, while a curious assembly of cogs and pulleys operated a system of fans, helping to keep the carriages cool despite it being the height of the hot season.

When Finley and Jacan weren't training or helping protect the convoy, they shared a smaller but still fairly luxurious carriage. The Royal Guard was less lucky, sleeping four to a carriage, and enjoying fewer amenities. The servant accommodations were even more crowded, with up to eight people occupying a single carriage. Macella felt guilty in her huge coach, knowing the servants' carriages must be unbearably hot—perhaps worse than the overcrowded rooms she'd once shared with her siblings.

The farther north they traveled, the more Macella's thoughts strayed to her family. Would they find her uppity and pretentious when they saw her in all her finery? Macella would've been comfortable sleeping under the stars with Aithan, but King Khari would never have allowed it. For his part, Aithan didn't seem to mind the unnecessary luxury of their transport.

"Do not poke a pixiu in the pouch," he told her when he lay beside her their first night on the road. "I enjoyed our nights beneath the stars immensely, but I could get used to sleeping like this."

Gradually, Macella had indeed gotten used to the comfort. She felt a little less guilty about it after spending time in the Crown's carriages, which were as far above her quarters as hers were above the servants' carriages. Queen Awa's transport was furnished almost entirely in satin and silks, all in shades of cream and ivory. Macella couldn't imagine how the servants kept it so pristine despite the dirt and dust of the roads, but she suspected there might be magic involved. Queen Annika's carriage was even lusher, if that were possible, her furnishings all rich blues and golds, and kept cooler than should've been possible given the heat of the season. King Khari's was largest of all, complete with garnet and gold furnishings and even a mahogany desk with built-in shelves of books.

Monarch Meztli had stayed behind to oversee matters at the keep, with the assistance of the small council. Some of the other resident nobles had remained at court as well, including Queen Annika's newly arrived cousin, Lord Kasper. Though Macella suspected the young queen and Lord Kasper were conspiring for the ailing Lord Theomund's position as Grand Treasurer, she was still relieved to have only one annoying transplant from Edgewood to contend with on this journey.

"Your mind is wandering, Macella," Finley scolded. "Start that sequence again."

Macella sheepishly refocused on the present, and the training session she'd been so eager for. She and Finley did not have long to work, as the sun was already dropping lower in the sky, and they would soon be forced to return to camp. They would need extra time to wash away the training session and dress appropriately for the evening.

Even before Aithan had warned her, Macella knew dinner would be a grand affair. Lucy had been harried that morning because the king had sent last-minute demands for an extravagant feast. That meant the servants would have to erect a huge pavilion and set it up to mimic a true dining hall.

"I apologize," Macella reset her position and began the drill again. "I am just dreading the silliness of this evening. It is such a waste of time and resources for us to have these elaborate meals—as if we aren't all sick of each other and wouldn't rather spend the time getting closer to our destination."

Finley grimaced, somehow making the expression elegant. "I must agree with you. I would much rather get to a place with an actual dining hall and proper ballroom."

"How are you not yet weary of parties?" Macella asked exasperatedly. "This journey has practically been nothing but one long ball!"

"You have grown accustomed to the good life, Lady Macella." Finley sniffed indignantly, tossing their hair. "May I again remind you that life in Smoketown and Duànzào is utterly devoid of entertainment?"

"Well, you are making up for it admirably," Macella teased. "I do not know how you charmed your way into an extended visit complete with a string of parties. It's honestly impressive."

"I do believe charm is my true gift," Finley mused, adjusting Macella's arm slightly and motioning for her to run the drill again. "Apophis's blessing is not nearly as useful to me as my innate people skills."

Macella rolled her eyes. "Most people would be awed and excited by the ability to shift their appearance at will."

"My dear, when this is my natural form, why would I ever desire to change it?" Finley replied incredulously, gesturing at themself with a grand sweeping motion. "It certainly wasn't my transfiguration skills that earned me this vacation."

Macella snorted a laugh. Finley was the most confident person she had ever met, and she loved it about them. They'd endured so much over a very long and arduous life, yet they carried themself with an unmatched lightness. It was heartening to know someone who was so secure in themself, despite the best efforts of the powerful to make them feel small. Not even the Crown could crush Finley of Fairdale.

"Your transfiguration skills rival any magic I've ever witnessed," Macella said. "Not even the Grand Mage can change her appearance at will."

"Grand Mage Kiama has bigger problems. She's probably still fuming about being left behind," Finley replied. "I know I would be. It is unheard of for the sovereign of Kōsaten to travel without their Grand Mage in attendance."

Macella sighed, reminded that the centennial tour hadn't changed the king's nefarious plans. Aithan had overheard King Khari and the Grand Mage discussing the trip. The Grand Mage had been incensed, but the king had quickly subdued her.

"If you should uncover the information I've asked for before we depart, you're welcome to join us," King Khari had said smoothly. "Otherwise, you will remain here where you can focus on your work. When I return, you will relieve me of my now long-standing disappointment, or I will relieve you of your duties. I have been patient, but I will not continue to be impeded by your incompetence."

Aithan and Macella had given the Grand Mage a description of Aithan's mother, claiming that his childish memories didn't include her name. They didn't know if there were records of the Aegis's appearance, but either way, the Grand Mage obviously hadn't been able to put the information to much use. Macella didn't know if the samples she'd ruined were at fault or if the magic necessary to create crossbreed children was truly that difficult. Either way, she knew the Grand Mage would eventually discover the secret to spawning Aegisborn children. And then their time would be up.

"I hope the Grand Mage is wasting her time fuming rather than completing the king's task," Macella told Finley, reluctantly sheathing her sword. The sun had dropped even lower, and they would need to make haste back to camp if they were to be decent for dinner.

"For her sake, she'd better not be," Finley rejoined darkly. "If she fails King Khari, it will likely be the last thing she ever does."

Chapter Twenty-Three

Macella was still thinking about those words when Aithan arrived to escort her to the pavilion for dinner. It was reassuring to lean into his familiar warmth and breathe in his familiar scent. It made her feel a little less terrible about the certainty that, no matter what happened in their rebellion against Khari, people were going to be hurt and killed.

"Every time you ride off with Finley, I wish I was in their place," Aithan said, planting a kiss atop her curls. "I have not had nearly enough time with you on this wretched journey."

Macella smiled softly, immediately soothed from her troubled thoughts. It was true that she and Aithan had less alone time than they were accustomed to. He spent much of his time diligently directing the Royal Guard in protecting their caravan from any dangers, human or demon. Yet he never asked his knights to do anything he would not do himself. He took as many night shifts and countryside patrols as any of the guards, while somehow keeping up with every new development or concern from the knights or the Crown. Furthermore, he still spent long, tedious hours in meetings with the king, assisting in her management of kingdom matters. He could probably allow himself more free time without anyone faulting him for it, but it simply was not his way.

"Every time you disappear into Khari's carriage, I wish I was in *her* place," Macella countered, running her fingers along his arm. "She keeps you away half the night, while I lie alone in bed, missing your touch."

"Hmmm," Aithan hummed thoughtfully. "Where exactly would you like me to touch you?"

Macella felt her cheeks grow hot. She'd meant it innocently enough, but now her thoughts turned in a more intimate direction. She was suddenly very aware of Aithan's biceps straining the fabric of his shirt, of his lips quirking into a knowing smile, and the way his orange eyes darkened with desire. She swallowed hard.

"That is not appropriate dinner conversation," she murmured, as the lights of the pavilion grew brighter ahead. "I will happily discuss it later."

Aithan breathed a low chuckle, kissing her temple, before brushing his lips against her ear. "I'm going to hold you to that."

Macella shivered as his breath brushed against her ear. Warmth pooled in her belly and spread across her skin. She contemplated turning around and leading him right back to their carriage. But it was too late. They'd drawn too near the pavilion and a servant was already approaching to escort them to their seats.

Tables covered in heavy, rich fabric had been arranged in a horseshoe, with the Crown seated at the very center, Captain Drudo standing at attention behind them. To Macella's relief, she and Aithan were seated at one of the side tables, rather than with the Crown.

They'd had a few more notable nobles join their party along the journey, and it was these guests who'd been placed in the seats of honor near the Crown tonight. The king had charmed her guests with the assurance that she valued their presence on her centennial tour and wanted them to witness an important announcement. Macella knew, however, that King Khari had strategically invited key allies to travel north, intending to show the northerners that many important citizens remained loyal to the Crown.

Soon, the other Aegises and a few regulars from the Crown's entourage joined Macella and Aithan's table. Macella half attended to their polite conversation. The majority of her mind was occupied with thoughts of where she would ask Aithan to touch her when they were finally alone. Beside her, Aithan's face remained blandly polite, but she could feel his attention on her, attuned to her mood, listening intently to her lascivious thoughts. She had a mischievous urge to slip her hand beneath the tablecloth and check to see just how attuned he was.

Aithan cut his eyes at her. Their warm orange hue had darkened to deep amber and taken on a crimson tint. Yes, he was absolutely in sync with her at present.

I hope no one asks me to stand any time soon—otherwise everyone will know exactly what has been on my mind, Aithan thought at her accusingly. Macella hid a smile.

A parade of servants entered the pavilion, filling it with the mingled scents of rich foods. The assembly ate in the candlelight as the sun disappeared and the evening deepened. The food was delicious, as always, but Macella only wanted the meal to end so that she and Aithan could be alone.

Unfortunately, when the meal was over, King Khari began to talk. She'd called this formal dinner for a reason, after all. As Macella daydreamed, the king lectured them all on the importance of this centennial tour, their mission in the north, and the legacy she hoped to leave behind when her reign finally came to an end.

"The gods favored me long before I came before them in pursuit of the blessed throne." King Khari's low, husky voice somehow rang through the pavilion. "From a young age, they showed me visions of a different world from the one I inhabited. A world that it was my Fate to forge and rule."

The tent was silent aside from the gentle breeze and the distant calls of night creatures. Nearly every eye watched the king intently and, seemingly, every mind was likewise engaged. But as Macella drifted in and out of her own internal fantasies, she noticed Queen Awa glance in her direction.

"There were those who believed in my cause and others who doubted me, but I never lost sight of my vision," King Khari went on. "I surrounded myself with my greatest admirers and most critical foes alike, because I knew that I would never allow such people to see me fail. And thus, I have attained a century of unmitigated success."

King Khari gazed around the room, her eyes lingering an extra second on Macella before resting on each of her current queens in turn. She regarded them with quiet curiosity for a long moment, saying nothing. The closer they drew to the north, the more introspective the king seemed to grow. Macella wondered if, in her way, King Khari was grieving the coming loss of her eldest queen. Surely sharing a century of life with another person had to have some impact.

"You are all here because I consider your good opinion to be valuable. You are among those I most wish to witness my success—those who will write and sing and speak of my legacy," King Khari intoned solemnly, gazing into her goblet. "My greatest admirers. My most critical foes."

The king let the silence stretch to an uncomfortable length. Macella could feel the tension in the air as everyone strove to remain as motionless as possible, no one daring to break the stillness.

Finally, King Khari lifted her head and smiled brightly. The assembled guests seemed to release a collective breath.

"I have accomplished many things I am proud of during my reign," King Khari boasted, unrolling a parchment she'd pulled from within her surcoat. "I am certain you won't mind indulging your king this evening as I detail a few that I hope will be remembered by the bards and scribes?"

Macella groaned internally. After her required history lessons and other training for her position as Royal Scribe, she could probably recite this list herself. She was definitely going to retreat back into her lustful fantasies rather than endure this self-gratulation. She glanced at Aithan, surprised to find him gazing at her, eyes full of wicked intent.

(38) *Keep your eyes on the king and try not to squirm*, Aithan thought. Macella felt a warm hand on her knee beneath the table. She tried to look captivated by King Khari's words, but her heart was racing, her attention focused on the progress of Aithan's hand.

She felt him stealthily gathering up her skirt until he was able to slip his hand beneath it. His touch on the bare skin of her thigh made her shiver. She willed herself not to move as his hand slid higher.

Open your legs, Aithan commanded mentally.

Macella held her breath and obeyed. Aithan slipped his hand between her thighs and ran his fingers lightly over her mound through the lace of her panties. Macella's stomach clenched. Tendrils of desire unfurled in her belly. She stared at the king without understanding a single word she spoke.

"By expanding the network of mages supported by the Crown, we have greatly improved quality of life throughout Kōsaten," King Khari claimed, scanning her parchment.

Aithan pushed her panties aside and pressed his fingers against her clit. Macella hurriedly took a sip from her goblet to stifle a gasp. No one at her table seemed to notice. Finley gazed indifferently past the king, their mind obviously elsewhere, whereas Jacan was focused on the young woman signing near the king. Everyone else seemed enthralled by the king's speech or their own drinks.

"Trade relationships across the kingdom are stronger than at any point in Kōsaten's history, as a direct result of the creation of the Crown and its reinforcement of our union."

Aithan moved his fingers deftly, expertly massaging her clit. Macella wanted to move her hips, wanted to pant and moan. She settled for gripping her goblet tightly with one hand, while the other made a tight fist in her lap.

His attention seemingly on the king, Aithan rubbed two fingers against her wetness, then used it to continue stimulating her clit. Macella choked on her wine, drawing a few brief glances from those around her. She gave what she hoped was an apologetic smile and covered her mouth with her napkin.

"Our kingdom has never been safer," King Khari asserted. "Our army, the Royal Guard, and the Thirteen protect us from every possible foe, be they corporal or ephemeral."

Aithan did not relent, his fingers moving in delicious rhythm against her clit. Macella shifted as subtly as possible. Her nipples stiffened and strained against her corset, her pussy clenching, seeking Aithan's probing fingers. She unclenched her fist and clutched his wrist through the fabric of her skirt—not trying to stop him yet needing something to hold onto to keep her from writhing in her chair.

"I solidified us after my predecessor's reign ended in discord and dissension," the king boomed. "I have kept us united, protected, and prosperous for one hundred years."

Aithan moved his fingers faster, applying firmer pressure to her clit. Macella's breathing had grown shallow. She struggled to keep it quiet, her grip spasming on Aithan's wrist. It took all of her willpower not to grind against his hand, to cry out her pleasure. The agony was absolutely delicious.

"My rule and my will shall keep us united, protected, and prosperous for the next century and every century thereafter until the gods end my reign."

When Macella thought she could not stand the delectable torment of Aithan's fingers for a moment longer, the pavilion erupted in applause. King Khari had finished her speech. Without any idea whatsoever of what had been said, Macella clapped. The feel of Aithan's fingers disappeared as he, too, joined in the applause. When the clapping tapered off, he took a swallow of wine. Then he wiped his mouth with his napkin, surreptitiously licking his fingers as he did so. He winked at Macella, making her flush again.

"Let us have some music," King Khari declared, with a wave of her hand. "More wine! More conversation!"

A few of the musical members of their party, including Jacan, had brought instruments in anticipation of the king's request. As they began to play, the mood in the pavilion lightened. The guests began to move about the tent, taking new seats, accepting fresh drinks, and engaging in more boisterous conversation. The most ambitious among them gathered around the Crown, vying for Queen Annika's and King Khari's attention, while Queen Awa watched on impassively.

Quietly, Aithan led Macella from the table and moved to the periphery of the space, making occasional conversation, before tugging her through an unseen opening near the rear of the tent. They emerged into the darkness, the merry sounds behind them fading as Aithan pulled her toward the nearby trees. He nodded at Sir Igor and Sir Citali, who were posted behind the pavilion.

"Lovely night for a walk, Lord Commander," Sir Igor said with a salute.

"Indeed," Aithan replied, smiling, and led Macella away from the noise and bustle of the tent.

They moved through the trees until the pavilion faded from view and the music grew distant. Suddenly, Aithan stopped and turned back toward her. Before she could speak, he crushed her against him, kissing her hard, his hands roaming greedily over body. Macella gasped, and he took the opportunity to deepen the kiss, his tongue exploring her mouth as he forced her skirt up to her waist.

Macella stood on tiptoe, wrapping her arms around his neck, and kissing him back eagerly. Her earlier excitement had returned with increased vigor, her body demanding the release she had been denied in the tent. She moaned against his lips, molding her body to his, grinding against the throbbing hardness of his erection.

"Fuck," Aithan growled, pressing her against the smooth trunk of a nearby tree. "I need you right now, Macella."

Macella bit his bottom lip and buried her hands in his hair. Aithan growled again and lifted her from the ground. He positioned himself between her legs, unbuttoning his trousers while his mouth trailed over her jaw and down her neck. Macella clamped her thighs tight around his waist. She moaned again at the feel of his hard cock pressed against her, every bit as desperate for him as he was for her.

"Take me," she begged, tugging his hair, and forcing his head back so she could look into his eyes. "I need you. Fuck me, Aegis. I am yours."

Aithan grunted and Macella heard a ripping sound as he tore through the lace of her panties, ripping them off completely. Then he was thrusting into her, and pleasure was igniting every nerve ending in her body.

She didn't feel the tree bark rubbing against her back, didn't care that they would have to return to the king's party before too many people noticed their absence. All that mattered was Aithan's steely cock inside of her, filling her, driving her toward an inevitable climax. He fucked her hard, his mouth on her neck, her collarbone, tracing the swell of her breasts above her bodice.

"Gods," Aithan groaned. "You are so fucking perfect."

Macella whimpered as a buzzing heat spread through her torso. She felt free and wild and ravenous. She clawed at his back, her fingers raking over the fabric of his shirt. Aithan managed to push his tongue inside the bodice of her dress and her corset to find her nipple. She couldn't hold on a moment longer—the sensation pushed her over the precipice.

She came in a spasming, shuddering torrent of ecstasy, moaning Aithan's name, and clutching his neck, holding him against her breast. He ran his tongue back and forth over her nipple, relentlessly thrusting deeper and faster, as wave after wave of pleasure washed over her.

Finally, when Macella felt as if she would completely dissolve into a puddle of bliss, Aithan came. His breath was ragged and warm against her skin, his hands clenching against her ass, a low growl escaping his lips. He whispered to her in his mother's ancient tongue, professing his love and devotion. Macella stroked his hair, relishing the moment.

Aithan held her to him for several long minutes, both of them catching their breath. Then, he set her down and sheepishly handed her the ruined lace panties. Macella giggled and stepped behind a tree to relieve herself, using the ragged panties to wipe away the mess. She tossed the tattered fabric aside as they made their way back to the pavilion.

Macella entered from the pavilion's proper entrance, trying to look as though she'd only stepped out for a bit of fresh air or to visit the privy. She found the party in full swing. Several people had decided to dance, the king and young queen among them. King Khari and Queen Annika were pressed close, swaying to a ballad. Annika rested her face against the king's chest. Her eyes were closed, her long lashes resting against her pale cheeks.

Though King Khari was murmuring to her young queen and wearing a loving smile, her eyes roved around the room. They paused on Macella, and the king's brow furrowed. Her ochre eyes trailed over Macella slowly from head to toe. When their gaze met again, the king's eyes were cold. Macella shivered, but held her head high, refusing to show any emotion.

Queen Annika lifted her head and said something to King Khari, and the monarch tore her attention away from Macella. Macella exhaled in relief. She picked her way through the crowd, rejoining Aithan, who had slipped back into the tent via the rear entrance.

It was several more hours before the festivities concluded. Aithan left Macella at the door of their carriage, promising to return as soon as he'd done a sweep of the perimeter and spoken to the knights on duty. Macella climbed into the carriage, looking forward to crawling into her makeshift bed and falling into an exhausted sleep with Aithan at her side.

But that was not to be. Macella had only just undressed when she felt a familiar ripping sensation. The feeling was hot, tugging at the back of her mind, beckoning her east. There was a rift coming, and it wasn't far from the caravan.

Macella sighed and slipped into a silk sleeping gown. It looked like she would be falling asleep alone again. Aithan would have to hunt and close the rift immediately. There was no way of knowing how long that would take.

Sighing again, Macella pulled the last of the hairpins from her curls, freeing them from their evening updo. Perhaps she would write or read for a while. The pull of the rift had chased away her exhaustion, and she felt a bit wound up. There was no way she would fall asleep any time soon.

Macella was startled from her thoughts by an abrupt knock on her carriage door. Moments later, King Khari flung the door open and climbed inside, closing the door behind her.

Chapter Twenty-Four

Macella's mouth dropped open, her mind blank (39). For once, she was at a complete loss for words.

"Relax," King Khari said lightly. "I am not here for horizontal refreshment."

"Y-your grace," Macella stammered, making a hasty bow. "I was not expecting to be honored with your company."

"The king has gone with Aithan to hunt the rift," Khari replied, laughing. "I might've kept up this ruse if I'd known how fun it would be, but this body feels all wrong."

In a flash of emerald, King Khari disappeared, replaced by a grinning Finley.

Macella clutched her chest, heaving a surprised breath. She didn't know whether she should laugh or scream. "Finley!" she managed to gasp, her heart still hammering and chest still heaving. "What the fuck?"

"My stars, you are a vision," Finley purred, looking Macella over. "I see why Aithan can't keep his hands off of you long enough to make it through dinner."

Macella blushed, pulling a blanket around her shoulders. "Finley, what are you doing here?"

"Your hospitality is deplorable. It is as if your time at the castle has taught you nothing," Finley declared matter-of-factly, despite the mischievous twinkle in their eyes. "I thought you might want some company since the rift has taken your Aithan and your hope of immediate sleep."

Macella supposed that all Aegises in the vicinity of a rift would feel much the same. It was an oddly sweet gesture from Finley, and utterly unexpected. Something else was going on.

Macella narrowed her eyes. "And why aren't you gone to hunt the rift as well?" she asked accusingly.

Finley feigned a hurt expression. "I thought you would be pleased that I stayed behind to entertain you."

Macella made a face and crossed her arms.

Finley sighed and held their hands up in surrender. Still, there was glee dancing in their orange eyes. "I thought it would be good for Jacan to assist Aithan on this hunt, without his teacher hovering around," Finley explained with a shrug. "Besides, I had other pressing matters that needed my attention. Like checking on my dear sister."

"Of course. I'm sure I am your top priority tonight. So, did you shift into Khari just to give me a heart attack?" Macella demanded, glaring at the other Aegis.

Finley only smiled. "Oh, that. That was just a first taste of vengeance."

Macella's stomach dropped. "Oh no. Finley, what have you done?"

Finley's smile widened. They sauntered to a set of cushions and gracefully draped themself across them. Begrudgingly, Macella settled into her bed to listen, pulling the blanket more tightly around her shoulders as she did so.

"Well," Finley began, "your mood must have been contagious this evening, because Annika and Khari were clearly feeling amorous as well. When we left the pavilion, I distinctly overheard the young queen arranging to visit the king's carriage for the night."

Despite every attempt to look aloof, Finley could not suppress their cat-that-caught-the-canary grin. Now that Macella's surprise and confusion had abated, she teetered between amusement and dread, wondering what very likely hilarious and dangerous thing her sibling had done. She raised an eyebrow, inviting them to continue.

"Of course, when King Khari heard that Aithan was off to close a rift, she demanded to accompany him," Finley continued smugly. "She dispatched an apologetic message to Queen Annika and hastily departed with the Lord Commander. A servant then delivered the king's very important message to the young queen."

Finley's eyes glowed jade and, just for a moment, their eyes went cobalt blue above plump, pale cheeks, their sleek silver mane transforming into a cascade of golden waves. Then Macella blinked against a flash of emerald, and they were themself again, beautiful and elegant. She shook her head incredulously.

"You didn't," she groaned.

"Don't ruin my story," Finley commanded, holding up an imperious hand. "I waited and watched until the young queen left her carriage to visit the king, then slipped inside under the guise of a servant, leaving the apology note from Khari among the queen's other correspondence. Honestly, she's a disorganized mess. I really don't see how she keeps track of any important papers."

Macella made a show of massaging her temples. Finley loved to milk a good story. As a writer, Macella could appreciate it. As a woman who'd had her night upended by her sibling's shapeshifting shenanigans, she wanted Finley to get to the point.

They sighed dramatically and continued. "Fine, I'll get to the best part. A short while ago, Queen Annika made her way to King Khari's carriage. She looked and smelled quite lovely—she must have mustered all of her seductive powers tonight. I almost felt bad for her when King Khari didn't answer her knock. I almost felt worse when she saw King Khari climbing into your carriage instead."

"Finley, you didn't!" Macella exclaimed. "You reckless, impetuous, evil mastermind! Why would you do such a thing?"

For a moment, Finley's laughing eyes went cold and hard. "If she can toy with my life, I can toy with her foolish heart."

Macella remembered the way Annika had robbed Aithan of his senses, engulfing him in a sightless, soundless bubble while he fought for his life. The young queen had manipulated the situation so that Finley had been turned into not much more than a rage-filled puppet. They had clearly not forgiven the violation.

Macella decided that she hadn't either. She unwrapped the blanket from her shoulders and tossed it at Finley, before snuggling into her bed. She propped herself on pillows to face her friend.

"Well, we have to make this look good, so I suppose you should stay awhile," she said finally. "Finish telling me the story of the time you convinced an entire regiment to duel for your affection. I might be able to work it into the scribe's next tale."

It was quite obvious at breakfast the next morning that Finley's act of revenge had the intended effect. Queen Annika was red-faced and silent all morning. King Khari was in a foul mood, snapping at everyone who dared cross her path. Lucy told Macella that some of the servants had heard the two monarchs engaged in a heated discussion well before they'd broken their fast. It was clear the conversation had not gone well.

Macella did her best to avoid both royals all day, instead spending her time with her books and papers, or running drills alone, at human speed. Jacan and Finley were off hunting for any crossers from the past night's rift, while Aithan stayed behind and stoically endured the king's ill temper. Though she succeeded in staying out of the way until late afternoon, it wasn't yet the hour of Nuha when the king found Macella polishing her sword.

(40) "Lady Macella, I need to stretch my legs a bit," King Khari said casually, though the look in her eyes contradicted her light tone. "Join me for a walk among the trees."

The star charm at Macella's throat went suddenly cold, making her shiver. She didn't need the charm's magic to know she was in danger. She could feel the menace radiating from the king. But it was clearly not a request, so Macella sheathed her sword and took the arm the king offered. Aithan fell into step a respectful distance behind them, gesturing for Sir Kamau to flank their other side.

King Khari looked back, her expression hardening. "You are not needed," the king snapped. "Either of you."

Sir Kamau looked surreptitiously toward Aithan, before saluting and turning back toward the convoy. The Lord Protector held his ground. He waited for Sir Kamau to move out of ear shot before speaking.

"Forgive me, your grace, but it is my duty to protect you," Aithan said. "We know not what dangers these woods hold."

"I can take care of myself," King Khari replied sharply. "You will stay and protect the queens. I command it."

Aithan gave Macella a quick, troubled glance, before smoothing his expression and saluting the king. He watched King Khari lead Macella away, his jaw tight. His orange eyes burned with suppressed rage.

I, too, can take care of myself, Macella thought at him. *I will be fine.*

If you are not back in a quarter of an hour, I am coming after you. Aithan's mental voice was curt and final. Macella took a steadying breath, sending what she hoped were calm and reassuring thoughts in return.

King Khari did not speak for a long time. Soon enough, they were moving through the trees, dappled sunshine offering dim light. Eventually, the king stopped. The trees had thinned, and it appeared they were nearing a clearing. Macella waited.

"In a few days, we will reach the outskirts of the northern region," King Khari began finally. "Soon after, we will conclude our tour in Highview, where we will announce Awa's retirement and our intended courtship."

"Yes, your grace," Macella replied, keeping her voice carefully neutral despite the pounding of her heart.

King Khari released Macella's arm and moved away. She paced for a few moments, her hands clasped behind her back. Finally, she stopped in front of Macella.

"I have always known what I've wanted," King Khari told her. "From a young age, I had visions of ruling Kōsaten. Though I was one of six children in a noble family and not high enough in the birth order to expect a grand title and large inheritance, I knew I was destined for more. I saw it so clearly."

Macella's heart was racing. She knew that the king had isolated her for a reason, but she could not determine where this conversation was headed. She felt tense and on edge.

"My older brothers didn't see my vision." King Khari spoke softly, her gaze distant. "Nor did my father—a violent, small-minded, self-important beast of a man. But it didn't matter. I did not need them. Others saw my potential. I found allies in more important families than ours. I became quite well-known in my community and then throughout Butchertown. Everything I had long dreamed slowly became reality. And before long, just as I had envisioned, I found myself seated upon the blessed throne. I united the kingdom by choosing spouses from every region to rule at my side. Everything I wanted, I took."

King Khari paused. She resumed pacing, gazing into the trees, as if hardly remembering Macella was present. She seemed so far away that Macella was startled by her next words.

"And now I want you," King Khari declared, stopping in front of Macella once more. "And it appears I will have you. But I must admit I have reservations. How could I not when my eldest queen has conspired against me and supported an Aegis insurrection? And you, my intended, happen to be quite close to several Aegises. Is that a fair assessment, Scribe?"

Macella swallowed hard. "Yes, your grace."

King Khari nodded. "You can certainly see my concern, can you not? I want our marriage to be built on trust and loyalty. I want it to be beautiful and fulfilling for us both. I want to show you how powerful we can be together."

The king stepped closer to her, and Macella felt a cold dread spreading across her skin. Her star charm was practically a block of ice against her flushed skin. The air around them seemed to shimmer and tilt, giving Macella an odd wave of vertigo. She felt the need to steady herself, but she was not near enough to lean against a tree, and the king stood just out of reach.

"I can give you a life beyond your wildest imaginings," King Khari promised, stepping farther away. "I can show you things no one else can."

The world stretched, taking the king with it. Suddenly, Macella was alone, barely able to glimpse King Khari standing far, far in the distance. Around her, the trees thickened and spread. Their leaves closed in, cocooning Macella in a quiet, green cave. She spun in a circle, gasping in surprise as the forest seemed to melt away around her.

Beneath her feet, the ground was replaced by fine, polished wood. The filtered sunlight of the afternoon became the warm, intimate glow of candlelit chandeliers. Macella was in the grand ballroom at Kōsaten Keep. Her tunic and tights were no longer—she instead wore a grand gown of garnet and gold, her neck, wrists, and hands adorned with gold and jewels.

"I can make you more than a queen," King Khari said, appearing at Macella's side. "I can make you a god."

The king gestured grandly around the ballroom, and Macella was shocked to see that they now stood upon a dais, surrounded by onlookers. She covered her mouth to stifle a scream. In unison, the crowd knelt, their heads bowed low. There were hundreds of them, in every direction, kneeling at her feet.

"I want to give this to you," King Khari said earnestly. "But I have to be able to trust you. I cannot handle another disloyal spouse."

The genuflecting crowd disappeared. The ballroom faded. Macella stood alone in utter darkness.

"I know that your heart belongs to Aithan of Auburndale." King Khari's voice cut through the darkness. "And I know that you have a soft spot for Aegiskind. After all, your writings forced me to reform Smoketown. You have proven that you have strong allegiances."

(41) The forest reformed around her, but it was not as it had been before. The trees were crooked and gnarled. The ground was cracked and parched. A harsh sun burned in a hazy gray sky. Sweat prickled on Macella's scalp.

"Your grace, what is happening?" she managed to whisper. "How is this happening?"

"I want to trust you, Macella," King Khari went on, ignoring her question. "But how can I be sure you will be true to me? Queen Awa conspired with Kiho of Russell to raise an army against me. And I have reason to believe that you and Aithan of Auburndale were among the last people to see Kiho alive."

Macella's heart stopped, her breath catching in her throat. Her charm was painfully cold, so cold she thought it might burn her skin. She went very still, disregarding the way the trees seemed to be reaching toward her with sharp, claw-like branches. She could not see the king. Her hands itched for her daggers, and her flames simmered beneath her skin. Macella fought to remain calm. Until she knew what the king was after, she would not reveal her fear or her secrets.

"Tell me, Lady Macella, can I trust you?" King Khari implored. "Can I trust that you are not another accomplice in the plot against me?"

While Macella had been listening to the king, thick vines had crept toward her feet from the gaps in the parched earth. Now they wrapped around her legs, rooting her to the spot. Macella struggled, but the vines only tightened painfully, climbing steadily higher.

"My king, I have never allied myself with Kiho of Russell," she swore, fighting to keep the vines from engulfing her arms. "Attempting to raise an army against you would be foolish and hopeless."

King Khari stepped from the trees. She was not alone. At her side was a creature Macella had only ever read about. The jorōgumo. As tall as Khari, the beast had the body of a spider and the head of a woman. Its face was obscenely beautiful juxtaposed against its arachnid body and long, segmented legs. Its strange eyes regarded Macella, dark markings beneath each one underscoring its frightening appearance. As it emerged from the trees, it opened its mouth wide. A torrent of insects and other pests flooded out.

Macella clamped her mouth shut, but inside, she screamed. The terror ripped from somewhere deep and primal. It actually hurt her throat to stifle it. She wanted to put her hands over her mouth, but her wrists were now bound by the creeping vines. She kept her mouth closed, but she could still hear her own terrified breathing.

Macella! Where are you?!

Aithan's voice cut through the panic clouding her mind. He must have heard her mental screams, or perhaps he'd decided enough time had passed to warrant following them. Macella immediately felt calmer.

She squared her shoulders and locked eyes with the king. "I met Kiho of Russell but one time, and I found them rather unpleasant," she rasped, her throat raw. "I had no role in their treasonous affairs."

King Khari regarded her coldly. Absently, she placed a hand on the jorōgumo's neck, patting it lightly. Macella shuddered.

"Perhaps that is true," the king allowed. "But that does not mean that you will not betray me in future."

King Khari's ochre eyes seemed to glow, as harsh and unforgiving as the sun in the slate sky above. Macella felt her skin begin to crawl. The back of her neck prickled.

"I have always been able to make people see matters as I do," Khari went on. "I've shown you how beautiful our life together can be. Allow me to illustrate how ugly it will become if you prove yourself disloyal."

Chapter Twenty-Five

Macella shivered, her skin feeling practically alive. Then she realized something horrible, and this time she actually screamed. It was not her skin that was crawling. There were things crawling on her skin.

Huge hairy spiders. Wriggling, writhing centipedes. Fat, slimy maggots.

Dozens of creatures swarmed over her body—the insects that had fallen from the jorōgumo's mouth. They skittered across the arid ground and swarmed over the creeping vines. She could feel them under her tunic and inside her boots. Macella felt vulnerable and violated. It was infuriating and revolting and degrading all at once.

A long, black scorpion crawled up her sleeve and Macella shrieked, hating herself for giving Khari the satisfaction. It was a visceral, involuntary cry of fear and humiliation and rage. Bound as she was by the vines, she could not even brush the pests away. She had to stand helplessly as they roamed over her body, as King Khari looked on impassively.

"After I became king, I invited my father and older brothers to visit me at court," the king said, still absently petting the jorōgumo. "By then, they'd come to see things quite differently."

Khari's hand stilled. Macella squirmed, trying to shake some of the insects loose. She could not stand the tickling brush of hundreds of tiny legs. Determinedly, she focused her attention on keeping her mouth clamped shut. She knew that if she screamed again, she might not be able to regain her composure. She would ignite and reveal herself to a dangerous enemy who distrusted her already.

"It was too late then," King Khari continued, her gaze fixed on a distant point beyond Macella. "I could not trust them. They had shown their perfidy and lack of faith. And so, I showed them the error of their ways."

Macella! Something is not right. I cannot find you.

Aithan's mental voice seemed very far away. Macella wanted to call to him, but she could not open her mouth and her brain seemed frozen, lost in this terrible moment. She was transfixed, completely at the king's mercy.

"My father's mind broke first," King Khari remarked, as casually as if she were talking of the weather. "I was disappointed. Here I had spent my entire life trying to gain this man's approval, and it took less than a day to turn him into a sniveling mess. He slit his own throat."

Macella felt a rush of revulsion. Hot tears spilled down her cheeks. Never had she wanted to hurt another person so badly. She believed she could cheerfully bludgeon Khari to death, laughing all the while.

"My second oldest brother hung himself after three days. The third eldest experienced cardiac arrest two days later." Khari ticked off each death on her fingers. "Finally, after a full week, my eldest brother fell upon his sword. I was impressed. But I had always admired him most, so I was not surprised by his resilience."

King Khari finally refocused her gaze on Macella. Leaving the jorōgumo's side, the king moved until she was standing before Macella again, close enough to touch. Or slap. Or stab. Macella's hands itched for her daggers—or perhaps that was just the itch of the centipede she'd crushed in her fist.

"It is a mercy that I bound you, dear Macella. I would not risk you harming yourself during such a brief, innocuous chat as this," King Khari mused in a low voice, as the jorōgumo scurried into the trees. "How long would it take to break your beautiful, brilliant mind, I wonder? What would it take to push you over the edge into madness?"

Suddenly, Macella felt cold steel against her throat. The king had drawn her sword so quickly Macella hadn't even seen her move. Khari watched her with a cold-eyed smile. She trailed her sword down Macella's throat and chest, stopping with the point at her heart. Macella dared not breathe.

The light overhead changed. Macella felt the splash of liquid on her shoulder. The fabric of her tunic sizzled where the drops landed, leaving jagged holes. Cold dread washed over her as she slowly lifted her head to look up. Macella's gaze locked with three pairs of hungry eyes. She would've screamed then, but all the air seemed to have been sucked out of her body.

The jorōgumo loomed above them, its long legs moving delicately across a massive web that surely had not been there a moment earlier. It had three sets of black eyes, each with red and yellow pupils that were too human for an insect but too demonic to be human. She realized now that the markings she'd noticed earlier must've been its additional eyes, kept shut until it prepared to feed. It watched her closely, opening its mouth slightly to reveal dripping fangs.

Macella struggled to free herself. Belatedly, she realized the thick vines had vanished. Instead, she was bound by the silky strands of the creature's web. It seemed that the more she squirmed, the more securely she was caught. She forced her muscles to stiffen, willed herself to die with dignity.

There was a sound like a snapping twig in the trees beyond them. The king spun away from Macella. Then there was a rustle of dry leaves. Khari stealthily advanced toward the sound, sword at the ready. Macella felt a swell of dread as the king circled the spot before obscuring herself behind a tree trunk.

Aithan stepped from the trees, his orange eyes scanning frantically. When he saw her, his expression shifted from worry to relief. He had not yet noticed King Khari, but he began to turn his head toward where the king waited.

And then Khari sprung forward, thrusting her sword into Aithan's gut. Surprised, Aithan did not even make a sound as he crumpled to his knees. The blade protruded from his back, surrounded by a growing red stain.

All of the light left the world. There was no sound, no color in the universe aside from the crimson spreading across Aithan's shirt. Macella's heart ripped with a sharp, serrated tearing so intense she thought Khari might have stabbed her too. She gasped against the pain, drawing in a ragged breath that burned her lungs.

An earsplitting shriek cut through the trees. Macella did not even realize that she was the source of the sound. Without knowing how she did it, she ripped her arms free of the web. Frantically, she tore at the sticky silk around her thighs. She would get to her daggers, and then she would plunge them into Khari's black heart.

Macella! Macella! Gods, where are you, Macella!

Macella's head snapped up. Aithan had fallen onto his side on the hard ground. Blood trickled from his mouth. His eyes stared sightlessly into the trees. Nonchalantly, King Khari jerked her sword free, and more blood poured from the gaping wound in Aithan's belly.

Macella bellowed a screeching roar of fury and despair. A ghost of flame flickered across her skin. The insects still clinging to her arms crumbled to ash.

Macella! Macella, answer me! I can smell you, but I cannot find you! Please—

Aithan's mental voice broke on the last word, raw with pain. His anguish drew Macella out of her own grief. Her skin calmed, the whisper of flame extinguishing. She drew a sharp breath, her eyes roaming the surrounding trees, then returning to Aithan's prone form. Something was not right.

Staring intently at Aithan's motionless body, she focused her mind. The call of his thoughts was not coming from the corpse before her. She cocked her head, reaching out to him. His mind caught hers instantly, his relief flooding into her.

Aithan? Macella knew that either her mind or her eyes were deceiving her. She hardly dared hope that it was her vision that was untrustworthy.

Vision. That was it.

Macella, thank the gods! Where are you? Are you hurt?

King Khari had boasted that she was able to make people see her *vision*. She had somehow driven several members of her family to madness when she—what was it she'd said—*shown* them the error of their ways?

I am not hurt, Macella answered. *I have only been fooled into believing I was.*

Aithan's confusion was clear in his thoughts, but Macella didn't have time to explain. King Khari had sheathed her sword and was advancing toward Macella again. The king hesitated, scrutinizing her expression.

Macella didn't bother masking the naked emotion on her face. After all, this is what the king had wanted. She'd brought Macella into the forest to show her the consequences of disloyalty. Macella would make sure King Khari knew how well she understood.

"You have made your point, my king," she whispered, her eyes locked on Khari's as she gave a careful bow, struggling to balance against her bindings. "I see your vision quite clearly, and I will not forget it when I am your queen."

For a long moment, the two women simply stared at one another. Macella felt the tears drying on her cheeks, the adrenaline in her veins beginning to subside. But not the rage. The rage burned hot in every fiber of her being.

"No, I do not believe you will," King Khari replied contemplatively. "I am glad we have an understanding."

King Khari stared at Macella for another long moment before adding, "Your mind is even stronger than I expected. I knew you were special. It is why I chose you."

The world around them grew hazy again as the king stepped toward her and took her hand. It took all of Macella's strength not to snatch her hand away and use it to drive a dagger through Khari's skull. Instead, she focused on the returning sounds of birds and forest creatures, on the dappled afternoon sunlight and the lush foliage.

"If you don't mind my saying so, you are quite lovely when you cry," King Khari remarked, kissing Macella's hand. "A pity that I won't often see you this way, since I will soon occupy myself with making you the happiest woman in Kōsaten."

By the time Khari had finished speaking, the world had returned to its normal state. There was no web, no skittering insects, no massive murderous spider woman looming overhead. Mere seconds later, Aithan appeared. He'd obviously been searching nearby. Sir Igor and Sir Griselda followed behind him.

King Khari smiled pleasantly at them, releasing Macella's hand. "Lord Protector, how unexpected," she said, her voice mildly reproachful. "I thought I gave you a direct order."

Aithan bowed stiffly. "Forgive me, your grace. I heard screaming and thought you might be in danger."

"Of course," King Khari agreed. "You are forgiven then. You have done your duty quite well. Fortunately, it was but a bit of confusion."

The king grinned at Macella, before moving toward Aithan. She stopped near him, gesturing over her shoulder flippantly. Macella felt her fingernails digging into her palms and realized her hands were balled into tight fists.

King Khari lowered her voice conspiratorially and leaned toward Aithan. "Lady Macella saw a spider. A big one."

With a chuckle, the king clapped Aithan on the shoulder, before strolling away in the direction of the convoy. Aithan nodded and the accompanying knights followed her. Macella and Aithan watched them depart in silence.

When Khari and her Royal Guard had disappeared into the trees and their footsteps were too far away for even Aegis hearing to detect, Aithan hurried to Macella's side.

Macella held up a hand to stop him. Letting out a strangled cry, she ignited in flames, and then vanished. Invisible, she unsheathed her sword. In a blind rage, she felt herself running effortlessly through the more advanced sword maneuvers Finley had been teaching her. She sliced through any foliage in her path, leaving deep gashes in the trees and severed branches in her wake. She felt hot tears spilling down her cheeks again, and she let them fall.

She had no notion of the passage of time. She did not stop when her arms began to burn; she relished the pain's reminder that she was in control of her own mind and body. Her breath came out in ragged sobs, her heart racing from the exertion. Macella pushed herself farther, willing her body to move faster, strike harder.

The clang of clashing steel suddenly rang through the trees. Macella started in surprise and found herself looking up at Aithan's sword. *Let me in*, he beseeched her, his expression troubled.

Chest heaving, Macella lowered her sword. She let herself materialize, and Aithan immediately pulled her into his arms. Racked with sobs, she felt her knees buckle. Aithan sank to the ground with her and pulled her onto his lap. He rocked her, stroking her hair, murmuring quiet reassurances.

They stayed that way a long time, Macella's face buried against his chest as she shared flashes of what the king had done. She felt Aithan's carefully compartmentalized fury. Though his focus was presently on comforting her, he was absolutely livid. Macella imagined that were it not for the magic binding him, his next interaction with King Khari would be violent.

Finally, when Macella was cried out, the two climbed to their feet and prepared to return to the convoy. Macella took a last look around, remembering how the forest had turned parched and hungry at the king's will. She remembered how helpless she'd felt, how her mind had been pushed toward a gaping maw of madness. Macella looked at Aithan, a certainty forming in her mind.

"King Khari must die," she growled. "I will baptize my blade in her blood."

Chapter Twenty-Six

The next stage of their journey was less eventful. King Khari had been perfectly affable since their encounter in the woods, showing Macella nothing but kindness. Macella tried to be equally pleasant but avoided the king as much as possible. When she wasn't training or talking with the Aegises, she stayed in her carriage, reading, writing, and—sometimes—plotting her revenge.

One bright afternoon, the caravan began to slow, pulling Macella from her solitary thoughts. She had been so engrossed in her book that she had not attended to their surroundings in quite some time. The volume she was reading was an interesting one that she was eager to finish. She knew that they would soon reach a decent-sized town and would subsequently be taxed with all the formalities of settling in at another noble's estate. There would be speeches and tedious hours receiving welcomes and introductions, not to mention the grand meals and inevitable balls.

Macella sighed and scolded herself internally. She knew she was very lucky to live as she did. She'd spent much of her childhood falling asleep to the rumbling of her own stomach. The very carriage she now rode in was larger than the bedroom she'd shared with as many as four siblings and niblings at any given time. The simple chiffon and lace blouse and skirt she wore at present was worth enough to feed her family of twelve lavish meals every day for a month.

Again, she noticed how frequently her mind drifted to her family as their journey brought them nearer her home. She sometimes found herself slipping into Shively's unique patois or using colloquialisms she'd nearly forgotten. Despite how much she'd changed since she left home, the community that shaped her was clearly still a part of who she was.

The slowing of their cavalcade drew Macella's attention to her carriage window. She was surprised to find the environs familiar. They were still more than another fortnight's travel from Shively, but Macella still knew this particular town well. She marked her place and closed her book as she watched the buildings of the town square pass by.

When the convoy drew to a complete stop, Macella swiftly alighted from her carriage, slipping away into the crowd of gawkers around the royal caravan. She knew their party would tarry here for an hour or so as the Crown sent servants to purchase and post, while they accepted gifts of welcome from merchants and wealthy townsfolk. Macella would be back in her carriage by the time the convoy started up again, ready to be escorted the rest of the way by whatever local noble would house them during their stay.

I am going to pay a quick visit to some old acquaintances, Macella thought in the general direction of the king's carriage at the head of the procession, knowing that Aithan had likely already anticipated her errand.

She walked quickly, aware of the stares she attracted, but relieved that she was not nearly as interesting as the Crown and their fine carriages. She wished she were wearing a tunic and trousers, but she'd dressed that morning knowing they would be in company by late afternoon. The scalloped neckline of her blouse accentuated her bare shoulders and collarbone, the coral color complementing the rich brown of her skin. Though the set almost looked like a single piece, the top was cropped just enough that when she walked, it showed glimpses of her midriff above the gentle movement of her skirt.

Many admiring, interested, or hungry eyes followed her progress. She easily identified those who wanted her purse more than her person. No matter. Her daggers were strapped to her thighs, and her keen senses assured her that she was more than capable of facing any would-be threats should they arise.

A few turns off the main road, Macella found an old but well-kept building. Music and raucous conversation drifted into the street, the place already bustling with activity. This time of year, the farmers and fisherfolk started their days before the sun, then drank and gamed away the hottest hours of the day. The best would pace themselves enough to sober up for another hour or two of labor in the relative cool of dusk. However, the clientele of this particular establishment was not typically the responsible type. These customers would be cheerfully whoring and gambling away most of their day's wages.

(42) Macella stepped inside, letting her eyes adjust to the building's dim interior. It was exactly as she remembered it. The front room had a high ceiling that was open to the second floor, allowing those above to watch the activity of the tavern if they wished. The room was crammed full of tables, their occupants drinking, eating, and playing card or strategy games. Scantily clad women sashayed around the room, flirting with the customers, and attempting to interest them in the other services the establishment offered. Beyond the bar, on the far wall, a veiled door led to an inner chamber.

Macella approached the veiled door, glancing up at the women leaning against the second-floor railings. She recognized a few faces, though there were several newcomers since she'd left the brothel some six or so seasons ago. Despite the noise of the tavern, Macella's superior hearing still picked out several familiar voices in the next room.

"Can I be of assistance, my lady?" a barman asked politely, appearing at Macella's elbow, and attempting to block her path with an apologetic smile.

Macella smiled complacently, still moving toward the veiled door. "I would just like to pay my respects to the madame."

The barman stumbled and scurried to keep up with Macella's confident stride. "I can escort you to her sitting room, my lady, and alert her of your presence."

"That won't be necessary," Macella said smoothly, resting her hand lightly on the man's forearm. "I used to work for her. I know my way around."

The barman gaped, looking over Macella's gleaming onyx and silver curls, glowing skin, and expensive attire with obvious skepticism. Macella stepped past him, slipping through the veil into an inner chamber that used to seem larger to her inexperienced eyes. It was sparsely furnished with a few tables and scattered cushions. Another door ahead led to Madame's rooms, while an archway to the right led to the staircase and the second-floor rooms for paying customers.

A half dozen women sat idly at the tables or draped across cushions. A large, noisy man Macella remembered as being an obnoxious regular sat on his own cushion, a woman she recognized perched on his lap. Everyone looked up when Macella entered the room.

"You lost, princess?" a woman with a pinched face demanded, looking Macella over with obvious distaste.

Macella smiled. "Sheena. You are every bit as rude as I remember."

Sheena looked so surprised that Macella couldn't help but burst into laughter. Several other women joined in, before hurriedly shushing one another and breaking into whispered conversations. Macella looked them over, recognizing several more faces.

"Ignore her, my lady. I heard there was a royal party coming through, and you look like you must be part of it," an older woman interjected, rising, and stepping forward. "You obviously have coin, and I'm not going to turn you away. I'll fetch Madame and get you upstairs and on your back before you can say cunnilingus."

The women cackled and hooted, encouraging their colleague's lasciviousness. The regular customer brayed laughter, smacking his lap mate's rear end appreciatively at the joke. The speaker preened, obviously expecting to either embarrass or intrigue the dainty, rich lady she perceived Macella to be.

"Esme, I am surprised by the offer," Macella replied with mock sincerity. "Didn't you once say that I didn't know my cooter from a hole in the wall?"

Esme narrowed her eyes and scrutinized Macella more closely. The others watched them keenly, no longer even pretending at their own conversations.

Esme tilted her head and then her eyes widened in surprise. "You're the one who ran off with an Aegis," she exclaimed. "Macella of Shively!"

The room burst into excited chatter. Several women bombarded her with questions, while others beckoned to the women lounging on the second floor. Macella laughingly dodged their questions about her whereabouts since she'd left after her very first night of sex work at the brothel. Many of the more seasoned whores had taunted her mercilessly, giving her filthy tasks to complete during the days before she began seeing customers. There seemed to be something about Macella that the other women had taken an instant dislike to. Back then, she'd only been away from home a few seasons and was accustomed to feeling herself an outsider. She'd endured their derision with resolute indifference.

When Aithan of Auburndale had arrived, they'd tried to scare her with stories of Aegises with monstrous desires and mutated genitalia. Macella had been shocked when he'd actually selected her as his companion for the night, and not a little terrified that there might have been some truth to the women's wild stories. But she'd held her head high and marched into his room, determined not to show any fear.

"Well, look at you now," Hacienda drawled from her perch on the obnoxious man's lap, her voice cutting through the chatter. "I suppose you think you're a fine lady, and we're all supposed to fawn over you."

Macella tilted her head, holding Hacienda's gaze. She maintained a polite smile, spine erect, her hands held delicately before her, fingertips pressed together lightly. She waited, letting the words hang in the air.

Hacienda glanced around, seeming to find reassurance in the spotlight of everyone's attention. "You're a whore, same as the rest of us, and always will be. We're not gonna act like you're pristine and spring flower fresh."

(43) The room was nearly silent, the onlookers intently staring between Macella and Hacienda. At some point, Madame had slipped into the room. She stood silently against the back wall, letting matters play out. Macella had spotted the madame immediately, but kept her attention focused on Hacienda.

Slowly and elegantly, Macella moved until she stood directly in front of Hacienda's cushion. She looked down at the other woman, ignoring the man she sat atop. Carefully, she straightened her lace gloves, ensuring that their delicate pearl buttons caught the candlelight.

"Actually, I've been told I smell like a stream, a crackling fire, an evening breeze, and very, very good pussy," Macella corrected coldly. "I would give you a sniff, but you'd immediately retire in shame, and then how would you feed yourself? I can't have that on my conscience."

This time, most of the other women joined in the laughter, Hacienda's customer guffawing loudest of all. Hacienda's face reddened, and she tried a retort that was lost in the clamor.

Macella turned toward Madame, but a clumsy hand grasped at her skirt. She looked down to see the obnoxious customer's meaty paw.

"I would gladly pay for a sniff under your skirt," the man leered. "You're not above making easy coin now, are you?"

Macella stiffened. "Remove your hand from my person or I will remove it from your wrist."

Again, the room was stunned into silence. The man gaped at Macella, his expression cycling quickly from surprise to disbelief to embarrassment to rage.

Face reddening, he clenched her skirt more tightly in his massive fist. "Now you listen to me, you s—" was all he managed to say before being cut off by his own screams.

In a fluid movement, Macella had slipped her hands inside her skirt. Lynn had been happy to update Macella's wardrobe with some special modifications to the pockets. In a flash, Macella's hands reappeared holding her daggers. She'd plunged one into the man's wrist, spearing it against the cushion without piercing it through, and pressed the other blade to his throat.

Hacienda shrieked and leapt from his lap, scurrying as far away from Macella as she could manage. The man swore and groaned but held very still against the points of Macella's daggers.

She bent toward him, dropping her voice. "Apologize," she hissed, pushing her iron dagger more deeply into his flesh.

"Please take it out," the man begged, clutching his wounded wrist with his free hand. "I beg your pardon, my lady. I have been deep in my goblet this evening and spoke out of turn. Please, turn me loose."

Macella straightened swiftly, stepping away from the blood spatter as she jerked her dagger free of his wrist. She pulled a silk handkerchief from her handbag, using it to wipe her dagger clean before tossing it at the bleeding man. Nonchalantly, she returned her daggers to their holsters.

"Put pressure on the wound," Macella commanded. "I haven't severed anything vital. Hacienda, take your client upstairs and nurse him back to health and happiness. I will, of course, cover the cost of your medical attentions."

Macella dug into her handbag and pulled a pouch from its depths. She tossed the pouch to Madame, who instinctively caught it. It clinked heavily against her palms. She raised an eyebrow at Macella.

"That should cover Hacienda's night and allow a generous tip to all the women for the warm welcome and diverting entertainment," Macella explained loudly enough for all to hear. "It should also compensate you for the great service you did me some six seasons ago when you sheltered me until Fate sent me Aithan of Auburndale. No matter how unpleasant my time here often was, I am grateful that it set me on the path to becoming my truest self. Please accept this token of my gratitude."

Madame regarded her shrewdly, then gave a curt nod. "I am glad you have done well for yourself. It seems you did not long tether yourself to that Aegis. It looks as if you've either married well or gained yourself a generous benefactor."

"You are partly correct," Macella replied, smiling at the sound of the veil swishing behind her.

Then she smelled a familiar scent and felt a familiar warmth. She watched everyone take him in as Aithan of Auburndale stepped into the chamber. Like Macella, the Lord Protector had been a different person before they'd left this brothel together. The change was deeper than the fine satin of his tailored surcoat or the polished leather of his boots. She could tell from their expressions that everyone in the room recognized the air of command that emanated from him, even as he nodded deferentially at Madame.

"Pardon my intrusion," he apologized in his low, resonant rumble. "Lady Macella, the Crown is preparing to depart for Laird Parul's castle and her grace, King Khari, wishes for you to join them in her carriage—to discuss logistics of our rooms and staff during our stay, I expect."

Macella suppressed a grin at the collective dropping of jaws that followed his words. "Of course, Lord Protector. I am quite finished here."

Macella bowed to the group, before turning to Madame once more.

"You have always thought too small," Macella told her. "And I have always refused to shrink. I do hope you are as happy with your decisions as I am with mine. Farewell."

She spun on her heel, taking Aithan's arm, and sauntering from the room. Heads held high and backs straight, they left the brothel together for the second and final time. They did not look back.

"I let you out of my sight for half an hour and you've already stabbed someone?" Aithan sighed, once they'd stepped out onto the sunny sidewalk.

Macella laughed. "It was barely a scratch. A mere warning, really."

Aithan shook his head. "You have an Aegis's temper, my little hell goddess."

"It is my nature then, and I cannot help it," Macella shrugged. "Have I truly been summoned to Khari's carriage?"

"I'm afraid so," Aithan replied. "However, the other members of the Crown will not be present. King Khari wants to speak with you alone during the short ride to Laird Parul's estate."

Macella heard and mirrored Aithan's displeasure. She would not soon forget her last private conversation with the king. She had woken several times wound in her sheets, struggling to free herself from the nightmare of the jorōgumo's web. Their conversation had been both traumatic and illuminating, and she hoped she never had to endure such another discussion for the rest of her long life.

"I will be just outside the carriage," Aithan said, his voice strained. "You need only think in my direction, and I will come."

Macella gave herself a little shake and forced a smile. "I will be fine. She knows that I took her threat to heart, and I've given her no reason to repeat the message."

Aithan's jaw was tight, his eyes gone hard. "Call and I will come."

Macella squeezed his arm. They walked the remainder of the way back to the convoy in silence. When they reached King Khari's carriage, Aithan handed her in, his hands lingering as if reluctant to let her go.

Chapter Twenty-Seven

King Khari looked up from her place at the small desk. She smiled warmly at Macella and gestured for her to take a seat. After another few moments looking over her papers, she stacked them with a sigh and joined Macella on a cushioned bench.

"Lady Macella, that color is enchanting on you," the king said, looking her over appreciatively. "You look positively mouthwatering."

Macella suppressed a shudder and smiled. "Thank you, your grace."

King Khari leaned against the seat back. She yawned lazily and crossed an ankle over her knee as the convoy began to move again. Macella waited.

"So, we have only just arrived, and you've already run off to a second-rate brothel?" the king inquired, her ochre eyes dancing wickedly.

Macella sat back as well, though she surely must've appeared much less relaxed. She did not believe that her visit to Madame was the reason King Khari had sent for her, nor did she think the king was angry about it. However, Khari was nothing if not mercurial. Macella could not lower her guard.

"I was calling on some old acquaintances," she told the king calmly. "I worked there for about a week some time ago."

"I know," King Khari replied breezily. "But I appreciate your honesty, nonetheless. How was your visit?"

Macella thought of the women's faces when Aithan came to fetch her and felt a petty thrill shoot through her. She couldn't suppress her grin. And she could tell that King Khari knew exactly what she was thinking.

"Satisfying," Macella answered truthfully. "I take pleasure in defying people's low expectations."

King Khari nodded. "That is a trait we share."

Macella remembered the story the king had told when she'd ensnared Macella in her mind. The king's family had not believed that she was destined for greatness, but Khari had proved them wrong. Then she'd imprisoned them in horrible visions, driven them mad, and let them kill themselves. Macella did not like the idea of sharing any traits with this cruel woman.

"I am glad you had a pleasant visit. I would have loved to see their faces when they saw you in all of your exquisite elegance. But now I want to speak to you about a few things, since we are firmly in the northern territory and soon to announce our betrothal," King Khari went on, fixing her gaze on Macella.

"Of course, my king," Macella responded seriously, rising, and taking a seat across the carriage, where she could face King Khari.

The king leaned forward, resting her elbows on her knees, and clasping her hands loosely before her. Macella forced herself to lean forward as well. It was imperative that she maintain the façade of pleasantry when in company with King Khari. Everything she did now would be seen as an indication of her suitability for the Crown.

Apparently, the king's thoughts had taken the same bent, as she said, "Everyone who we encounter on this journey will remember you, even if they do not. They will rack their feeble brains to recall the slightest impression they had of the woman they did not yet know was to be queen. Perhaps they'll recall a curly-haired beauty with a nice smile, or a kind woman who'd stopped to help a beggar."

The king took Macella's hands in hers, gazing into her face with an intense possessiveness. Macella had to consciously relax each finger, to remind herself to breathe and look flattered. She hoped the rush of heat to her face looked like a prim blush and not like the rage she felt at Khari's audacity.

"You are the rose I've plucked from obscurity, the erudite adventurer from the poorest part of the northern region," the king declared. "That is what they must remember. That is who you must be. Do you understand, my lady?"

The intimacy in her voice made Macella nauseous. Rage and fear fought for prominence in her racing thoughts. If there was one thing Macella believed belonged fully to herself, it was her story. Now, King Khari was perverting it, contorting Macella's story to fit her own twisted vision.

"Of course, your grace," Macella managed. "I will strive to represent you well at all times."

King Khari squeezed her hands. "I have no doubt. Show them your petals unless they earn your thorns, my northern rose."

Macella suppressed another shudder by squeezing the king's hands in return. Again, the possessive undertone. *My* northern rose. If anyone had earned a glimpse of Macella's thorns, it was King Khari. And how Macella ached to show her just how sharp they could be.

She exhaled to steady herself, wetting her lips with her tongue to distract Khari's attention from the anger that must have shown in her eyes. Not yet. She had to bide her time until they had a plan for besting the tyrant. Until then, she must preen her petals and conceal her thorns. Until then, she must be King Khari's prize—the key to winning back the north's loyalty. The king's northern rose, picked from the gutter and planted in a gilded cage.

King Khari cleared her throat and straightened, releasing Macella's hands. She seemed to shake herself a bit, and her expression lost some of its intimacy. She smiled, but it did not reach her eyes.

"Additionally, now that we are in her home region, it simply will not do to continue confining Queen Awa to her carriage or my company," the king explained nonchalantly. "I do not trust any of her former companions, aside from you. Thus, I would consider it a great favor for you to give her as much of your time as you can spare."

There were few things at that moment that could've distracted Macella from her simmering rage, but somehow Khari had landed on one such thing. Macella blinked in surprise. For months, Queen Awa's entourage had been gradually sent away under one guise or another, always to some coveted or advantageous position that guaranteed they would dare not ask any questions about Awa's sudden confinement. Macella had, of course, remained at the keep but had not been allowed to visit her friend.

"That is very thoughtful of you. I would like that, your grace," Macella said, letting genuine gratitude saturate her words.

"It will be nice for the dignitaries of the north to see how close the present and future queens are," King Khari mused. "You will be a model of regal grace—the incumbent queen graciously passing her crown to her humble successor. This story rivals your best, Scribe."

Macella gritted her teeth, her gratitude turning to ice in her veins. Once again, King Khari had alighted on the precise words to affect her. She felt her own careful smile turn sinister.

"I believe we must wait and see, my king." Macella let her voice drop to a purr. "Much remains to be written."

Khari chuckled, her eyes warming once more. "As irresistibly beautiful as you are, it is that fire that truly captivates me. I pray it never cools."

Alright? Aithan whispered in her mind. Though Macella knew he'd been anxiously listening, the reminder calmed her taut nerves.

She lowered her eyes, looking up at Khari through her lashes. "If this is the kind of adulation I can expect during our courtship, I am not sure my pride can handle the temptation," Macella teased. "I shall become an obnoxious peacock."

Quite alright, she thought at Aithan as King Khari laughed and relaxed, looking pleased with Macella's flirtation.

"My dear, you have no idea what is in store for you," the king promised. "Just you wait."

Macella knew that it was not meant to be a threat, but she could not help but feel a stab of fear. She wondered how Khari's other spouses handled this emotional minefield. Did they constantly teeter between terror and fury? How did Annika manage to appear so enamored with Khari? Was she too stupid to sense the depth of the danger, or was she much, much smarter than she appeared? If her adoration of the king was an act, then she must have some extremely ambitious schemes of her own.

The convoy began to slow and Macella could see they were approaching the wide gravel drive of a well-manicured estate. It appeared their little parley would soon come to an end. Macella was eager to escape to her rooms, where she could parse her feelings in private.

"Alas, time with you always flows too quickly." King Khari sighed, glancing through the window at the sculpted hedgerows.

"It is a blessing, then, that we will have so much of it ahead of us," Macella replied sweetly.

"Yes, that brings me to a final matter you must consider." King Khari clapped her hands as if she'd nearly forgotten. "You must have companionship at court. Those you trust, those you wish to elevate, those you enjoy. Think on who you would invite. Of course, we will find positions for any among your family you wish—at least a few squires, cupbearers, etcetera—but your entourage should be your trusted advisors and friends."

Macella had avoided thinking about such arrangements. She'd hoped that, since she and Aithan were already established at the castle, there would be no need for further companions. Of course, she knew that it was customary for family members to receive prominent positions at court. It was a double-edged sword, however. Your family members would earn wealth and status but could be used as pawns to control you.

How could Macella bring anyone else into that nest of vipers? On the other hand, how could she deny them such a life-altering opportunity? It would be impossible to avoid. The only solution was to surround herself with people she trusted and lean on their support as she cleared the viper's nest.

"Thank you for this wise counsel, your grace," Macella said, bowing her head deferentially. "I will let it guide me as I compile my list."

"Good," King Khari answered, glancing out the window once more. "You should begin extending invitations soon so we can start the necessary arrangements."

Macella nodded. "I will be prepared to do so as soon as we make the betrothal announcement. I would not want to jeopardize the surprise by revealing it to my friends too early."

The king planned for them to visit Shively, invite Macella's family to join the convoy to Highview, and then make the dual announcement of Awa's retirement and Macella's ascension. She had at most another two months before everyone would know her as the king's future wife. She wanted these final weeks of anonymity to pass as slowly as possible. She already had doubts that it wouldn't immediately spread from her family to the rest of Shively.

"No need to wait, my dear," King Khari assured her, waving a hand dismissively. "I have no doubt that much of the kingdom will know our good news well before the official announcement. These things have a way of getting out."

Macella's stomach dropped. She should've thought of that. The small council had known for months; it was a miracle one of them had not already leaked the information. Perhaps they had. Perhaps today's tête-à-tête with the king was a preemptive measure to alert her that she was already being observed. She must be on constant guard. It seems her story would inevitably be told by others. She would have to discern how best to take control of the narrative.

The carriage stopped before the broad front entrance of an imposing castle constructed from large, clay bricks in various shades of brown. Aithan helped her from the carriage, squeezing her hand and looking her over quickly as if checking for damage. Then they were caught up in the introductions and arrangements as the Crown's convoy settled into their accommodations.

After a bit of initial confusion, Macella and Aithan were given a suite of rooms nearest those prepared for the Crown. Obviously, the Protectors of the Crown had never before had a partner or many belongings of their own. Macella stifled a smile at the apologetic overtures from the staff as they scrambled to rearrange lodging. Before the scribe's writings, an Aegis would never have been treated so well. Though Macella knew there was still much to do, she would take comfort in the triumphs they'd already won.

In the end, Captain Drudo took up residence in the small room adjoining the king's chamber which had been meant for the Protector. Macella doubted that the captain would spend many of his free hours in the little room if Finley had their way. They'd kept up a steady flirtation for weeks. Macella thought Finley might be more taken with the young captain than they realized.

While Aithan held counsel with Laird Parul's knights, head servants, and the Royal Guard to arrange the particulars of the Crown's protection during their few days' stay, Macella relished the privacy of their rooms. She sent Lucy away, insisting she'd unpack their trunks herself. Laird Parul's servants had left a large basin of sage-scented warm water and towels in their washroom, which Macella promptly took advantage of. Once she'd freshened up, she helped herself to wine and fruit from a platter the servants had left and wandered through their rooms, examining their temporary living space.

Macella had missed doors and walls and floors that didn't move. Her carriage was luxurious, and she frequently left it for walks and rides in the countryside, but it still felt confining after a while. It was freeing to stretch and take up space. With hours before dinner, she wrapped herself in a satin dressing gown and lay across the bed. It was large, with an ornate iron frame, and draped with gauzy white fabric. Macella gazed up at the bedframe's swirls and spirals, enjoying the sensation of a bed that held still.

"I will never get used to how perfect you look when draped in satins and silks," Aithan rumbled as he entered the room. "I told you long ago that you were meant to live in luxury. You were born to be a queen."

Macella sat up, letting her dressing gown slip off of one shoulder and watching Aithan's gaze fall hungrily to the bare skin it revealed. She smiled at the thrill his expression sent through her body.

"I told you long ago that I was meant to be wherever you are," she replied. "So, come and join me."

Aithan crossed to the bed and leaned to plant a kiss on her lips, then her bare shoulder. "Don't move."

He disappeared into the bathing chamber, where a servant who preceded him into the room had left fresh water. Macella stretched out again and waited, curls fanning out around her, letting the afternoon's tension drain from her body. She hadn't dared hope she'd have any alone time with Aithan until well past the dinner festivities, but it appeared she was in luck.

Soon enough, Aithan reappeared, clad in his own crimson dressing gown. His wet hair looked steel gray, falling in waves around his shoulders. He took in the ornate bed frame before looking down at her with burning eyes.

(44) "I have an idea," he murmured, one side of his mouth quirking up in a libidinous grin. "May I try something?"

Macella wasn't sure what he was up to, but anything that came with that look in his eyes would undoubtedly be pleasurable. She nodded her consent, returning his lustful gaze. She could already feel a flutter of excitement in her belly.

In a swift movement, Aithan untied the belt of her dressing gown and pulled it free. His eyes raked over her naked body beneath, darkening with palpable desire. He sat beside her on the bed, trailing his hands over her stomach, between her breasts, across her collarbone, and then down her satin-clad arms. Macella shivered with delight.

"This bed frame could be very useful," Aithan said, pulling her wrists above her head.

Deftly, he used the belt of her dressing gown to tie her wrists together and then to the iron headboard. Macella gave the binding a cautious tug and found that she could not easily free herself. She felt another thrill of excitement at the discovery.

"Alright?" Aithan asked.

"Quite alright," Macella breathed, biting her lip, and gazing up at him.

Aithan smiled and stood. Eyes locked with hers, he untied his dressing gown and let it fall open. Macella took in the glory of his incredible, naked body. He was a masterpiece of golden skin and chiseled muscle. She never tired of drinking him in—her thirst for him was never satiated.

His cock swelled under her gaze, rising to the tenor of her lustful thoughts. Macella squirmed at the answering throb between her legs. Aithan sat beside her again, and she involuntarily flexed against her satin restraints. The pull to touch him was difficult to resist.

"Patience, daughter of Hades," Aithan teased with a sly wink and a salacious grin. "Your Aegis temperament is on full display today. Most of us do so love to fight and to fuck. I am glad it was me and not some other Aegis who walked into that brothel your first night."

Before she could retort, Aithan covered her mouth with his, kissing her deeply. As his tongue probed her mouth, he ran a hand over her breast, brushing a light circle over her nipple, and then across her belly. With excruciating gentleness, he slid his fingers through her pubic hair. She lifted her hips toward his touch, but Aithan chuckled and pulled away.

"Patience, wife." Aithan grinned. "It will be worth the wait. I am going to try your Aegis temper now, and you are going to love every minute of it, little hell goddess."

With that, Aithan pulled the belt of his dressing gown free and tied it over Macella's eyes. In the sudden dark, Macella's need spiked. She could feel the warmth of Aithan's skin, knew he was nearby, naked, and full of wicked intent. And yet she could not move, bound to the bed frame as she was, could not even see to brace herself for whatever he would do next.

"That nickname better not stick," Macella said breathlessly, trying and failing to sound firm. "It sounds far too dark and wild to describe me."

"I disagree, little hell goddess," Aithan breathed against her ear.

Macella jumped a little and shivered again. She hadn't realized he was so close. The heat of his breath sent electricity buzzing over her skin. He brushed his lips over her earlobe, then down her neck, before trailing his tongue along her collarbone. Macella's nipples stiffened, and she let out a gasping whimper. Then he was gone.

"I know exactly how dark and wild you truly are," Aithan murmured from somewhere near the foot of the bed. "It is why we match so perfectly, why our bodies and our spirits connect so seamlessly."

The slight shifting of the bed under his weight was the only preparation Macella had for the sudden exhilarating feel of his tongue moving along the inside of her leg. She spasmed, moaning as he licked his way up to her inner thigh. When he reached her apex, he flicked his tongue over her clit only once before tracing his way down the inside of her other leg. Macella squirmed, her pussy throbbing in protest.

"The darkness in me calls out to the dark in you," Aithan murmured. "The wildness in me draws out the wild in you."

His tongue flicked across her clit again, just once, and then it was tracing a line along the crease of her hip and over her waistline. Macella's hips bucked. The insistent throbbing between her legs was maddening. Her nipples felt almost painfully stiff. She squirmed, letting out a moan of pleasure and frustration.

"Do you not feel it, my hell goddess?" Aithan growled against her skin. "My underworld queen, do I not drive you wild?"

A shift in the mattress and Aithan took one taut nipple into his mouth, sucking gently. Macella's entire body quaked. She cried out, thrusting her hips upward. Aithan held her nipple between his lips and flicked his tongue, eliciting another cry from Macella as her pussy clenched and the buzzing spreading over her skin began to pool in her belly. She tugged against her restraints, both exasperated and excited by her inability to see or touch him.

"Show me," Aithan commanded, his lips suddenly at her ear again. "Show me how wild I make you feel. Make me believe it."

Macella turned her head, wanting to kiss him, but he was gone. She whimpered, writhing against the soft bedding. Her own breath sounded loud in her ears, and she could hear the faint squish of moisture as she pressed and rubbed her thighs together, trying to soothe the agonizing pulsing in her core.

"Aithan, please," she moaned. "I want you so badly."

His tongue traced her areola before he sucked her other nipple into his mouth. A symphony of sparks exploded deep in her core. If he didn't touch her, lick her, fuck her soon, she would surely spontaneously combust.

"How badly?" Aithan asked, sliding a hand across her hip and around to cradle her ass.

Macella strained toward him and found he'd stretched out beside her. He pressed her to him, his grip tight on her ass, his mouth steadily working on her nipple. She writhed against the hard press of his body, aching at the stiffness of his cock against her leg.

"I need you, Aithan," Macella half-moaned, half-whimpered. "I need you inside of me right now. Please."

Aithan rolled her onto her back, positioning himself on top of her and kissing her fervently. Macella rolled her hips, feeling the hard promise of his cock so close to where she needed it. She shuddered, the buzzing in her torso becoming frenzied, the throbbing in her pussy reaching a fever pitch.

"Wild," Aithan whispered, breaking the kiss, and biting her neck. "My hell goddess, my queen, my wife."

Macella gasped, clamping her thighs around his waist, and lifting her hips, trying desperately to guide him inside her. She felt every bit as wild and dark as the underworld queen. She might balk at being King Khari's northern rose, but she would gladly be Aithan's hell goddess. She would be anything he wished.

"Yours," Macella panted. "I am yours. Take me. Fuck me, Aegis."

Aithan thrust into her, hard and sudden and deep. Macella screamed raggedly, unable and unwilling to contain her ecstasy. The sensation of him inside her was so exquisite it was almost painful. The pulsing, buzzing, chaos spread through her torso, radiating from the place deep inside her that Aithan filled, thrusting mercilessly, stroke after stroke hitting the exact spot deep within her that had been waiting for this moment.

She came hard, calling his name as wave after wave of rapturous bliss washed over her. The satin around her eyes was wet with tears and still she was coming, her orgasm refusing to release her after the endless anticipation it had waited through.

Aithan did not relent. He lifted her hips, moving to stand on his knees, steadily thrusting into her, not allowing her to escape. She kept her legs clamped around him, her head thrashing against the pillow with each long, deep stroke. The new angle changed the sensation, somehow allowing for still deeper access. Macella felt lightheaded and had to remind herself to breathe between moans and cries. Her entire body shook uncontrollably, her bound arms gelatinous and tingling.

"Fuck," Aithan gasped. "Gods, you feel amazing."

He let her hips fall back to the bed, lowering himself onto her once more, his hands clenching her ass, no space between them as he drove into her. Finally, with a growl and a curse, he came, clutching her hips, his mouth on her neck, biting and sucking as his body racked with tremors. Macella shuddered, satiated, and utterly wrung out.

After a few minutes of simply bathing in the afterglow, Aithan whispered an apology as he hurriedly untied her wrists and removed her blindfold. He rolled to one side to allow her free movement, rubbing her arms, and looking into her face.

"Alright?" he whispered.

Macella lifted her head and kissed him softly. She reached a hand up to cradle the back of his head, holding him to her. Then she flopped back onto the pillow, letting her arm fall back to the bed. The feeling hadn't quite returned to her limbs. She smiled lazily.

"Quite alright," she replied.

Chapter Twenty-Eight

They lay in bed for a long while, her relaying the particulars of her conversation with King Khari, him filling her in on the details he'd learned of Laird Parul's castle and its inhabitants. They'd visited so many nobles along this journey that grand castles had lost some of their luster, but Macella knew that these northern lords would be the most important to understand. After all, it was their interests she was supposed to represent when she became queen. Theirs and, she was determined, the commonfolk so often overlooked and unheard.

Laird Parul and their new wife governed the township of Nulu, a fairly prosperous fishing community that, like its nobles, was only recently founded. The waters in the north were known to be treacherous, but Parul had pioneered a method for navigating the rough waves and had been rewarded with a massive catch. Soon, they'd settled near the coast, established a fishery, and begun attracting others to the area. The Laird of Nulu had petitioned the Crown for recognition less than a decade ago, and their establishment was already well on its way to becoming one of the wealthiest towns in the north.

(45) As such, they were clearly eager to impress the Crown during this inaugural visit of the royals to the township. Macella was surprised by the splendor

as Finley escorted her to dinner that evening. Laird Parul's castle was certainly not as extravagant as Kōsaten Keep, but its owners had clearly put a great deal of money and effort into making it fit for nobility.

"This place has a uniquely refined flair, doesn't it?" Finley purred, their eyes following Macella's. "Not at all like that gods-awful gaudy mess in Avondale."

Macella snickered, muffling the sound in the lace of her gloved palm. "You must behave yourself tonight! I am playing the future queen, and I cannot be seen giggling and gossiping all evening."

They stopped near the doors of the dining hall. Macella admired the silk wallpaper, another of many beautiful touches she'd noticed along their route. The corridor was softly lit by candles in gold sconces that had been molded into intricate loops and swirls. Against the deep violet of the wallpaper, the sconces looked both elegant and whimsical. Macella decided that she liked Laird Parul. They'd built a beautiful home out of nothing but ingenuity and determination, had made peace with the untamed sea and made this land their own. That was a story Macella would love to tell.

"I shall be the picture of politeness, your grace," Finley drawled with a saucy sidelong glance. "Do I not look the part of the refined socialite?"

That was an understatement. Finley looked exquisite in a jacket with a high collar that framed their lovely face, their silky silver hair stark against the emerald fabric. The jacket flared into a ruffled train that whispered against the polished stone floor. Their black blouse and corset accentuated their small waist and their legs looked long and graceful, clad in black tights and extended by high-heeled leather boots. Macella briefly leaned her head against their shoulder, breathing in their honey and hazelnut scent. It had become a comforting smell, like Aithan's smoky sweetness.

"You look lovely and incredibly dangerous," Macella replied honestly, squeezing Finley's arm.

Finley tittered a delighted laugh. "That is precisely what I was going for! You truly see me, dear Macella."

They stepped into the dining hall, joining the queue to greet the laird and lady of the estate. The room was long with a vaulted ceiling tastefully hung with more artfully sculpted gold chandeliers. The rows of long tables were laid with heavy violet fabric and gold candelabra centerpieces. Macella loved it immediately.

"You look enchanting as well, darling," Finley added, looking Macella over approvingly.

"Thank you, sweetness." Macella smiled, preening a bit for their amusement.

Where Finley had gone for the dramatic, Macella had chosen a demure look that evening. Her gold dress featured a snug bodice that flowed into a loose skirt of silk and lace, which wrapped around her waist, and was secured with an elaborate bow. The dress moved as she did, occasionally revealing a length of brown leg through the natural slit formed by the wrapped fabric.

"I would hate not to look my best in a room like this," Macella added. "I am impressed."

"They do have good taste," Finley remarked as they caught sight of the castle's owners, standing at the head of the room greeting their guests.

Laird Parul and their wife, Lady Seondeok, were a striking couple. They'd attired themselves in the king's garnet and gold, and the colors complemented both of their skin tones nicely. Laird Parul was tall and leanly muscled with dark red-brown skin and thick, chin-length black hair that fell into their wide brown eyes. Their wife was wispy with porcelain skin, hooded eyes, waist-length black hair, and a smile that held a hint of mischief.

"I am already beginning to like them," Macella agreed, following Finley's gaze.

She might've said something else then, but her eyes landed on someone entirely unexpected. Among a group of the castle's mages, Macella spotted pale skin and long ginger hair. When the woman lifted her head, she revealed plump cheeks and familiar gray eyes.

Aisling. The sorcerer who had given the prophecy about Macella and Aithan's Fate. The one who had foretold Macella's discovery of her Aegisborn nature.

As if sensing herself being watched, Aisling met Macella's gaze—blankly for a moment before her eyes widened in recognition. Macella smiled, but Aisling looked away quickly, turning her back to the queue.

The king's voice drew Macella back to the line. "May I introduce Finley of Fairdale, one of our great Aegis warriors."

King Khari and her queens stood beside their hosts, meeting and introducing in turns as the castle's guests and the Crown's convoy converged. Those who'd already been introduced, and those who didn't warrant introductions, were seated at the long tables, enjoying wine, bread, and cheese. Macella spotted Aithan and Captain Drudo across the dining hall, their eyes scanning the room. The captain looked resplendent in his dress uniform, his dark hair shining in the candlelight. Aithan's golden skin glowed against his crimson jacket, his hair falling in loose waves around his shoulders. Macella was sure her eyes weren't the only ones on the two—they were by far the most handsome men in the room.

"And it is my pleasure to bring to your particular notice the Lady Macella of Shively, Royal Scribe and personal favorite of the Crown," King Khari said smoothly, taking Macella's hand and kissing it before presenting her to Laird Parul and Lady Seondeok.

Macella bowed. "Thank you for having me, my lady, my laird."

"We have heard much of you." Laird Parul smiled, their voice warm and husky. "The lords who visited the capital returned full of praise for the striking beauty from our very own region. I see now that they did not do you justice."

Macella blushed as Laird Parul kissed her hand. Lady Seondeok shook her hand next, her shrewd eyes studying Macella with bright interest. Up close, the couple were even more striking, their faces open and generous, their smiles genuine. Macella decided she had been correct in her positive assessment of them.

"I am sure they embellished my merits," Macella objected, her blush deepening. "And you flatter me because you are such gracious hosts. I am very pleased to make your acquaintance."

They're not embellishing at all. You are breathtaking, and the laird and lady genuinely find you stunning. They'd also like to bed you.

Aithan's voice in her mind was amused. Macella stifled a laugh, cutting her eyes at him reproachfully. He was still innocently scanning the room for threats, but he flashed her a quick wink when their eyes met. Macella's cheeks grew hotter, Aithan's effect on her instantaneous as always.

"We hope to get very well acquainted with you while you are with us, Lady Macella," Lady Seondeok said, and Macella used all her willpower to smother a laugh at the unintentional double entendre. "It means a great deal to us having a true child of the north in favor at court. We would be honored to be counted among your supporters and friends."

Laird Parul nodded their agreement. "We know what it is to fight for survival against the harsh terrain, to pull ourselves up the ladder with only wit and willpower. We believe you can do much good for the region. If we can ever be of assistance, please consider us honored to do so. We are at your disposal."

The intensity of their words struck Macella with a peculiar sensation—something akin to hope. These people saw themselves in her, believed her to be worthy to represent their interests before the Crown. She'd been so lost in the fear and danger of her rise to queen, she hadn't had room for this hopefulness.

"I will strive to prove myself worthy of such friendship," Macella replied earnestly, shaking each of their hands again before letting Finley lead her away.

As the nobles turned to the next guests, Macella could feel the king's eyes on her—coldly assessing.

All through dinner, Macella snuck glances at the table where Aisling sat, but the sorcerer never returned her attention. She saw Aithan's eyes stray in the same direction several times and wondered when he'd known of the young sorcerer's presence. She wondered how Aisling had managed to get a position here, apprenticing to be a real mage. It was rare for a sorcerer who had not attended a mages' academy as a youth to get an apprenticeship under a reputable mage. Clearly Aisling's lot in life had improved since they'd seen her last.

After the meal, the conversation grew more boisterous as well-dressed servants refilled goblets and offered an assortment of sweets and pastries. Macella was absently staring at her, when Aisling rose, heading toward a smaller doorway on her side of the room. Right before she stepped through it, she turned and locked eyes with Macella. She motioned for Macella to follow before disappearing into the corridor.

Take Finley, Aithan whispered in her mind.

"Finley, I need a breath of fresh air," Macella remarked, turning to interrupt their conversation. "Walk with me?"

She didn't wait for their answer, her eyes on the door Aisling had left through. Finley was at her side in an instant, taking her arm and letting her guide them from the room. The door led to a dim hallway that ended in a lanai which opened onto a garden. Finley and Macella stepped out into the warm evening air.

Strange, sculpted foliage loomed above them. Vines, cacti, gnarled trees, and other northern plants had been shaped into a maze of reds, browns, and oranges. Beautiful flowers in all manner of colors bloomed in the bushes, filling the night air with their sweet scents. Ahead of them, Macella spotted a flash of ginger hair disappearing between two curved trees that formed a natural archway.

"Why have we truly come out here?" Finley demanded, lifting a perfectly sculpted eyebrow. "It had better be good because I was in the process of securing the affections of two northern knights."

Macella scanned the darkness, searching for any movement around the archway Aisling had taken. "You shall certainly have them now. Your departure mid-flirtation will only heighten their desire. I've found that the anticipation makes the acquisition all the more pleasurable."

Finley barked a laugh. "You naughty thing! I am constantly caught off guard by the things you say. And I am not easily surprised."

"It's one of the many reasons I'm your favorite," Macella replied, planting a quick kiss on Finley's smooth cheek, and releasing their arm. "Now, I am going to have a private word with an old friend. If anyone else attempts to enter the plant maze, alert me."

Finley nodded, orange eyes on the looming foliage. "Be quick and be safe. I would hate to repay Laird Parul's hospitality by having to murder someone on our very first evening under their roof."

Macella waved in acknowledgment before stepping into the maze. Inside, the evening was darker and quieter, the plant walls blocking the lingering sunlight and muffling the sounds of the after-dinner revelry. Macella glanced around, gaining her bearings. There were three paths to choose from, with no discernible difference between them aside from their direction.

"Aisling?" Macella called quietly, feeling suddenly less sure of the woman's intent. "I mean you no harm and I hope you bear me no ill will."

A throaty laugh greeted her words. Then, the grass to her left rustled and a trail of glowing footprints appeared. Macella followed them deeper into the maze. When she looked behind her, the footprints had disappeared, leaving no evidence of the route.

"Sorcerers," she grumbled beneath her breath. She thought she heard another throaty laugh.

After an incomprehensible sequence of twists and turns, Macella found Aisling sitting beside a sculpted stone fountain, its center a statue of Shiva, water pouring from his open palms.

Aisling leapt to her feet, smiling, and stepped toward Macella. "I never thought I would see you again," Aisling said, stopping a few steps from Macella. "I do not think I wanted to, but now that I see you, I am glad."

"That is surprising, indeed, since your last words to me were that you wanted to know nothing of us and our dangerous Fate," Macella replied, smiling despite herself. "You look very well."

Aisling twirled in a circle, her pale cheeks rosy with delight, the breeze wafting the faint scents of heather and freshly baked bread as she moved. "I've gotten quite fat and happy. And I owe it to you and your Aegis."

Aisling explained that after Aithan had uncovered her fraudulent use of sorcery—exorcising "demons" from people she'd herself afflicted—she'd been forced to reflect on her choices. She'd realized that she no longer wanted to live a life of deception and solitude.

"Your Aegis said that, if I found an honorable way to live this life, the right people would find me and I would not be alone." Aisling spoke the words solemnly, as if she'd recited them many times. "So, I tried to find a respectable path. I used my gift honestly, even when people despised the truth. With the money the Aegis gave me, I was able to get by for a while, even when people refused to pay for an unpleasant fortune."

Macella felt a swell of pride. Aithan, her Aithan, was so kindhearted and wise. He'd shown Aisling mercy, even though she was guilty of crimes that could've caused serious harm. He had offered her a second chance, and she'd clearly made the most of it.

"Is that how you found your way into Laird Parul's service?" Macella asked, gesturing around them to indicate the lavish estate.

Aisling nodded happily. "I foretold Laird Parul's marriage to Lady Seondeok, and they remembered me when they wed. Now I am apprenticing to be a true mage. I never would have found this path had I not encountered you and your unsafe Fate."

Macella made a mental note to add Aisling's tale to their list of victories. When things grew difficult and terrifying, she would need to remember all they'd accomplished. They had already helped some of the kingdom's discarded and mistreated citizens. They had already made a positive difference.

"I will pass your gratitude along to Aithan of Auburndale," Macella promised. "But I am sure he would like to hear it from you. You should join us for a drink tomorrow. Though we are staying but a short while, he will make time for his friends."

Aisling's eyes grew wide. "What are you even doing with the Crown's convoy? I've been eavesdropping as best I could and listening to all the gossip, but nobody has known much about the two of you!"

Macella laughingly led Aisling back to the fountain and took a seat on its edge. She noticed that Aisling always kept space between them, ensuring they never touched inadvertently. Macella understood why. The last time Aisling had touched her skin, the sorcerer had been possessed by a vision. Afterward, she hadn't remembered the prophecy she'd delivered.

"Aithan of Auburndale had the great honor of being named Protector of the Crown during the cold season," Macella explained. "I have been appointed Royal Scribe and…find myself in the king's favor."

Aisling's mouth popped open in a comical expression of surprise. Macella stifled a laugh. Aisling snapped her mouth shut and hastily jumped to her feet again.

She bowed clumsily, her face reddening. "My lady," she sputtered, her pale cheeks gone crimson with embarrassment.

"We are old acquaintances and need not stand on such ceremony," Macella demurred, waving the formality away. "Please treat me just as you always have."

Aisling started to retake her seat, but her feet tangled in her skirts, and she stumbled. If she fell now, she would likely hit her head against the fountain's stone edge.

Macella sprang to her feet and grabbed the other woman's arms to steady her. Aisling tried to flinch away from her touch.

But it was too late.

Chapter Twenty-Nine

―――~⊱❦⊰~―――

The sorcerer went completely rigid, her eyes blank and white. (46) A jolt of electricity shot through Macella's palms. She couldn't pull away, could not look away from Aisling's sightless eyes.

"Aisling?" Macella whispered, knowing even as she spoke that it was futile. Aisling could not hear her now.

Instead of replying, Aisling tilted her head one way and then the other slowly, as if testing out the movement. She inhaled sharply, sucking air through her mouth, then her nose. She blinked rapidly several times, her head moving continuously, turning this way and that. When she opened her eyes a final time, they'd gone entirely black. Her head settled, still slightly tilted, and her nose twitched as she sniffed the air. Then her black gaze focused on Macella, and her mouth opened in a horrible approximation of a smile.

"*Macella of Shively, born of Matthias and Lenora, Magic and suffering. Macella, orphan abomination, blood of Hades.*"

Macella's heart froze. This was not Aisling's voice. It was not even the chilling raspy falsetto with which she'd delivered the prophecy when they'd last met. No, this was not a human voice, but Macella knew it well. It still spoke to her from the shadows of her nightmares.

Aisling nodded, the movement of her head exaggerated and grotesque, that profane mockery of a smile still on her face. Macella wanted to speak, but her throat felt tight. She could hardly breathe.

"***Crossbreed desecration. My blood flowing naturally through your veins. You have grown stronger, daughter of mine.***"

Macella swallowed against bile. It was one thing for Aithan to call her a child of the dark god who owned her soul. It was another thing entirely to remember that she'd been born belonging to Hades, had inherited his blessing naturally. She and Aithan were different from the other Aegises in fundamental and unclear ways. She had no idea how that might manifest throughout their long lives.

She'd never heard of living Aegises communicating with the gods after their trials had ended. However, Aegises did not often talk about their experiences, so she had only the stories of her own acquaintances to judge by. Not even the vast collection of books in the library at Kōsaten Keep held much information about Aegiskind.

Macella swallowed hard and forced her lips to move. "Hades, Lord of the Many Dead, King of the Underworld. What would you have from me?"

Aisling's mouth opened wider as Hades laughed, the sound like a spine cracking against a noose. Macella wanted to move away, to flee the hedge maze entirely, but she was rooted to the spot. She could feel her flames whispering over her skin, her eyes mirroring Aisling's shining onyx sockets, but she could not look away, let alone escape.

"***Curious little crossbreed. Dauntless, foolish, amusing little abomination.***"

Macella took a deep breath, realizing she had momentarily forgotten how to acquire oxygen. She had spent immeasurable time with Hades, facing his trials, but all she remembered of the dark god was a nameless terror. His presence could mean nothing good.

Again, Hades widened Aisling's smile. The expression had become obscene, so contorted and unnatural it was sickening. Macella's stomach churned.

"What can I demand from you that is not already my own? What could you offer that I have not already claimed? No, child. I am here not to take but to give."

Macella didn't think that it could get worse than Hades wanting something from her, but she was wrong. Hades giving her something was perhaps more dangerous. His last gifts had cost her soul. What would she owe him for further favor?

"I bring you warning, crossbreed. A chance to save the realms to which you belong."

Macella felt a shiver of dread. "Realms? As in this and the Otherworlds?"

Hades nodded Aisling's head again, still smiling. To her horror, Macella realized that Aisling's feet no longer touched the ground. She floated inches above the cobblestone, formless shadows stretching beneath her in all directions.

"The Otherworlds are restless. The child of Apophis disturbed ancient beings that dwelled beneath the worlds even before we gods. Thus, our annual slumber was insufficient, Persephone taken too soon."

Macella's veins filled with ice. Though she'd already known or suspected as much, it felt far more devastating hearing it from the mouth of a god. The cold season had been too short. Since Hades's wife Persephone only spent the cold months with him in the Underworld, the brevity of the season was a personal affront to the god. Kiho had attempted to open rifts, to intentionally summon demons into the human realm, and those actions had consequences.

Aisling rose further, her smile morphing into a snarl. Her eyes glowed, her ginger hair billowing around her like flames. Macella suddenly noticed that it had grown cold, the stifling heat of the season replaced by a glacial breeze.

"The balance is broken. Your world will break next."

"Why would you warn me when you could simply let the human world fall? Your legions could reclaim it," Macella asked, fear and suspicion warring for dominance in her mind.

Aisling's eyes flared brighter, and she lifted several feet higher. Hovering above Macella, she tilted forward at an impossible angle, her body a stiff plank. She bared her teeth.

"Do not presume to know the ways of gods, crossbreed. I do not need or want this world. I want what is mine. Do you believe we earned nothing in the treaty with your first human king? The dead are ours and belong in our realms. That is balance."

Macella felt Hades's rage in the air. The temperature dropped further, raising goosebumps on her skin despite her natural Aegis resistance. Her brain struggled to make sense of the god's words. When Khalid brokered the deal with the gods, the dark gods agreed to bless Aegiskind in exchange for ownership of their souls. Now Macella realized that there was more to it.

"The dark gods do not want souls to escape the Otherworlds," she ventured, carefully considering each word. "You bless us willingly because we monitor the veil—not just to protect our world, but to keep your subjects in your domain."

"I am charged with ruling the Underworld, as the other dark gods rule their realms. That is my purpose. That is my will."

"We stopped the one who disturbed your demons' slumber," Macella blurted, recognizing the feebleness of her argument even as she spoke. "And the Thirteen are complete again. What else must we do to restore the balance?"

"Your king believes herself a god. She blasphemes, believing she can create life. She believes she can evade death. She threatens the balance."

Khari. Of course. The constant thorn in Macella's side. Hades somehow knew the king was planning to breed her own Aegisborn army. He knew of her ambitions—probably knew much more than Macella did.

I can make you more than a queen, King Khari had promised when she'd taken Macella into the woods to threaten her. *I can make you a god.*

"The blasphemer must be stopped. Child of both worlds, you and the son of Lucifer must stop her. Only you can."

A weight like a sack of stones settled over Macella's shoulders. Her betrothal to King Khari, her life at court, her role in the reformation of the kingdom—it was all so complicated and dangerous and important. And now Hades was confirming that the very survival of their world was at stake. When she'd dreamed of her Fate being bigger than Shively, this was not what she'd imagined.

"I offer a gift to aid you in your task."

Macella tried to back away, but still could not move. She'd been holding her hands aloft since Aisling rose out of reach. Now, she tried to lift them to shield herself, but it was useless. Until Hades released her, she would be frozen in place.

With her attention so focused on the floating sorcerer, Macella had not noticed the movement of the shadows on the ground. They'd crept closer to her until they'd completely surrounded her. Now, in a sudden rush, the shadows engulfed her, merging with her simmering onyx flames. Macella felt as if she'd been plunged into an icy lake. The sensation was so frigid that it burned.

Then it was gone, disappearing with the shadows as her flames absorbed them. She gasped, shivering violently. Despite the way the shadows had caused her flames to flare higher, Macella felt cold through and through.

"What have you given me?" she stammered, her teeth still chattering from cold.

"*You will discover it when you need it. Restore the balance, crossbreed.*"

"What if I cannot?" Macella croaked, hating the quaver in her voice.

"*Your realm will burn. Everyone you know will have the flesh carved from their bones and their entrails devoured. The screams of the dying will serenade you at night and the lamentations of the damned will haunt your days. Ammit will grow fat on human hearts and the air will ring with an exquisite symphony of suffering. Your world will collapse into meat and viscera, and the gods will start again.*"

Aisling's eyes went white. She collapsed before Macella could fully catch her, falling to her knees on the cobblestones. Around them, the shadows faded into twilight, the air abruptly warmer.

Half carrying, half dragging her, Macella got Aisling to the fountain and propped her against it. The sorcerer's eyes were closed. Her breathing was steady, but her skin was far too pale. Macella cupped water from the fountain in her hands and poured it over Aisling's face.

Aisling's eyes snapped open, round and back to their normal gray. She looked around frantically, her eyes snagging on Macella's hands. She scrambled away, scooting across the cobblestones.

"Please don't touch me!" Aisling pleaded. "That was worse than last time!"

Macella held her hands up placatingly, keeping her distance. "It was worse for me too."

Suddenly exhausted, Macella lowered herself to the ground. They sat in silence awhile, the last light of dusk fading around them. Macella did not know what Aisling was thinking, but her own mind was racing.

She was so tired of being threatened and manipulated. She was tired of being told what to do. It seemed that others were determined to dictate her story. Everyone had an opinion on her Fate.

Then she remembered the way Laird Parul and Lady Seondeok had looked at her while pledging their support. She remembered the way Jacan had knelt before her and thanked her for what she'd done in Smoketown. She remembered she'd helped change Aisling's life.

Macella was not a pawn or a puppet. She was the scribe, and her words were powerful. She was powerful.

A flare of black anger washed over her, hot and raw. Her Fate was *hers*. She was the scribe. She wrote the stories. She enchanted people with her words, swayed their emotions, shaped their thoughts. It was time for her to reclaim her story.

"Aisling, how would you like to study beneath the finest mages in Kōsaten and serve as personal mage to the queen?"

Chapter Thirty

Dearest Zahra,

By the time this letter reaches you, my good news will be rapidly spreading across the kingdom. I am to be wed to King Khari. I can hardly believe it myself. Forgive me for keeping my joy a secret. I am sure you understand why I could not reveal my betrothal earlier. I cannot wait to give you all the details. Please tell me that you'll accompany your father to court to congratulate the king. And perhaps you would be willing to stay a while?...

Macella would've been happy to stay much longer at Laird Parul's estate; however, King Khari was eager to accomplish the objective of their journey. Thus, after only three days in Nulu, the convoy departed for Shively. The only good aspect of drawing nearer to home was that King Khari had made good on her promise of giving Queen Awa more freedom. She and Macella walked or rode together daily, often taking meals together as well.

Despite the pleasure of these visits, neither woman was in the best spirits. While Macella grew more anxious with each passing day, Queen Awa seemed to grow sadder. The elder queen insisted she was looking forward to retirement, but whenever they spoke of it, she became quiet and distant. Macella found herself missing the cheerfulness of Laird Parul's home more than she'd expected.

Fortunately, Lady Seondeok had charmed the king into a promise to visit again on the return journey. To ensure they courted as many nobles as possible, they weren't staying a second time at any other estate. The route was carefully mapped so that they would visit every important house between Pleasure Ridge Park and Highview over the course of the trip. Thus, revisiting Nulu was another obvious favor for Macella. King Khari had noticed her enjoyment of the castle and its hosts and wanted to please her. The second stay would serve another purpose as well; when they returned, Aisling would join the convoy and become the first official member of Macella's entourage.

But first they had to achieve the purpose of this journey, which meant that a mere ten days of tireless travel later, Macella found herself back in her hometown. She insisted on going alone to speak with her parents before introducing them to Aithan and King Khari. She wanted to get it all over with as quickly and painlessly as possible. So, once she'd had time to prepare her family, the king and the Lord Protector would join her at her parents' home.

The neighborhood where Macella found her family was a far cry from the one in which she'd grown up. She'd known from the directions in their letters that her family had relocated, and she'd been glad about their improved situation. It seemed that with the regular money she sent home, they'd been able to move up in the world. According to their correspondence, they had purchased the land they'd long farmed for a wealthier family. Her mother had even hired a few workers of their own, allowing her parents and siblings to spend less time in the fields.

Macella realized that her parents had been reserved about their change in fortune. Struggling to raise ten children, her adopted mother had always been able to stretch their meager income a long way. If the new neighborhood was any indication, with a steadier and more abundant source of funds, the woman could do wonders. When Macella had lived at home, her family members only visited this part of town to pick up extra work or deliver herbs.

Macella's carriage halted before a large stone cottage covered in climbing vines and surrounded by sculpted shrubbery. Several other buildings sat farther back on the land—a barn, a workshop, a few smaller cottages that likely housed some of her adult siblings. A handful of children chased one another through the yard, while a big black dog lay in the shade of the main house, panting in the afternoon heat.

It wouldn't have mattered what home she returned to, Macella knew that she would always feel out of place. So, she would get this fuss over with and return to their much easier written relationship. She had grown used to the pleasant blandness of letters to and from her mother, crammed with bits of news and requests from her siblings. They treated her like an odd but harmless benefactor, and she was happy with her role. However, since they had not been in each other's company since she'd left home, she dreaded the inevitable awkwardness of the interaction.

"None of this matters," she whispered to herself as the footman helped her from the carriage.

She'd dressed simply in a lightweight sepia summer dress with loose sleeves and a ruffled, flowing skirt. The wide neckline bared her shoulders, the corseted bodice accentuating her waist and bosom. She hoped the fineness of the fabric and the quality of the workmanship didn't make her appear uppity. Nervously, she touched her star charm where it rested against her throat.

"Beg pardon, m'lady?" the footman inquired, but Macella just shook her head.

He'd already announced her arrival to the household and now someone was stepping onto the house's low porch. Macella almost didn't recognize her adopted mother, Babette, without a head wrap, a baby on her hip, and a basket in her arms. The neatly dressed woman awaiting her seemed far more refined and rested than the mother Macella remembered.

"Maman," Macella said, opening her arms for an embrace.

"Macella," Babette replied with a stiff bow. Ignoring Macella's outstretched arms, Babette shook her hand. "Come in. Let me show you the house."

Swallowing a lump of embarrassment, Macella stooped to pat the dog. She took a moment to smooth her facial expression, before rising and following her mother into the cottage. She found the inside to be as neat and refined as Babette herself. The furnishings were simple but elegant, and there were touches of luxury that alluded to their newfound wealth in subtle ways. A mahogany dining table made of wood that had to be imported from the logging settlements in the west. A colorful tapestry that was handmade only in southern Kōsaten. A housemaid, rather than one of her siblings, scrubbing dishes in the kitchen.

Most telling was the amount of space. Macella remembered the entire family being crammed into a few small rooms. She'd never had a moment to herself, though she'd felt constantly alone. This new cottage boasted four bedrooms, in addition to the kitchen, parlor, dining room, washroom, and study. The siblings still residing at home had their own beds and appeared to live only two or three to a room.

"Where is Papa?" Macella asked as they peeked into the study. "I hoped to speak to you both."

Babette smiled tightly. "He is very busy. There's so much to manage with the farm and our budding business. I always said it doesn't make sense how many magical herbs we ship out of Shively only for them to be sold for thrice as much elsewhere. Now, we're selling our own herbs and mixing our own tinctures and cutting out the unnecessary brigand who has been feeding off of our labor."

Macella heard the pride in her mother's voice and tried to feel happy for her family, instead of feeling sorry for herself. She'd come home a wiser and wealthier woman, with incredible news to share, and her father couldn't even be bothered to see her. If they could afford workers and servants, he should be able to spare an hour for the person who'd helped make all of this possible.

"This is lovely," Macella said, as they sat down in the parlor.

"Yes," Babette replied, looking pleased. "We've invested the little gifts you sent us well. I suppose it is nothing to you, but it is so nice to own our home and land, to pull ourselves up in the world."

"Ça c'est bon. I am glad to see you all doing so well." Macella smiled, realizing she had already begun to slip back into the local dialect. "What good is good fortune if I cannot share it with anyone? Speaking of which, I actually have some important news to share."

"So do I!" her mother interrupted. "I know I've kept you abreast of how well your siblings and niblings are doing—Lisette, Martine, Sebastien all married; Remy established at the best fishery in Nulu; Fabien and Flavia learning to run the herb farm; Henri and Etienne training as apothecaries. But I haven't told you dear Charlotte's news."

Macella suppressed a sigh. Her family had never bothered to listen to her before. Why would she expect that to change? She would have to wait through her mother's endless gossip before she could share her own news.

"How is Lotta?" Macella asked, smiling despite her annoyance. "Still planning to teach at the primary school?"

Charlotte, or Lotta, was about ten years younger than Macella—or so they'd thought. Of course, Macella had since learned that her Aegisborn nature masked her true age, and thus, she was actually twice as many years Lotta's senior. Still, she had fond memories of her younger sister. Lotta was one of the little ones who most enjoyed Macella's stories. Quiet and pliable, Lotta had always seemed fascinated by Macella's refusal to conform to expectations. Lotta was sweet to everyone, but she seemed to have a particular affinity for her strange, adventurous, storytelling older sister.

"*Charlotte* is incredibly well." Babette placed an added emphasis on her daughter's given name. "She is recently betrothed."

"She's not even twenty," Macella blurted, before catching herself. She and her mother had never seen eye-to-eye on matters of matrimony. "I mean, how good of her to know her own mind so young."

"Yes, she is a very good girl," Babette answered, her eyes tight. "We made her a fine match. She will have a fine establishment with Gaspar."

"Gaspar the blacksmith's son?" Macella asked, dismayed.

She needn't have asked. There was but one Gaspar in Shively, and everyone knew him because he was rich, talented, athletic, and handsome, and if you gave him a chance, he'd boast about those attributes ad nauseum. Macella's mother had long cherished the hope of marrying into the blacksmith's family. When the blacksmith's daughter, Elinor, had broken up with Macella, Babette hadn't spoken to Macella for weeks. It didn't matter that Gaspar had made Elinor a more beneficial match, Babette still blamed Macella for letting such a catch escape her. Even though Macella disagreed with Gaspar's snobbish reason for interfering, she hadn't been too upset about the breakup. She'd had liked Elinor, but she hadn't wanted to marry her, and she'd despised Gaspar for being a self-important prat.

"Gaspar has inherited his father's forge," Babette boasted. "The old man retired over the cold season, and Gaspar took over. Charlotte is going to be the blacksmith's wife. We are so proud of her."

Macella ignored the veiled jab. "I hope they find happiness in one another. You will have to give them my congratulations."

"You can give it to them yourself," Babette replied. "They'll be here any moment."

Macella bit back a groan. All she'd wanted was to tell her parents about her betrothal and prepare them to receive a visit from King Khari. She was already dreading having to play the lady for the entire afternoon. Now, she'd have to endure the pompous remarks of her ex's brother on top of everything else. Lovely.

"I had hoped to speak to you and Papa privately about a matter of some importance," Macella protested.

"Your papa will likely be with them." Babette shrugged. "He and Gaspar often walk here together for their midday meal."

"Yes, but, Maman—" Macella tried, but she was interrupted by the sound of voices and footsteps in the hall.

In the next moment, the parlor door was thrown open, and Gaspar burst into the room, Charlotte, Macella's father, Tomas, and a couple of children trailing behind. Macella stood to greet them, turning first to Tomas, and extending her hand. He took it hesitantly, releasing it almost instantly and moving away.

"Macella, is that you, mon ami?" Gaspar grinned, taking her hand for a vigorous shake. "I never thought I'd see the day you'd look the proper lady."

"And I never imagined you'd honor my family with your hand," Macella replied icily. "I seem to recall you being quite concerned with your sister marrying into our station."

Gaspar blinked, clearly thrown by her bluntness. Macella took advantage of his confusion, turning to her sister and extending a hand. Charlotte ignored it, wrapping her in a hug instead. Macella hugged her back, the knot in her chest loosening ever so slightly as she squeezed. Charlotte smelled familiar, sweet and warm, like cherry blossoms and cinnamon.

"You look different," Charlotte said, stepping back to scrutinize Macella more carefully. "Not just your fine clothes—your eyes, your hair. You're different but it's a good kind of different, cher."

Macella's heart warmed at the endearment. Though they shared no blood, Macella and Charlotte shared enough physical features to pass for birth sisters. Charlotte's curls were tighter and her skin a bit darker, but she had Macella's dimples, full lips, and dark eyes. Charlotte was also more petite, her stature always seeming a proper match for her unassuming personality.

"I'm sure she's using the finest beauty products the kingdom has to offer, and the talents of the mages besides," Gaspar chimed in, laughing mockingly. "Life at court has its perks, right, Macella? Have the royal mages put a gris-gris on you to cover your flaws? If you stay away from the palace too long, will you turn back into the coarse ballbuster we all remember? I'm surprised you'd risk it. So, to what do we owe the pleasure of this visit?"

Macella gritted her teeth. Only the anxiety in Charlotte's eyes kept her from snapping at him.

She took a steadying breath and turned to her parents. "As I wrote, I wanted to speak to you today regarding an important matter," she said. "I'd hoped we could speak in private."

"Bah! There's no need to stand on such ceremony," Gaspar interjected. "We are almost family. We need have no secrets from one another."

"Congratulations on your betrothal," Macella said through clenched teeth. "However, this matter is confidential—"

Gaspar snorted. "Is it a matter of national security? Some intel from your Aegis lover? I have to say, I am glad my Elinor didn't marry you. You are too ambitious for her. However, I'm impressed at what you're willing to do to climb in rank and pleased to be joining our families for your rise to the top."

Charlotte gasped and covered her mouth. Macella glared from Gaspar's haughty face to her parents' stern indifference. She didn't know whether to be angrier about his insulting insinuations or his openly mercenary scheming with her parents.

"Macella, you should be pleased at all the good you've done your family," Babette scolded. "Your rise in rank was the only way we ever could've secured such an advantageous match for Charlotte. She's a very sweet girl, but she's not as capable as the rest of you, pauvre ti bête. She needs taking care of. You've secured that for her."

Macella looked at Charlotte. Her sister was staring at the ground, silent, her shoulders slumped. Macella felt a flash of hot anger.

"She's going to make a charming little wife," Gaspar declared, wrapping an arm around Charlotte's shoulders. "I am really getting lucky here. I never would've considered her as an option before. I thought I'd end up with some spoiled, over-educated tradesman's daughter, but now I get the status without the obnoxious upbringing. My Charlotte is so quiet and docile."

Macella stepped closer to Charlotte, ignoring Gaspar's possessive stance. "Are you pleased with this match, petite cher?"

Charlotte gave Macella a wide-eyed shrug, glancing furtively at her parents then back at her feet. "It is a good match. I will have a good home, and I won't be a burden to my family. That is enough for me. I'm not adventurous like you, Macella. I'll never go out into the world and make my own way."

"Absolutely not," Gaspar agreed, his grip visibly tightening on Charlotte's shoulders. "Not a lot of folks would take Macella's path—leaving a whorehouse to take up with an Aegis. But she always was different."

Macella looked again from her sister's fiancée to her parents. Nobody looked as enraged as she felt. If anything, her mother looked a bit embarrassed, but probably only because of Gaspar's references to Aithan of Auburndale.

"What's he like, your Aegis?" Gaspar lowered his voice conspiratorially. "I bet he's nothing like the pretty stories from all the society papers. I made Charlotte stop reading them. It was filling her head with nonsense. We all know Aegises to be beastly, subhuman brutes. They give me the frisson! However did you tame one?"

Macella's blade was at his throat before she formed her next thought. Her mother cried out and started forward, but Tomas held her back. Charlotte stepped forward instead, placing a gentle hand on Macella's arm.

"It will be a good life for me, Ella," Charlotte said quietly. "It's the best I could hope for. Please don't ruin it."

Macella held her dagger steady but slid her eyes to meet her sister's. "You deserve better. You can have better. Come and live at court with me."

A chorus of exclamations filled the room. Macella ignored their protests, keeping her attention on Charlotte. Her sister looked as if she was afraid to consider Macella's offer. She looked afraid to hope.

"What would I do at court?" Charlotte whispered.

"Whatever you'd like," Macella said. "You can study a trade, or you can simply be a member of my entourage, dedicated to keeping me company, amusing yourself, and eventually finding yourself a *worthy* spouse. Or both. Or neither. It will be up to you."

"You cannot seriously be considering this," Gaspar exclaimed, his eyes still on Macella's dagger. "You have no idea what sort of perverse lifestyle she's living, Charlotte! Babette, Tomas, we have an agreement. Charlotte is mine."

Macella's parents were babbling their apologies and concerns. One part of Macella's mind registered that her father wanted Charlotte to go through with her marriage to Gaspar, while Babette sounded intrigued by the idea of Charlotte finding an even wealthier spouse. Another part of Macella's mind was waiting for Charlotte's decision. Most of her mental capacity, however, was devoted to containing the hot anger she felt, suppressing the desire to press her blade deeper into Gaspar's flesh.

"I would like to come with you, Ella," Charlotte confessed miserably. "But I cannot break my commitment to Gaspar. It wouldn't be honorable."

Gaspar heaved a triumphant sigh. "That's right. Now remove that dagger from my throat unless you really mean to offend me."

Macella couldn't help herself. She smiled. For a moment, Gaspar's eyes reflected real fear, but then he seemed to remember that he was supposed to be superior.

His lips curled into an ugly sneer. "I recognize this workmanship. My father made that dagger. You're not fit to wield it," Gaspar snarled.

"You have insulted me repeatedly, and now you will atone for your vulgarity, or meet me in combat," Macella growled, still smiling wickedly. "You will apologize to me, retract the insults you made to Aithan of Auburndale's good name, and you will release Charlotte from your betrothal."

Gaspar laughed, baring his teeth. "Allons! I will meet you in combat, and when I defeat you, I will take my wife *and* my father's dagger. And you can throw in a hefty contribution to Charlotte's dowry for my trouble."

Chapter Thirty-One

Macella's parents and sister protested in vain. Gaspar would not apologize and Macella would not relent. Soon enough, they stood in the yard, facing one another, while a circle of onlookers watched. Macella thought they were all family members, but she couldn't be sure. Inevitably, this story would spread, so she had better make it good.

(47) Macella pulled her curls into a bun and tied her skirt high enough to allow for unobstructed movement. Her sword lay against her back, her daggers secured on her thighs. She knew that Gaspar was no match for her, she needed only decide how much to hold back. How much humiliation did he deserve?

"You have insulted my honor and grossly undervalued my sister," Macella declared, reaching behind her head, and grasping the pommel of her sword. "You can apologize now and release my sister from your engagement, and we can part as polite acquaintances. Otherwise, I will exact payment from your flesh."

Gaspar glared at her, his hand on the hilt of his own sword. Like his sister, Gaspar was tall and lean with golden brown skin and dark curls. However, while her natural beauty made Elinor more gracious, Gaspar's physical attractiveness had only served to make him more insufferable. He knew that his social status and good looks ensured he would always get what he wanted. Now, Macella was challenging that, trying to take what he believed himself entitled to. She watched his handsome face contort with anger.

"You are a putain and a whore who thinks you're a real lady because you fucked your way into a place at court," Gaspar spat. "You're ruining the only good thing you've ever done for your family in your useless, repugnant life. You have always thought yourself better than your station. I will teach you your place."

Macella unsheathed her sword and slid into a fighting stance. "We will see who learns a lesson."

Gaspar advanced immediately. He'd trained with weapons his entire life and was quite skilled. If Macella were a regular woman, she might be facing a worthy adversary.

She watched as Gaspar charged at her, his movements appearing slow and obvious in comparison to the training partners she was used to. Distantly, she registered the sound of approaching hooves, and sighed inwardly at the ever-growing audience. She would make this quick then.

Effortlessly, Macella dodged Gaspar's strike, parrying his blade and pivoting around him. Before he could turn around, she spun and raked her blade across his back, carefully cutting a gash deep enough to draw blood, but not to cause lasting damage. The onlookers gasped and Gaspar roared.

"Yield," Macella commanded. "Apologize to me, retract the insults you made against Aithan of Auburndale's good name, and release Charlotte from your engagement."

Gaspar roared again, lunging for Macella, slashing viciously. Macella thought she heard her sister cry out in alarm. She dropped low, swiveled, and swiped at his calves, leaving another set of bloody gashes. Gaspar stumbled, catching himself on one knee. Macella rose and kicked him in the center of his back, sending him sprawling face first into the dirt. This time, she thought she heard Charlotte let out a startled whoop of laughter. Gaspar scrambled to his feet, cursing, and wiping his filthy face with his sleeve.

"Yield," Macella repeated. "Apologize to me, retract the insults you made against Aithan of Auburndale's good name, and release Charlotte from your engagement."

"Go to hell, mongrelfucker," Gaspar spat, charging at her again.

This time Macella lunged forward as well. She sliced three red gashes across his abdomen before he could lower his blade to deflect her attacks. By the time he'd taken a defensive stance, she'd added wounds to both arms, and knocked his sword into the dirt. Before he could recover, Macella swept his feet out from under him. He fell hard, his back and head thumping against the packed earth.

Macella put her foot on Gaspar's chest and the tip of her sword against his throat. "Yield. Apologize to me, retract the insults you made against Aithan of Auburndale's good name, and release Charlotte from your engagement."

Gaspar glared up at her through dirt and blood. The enraged mask he'd worn throughout the duel was beginning to slip. Beneath it, Macella saw a newfound fear: the idea that he might not be superior to everyone else.

"I yield," Gaspar croaked, as the crowd drew closer to hear his words. "I deeply apologize for insulting your honor, Lady Macella. I retract everything I said or implied against Aithan of Auburndale."

Gaspar swallowed hard, his expression pleading. It was the final concession that would hurt him most. He wanted to be a man of rank and still have a kindhearted wife he could consider to be beneath him. He was begging Macella to allow him to return to a life where he always got what he wanted.

Macella curled her lip, narrowing her eyes. She shifted her weight, driving the point of her sword deeper into the flesh of his throat. Gaspar squeezed his eyes shut for a long moment. Macella thought he might be fighting back tears.

"I release Charlotte from her commitment to me," Gasper conceded finally, his voice lifeless. "Our engagement is terminated."

Macella sheathed her sword and removed her foot from Gaspar's chest. While her family members exploded into excited chatter, she held out a hand to help him up. Gaspar looked as if he'd rather die than accept her help, but he knew better than to refuse.

"You are forgiven," Macella said, practicing her cold, queenly smile. "Our families have always been great friends, and I hope we shall remain so. And, by the way, Elinor forged my dagger, not your father. Stop underestimating the women in your life."

Luckily for Gaspar, he was spared the necessity of responding by the interruption of a loud, slow clapping. Though she hadn't noticed their final approach, Macella saw the riders on horseback she'd heard at the start of the duel. A hush fell over the onlookers as they noticed the new guests.

Three knights of the Royal Guard in their telltale garnet-studded armor sat atop beautiful chestnut steeds. A fourth chestnut held a finely dressed servant carrying the Crown's banner. Aithan of Auburndale looked stoic and imposing on Jade's gleaming ebony back.

The final rider was King Khari, resplendent in garnet and gold, astride a rare Akhal Teke—a beautiful breed of horse with a metallic gold coat.

Macella's family and nosey neighbors alike dropped to their knees to bow before the king. Macella tossed Aithan a questioning glance. How had she not noticed their approach?

King Khari did not wish to be noticed, so she ensured we wouldn't be.

Macella shuddered. The king had proven she could manipulate the mind and distort a person's reality, but this was something more. How had she concealed six extremely noticeable people on horseback from an entire crowd of onlookers? Could Macella ever trust her senses around the Crown?

"My family," Macella said, recovering herself enough to remember her duties. "It is my great honor to present to you her grace, the supreme sovereign of Kōsaten, King Khari."

Smoothly, the king dismounted, the other riders following suit. She moved to stand at Macella's side, Aithan close behind them. The knights took strategic positions around the perimeter.

"My king, may I present my parents, Babette and Tomas de Pointe." Macella gestured to where the two knelt.

"Please rise," King Khari commanded them. "Thank you for receiving me."

Macella felt a tinge of amusement at the tongue-tied greetings her parents managed to fumble out. Babette was not easily rattled and almost always managed to work any given situation to her family's advantage. Now, however, she seemed truly speechless.

"Maman, Papa," Macella interrupted their stammering. "I would also like to introduce my partner, Aithan of Auburndale."

Reluctantly, her parents dragged their attention away from the king. They looked up at Aithan, who bowed his head in polite acknowledgment. Macella saw the pleasure drain from their expressions.

"It is an honor to meet you," Aithan said, wisely refraining from attempting to shake hands. "I have heard a great deal about you both."

"Thank you, Lord Protector, Lady Macella." King Khari easily took control of the conversation. "We are so pleased to meet your loved ones. And so...surprised to be treated to an exhibition of your combat skills. Please rise, everyone."

The dozen or so folks who'd been kneeling in the dirt now stood. They gaped between Macella and King Khari, committing every detail to memory. This story was getting better and better—they'd gotten an unexpected duel between the local outcast and a man who was practically Shively royalty, followed by a visit from the actual king. They'd be talking about this for years.

King Khari stepped forward, smiling magnanimously. She stopped before Gaspar, beckoning for him to rise with the others. Once he was on his feet, the king shook his hand. Gaspar's face went gray as a sharp snap cut through the silence.

"If you so much as frown in Lady Macella's direction ever again, I will have you boiled alive," King Khari promised, her voice deadly calm. "The only reason you are surviving today with only a few fractured phalanges is because I wish to make a favorable impression on my future in-laws."

"Your in-laws?" Gaspar said stupidly, clearly struggling to keep up with his rapidly changing reality.

"Lady Macella, have you not given our family the joyous news?" King Khari asked, her ochre gaze still on Gaspar.

"I haven't yet had the opportunity, your grace," Macella replied, untying her skirt, and freeing her curls from their hastily tied bun. "The blacksmith intruded upon our reunion."

"Pity," King Khari intoned, hands now clasped behind her back. "This is not how I envisioned this conversation. I planned to gallantly ask your parents for their blessing on our courtship. I brought a rare wine to toast our good fortune."

King Khari gestured to the servant, who scurried forward holding a polished cask. At the king's nod, he handed the cask to Macella's parents. Tomas and Babette stared in open-mouthed astonishment. The servant had to clear his throat to prompt Babette to take the wine.

"I am so sorry, your grace," Macella murmured. "This is not how I intended to introduce my family to your notice."

King Khari turned a benevolent smile in Macella's direction. "I do not blame you at all, my dear. I only regret that this imbecile ruined our moment."

The king slowly turned her head back to Gaspar. He seemed to shrink under the weight of her glare. Shivering, he watched King Khari with panicked, bulging eyes.

"Disappear before I have time to reconsider this mercy," the king commanded, her husky voice dripping with venom.

Gaspar didn't hesitate. He bowed, backing away from the king until he'd cut through the circle of onlookers. Then he turned and fled, practically running. Macella turned away to hide her satisfaction.

"Lady Macella, Tomas, Babette." King Khari smiled magnanimously at them all. "Shall we go inside and properly discuss our good news?"

It was humiliating how differently Macella's parents treated her during her second conversation in their parlor. Suddenly she was "dear Lady Macella" and even "dearest Ella." Babette ordered the housemaid to bring a fresh loaf of bread, cheese, and tea, and served them on a fine set of dishes Macella had never seen before. She remembered eating from earthenware bowls and drinking out of tin mugs, all chipped and scratched and mismatched.

Macella let herself get lost in reverie, preferring it to engaging with her parents' officiousness. She wasn't sure if King Khari was enjoying their conversation, but she still managed to be effortlessly charming. Aithan stood near the parlor door, observing in silence. Macella made a conscious effort not to hear his mind—she didn't want to know what he thought of her parents' unpolished manners and obvious insincerity.

"Our Ella has always had a strong mind," Babette was saying with a too-big smile. "We knew she was going to get out of this poor village and make something of herself."

Macella resisted the urge to snort into her teacup. Apparently, the many times her mother had called her obstinate, headstrong, and foolish, she'd been admiring Macella's strength of mind. And while her parents had indeed expected her to leave Shively, they certainly had not expected her to do well for herself.

"Even when we were living in a tiny home, six to a room, with hardly enough food to go around, dear Macella behaved as if she were above it," Babette went on, after King Khari had complimented the cottage. "She was always scribbling and reading and telling stories."

"That does sound like the Lady Macella I've come to love," King Khari said, patting Macella's hand affectionately. "Would you agree, Lord Protector?"

Macella would have been annoyed with the king's use of the word love and her possessive touch, but she was pleased that King Khari was refusing to allow her parents to ignore Aithan's presence. They hadn't yet spoken to him, hadn't offered him a seat or any refreshment. Macella wanted to believe that they were being mindful of his responsibility to stand guard, but she knew better. They could hardly stand to look at him.

"Lady Macella has a brilliant mind, courageous spirit, and a loyal heart," Aithan replied. "Even toward those who do not deserve her love and kindness."

His gravelly voice was even and polite, but his meaning was clear. Macella's heart swelled. He hadn't spoken more than three sentences to her family and was already standing up for her. For a moment, she wondered what awful thoughts he might be hearing from them, then decided she was glad she did not know. For once, she was glad she couldn't hear human minds as Aithan could.

She didn't have to hear her parents' thoughts to know that they, too, had understood the meaning beneath his words. Her mother's smile was strained. Tomas, always a man of few words and fewer opinions, stared at his shoes.

"Well said, Lord Protector." King Khari nodded, smoothing easily over the awkwardness. "She was a born queen. It is hard to believe her modest beginnings. This is a sweet little cottage, however. It will be a nice rental property or a fine inheritance for one of your other offspring once you move into your new estate."

Tomas' head snapped up, and he joined his wife in gaping at the king. Macella turned questioning eyes on Khari as well. This was not a part of their planned discussion.

"I dispatched royal solicitors well before we began our journey northward," King Khari explained. "They were charged with finding suitable accommodations for Queen Awa, as well as for your family. You will soon be in an entirely new station. You cannot continue residence in such modest lodgings."

Apparently, the king's solicitors had found a quaint, uninhabited castle with ample grounds and more than enough space for Macella's large family. They'd hired workers to do renovations and repairs, so by the time Macella's parents returned from accompanying the royal caravan to Highview, the property would be ready for their habitation. It would be fully staffed and furnished in the latest fashion.

"Of course, as the new Lord and Lady of Shively, you'll have new duties, for which you will be handsomely compensated," King Khari continued, obviously relishing their reactions. "You will receive a monthly allowance this first year that should be more than sufficient for the management of your household and property, until you've established proper taxes and tithes to support Shively's management. Don't worry about the debt; you'll eventually repay it through Shively's annual tithe to the Crown, which I'm sure will grow much larger under your stewardship. I can already see how well you manage money. The warden of Shively now serves you, of course, and one of my solicitors will offer counsel as you restructure the town's leadership. Your new role does not preclude you from earning coin in other ways—such as your herb farm and budding apothecary. And, of course, the estate and requisite titles will belong to your family for time immemorial."

Her parents were effuse in their gratitude. Even Tomas was compelled to speak. Macella tuned out as they discussed particulars, but she was glad to hear that the king had supplied a core staff familiar with nobility and even an etiquette coach to train her family in the customs of their elevated station. Knowing some of her siblings, the coach would certainly have their hands full.

Macella hoped this made her parents happy. At least she could rest assured that they'd been well-compensated for taking her in as a child. She was sure they would never acknowledge that she'd been adopted, especially now that she'd proven herself valuable. They had never loved her, but they'd kept her alive, and that was worth something. Macella considered her debt paid.

"Are you pleased, Lady Macella?" King Khari asked, drawing her back into the conversation. "This will benefit not just your family, but all of Shively."

Macella smiled at the king, her mind scrambling to process the words. Her family would join the nobility, meaning Shively would finally have a direct voice in kingdom politics. It would mean good jobs for the working class, as her family would have to hire at least a few dozen additional staff members to tend and manage their new lifestyle. Eventually, her family would begin entertaining other nobles, intermarrying and growing Shively's upper class. The city would attract more people, more businesses, more amenities.

This was precisely the kind of impact she wanted to have in the kingdom, making life better for those most in need. How fitting that she should start with her own family, her own humble home.

She nodded at the king. "I am very pleased, your grace," Macella assured her. "Forgive me for my silence. I am simply struck speechless by the magnitude of this opportunity."

King Khari beamed. She and Macella's parents chattered on, discussing the trip to Highview, and which family members would take positions at court. Eventually, all was settled, and King Khari took her leave. Macella walked the king back to her horse.

"Your mother will have no trouble governing the city. She is shrewd," King Khari mused, kissing Macella's hand before mounting her horse. "Forgive me for saying so, but you bear very little resemblance to either of your parents, in person or in temperament. You don't seem to belong here."

Macella shrugged. "Thank you for honoring my family with this visit, your grace."

She turned away from the king, who was soon occupied with the knights and servant as they prepared to depart.

Aithan brushed his lips over her temple, giving her a concerned look as he shouted orders, and a stable hand passed him Jade's reins. Macella smiled sadly and shook her head.

I can stay behind and ride back with you, Aithan thought at her.

Macella shook her head again. *I will be right behind you. I am just going to say goodbye to Lotta.*

She felt him watching her as she headed back to the cottage. She let herself in, wondering where Charlotte might have gone. Rather than talk to her parents again, she decided to search for her sister on her own. She'd checked the kitchen, dining room, and parlor when she heard voices from the study. The door was open only a few inches, obscuring who was inside. Perhaps Charlotte was talking logistics with their parents. Macella approached the door quietly, wanting to be sure her sister was present before interrupting.

"I told you she would be worth the trouble, cher!" Tomas was saying. "You didn't even want to take her in."

"You said nothing of the sort, Tomas de Pointe," Babette shot back. "You said she wouldn't be any more trouble than the rest, and at least she came with coin. And you only said that because you were salivating for that purse and knew you wouldn't be the one minding her anyhow, since you never saw fit to help me with the child-rearing. I swear you haven't got one fatherly bone in your body."

Tomas huffed indignantly. "Well, I was still right. A queen, Bette! Our kid is going to be queen."

A smile tugged at the corner of Macella's mouth. She'd never heard her father talk about her this way. She knew she should leave—obviously Charlotte wasn't in the study—but she lingered, wanting to hear her mother's response.

"I wish it was one of our own," Babette replied. "But I won't poke a pixiu in the pouch. Let's just pray the king doesn't come to her senses and change her mind."

Tomas laughed. "You saw the way her grace looked at Macella and the way the girl carried on. She seemed almost normal, though she still gave me the frisson. Either she's learned to hide her strangeness, or the king has fucked it out of her. Macella won't give her any reason to back out now."

Macella's smile froze. She'd never heard her father speak of her this way either. Now she really wanted to walk away. But she didn't.

"Don't be crass!" Babette scolded. "Besides, she's still as strange as ever. You forget that, besides the king, she brought that beastly Aegis. After that blue-haired woman left her here, I prayed I'd never see one of their kind again. And now we'll never escape them because she's partnered up with one. I told you that any child even the Aegises didn't want had to be unnatural. And she's proven it. Raised by decent folks and still ran away to take up with a mongrel."

Rage and shame battled for dominance in Macella's mind. Ears pounding with blood, she willed her feet to move. How stupid she had been to think for a moment that her family might have kind things to say about her. Stupider still, she'd thought her elevated rank might make them accept her. She didn't need their approval or validation, but here she was hoping for it anyway. Like a fool.

"Can we just enjoy this moment, cher?" Tomas said beseechingly. "It's not every day one becomes wealthy and titled."

Babette let out a squeal and a laugh. The subsequent giggles and murmurs were muffled. Macella left them to their celebrations.

Chapter Thirty-Two

Macella would see Charlotte soon enough, since her sister and a few other family members would join the convoy to Highview. There'd been enough family time for one day. She was relieved when her carriage pulled away from the cottage.

She slumped against the cushioned bench. She felt heavier than she had that morning. She dug through her handbag for a silk handkerchief, then irritably dashed away her tears. A coin fell from the silk and landed in her lap. Absently, Macella began to roll the coin across her knuckles in an anxious gesture she'd picked up as a child—she wasn't sure who'd taught her the trick.

"Illegitimi non carborundum," a voice said, startling her. "We used to say that in Smoketown. Don't let the bastards grind you down."

The coin stuttered and fell from her fingers when Macella looked up in surprise. Shamira sat across from her, looking for all the world as if she'd been there the entire time. She was watching Macella with a mixture of vexation and sympathy.

"Have you been around all afternoon?" Macella sniffed, picking up the coin again. "How much of my family's awfulness did you witness?"

"I couldn't help it," Shamira replied, looking sheepish. "When I cross into this realm, you're often the easiest person for me to locate. And it's even easier if you are experiencing heightened emotion."

Macella laughed bitterly, trying and failing to smoothly reverse the direction of the coin across her knuckles. "Good to know that I send out a ghost-summoning distress signal. Well, I suppose I should apologize to you in advance for disturbing you, since this is how I typically react to my family, and I'll be around them a lot over the next month."

"This is not your family," Shamira insisted earnestly. "I am sorry you cannot remember the parents who loved you, and I'm sorry they were taken from you. But they're still inside you. I can see traces of your father in your face. And he used to do that same coin trick."

Macella tossed the coin aside, feeling somehow more miserable. "He must've taught it to me, but I don't remember it at all. How can I claim a family I have no memory of?"

Shamira frowned. "You don't have to remember them to honor them. And you still have a family. You have built that for yourself. Aithan of Auburndale, Finley of Fairdale, Zahra, Awa, and a dead woman who is grateful to have known you, even if we met again far too late."

Macella wiped at her eyes, taking a deep breath. "I had no idea you were capable of saying kind things without sarcasm."

Shamira shook her head in exasperation. "You are the prototype of an annoying younger sister."

"And yet you love me." Macella grinned, feeling a bit better. "You have been with us more of late. Is it becoming easier to stay in this realm? It certainly can't be because we're any closer to defeating Khari."

Shamira's expression shifted into something unreadable. "Not exactly. But Awa needs me right now. So, I am here and here I shall stay."

And stay she did. Over the whirlwind travel of the next few weeks, Shamira was a constant presence. Macella spent much of this time with the elder queen and her dead lover. Nonetheless, the nearer they drew to Highview, the more melancholy Awa grew. However, when Macella questioned her, the elder queen only said she was mourning the end of her long reign, but still eagerly anticipating the peace ahead.

By the time they reached Highview, Macella was as quiet and pensive as Queen Awa. Aside from having to say goodbye to her friend, there was plenty for her to brood over. Many of the northern nobles were also assembling at Highview Castle at the Crown's invitation, where they'd be hosted by Awa's relative, Lord Moussa. They'd join a private meeting in which Awa and Khari would officially declare the elder queen's retirement. A special luncheon in her honor would follow.

And then Macella's life would change forever, because the next day would hold a grand feast and ball, and King Khari would announce their courtship. The king would say some pretty words, and Macella would gracefully accept the honor of betrothal. She'd spend the rest of the evening being bombarded by the attentions of every nobleperson in northern Kōsaten.

And she would need to grow accustomed to it. This was only the beginning.

Perhaps her dread made the days pass more quickly, or perhaps Chronos, Zurvan, Etu, and the other gods of time were playing a cruel joke. Either way, she soon found herself surrounded by nobles, toasting the now former queen's health. The great hall of Highview Castle rang with cheers and well wishes, as well as an undercurrent of murmured conjectures.

Macella thought her parents might burst before the afternoon concluded. They couldn't help but overhear the whispered wonderings about King Khari's next spouse. Every eligible person between fifteen and fifty jockeyed for the king's attention, hoping that she'd planned this visit with the intention of finding a new partner. Macella's parents were under strict orders not to spoil the surprise before the king's announcement, but their smug expressions should've been enough to make the other guests suspicious.

"Lord Ngozi passes through Shively on occasion, always fussing with his fool of a daughter," Babette whispered loudly. "Now he's trying to push the girl on dear King Khari. As if the king would choose such a silly, crooked-nosed thing."

Charlotte hurriedly distracted her mother with an unrelated question, while Macella pretended she hadn't heard her at all. Her mother and sister chattered about Highview Castle's amenities—her mother already deciding that everything about *their* new castle would be better—but Macella couldn't pay attention to any of it. She watched the Crown, anxiously cataloging their interactions, mannerisms, and looks. By the next sunset, she would be thrust into their world.

She wasn't ready. She'd never be ready.

Macella did not linger after the meal, feigning a heat-induced headache to escape her mother's meddling and the polite attentions of the other guests. She craved solitude. Back in their borrowed rooms, she could wallow in her fears without being observed. She didn't know when Aithan would be free to join her, and for once she didn't mind. She wanted to be alone with her misery.

The hot season in the hottest region of the kingdom was not a pleasant place to be anxious and irritable. Highview Castle didn't have as much magical climate control nor the latest technological advancements of Kōsaten Keep, and the northern environment was far less forgiving in general. After a cool bath, failed attempts at reading and napping under whirring fans, and a fair bit of crying, Macella was exhausted. Perhaps she'd had enough alone time. She'd planned to spend the remainder of the day alone in her rooms, but maybe she should find Finley instead. They always managed to cheer her up.

She'd just decided on that course of action when there was a sharp knock at her outer door. She groaned, her patience long gone for the day. Something told her that it wouldn't be anyone so welcome as Finley.

Macella was not surprised to find King Khari at her door. Tomorrow, their betrothal would be made public. Of course, the king would have last-minute advice or concerns to discuss. Macella led Khari into her quarters' sitting room and poured them each a goblet of wine.

"Lady Macella, I will not waste your time on your last evening of relative freedom," King Khari began with a wry smile. "This time tomorrow you will be known as the next queen of Kōsaten. I am sure you have much to reflect on. I do not mean to keep you from it, only to give you a few additional points to consider."

Macella sipped her wine, willing her face into a serene mask. Tomorrow and tomorrow and tomorrow. Tomorrow, she would allow this woman to claim her anonymity. From that point on, she would be under a magnifying glass, her every word and expression scrutinized. Tonight, she would not bother trying to craft the perfect words. She waited for the king to continue.

"I have watched you on this journey and have been impressed with you at every turn," King Khari complimented, smiling her cold-eyed smile. "You have charmed everyone you've met. These northern nobles, especially, have been very taken by you. You have already proven yourself an invaluable asset."

The praise made Macella think of her parents. Like them, King Khari valued Macella only as she was useful in promoting their success. None of them would ever see her as an equal, as a person with inherent worth.

"You will be quite the rose in my cap, forgive the expression," King Khari continued. "It is unfortunately an apt one. You will be an adornment, a complement to my power. You will have all you can ever wish for; everyone you care for will be richly rewarded. And you only have one job—to remain an asset to me."

So, they'd reached the crux of this little tête-à-tête. Macella should've expected this. Though the king had already warned her about being queenly, trustworthy, and loyal, she hadn't yet cautioned Macella about ambition. Macella had worked hard to court the northerners' good opinions, knowing it was what King Khari expected of her, but she'd noticed the king's calculating gaze on her during these exchanges. Now, she realized Khari had been watching for any indication the northern nobles were *too* taken by Macella. It must be exhausting always searching for signs of treasonous intent.

"I would simply request that you remember, it is not only you who will suffer my displeasure if ever you should cease to be an asset," King Khari finished at last. "Finley, Charlotte, Zahra, Aithan—even people you hardly care for or only briefly knew, like the madame at that shitty brothel, the blacksmith's daughter, your servant Lucy, or our dear high tailor—they are all at my mercy. And even once we are wed and the magical bindings preclude me from harming you, it will not protect them. You are well aware of the sights I can show them."

Though Macella had considered all of these threats a million times over, she couldn't suppress the thrill of terror that shot through her body in response. An image of Charlotte suspended in the jorōgumo's web sprang unbidden, to her mind. Then Charlotte became Zahra, and then Finley. Worst of all, Aithan lay before them, Khari's sword driven through his torso. If Khari attacked him, he would be powerless to fight back against the magical binding tethering him as Protector of the Crown.

Macella drained her goblet, closing her eyes and willing away the anger and despair tugging at the edges of her consciousness.

Exhaling, Macella opened her eyes and met Khari's hard gaze. "I am perfectly aware of the responsibility I bear, my king. I shall strive to be Kōsaten's greatest asset."

King Khari stared at her a long moment before replying. Macella didn't bother masking her exhaustion and dejection. She could let the king see the brokenness, the defeat. Khari liked that. It was power, determination, and rage that Macella must keep hidden. She must appear the beautiful, pliable, northern rose. Simply an adornment for the king.

"Good," King Khari said finally.

The king rose to leave, gesturing for Macella to stay seated rather than see her out. As she swept past her, the king rested a hand on Macella's shoulder. She paused, producing a box from the folds of her robe, and setting it on a side table.

"I nearly forgot, a gift for tomorrow. I know they'll look lovely on you."

With that, King Khari strode from the room. Moments later, Macella heard the chamber's outer door click shut. Sighing heavily, she poured herself another goblet of wine.

When Aithan arrived a short while later, he took one look at her and said, "Let's go for a ride."

Macella slipped into a pair of soft, wide-legged pants that looked deceptively like a skirt, a loose blouse, and, at Aithan's insistence, a lightweight, hooded cloak. Similarly concealed, he led her through a series of dark corridors and out through a rear gate of the castle grounds, which happened to be guarded only by Sir Igor and Sir Griselda. Jade and Cinnamon waited for them just outside the gate.

Macella couldn't help but smile. Of course, her Aegis had known she'd need an escape this night. Cinnamon nickered an affectionate hello as she pressed her face into his mane. For a moment, all was well.

They were quiet as they rode through the slums just beyond the Highview Castle grounds. People were venturing out into the streets now that evening was approaching and bringing relatively cooler temperatures. They cooked and sang and laughed and washed and scolded their children. Some sold meager wares they'd made or the rare plants they'd managed to grow. They reminded Macella of the people she'd grown up with in Shively, hardworking and poor. These people relied on day work at the castle or the whims of rich folks passing through. Meanwhile, nobles like Lord Moussa—Awa's relative who owned Highview Castle—feasted inside the castle walls, wasting more than these poor souls could ever hope to earn.

"These people are like me," Macella sighed, feeling Aithan's eyes on her. "Overlooked by the wealthy and powerful unless they can be used as pawns. They do not see us until we prove ourselves valuable to them."

She knew Aithan had heard her troubled thoughts and read her mood since he'd proposed this little excursion. Most likely, he'd caught her despair even during Awa's retirement luncheon. But he'd given her space and allowed her to grieve as she saw fit.

Now he spoke up. "That is what the wealthy and powerful believe. But that is not who you are at all. Come, I have something to show you."

He urged Jade into a trot, and then a gallop after they'd escaped the busy streets, leading her away from the city and into the backveld. Unlike in other parts of Kōsaten, there weren't thick forests and shimmering lakes covering the terrain. Instead, the foliage consisted of sharp, scraggly bushes and bare, crooked trees. Everything was colored shades of brown, red, and orange. Still, there was a unique beauty in the natural arches, mesas, and dunes. Macella felt the pull of the land soothing her. There was something about an environment that refused to bend to human will. The northern landscape was content in its own identity, full of untamed marvels and surprises.

After three-quarters of an hour, they stopped. Macella drew in a sharp breath, stunned. She looked around in silent awe.

"This is why it is called Highview," Aithan explained. "Whenever I'm led to this region, I make it a point to find spots like this one."

Macella knew they'd been traveling a steady incline, but she hadn't realized how high they'd climbed. Now, they looked out from a mesa's edge so far above the city that Highview Castle looked like a dollhouse. They could see for leagues in every direction, to the lights of other cities, and even—she thought—the distant blue-green of the ocean. The land was an endless expanse, wild and pure.

"This is who you are, my hell goddess, my Macella," Aithan said. "You are untamed. You are not what they see, nor what they want you to be. You are so, so much more."

Macella exhaled heavily, her eyes stinging with the threat of more tears. She slipped from Cinnamon's back, landing silently on the hard earth. She ventured nearer the cliff's edge, gazing out into the seemingly infinite vastness. In the setting sunlight, the terrain was awash in pinks and purples, a starless cosmic sea. The world suddenly seemed much bigger than she'd realized, and humans were so very small.

Aithan was at her side in an instant, moving as silently across the gravelly dirt as if he were on plush carpet. He took her hand, intertwining their fingers.

"I am afraid, Aithan," Macella whispered, still staring into the distance. "I don't know if I can do this, if I can be what everyone needs me to be. I'm afraid of losing myself. How long can I play their games before I become someone—something—else? Who am I to rebel against gods and kings?"

To her surprise, Aithan laughed. "Of course, you're afraid. I would question your sanity if you weren't absolutely petrified. But you are exactly the right person to stand up for the multitudes neglected and oppressed by gods and kings."

When Macella shook her head, he tugged her to the cliff's edge, pulling her down to sit beside him. They dangled their legs over the side, and the excitement of being practically suspended in the sky took Macella's breath away.

"You have already begun, my love," Aithan insisted. "Without hesitation or consideration, heedless of your own safety, you have been rebelling against injustice since the moment I met you. Our society told you that I was a monster, no more than a subhuman attack dog. You saw beyond that and treated me accordingly. You ignored the disapproval of others and demanded to accompany me on my travels."

"Stubbornness and spite can only take a person so far," Macella rebuffed, rolling her eyes.

"Well then, it's a good thing you have much more than that," Aithan shot back. "Stubbornness and spite didn't make you throw yourself at that lamia in Hurstbourne. You hadn't tapped into your Aegis gifts yet; I'd barely even begun training you in combat. But you didn't hesitate to try to save that child."

Macella opened her mouth to protest, but Aithan pressed on. "You saved my life during the battle with Kiho, then again when you followed me into Duànzào—literally challenging the gods in the process."

She tried to brush off his words, though they were starting to sound logical. "You are leaving out key details and making me sound much braver than I was! I couldn't just leave you there."

"But you could've left the children of Smoketown to their horrible fates, like so many others have done for centuries," Aithan countered. "Instead, you used your gift with words to their advantage, and you did it before marching into the mountains toward near-certain death. You made sure that, no matter what happened to you, life would improve for those children."

Macella threw up her hands. "I just try to do what's right and what I must to survive! I'm not trying to be heroic."

"Exactly," Aithan replied. "That is just who you are. And you are who we need standing against gods and kings."

He took Macella's face in his hands, gazing intently into her eyes. She felt the tears spilling over, even as her chest swelled with love at the force of his conviction.

He planted a soft kiss on her lips, then kissed her tear-streaked cheeks. "I know who you are, Macella of Shively," he assured her. "I will not let you lose yourself. I will not allow them to change you, to take you from me."

Macella saw the sincerity in his eyes, felt it in his touch, and the tenor of his voice. She kissed him, throwing her arms around his neck and pressing her body closer to his. In the distance, coyotes yipped, and birds of prey screeched as they careened over the arid landscape. And, in the midst of the natural majesty, a pair of lovers kissed on a cliff's edge, unperturbed by their tenuous perch and the treacherous terrain ahead of them.

Chapter Thirty-Three

Lost in one another, Aithan and Macella kissed until the sun disappeared and the sky darkened from indigo to obsidian. (48) A blanket of stars settled overhead as Aithan pulled her away from the precipice, then laid her down on a bedroll from Jade's saddlebag. Macella gazed up at the ceaseless starry sky, feeling Fate settle into her bones. She was precisely where she was meant to be.

Macella reached up and untied Aithan's hair, letting the silver silk of his tresses fall around her face. She breathed in the scent of him, always smoky and sweet and inviting. Burying her hands in his hair, she pulled his mouth down to meet hers.

Aithan slid his tongue into her mouth, kissing her deeply as he pressed his body over hers. Macella sighed against his lips, loving the familiar weight of him, the feel of his hard muscles and calloused hands. Her hips lifted involuntarily, rubbing against the stiffening length of his cock straining against the confines of his trousers. Aithan groaned, the sound vibrating in her mouth, tugging at the tendrils of pleasure unfurling deep in her belly.

He snaked a hand between their bodies, sliding his palm over the warmth between her legs. Macella shuddered, moaning as he massaged her mound through the thin, soft fabric of her pants. Writhing, she held him more tightly against her, arching her back and biting his bottom lip.

Growling, Aithan broke the kiss, and knelt to yank her pants and panties down, over her boots and off. Tossing them aside, he buried his face between her thighs, sucking Macella's clit into his mouth. She cried out, clutching his head, her hips bucking. Aithan gripped her ass, his nails just barely biting into her skin.

The stars were above and below and inside of her as he feasted upon her, the relentless, gentle sucking on her clit obliterating her equilibrium. His mouth was the axis on which the world turned. All Macella could do was hold on as he carried her into sweet oblivion.

Aithan kissed her thighs as her orgasm subsided, looking up at her with burning orange eyes. As always, she marveled at the surge of love and lust she felt under that gaze. She sat up, grabbing his shirtfront and hauling him up to kiss her. She fumbled with the buttons of his trousers until he took over, deftly loosening them.

Macella pushed him onto his back, letting him shimmy his pants past his hips, before straddling him. The rocky ground poked through the bedroll, digging into her knees, but she hardly felt it. She took his stiff, throbbing cock in her hand and positioned it against her eager wetness. Slowly, she took him inside of her, lowering herself a millimeter at a time until he filled her completely.

Aithan groaned, his burning eyes rapt, watching her take him into herself. As she began to rock her hips, she pulled her blouse over her head. Aithan sat up, the sudden change in angle making her cry out. She helped him pull off his shirt, while he undid the clasps of her binder.

Lowering his head, Aithan took one nipple into his mouth, teasing the other between his thumb and forefinger. Macella's body spasmed, and she threw her head back, letting her cries join the calls of the other night creatures.

She rode him hard, clutching his head while his tongue flicked over her nipple, firm and fast. The euphoria of release, the abandon of this wild, timeless place, the grief of this last night of freedom—it all flooded into the wave of sensation threatening to pull her under.

"Fuck," Aithan gasped, flopping back onto the bedroll, his hands clamped around her hips. "That's it. Take what's yours."

Macella arched her back, screaming up at the stars, her hands tangled in her curls, breasts trembling as she came in a torrent of spasming hips and shaking legs. Aithan thrust his hips up, pressing her down, deepening their union. His orgasm came on suddenly, spurring Macella higher, her pleasure almost painful. She gave in completely, letting her body take control, dissolving into nothing but primal need and instinct.

Afterward, they lay side-by-side, gazing up at the twinkling sky. Macella smiled to herself, imagining some cosmic beings staring back at them, laughing at the woman clad only in a pair of riding boots and her companion with his trousers around his knees.

Aithan let out an amused grunt. "We certainly gave them a good show," he chuckled. "Now let's get you back to civilization. You need your rest. We have a bigger show to put on tomorrow."

Macella slept far better that night than she'd expected and woke rested and resolute. She rose early and began to write, scribbling frantically, revising and rewriting. When evening arrived and she stood alone outside of the great hall, the words were clear and true, imprinted on her memory.

All too soon, Macella heard the herald's resonant cry. "King Khari of Kōsaten is honored to introduce her intended bride, the Lady Macella of Shively!"

A hush fell over the ballroom as a pair of smartly dressed servants pulled open the huge doors. Macella could hear each of her footfalls on the patterned tile. Taking a deep breath, she willed her legs to carry her forward.

(49) Macella stepped into the silent room, feeling every eye on her, hearing every gasp and exclamation as the partygoers took her in. King Khari stood waiting for her on the steps of the dais, looking regal in a garnet tunic embroidered

with gold lions beneath a magnificent golden robe. Behind her, Queen Annika, and the now Lady Awa sat with Awa's relative, Lord Moussa, on grand thrones.

Gods, Macella. You are celestial.

Aithan stood on the dais behind the king. Macella was glad. She could pretend she was walking to him, that none of these other people mattered, that this was not the moment she condemned herself to a truly treacherous path. She could do this because her Aegis would be with her every step of the way, no matter how perilous the road.

Wherever you go, there go I, he whispered in her mind.

Macella could feel Aithan's admiration and sensed that it was echoed throughout the room. Every person in the great hall watched her progress across the polished tile. She risked a glance around and drew in a sharp breath. The looking glass in her chambers had not done her justice.

The walls of the ballroom had been covered in mirrors, making the room appear endless. The floor was obscured by a conjured fog that wafted in a gentle breeze. The warm glow of candlelight flickering from crystal chandeliers glimmered in the reflections like a sea of stars.

And in the middle of all of it, Macella shone like the setting sun.

Her rich brown skin glowed against the deep crimson of her gown. The bodice hugged her torso, its lace overlay molded into the shapes of blooming roses, its wide neckline baring her collarbone and shoulders. It featured a billowy skirt of sheer crimson muslin layered over chiffon. The fabric fluttered and clung to her in turns, revealing and concealing her curves and glimpses of skin through a thigh-high slit. Crimson chiffon rose petals nestled in the skirt's folds.

The royal stylists had braided Macella's hair away from her face, sweeping it up to form a crown of curls, held in place with diamond and garnet-encrusted hair clips. A few curly tendrils were loose, arranged to frame her shimmering cheekbones and kohl-lined eyes. Garnet and diamond earrings dangled from her ears. Along with the matching hair clips, they'd been a gift from King Khari, left in the wake of last night's threat.

Around her throat, Macella wore her braided leather choker, the star charm ice cold against her throat. She cherished the chilly reminder of her Fate and her duty. She wore a token of love that a small boy had once clung to while lying beside his dead mother. She carried the rage and responsibility of orphaned children, murdered parents, and stolen love stories. Macella must always remember that she was playing the rose of the revelry only as a means to right the wrongs these royals had wrought.

The glimpse she caught of her face was exactly the one she meant to show. Her eyes and cheeks were dusted a shimmery gold, her lips the same deep crimson as her gown. She looked lovely and unafraid, the set of her shoulders confident, her movements graceful. In other words, she looked like a queen.

As she neared the dais, she quickly scanned the ballroom for other familiar faces. She spotted Finley and Jacan among a group of northern knights and nobles, Finley grinning proudly, while the younger Aegis's mouth had fallen open in awe. Macella's family sat nearest the dais, with a few prominent members of Awa's family. Macella saw Charlotte watching her in wide-eyed wonder beside their parents, who looked somehow both pompous and petrified amidst all the grandeur of the evening.

Finally, she stopped before the dais, kneeling at King Khari's feet. The skirt of her dress spread out around her, seeming to float in the conjured fog. The king descended the steps and extended a hand to Macella. As she rose to take it, she caught a glimpse of Queen Annika, glaring from her seat beside Lord Moussa.

A quartet of musicians began to play, their bard crooning a sultry tune, as King Khari twirled Macella about the room. Hushed whispers followed as they danced, their feet seeming never to touch the floor, the fog swirling around them, adding a dream-like quality to their movements.

As the song concluded, King Khari dipped Macella so low that the fog swirled around their heads. Macella lifted her knee to the king's waist, the slit of her dress falling open to showcase one shapely brown leg. They held the pose for a long moment, the room exploding into clapping and cheers.

"Perfect, my northern rose," King Khari whispered, and then she brushed Macella's lips with hers.

A crackle of electricity sizzled around them, and for a moment there was nothing but the two of them, suspended in complete darkness and swirling fog.

Khari's lips were soft and warm. She tasted of pomegranate, metal, and ash. Kissing her felt like falling, careening toward certain death.

Then the moment was over, and they were standing in Highview Castle's great hall, hand-in-hand, receiving tumultuous applause. Macella's smile felt frozen on her face, her lips still buzzing. The faces around her blurred into a featureless mass, only Aithan's stoic expression making any impression.

Finally, King Khari lifted her hands for silence. "Thank you all so much for sharing in our great joy. I had no notion of finding such a woman, but the gods are good and continue to grant me their favor. They sent me this remarkable rose from the north, and I knew immediately that I must pluck her and plant her at my side. Many of you have met her, so you understand my enchantment. I know that she will represent you well as a member of the Crown."

Again, the room erupted in applause. Servants were moving quickly, filling and refilling goblets of wine. One appeared before them, carrying a silver tray bearing two crystal goblets of dark, red wine. They took the goblets, King Khari raising hers in a toast.

"A toast to my northern rose and your next queen, the Lady Macella of Shively!" the king proclaimed.

Macella felt a bit lightheaded. The multitude of faces seemed to swirl around her, their smiles more like leers. The cheers were too loud, the fog too thick, the candlelight too bright. *My northern rose*, the king's voice echoed over and over in her mind.

Savior of Smoketown, crossbreed abomination, defier of gods and kings. Child of Hades, daughter of Matthias and Lenora, the Shield's Scribe, Aithan spoke firmly through the haze in her mind. *My Macella, my hell goddess, my love, my wife, my life.*

(50) Macella found his orange eyes and did not look away. The disorientation and noise receded. She took a deep breath, straightening her back and squaring her shoulders.

When she looked around the room again, she saw the faces of her friends among the northern nobles, heard the genuine congratulations reverberating from many of the guests. She thought of the wild, untamed landscape from the night before. Her smile grew.

The king reached for her hand, preparing to lead her to the dais and begin the feast.

Deftly, Macella stepped away, lifting her goblet, and raising a hand for silence. The crowd quieted.

"A toast to King Khari of Kōsaten, our wise and favored supreme sovereign!" Macella declared, and the guests cheered and drank.

King Khari smiled magnanimously, preening for her guests. Macella sipped from her goblet before raising her hands again. The king eyed her uneasily, but Macella pretended not to notice.

"It is a great honor to be chosen for such an important undertaking," Macella continued. "I assure you that I do not take this honor lightly. As her grace said, I am a true northern rose. I grew in the harsh Shively soil, among so many others struggling to survive without the resources needed to thrive. I knew that Fate insisted on my survival for a reason, and I have since learned what that reason is."

The room was utterly silent, the guests enthralled. King Khari's smile was frozen on her face, an undercurrent of anger simmering beneath. She had not planned for Macella to speak. Apparently, she'd forgotten that her betrothed was an experienced storyteller.

"Throughout Kōsaten, I've encountered others like me—poor and forgotten people seeking better lives. I have carried their stories with me, and I will not forget them when I am queen. I will make sure their voices are heard," Macella promised, lifting her chin. "Already, the Crown and I have worked to secure a brighter future for the children of Smoketown. With our improvements and renewed focus on the children's well-being, we can officially announce an end to Aegis recruitment. You no longer need sacrifice your offspring for our kingdom's protection. Instead, we will focus on the many trainees already inhabiting Smoketown, ensuring they are properly cared for so that they might mature into brave and mighty warriors, like the Aegises here with us tonight."

Macella lifted her goblet toward Jacan and Finley, then to Aithan. Hesitantly, the guests followed suit, applauding the three Aegises politely. The air in the room seemed heavier, but Macella felt increasingly relaxed. It was well past time for the wealthy and powerful to experience some of the discomfort that plagued their subjects every day.

"I vow to serve *all* of Kōsaten's citizens so that the peace and prosperity that we in this room enjoy is spread to those most in need," Macella continued. "However, my roots tether me to the plight of the north. That is why her grace, King Khari, and I will partner with my dear parents, Lady Babette and Lord Tomas of Shively, to revitalize the region and ensure its people reap the rewards of their labors. To that end, we will immediately begin the construction of a northern mages' academy, as well as a hub for the trade of magical plants and medicines—the proceeds of which will be reinvested in the poorest communities in the region."

This time, the applause was more genuine. There were only three other truly reputable academies in the kingdom, and neither was anywhere near the region where so many crucial plants were grown. Having such an academy would elevate the north's reputation, make it easier for its young sorcerers to rise to true magedom, and guarantee more jobs and resources would be devoted to the region. The northern nobles were looking at Macella with a newfound respect.

"I look forward to working with all of you to make our great kingdom a more just and balanced place," Macella finished. "I will strive to be Kōsaten's greatest asset."

Macella took King Khari's arm amidst the roar of applause that followed her words.

The king's smile was tight as she led Macella up the steps of the dais, to their empty thrones. It was a beautiful, uncomfortable seat—an apt metaphor for the evening.

Macella gazed out over the room. She could feel Aithan's protective presence behind her, could see Charlotte, Finley, and Jacan beaming up at her. She'd enthralled the room with her words, showing them her petals while pricking them with her thorns.

She had reclaimed her story, and it had only just begun.

Chapter Thirty-Four

―――⋙✦⋘―――

Their stay at Highview Castle passed in a blur of celebrations. Finally, the convoy prepared for the return journey. On their final night, King Khari proposed a quiet drink to say farewell to Lady Awa. Aithan and Macella accompanied the king to Awa's new home—a lovely cottage on the outskirts of the castle's grounds.

Awa hadn't wanted to live in the castle itself, preferring solitude to another courtly life. Her cottage was self-contained enough to give her the privacy she craved, yet without sacrificing any comforts. She had a small staff of servants, a well-stocked library, and even her own stables.

Though King Khari did most of the talking over drinks, Macella's attention stayed on Awa. Something seemed to be troubling the former queen. Macella had hoped that she might see her friend at peace before they departed. She'd thought that this sweet little place might give Awa a sense of freedom and hopefulness. Instead, the former queen only seemed tired and sad.

"We will leave you to your new life, my love," King Khari said eventually, rising and moving to Awa's side. "Thank you for your many years of companionship. I pray your final days are as pleasant as the time we shared."

(51) Macella's star charm went cold, and she saw the moment unfold as if in slow motion, yet she could not stop it. On some level, it felt as if she'd been expecting this, waiting for King Khari to strike. The syringe was in the king's hand in the next breath. Had it been concealed up her sleeve? No matter, because the king was stabbing the needle into Awa's neck, murky liquid disappearing as she pressed down on the plunger. The former queen's eyes were fluttering closed, almost in resignation.

A roar echoed through the room. Aithan was faster than Macella, but somehow still not fast enough. He lunged for King Khari, unsheathing his sword with one hand, his other arm stretching before him.

An electric crackling filled the air as Aithan's palm connected squarely with King Khari's sternum. A whoosh of air escaped her as the force of the blow sent her sprawling. She flew back several feet, landing on her rear and sliding across the polished floor.

Aithan roared again, this time in pain. He crumpled to his knees, chest heaving, dropping his sword to clutch his other arm. He pushed his sleeve up roughly, almost tearing the fine fabric. Crimson veins bulged from his skin, climbing from his palm up his forearm, and spreading slowly toward his bicep.

Lady Awa slumped forward, the syringe protruding grotesquely from her neck. Her breathing was labored, her downturned eyes blinking slowly. As if deciding to take a nap, the elder former queen folded her arms on the table and let her head fall onto them.

"Aithan!" Macella cried, running to his side.

She knelt next to him, extending a hand toward the angry crimson veins. She felt a whisper of fire rising, unbidden, to her palm. A flicker of shadow danced over her hand, startling her into pulling away. The heat faded from her palm, the shadow disappearing.

"That is impossible," King Khari growled, struggling to her feet. "You cannot raise a hand against me."

Macella and Aithan both turned their attention to the king. She stood a few feet away, breathing hard, her expression livid. The skin peeking above her blouse was an angry red that would obviously turn purple and bruised.

Macella stood slowly, her hands instinctively lifting in a placating gesture. "Instincts, your grace," she said quickly. "Aithan of Auburndale has trained extensively to protect the Crown from danger. Perhaps your actions confused the binding, allowing Aithan to strike you in defense of the queen."

"She is no longer the queen," King Khari spat.

Though her voice dripped venom, Macella could see the king calming. She was considering Macella's words, trying to find a way to accept them. Macella knew Khari would prefer any alternative to her magical protection's fallibility. She could use that in their favor.

"Yes, and so he suffers," Macella replied, gesturing at Aithan's arm. "Awa has only just retired, and you have attempted serious harm. The magic simply adapted to this unique situation. The binding holds."

King Khari looked at Aithan's arm, where the veins had ceased to spread. They were beginning to turn into jagged wounds, welling with blood.

Aithan's jaw was clenched, his mouth pinched. "What have you done to Lady Awa?" he demanded through gritted teeth.

King Khari's face softened, going almost tender as she looked at her former queen. She moved to Awa's side and rested a gentle hand on the sleeping woman's shoulder. Awa didn't move, but Aithan tensed as if prepared to defend her from further harm. Macella shot him a warning glance.

"You must know that I could not allow her to live," King Khari said softly, still gazing at her former spouse fondly, as she removed the needle from her neck. "Even without her alleged treason, she is too dangerous. She knows too much. As do the two of you."

The king turned her ochre eyes on them. Aithan lurched to his feet to stand in front of Macella. The only sounds in the room were Awa's steady breathing and the irregular patter of blood hitting the floor as it dripped from Aithan's wounds.

Macella stepped carefully to his side, one hand on his good arm, her eyes on King Khari. "Tell me what the poison will do to her," she whispered, holding the king's gaze.

King Khari studied Macella for a long moment before she responded. "We loved one another once. I owed it to her to do this myself and to make it gentle. She simply will not wake. And eventually, she will perish."

The horror of the moment threatened to consume Macella, but she would not let it. There was no room for grief or anger or despair, only survival. Everything else could wait until after. But first, she must ensure they lived to see said after. Beside her, Aithan simmered with rage and frustration as he understood what she meant to do—what they had to do.

"Queen Awa was ill when you married her," Macella began, ignoring the bile rising in her throat. "A carcinoma, perhaps. The gods' blessings saved her, kept her healthy throughout her reign."

King Khari's eyes narrowed, understanding dawning. She looked at Macella with renewed interest, scrutinizing her even more closely. Finally, she nodded for Macella to continue.

Macella closed her eyes, letting the tale spin itself. "You both have always known that her retirement from the Crown would mean her immediate death. So, she continued to rule, even after she grew weary of life at court. She couldn't bear to leave you to deal with that grief alone."

Macella felt Aithan's big, rough hand taking hers. He intertwined their fingers, giving her hand an encouraging squeeze.

She took a steadying breath. "Once Queen Annika joined the Crown and the two of you grew to love each other, Awa began to talk to you of her desire to take her rest," Macella continued. "Still, she would not leave you until she knew you'd found someone suitable from the north, someone who would rule wisely in her stead, and who could help fill the hole she'd leave in your heart."

Macella opened her eyes, meeting the king's gaze. King Khari was smiling a satisfied, triumphant smile. It made Macella want to scream. Instead, she clung to Aithan's hand, using the anchor of his love to ground her. She returned the king's smile.

"And then the gods sent me exactly what I needed," King Khari finished the story. "A rare rose from the north."

But this was Macella's story. She was the scribe. She decided how this all ended.

"Fate sent you exactly what you needed—exactly what you deserve and what Queen Awa wanted you to have," Macella corrected. "Me."

If the king heard the deep conviction and deeper meaning in Macella's words, she wasn't bothered. In fact, King Khari was looking at Macella with something akin to pride. It made Macella's skin crawl.

"You continue to exceed my expectations, Lady Macella," King Khari praised, clasping her hands behind her back. "You truly were destined for greatness."

King Khari let her gaze settle on Lady Awa for a last, long look. The king's eyes glistened with candlelight or, perhaps, unshed tears. Before Macella could decide which, Khari straightened her back, adjusted her crown, and turned away.

"I trust that you two can clean up here." King Khari gestured at Awa with a dismissive hand. "And the Lord Protector may have the remainder of the night off to heal and compose himself."

With that, King Khari left the elder queen's quarters, her boots sounding heavy against the wood floors as she walked away from her oldest companion.

When her footsteps had faded, Aithan pulled Macella into his arms, crushing her against his chest. She gave a long, shuddering sigh and leaned into his warmth. They stood that way for a long time.

Finally, Macella pulled away, brushing tears from her cheeks. "Let me see your arm," she demanded, gingerly taking Aithan's injured wrist in one hand.

He winced as she lifted it. The cuts were deep and still bleeding. They would need to be cleaned, stitched, and wrapped immediately. Macella used her other hand to adjust Aithan's elbow, trying to get a better look at the gashes on his biceps.

The warmth she'd felt earlier spread from her palm, accompanied by flickering shadows. Instead of pulling her hand away this time, Macella instinctively moved her hand over Aithan's arm, hovering just above his wounds. She felt her eyes shift into their hellform, glowing onyx, whites disappeared.

"What new wonder is this?" Aithan asked, his voice low and hushed.

The shadows grew thicker, dancing from her hand and over Aithan's bloodied skin. They appeared to seep right into his wounds, bathing his arm in shifting darkness. Aithan shivered.

Macella started to pull back. "I don't know what—"

"Don't stop." Aithan caught her wrist so she couldn't move away. "I think—I think you are healing me."

He was right. As they watched, the shadows flickered across flesh that was scarring over, and the bleeding stopped. Macella's arm felt cold, the warmth fading from her palm. With the cold came a wave of nausea. Macella quickly took a seat across from Awa. She poured herself a cup of water, sipping as she focused on fighting the queasiness. Slowly, the sick feeling subsided.

Aithan watched her without question, listening to her mind and recognizing that it would be a bad time to ask her to speak. His eyes wandered between anxiously scrutinizing her expression, to marveling at the tender new scars on his arm. Even with a mage's attention and his enhanced healing abilities, it would have taken days for his wounds to improve this much.

"It seems we've discovered my new gift from Hades," Macella said finally. "My flames conceal, my shadows heal."

Aithan nodded, his orange eyes wide. "A god gift, indeed."

The thought struck them both at the same instant. Without a word, Aithan lifted Awa from the table and carried her into her bedchamber. He laid her on top of the bedclothes, then moved to give Macella room.

Macella extended both her hands, waiting for the warmth to come. It was more difficult this time, the heat building slowly. Finally, the shadows crept from her hands to flicker across the former queen's ebony skin.

The minutes stretched, dragging by as Macella struggled to hold on to the shadows. She knew she could do this. She pushed harder, willing heat into her palms. The room tilted dangerously around her.

Awa's dark eyes opened. She took a long, slow breath.

Her gaze met Macella's. "Stop," she whispered. "Let me go."

"Awa!" Macella gasped. "Don't try to talk. I am going to heal you. Just hold on."

Macella swayed a little as she focused more intently on the heat in her palms. Aithan took her wrist, pulling her hand away from its position above the former queen. Macella jerked toward him, her mouth open in protest.

Then she saw the mournful look in his amber eyes. She felt tears pricking her own.

"She doesn't know what she's saying," Macella hissed, rubbing angrily at the tears spilling down her cheeks. "It's the poison. She's not in her right mind."

"I can hear her mind quite clearly now that she is no longer queen," Aithan replied gently. "She is in full possession of her senses. She knew this would happen."

Macella spun back toward the former queen—toward her friend. "You knew she was planning to kill you? Why did you not confide in us? We could have done something! We could have stopped her."

Awa smiled, the rare expression tragic in its beauty. "This is where my story was always going to end. Your story must continue. You are exactly what I wanted for her—exactly what she deserves. You are her destruction."

Macella felt sick. The chill in her palms had spread up her arms, leaving a trail of goosebumps. Nausea filled her throat with acrid bile, and she felt unsteady on her feet. But none of those things hurt as badly as her heart. She took Awa's hand in hers. Aithan wrapped an arm around Macella's waist, and she leaned gratefully into his warmth.

"I will stay with her until the very end," said a familiar voice from behind them. "And then I will welcome her to Otherworld. Just as she and I have discussed."

Awa smiled as Shamira moved to her bedside. Macella sniffled, looking between the two women. Realization dawned.

"You knew, too?" she accused. "Shamira, how could you let her do this?"

Shamira sighed. "I didn't agree at first. But the decision is hers. And deep down, I'm a selfish bitch."

"She doesn't belong to Kali," Aithan said when Macella relayed Shamira's words. "She will not pass into your Otherworld."

"I have the favor of the gods of light," Awa replied simply. "When they welcome me, I will ask this one last gift. We don't know what will happen, but it is worth the risk."

"You will have to say goodbye to both of us, little sister," Shamira said, giving Macella a sad smile. "It is Awa, not my vengeance, that has truly tethered me to this realm. I will wait with her until her final breath, and then I will let go of this plane forever."

Macella sat beside Awa on the bed, unable to trust her legs any longer. She felt ill and exhausted and extremely afraid. Aithan stood beside her and stroked her back. Awa squeezed Macella's hand, her grip surprisingly strong.

"I know you can do it, Scribe. Finish the story," she whispered.

Macella thought of Awa often. Back at court, there was much to remind her of her fallen friend. The former queen had not awakened the morning following their farewell visit. By the time the royal caravan arrived, notice of her death had already reached Kōsaten Keep. Macella crafted the official announcement for the royal bulletin, telling the kingdom the tragic tale of Awa and Khari's doomed love, haunted by the specter of her illness.

She often second-guessed her decision to respect Awa's wishes and not heal her, but she knew that it hadn't been her choice to make. The elder queen had lived several lifetimes and was ready for her next adventure. Nevertheless, Macella missed her and the balance she brought to the Crown—both as a counter to Khari and Annika and another soothing presence for Meztli.

Surprisingly, however, there were additions to her life that soothed the loss of Awa and Shamira. She'd taken King Khari's advice and filled her entourage with trusted advisors and friends. Aisling was a jolly, gossipy delight who was beside herself with the excitement of apprenticing for the kingdom's best mages. Once Lynn had fulfilled Macella's request of furnishing her novice mage with an array of full-length gloves, Aisling was able to comfortably interact with Macella, and the two got along quite well.

Charlotte was agreeable company, falling neatly into the role of Macella's protégé. Macella enjoyed watching her little sister come out of her shell and discover her true self. Charlotte took immediately to the Aegises, shyly befriending Finley and, until his departure for patrol, Jacan. Most of all, she admired Aithan, enamored with and intimidated by him in turns. For his part, Aithan seemed quite a natural at playing the big brother, teasing and teaching the timid young woman, subtly helping her ease into life at court.

Finley was another source of joy entirely. The king accepted Macella's proposal of them remaining at court as a member of her entourage. If another neophyte crossed into Duànzào, Finley would retrieve them after their training with Diya and Kai, then escort them to court for presentation to the Crown, continuing their education during the journey. Other than that, Finley would reside permanently at the keep, supporting Aithan and the Royal Guard. When Macella had relayed the invitation to Finley, they were silent for a full minute, before grabbing Macella and kissing her firmly on the lips. Finley had been in high spirits ever since, providing constant cheer and amusement to the future queen.

It still felt odd for Macella to think of herself in those terms, but she grew more resolute each day. She was surrounded by people who loved and believed in her, and they were not the only ones who did. Laird Parul and Lady Seondeok wrote to Macella often, helping her stay abreast of developments in the north. Moreover, Zahra was officially handing her badge over to Lailoken and moving to court as Lady Zahra of Shelby Park, western advisor, and companion to the future queen. As if Zahra's presence weren't invaluable enough, she provided Macella much-needed supporters in Queen Annika's home region.

Even Macella's parents, false as they were, genuinely took her guidance in the management of Shively, slowly improving life for all of its inhabitants. Her mother was personally overseeing the establishment of the northern mages' academy, while her siblings Henri and Etienne supervised the herb and apothecarial trade. And it all translated into more jobs and more coin for Shively's population and the north in general.

Most importantly, there was Aithan—always at her side, reminding her who she was, tethering her to truth and love and integrity. She might have been the face of their little rebellion, but Aithan of Auburndale was the heartbeat, steady and strong. He never wavered in his conviction that they would succeed, because he never wavered in his belief in her.

Macella held tight to Aithan's certitude. He had to be right. They'd accomplished so much already. Aisling and Charlotte were constant reminders of their many triumphs, not to mention the positive updates they received from Smoketown. There was hope and possibility where there'd previously been nothing but despair and resignation.

Of course, there was still plenty of cause for despair. Grand Mage Kiama was once more in the king's good graces, which could only mean she had discovered the secret of creating Aegisborn children. Surely, they'd force Aithan and the other Aegises to provide more samples soon. How long would it be before King Khari had Queen Annika carrying a child of the king's blood and Aithan's abilities? Worse, would Macella also be expected to help birth Khari's crossbreed army?

Macella didn't know if she could even bear children or if her own Aegisborn nature would counteract the magic. What would happen then? Would the king discover what she was? Or would that discovery come the minute Macella married Khari and received the blessings of the gods of light? Could she even receive those gifts with her soul already pledged to Hades? Perhaps the process of joining the Crown would hurt or even kill her. There were so many unknowns.

"We are more powerful than anyone knows," Aithan reminded her often. "We are so much more than they realize."

Again, his surety was well-founded. Macella, despite her terror and devastation, had broken free of Khari's mind-manipulating illusion on that terrible day in the woods when the king had revealed her god gifts. When Khari attacked Awa, Aithan had raised his sword against the king, defying magical binding from the gods themselves. Time and again, they'd fought for their lives, and come out the other side stronger.

Who knew what all they could do, together?

> *The Crown serves the people, at the people's will. Now the people prepare to employ a new monarch to shoulder the duty of securing Kōsaten with protection, peace, and prosperity. Lady Macella of Shively, the king's betrothed from the north, has already established herself as a champion of the commonfolk. Her relationships with sex workers, Aegises, and the poor challenge us all to reflect on the prejudices that infect the very bones of our society. Perhaps our new queen will usher in a new age in Kōsaten's illustrious history—one in which all of its citizens know what it is to be seen and safe.*

-*Excerpt from Royal Bulletin, Harvest Season, Year of the Serpent*

Glossary of Proper Nouns

Aegis (ē-jis): (from Merriam-Webster)

Aegis has Greek and Latin Roots. We borrowed aegis from Latin, but the word ultimately derives from the Greek noun *aigis*, which means "goatskin." In ancient Greek mythology, an aegis was something that offered physical protection, and it has been depicted in various ways, including as a magical protective cloak made from the skin of the goat that suckled Zeus as an infant and as a shield fashioned by Hephaestus that bore the severed head of the Gorgon Medusa. The word first entered English in the 15th century as a noun referring to the shield or protective garment associated with Zeus or Athena. It later took on a more general sense of "protection" and, by the late-19th century, it had acquired the extended senses of "auspices" and "sponsorship."

Pronunciations include dictionary style and the author's attempt at phonetic spelling.
Aisling [ash-liŋ; ash-ling]: (Irish) a dream or vision
Aithan [ā-than; a-than]: (Greek) firm, strong

A SAGA OF SOVEREIGNS AND SECRETS

Annika [an-ik-ə; an-ick-uh]: (Swedish) grace

Anwansi [än-vän-sē; on-von-see]: (Igbo) uncanny, magic

Anwir [an-wɪr; an-weer]: (Welsh) liar

Awa [ä-wə; ah-wuh]: (Arabic) beautiful angel, night

Citali [sē-tä-lē; see-tall-ee]: (Aztec/Nahuatl) star

Cressida [kres-ə-də; kres-uh-duh]: (Greek) gold

Diya [dē-ə; dee-uh]: (Sanskrit, Arabic) light, glow

Duànzào [dü-in-zaủ; doo-in-zow]: (Chinese) The Forge

Drudo [drü-dō; droo-doh]: (Italian) strong, defender, loyal, faithful

Epanofório [ā-pän-ō-fȯr-ē-ō; a-pon-o-for-ee-o]: (Greek) cloak

Finley [fin-lē; fin-lee]: (Irish, Celtic, Gaelic) a hero or battle warrior with fair skin

Gabriela [ga-brē-el-ə; gab-ree-el-uh]: (Hebrew) God is my strength

Griselda [grɪ-zel-də; griz-el-duh]: (German) gray battle

Igor [ē-gȯr; ee-gore]: (Russian) warrior

Jacan [jak-in; jack-in]: (Hebrew) trouble

Kai [kī; kye]: (Hawaiian, Japanese) of the sea; keeper of the keys

Kamau [kə-maủ; kuh-mow]: (Kenyan) quiet warrior

Kasper [kas-pər; kas-per]: (Polish) treasurer

Khalid [kä-lēd; kah-leed]: (Arabic) immortal, eternal

Khari [kä-rē; kar-ee]: (West African) kingly

Kiama [kē-ä-mə; kee-ah-muh]: (Kenyan) magic

Koroibos [kȯr-ə-bəs; kor-uh-bus]: (Greek) fool

Kōsaten [kō-sə-ten; ko-suh-ten]: (Japanese) intersection

Kiho [kē-hō; kee-ho]: (African, Japanese) fog; hope or beg or sail

Lenora [lə-nȯr-ə; luh-nor-uh]: (English, Greek) light; compassion

Macella [mä-sel-ə; mah-sel-uh]: (French) she who is warlike

Maia [mī-ə; my-uh]: (Greek) mother; one who has unconditional love like a mother

Matthias [mə-tī-əs; muh-tie-us] (Hebrew) gift of God

Meztli [māz-lē; maze-lee] (Aztec/Nahuatl) moon

Omari [ō-mär-ē; o-mar-ee]: (Swahili, Egyptian) God the highest; highborn

Quirino [kwē-rē-nō; kwee-ree-no]: (Italian, Latin) spear

Rhiannon [rē-an-in; ree-an-in]: (Welsh) divine queen

Shamira [shə-mi-rə; shuh-mere-uh]: (Hebrew) guardian, protector

Theomund [tē-ō-mənd; tee-oh-muhn]: (Anglo-Saxon) wealthy defender

Tuwile [tū-wē-lā; too-wee-lay]: (Kenyan) death is invincible

Valen [vä-lən; vah-luhn]: (Latin) healthy, strong

Zahra [zä-rə; zah-ruh]: (Arabic) bright, brilliant, radiant

Aisling's Prophecy

Impossible children, unbearable pain
  Suppressed so long, love blooms again
  Baptized in blood, forged in flame
  Stars align, prophets proclaim
  Love leads wanderers to their truth
  Unknown power now unloosed
  Darkness gathers, trouble brews
  Predator or protector, one must choose
  Fools fight for fortune, the peaceful court war
  Not one prepared for that which is in store
  A shield
  A scribe
  A sword
  A pen
  Against hell's fury
  Against our end.

KŌSATEN
CLOCK

TIME	HOUR OF	TIME	HOUR OF
2400	NÓTT (NORSE GODDESS OF NIGHT)	1200	HELIOS (GREEK GOD OF THE SUN)
0100	KHONSHU (EGYPTIAN GOD OF THE MOON)	1300	TAWA (HOPI GOD OF THE SUN)
0200	EREBUS (GREEK GOD OF DARKNESS)	1400	ARINNA (HITTITE SUN GODDESS)
0300	NYX (GREEK GODDESS OF NIGHT)	1500	XIHE (CHINESE SOLAR GODDESS)
0400	MÊN (PHRYGIAN LUNAR GOD)	1600	NUHA (ARABIC SUN GODDESS)
0500	ZORYA (SLAVIC GODDESS OF DAWN)	1700	LIZA (WEST AFRICAN SUN GOD)
0600	RA (EGYPTIAN SUN GOD)	1800	MAWU (DAHOMEY GODDESS OF SUN AND MOON)
0700	SOL (ROMAN SUN GOD)	1900	SHALIM (CANAANITE GOD OF DUSK)
0800	SURYA (HINDU SUN GOD)	2000	FATI (POLYNESIAN MOON GOD)
0900	INTI (INCAN SUN GOD)	2100	TÔLZE (MARI MOON GOD)
1000	LUGH (CELTIC GOD OF SUN AND LIGHT)	2200	SOMA (HINDU MOON GOD)
1100	MITHRA (IRANIAN GOD OF SUN AND LIGHT)	2300	IX CHEL (MAYAN MOON GODDESS)

ACKNOWLEDGEMENTS

Thank you, thank you, thank you to every reader who has picked up the Aegis Saga. It has been surreal hearing from readers who care about my characters and their world. A huge thank you to my beta besties: B.W, M.M., C.R, L.H., K.W., and C.J. You ladies rock. To my amazing editor, Shannon Cave, thank you for making my story shine! And, most of all, thank you to my partner in crime and in life, who continues to read every word, give me honest feedback, and cheer me on, while enduring my angsty artist shenanigans. I love you.

SERIES INFORMATION

Craving more Macella and Aithan? Get an exclusive bonus scene from Aithan's POV by visiting http://ajshirleyauthor.com/get-the-a-saga-of-sovereigns-and-secrets-bonus-chapter/.

Macella and Aithan's prophetic journey will conclude in...

A SAGA OF SMOKE AND SACRIFICE

Printed in the USA
CPSIA information can be obtained
at www.ICGtesting.com
LVHW041930011024
792665LV00008B/62